1234
5TH AVENUE

1 2 3 4

5TH AVENUE

BY NINA LOURIK

Pentland Press, Inc.
England • USA • Scotland

PUBLISHED BY PENTLAND PRESS, INC.
5122 Bur Oak Circle, Raleigh, North Carolina 27612
United States of America
919-782-0281

ISBN: 1-57197-138-6
Library of Congress Catalog Card Number 98-067432

Printed in the United States of America

For Melanie Lourik, my mother

Preface

ONE SUMMER DAY MY GRANDDAUGHTER, CORI, RODE over on her bicycle with a lined composition notebook in one hand and a pencil in the other and announced, "Gramma, I want to be a writer."

At first I was astonished. "When I was twelve, same as you, I knew that I wanted to be a writer. The best things to write about are your experiences — true to life happenings," I said.

Cori put a half smile on her face and opened her notebook saying, "I know Gramma. That's why I'm here, so you can start talking and tell me your story — stories."

"There are so many, I wouldn't know where to start."

"At the beginning, Gramma. Come on, you can do it, just start."

Cori. Self-assured Cori. Every whim of hers had to be satisfied now. Not later, not tomorrow, but immediately. Something else could come up a half hour from now.

The announcement that Cori wanted to be a writer should not have surprised me because she always had her nose in a book. Even on holidays when she and the rest of her family came to dinner, a book accompanied her. She memorized the first book she really liked when her brother read it to her a few times. She was four years old. I thought she was reading word for word, but her brother whispered to me, "She can't read, she memorized it." Smart, determined, "I'll-show-you" Cori.

And so I began at the beginning. A half hour later I realized she was mesmerized and was not taking any notes. I stopped and asked why she wasn't writing. She handed me the notebook and pencil and said, "You do it Gramma, write your story."

She was right, it was time. My parents were gone, as were my brother and three sisters. I was the only one left of our Russian family. If I didn't tell it, it would never be told. The entire town of Lily, Indiana expected me to write so they could one day read about their town and its people (all immigrants from mostly Baltic countries) and how they all survived the Depression years. Most of them were employed at the Midwest Corn Products Company, just down the road and across the railroad tracks. When they looked out their windows all they could see was the factory, a few trees, tall weeds, and the railroad boxcars as far as one could see in both directions.

My notes are yellow with age but the memories remain. I can hear the switching of the raw corn-filled boxcars that came in every evening. Banging and clattering, boxcar after boxcar, one by one, went into the yard to be emptied then sidetracked to await the women who came each morning to find raw corn left in the cracks of the boxcars. These women would fill their sacks to feed their farm animals, to fatten them to be eaten, in order to survive a life not much different from the sparse existence they left behind in Russia, Latvia, Poland, and the Ukraine.

There were also a few Irish and one very handsome man from Turkey. Oh, my gosh, I almost forgot! There was one man who never spoke to anyone and always lowered his eyes when he passed you. He was never without his cap which the children thought had a snake wrapped up inside, it looked so stuffed. And a housekeeper who lived with him who was always drunk. She was a gypsy.

Russia

THE FACTORY WHISTLE BLEW. ITS LOUD RESOUNDING tone told the women their ten-hour workday was done. They could now go home to their loved ones and to the bread, cabbage, and potatoes that awaited as their dinner. As far as they could remember, this was their standard food. They did not need much. As long as these staples filled their kitchens, they would never be hungry. These staples filled the bellies of the peasant class in Russia and afforded their survival of the past war and revolution.

One of these women was hearing the whistle for the last time. She did not go directly home. Her weary heart was sending her on a farewell mission.

Nadia Alexandrovna was standing in the empty corridor of the small building which housed the offices of the army clothes factory where she had worked for the past seven years. She was waiting. Her blue-green eyes had a troubled faraway look. As she leaned her head against the cold stone wall and closed her tired eyes, she reminisced the past long nine years of her life in Russia. She waited outside the closed door for Stephan to return to his office.

Her thoughts took her back to an early spring day in 1913 when her husband, Alexander Ivanovich, came home to stay after serving three and a half years in the Russian Army. He was proud of the position he had held while in the Czar's service. He ordered the food his comrades ate each day.

Nadia looked very happy when Alexander removed his lieutenant's uniform to don his peasant clothes. He was going back to work for the Pon, the landlord appointed by the Czar to oversee the farmland, and life would be as it should be. Then his wife gave him the letter that was waiting for him to open from his brother, Vassil, in America. A paid ship-card to the United States was enclosed. Vassil Ivanovich had left Russia just six months before and already he had earned enough money to be sending passage to his brother.

"I will not go," Nadia remembered her husband saying. "I will sell this ship-card and we will live good this winter with $200 cash money. No, I will not go."

Alex put the letter and ship-card in his uniform pocket. He would think about it later. Right now it was time to sing and dance and get drunk. Every eligible man was required to serve three years; he had served three and a half and was glad to be home. When his family and neighbors gathered at their meager home that evening, Alex learned that most of the young men in their neighborhood had left for America. Why should they work for the Pon for $30 a year when they could earn that in a week in the Land of Plenty?

Alex went to work plowing the fields with two horses, twelve hours a day. The surrounding three thousand acres belonged to the Pon. However, the house and an acre of land it stood on was now owned by Alex. The neighbors were given the same. Everyone worked for the Pon. Their own fields were tended to in their spare time. Life was a little better now. But Vassil wrote again of the plentiful jobs and high wages in America. Five weeks later, Alex left for the United States.

Nadia took her husband's place in the fields, leaving her daughter, Vera, with Alexander's mother who lived on the adjoining acre of farmland in the Hgrudinska Hgubarnia in White Russia near the Polish border between Grodno and Brest Litovsk in Choplee, a village of Matasie. The nearest big town was Chamensk Litowske.

Oh, Alexander, if only you could have taken us with you then. I know we did not have the money for our passage and never would have had on the $30 a year the Pon was paying you. I was glad you were gone when word came for you to put on your uniform and return to the army. It was too late to turn back, you were already on board a ship to America.

The Pon increased wages to a dollar a day in hopes that the young men would stop leaving for America. Nadia wished her husband had not left the country. They could fare very well in Russia on a dollar a day.

Our daughter, Vera, was almost three years old when you left. She still remembers the silly expressions you made with your face to make her laugh. We thought we would join you in about six months, but war broke out and our land was the front line. We walked northeast for one month with your mother, father, brother, and sister; then we

*boarded a train along with hundreds of other peasants who
were forced to leave their homes.*

*I still do not know if your brother is alive for he and
your family left the train in the hilly state of Ufa. Grisha,
your young brother, had scarlet fever. There was an
epidemic. Your family went to care for him in the army
barracks that were set up as hospitals. It was a blessing
when the doctors stopped the trains to check the sick at
many, many stops. Then we were able to open the boxcar
doors for air and food; it was very crowded with cold,
hungry, sad, and sick people.*

Nadia came back to reality when she heard the
outer door open. It was not Stephan. It was only the
cleaning woman. She went to the first office to begin
her work. Nadia went back to remembering the train
ride that took one month to reach Omsk in
southeastern Sibirskya (Siberia). There they were
given government homes to live in and soup and
bread to eat. They were a great distance away from
their homeland. Vera was sick with a combination of
scarlet fever and chicken pox. Nadia slept in the same
hospital bed with her daughter for six weeks until
Vera recovered. Vera was cared for by neighbors
while her mother went to work in the army barracks
which accommodated the wounded soldiers in the
city of Omsk.

Nadia remembered the city of Omsk for its
cleanness. A watchman was assigned to each block of
the immense housing project to keep the streets clean
and to see that the people washed their windows
regularly.

There was so much plate glass in Omsk that Nadia
remembered it as the City of Mirrors. Each building in
the project had a store on the ground floor and the
entire front was plate glass. The city sparkled,

especially in winter when the snow was reflected in the mirrors. The weather was another story. There were only three months of summer. It snowed in August.

The long awaited ship-card from Alexander finally came. Nadia was given permission to leave for Arkhangelsk (Archangel) with her daughter. They found the port closed to all ships. There was no train available either; all trains were being used by the army. World War I was formidable. They had to wait until the war was over before they could leave for America. Nadia hid her ship-card among her belongings, left her daughter to be cared for by neighbors again, and went to work as one of many cooks for the Russian soldiers.

The women were doing all the work in Russia then, even office men went to war. Summer came and Nadia learned she could earn more money loading brick and coal on barges. The work was very hard. Winter soon came again and Nadia, along with a great number of other people, was unemployed. The port was completely closed when the snow and cold descended upon the city, freezing the waters of the White Sea.

Six hundred women were needed to sew army clothing in the city of Vologda, far, far south of Archangel. In order to get there Nadia had to sell her and her daughter's ship-card, which brought her $300.

She wrote to her husband asking him to come back to Russia, there was plenty of work in the city. Alexander wrote that he would not come back. He knew he would surely have to go off to war if he did return. He would wait until they could join him in America. The fact that Alexander was not a citizen of the United States made him exempt from serving in the army.

The war came to an end. Alexander sent ship-cards for them again. Vera just made it for half price passage. She was now eleven; children had to be under twelve to travel at half price.

Now here we are in Volagda. I have just quit my job in this factory and I have come to say goodbye to Stephan. He has been very fortunate to hold such a high position here as production manager. He did not have to go off to war for very long. Not so fortunate for me; it will be very hard to leave him.

Nadia and Stephan met by chance in the same factory where Nadia worked. She accepted and returned his affections, thinking she would never see her husband again when he stopped writing. The uncertainty and great distance between them brought out the weakness a woman experiences when faced with the unfortunate circumstances of war and separation. In the beginning of the war Stephan was wounded in one leg. He walked with a slight limp. When he recovered, he was assigned the high position in the factory where army clothes were sewn—and would never cease to be sewn—for all of Russia.

The door opened again. She looked down the corridor. It was Stephan. "Nadia, what are you doing here?" He took her arm and opened his office door. They stepped in and he locked the door behind them.

"I will not see you anymore," she said, finding it hard to believe the day had come for them to part.

He laid some papers on his desk, turned to her and said, "Here, here. I will have no excuses. Do you want me to die?" Stephan took her in his arms and kissed her. As he was about to release her, she pulled herself to him hard, kissing him for the last time, she thought.

He hugged her and stroked her hair, then kissed her forehead and both cheeks. She was afraid to open her eyes. She could not bear to hurt this man who loved her.

"My dear love, my heart, you are the warmest woman in all Russia." He kissed her again. "Now what is this that you say you cannot see me anymore?" he asked. His arms still encircled her.

Nadia took his hands in hers and said, "I have something to tell you. I have a letter from Alex and a ship-card for Vera and me. He wants me to start for America but he wants us to go to his homeland first and see if his family is all right." She kept her eyes fixed on his hands as she held them tightly.

"I will not let you go," he said as he embraced her again. "He has waited too long to send for you."

"You must listen to me," Nadia said as she began to cry. "I knew this day would come and now it is here. I must go for Vera. She remembers her father. We cannot think of ourselves. We must say goodbye. Vera thinks and speaks of nothing else but America and her father. It is her dream. She even insisted we have our picture taken to send to her father. She wanted him to know how very beautiful she is. I did not think the photo would reach him because he moved as we were traveling, but the letter and photo were sent to people who kept forwarding it until he was found in the state of Indiana in America. He has a job and a house for us to live in that he bought for us. Vera is so happy, she hasn't stopped jumping up and down and clapping her hands and hugging herself with joy." Nadia sat down in a chair and began wiping her tears. She added, "Her playmates call her Vera Americanovna instead of Vera Alexandrovna."

Stephan looked out the window. "I cannot live without you," he declared. "Stay here, I will take care of you and Vera. I promise you we will have a good life now that the fighting is over. You could get a divorce."

"But we could not marry for seven years. And you don't know my Alex. He would come back and kill us both. No, I must think of Vera. It would not be right. She so wants to go to America. You have an important job here. You must think of yourself and your mother and father too.

"Alex used to tell me he would give me permission to have an affair with another man any time, as long as I asked him first. But he would kill me and him if I did it without him knowing. I know you are probably wondering what he's been doing all these years. He probably found someone else or he would have sent for us sooner, and he stopped writing all of a sudden."

"We could go to Poland, my country. My mother and I just came to visit her relatives here; the war made us stay. She will be going back to find my father," Stephan pleaded.

He walked over to Nadia and knelt in front of her. She took his face in her hands and kissed his eyes, his cheeks, his lips. "My love, my heart," she said, "we have to say goodbye. Help me. Do not make this so hard for me. My heart hurts." She buried her face in his chest and sobbed.

Stephan caressed her thick braid of hair and tried to comfort her. "Please my beloved, do not cry anymore. We will talk about this later. Come, let us go to my place." They left the building together.

Nadia agreed to divorce Alexander and make Poland her new home. She agreed to ask Vera to go to

Poland with them where Alexander might never find them.

Poland, the country she was taught to despise from early childhood. The country that was spat on by every Russian living in Belorussia. The land whose people the Belorussians were seldom permitted to marry. The Poles took our land away! This is Russian land! We will never be Poles. Now Nadia was going against tradition by choosing to divorce her husband and marry a Pole.

Tradition does not govern the heart, only the mind. One cannot sternly affirm 'I cannot love this man or woman because he or she is not like me, my country does not approve of his country.' The heart rules all ties and only a strong will tells you to do otherwise and even then, the love still remains and tortures the mind and the heart until the end of time.

So, this war-torn woman who had laid awake nights with dreamy thoughts of wealth in America had, in a matter of a few hours, changed her mind while she lay in her lover's arms and let the heat of passion decide for her.

But when she saw her daughter and how happy she was about going to America, she could not stay. The next morning they packed their meager belongings into the one valise they owned, making sure the ship-card was in a safe place, and walked southwest.

Vera saw her mother crying. "Do not cry Mama. I do not want you to be sick. It will be better for us in America. You will see," Vera explained as she took the valise from her mother's hand.

"But I am afraid he will kill himself if we leave him," Nadia said as she turned her head away from her daughter.

"Oh, Mama, no he won't. He just says that. You want to go to America don't you?" Vera asked, wishing her mother would stop crying because she herself was so happy.

"Yes, we have waited and suffered so many years here that we must go to your father now," Nadia agreed. She reached into her pocket for her handkerchief, sighed heavily and lifted her head, resolved that, for Vera's sake, she had made the right decision.

They did not walk far that day. Nadia had very little sleep the night before and she was tired. She felt the tears trickling down her cheeks again as she thought of Stephan, how kind, loving, and generous he had been to her for the past five years.

I will pray for you, my heart, please do not destroy yourself. If I find my love for Alexander is dead, I will be back to find you.

Another deep sigh. Then she remembered that Alex was her first love, that they had been happy together, and time would heal the wounds she and Stephan would suffer for awhile. Her first duty was to her daughter because she loved Vera dearly. But she would never forget the adoration Stephan had given her, knowing she just had to close her eyes to feel his arms around her and to see his green eyes that almost shut when he smiled and the way he ran his fingers through his light brown hair to push the curls off his forehead.

She prayed God would give him strength to go on with life and would soon find someone to take her place. She thought perhaps that he was already making plans to return to Poland and his family.

All will be well. It has to be. It is time. No more suffering. No more tears. America!

The train station was very crowded with people still returning to their homelands after the turmoil of war and revolution. Soldiers in uniform were everywhere. People were either coming home or going to a new home in faraway places. They could not get train tickets; they knew they would probably have to walk the entire distance to White Russia, to a homeland they had not seen for nine years, to find Alexander's family and hers, and then on to America. They would try again at the next station.

For two months they rode trains for short distances and walked when they had to. Nadia knew she was going to have a child. Vera had to be informed of the situation because they could not continue their journey. They stopped in a city about fifty miles from their destination to spend the remaining confinement. America would once again have to wait.

Nadia wrote her husband saying Vera was sick with influenza and that they had to rest awhile. Nadia found work in a Turkish bath establishment and sent her daughter to school. When Vera was informed of the new situation, she tearfully asked, "What are we going to do Mama? What are we going to do?"

"We will see daughter. We will see," Nadia replied, looking away. Far away.

She wrote to Stephan asking if they could return, mentioning nothing of her conception, saying only that she had changed her mind, was tired of traveling, and wanted to be his wife. When a letter came from Stephan's coworkers with the news of his suicide by hanging, Nadia deeply regretted their quick departure. Even Vera was mournful for her selfish desire of wanting to fulfill her childhood dream of America.

There was no turning back now for them, only a long, long wait and a choice still to make between Russia and America. To take one's life is against God's will, yet the weak cannot wait for God to decide when to take their breath away. Nadia knew how deeply Stephan loved her, but she remembered when they first met how much Stephan's voice reminded her of Alexander. The first time she lay in his arms, she still thought of Alex, her husband. But time erased his image and she saw and felt only Stephan. But the shock and realization that she was carrying his child, a child she knew could never accompany her to America, brought her suffering more than anything she had experienced in the past ten years. More suffering than hard work, leaving her home, severance of kin, hunger, sickness, the sights and sounds of war, insufficient funds, unemployment, concern for her daughter while she worked, and wonderment of ever seeing America, leaving Stephan, and now the uncertain future once again and again and again.

The child was born in early spring. Nadia placed the infant on the doorsteps of an orphanage, but when no one came out to get the crying baby, Nadia went back and picked up the frail child. She realized she could not part with this product of the love she had left behind and would never see again.

They continued their walk to Alexander's parents. Nadia thought perhaps her sister-in-law, Irina, would be married now and she might take the child who was born under such unfortunate circumstances. Nadia paid a woman she met in a bakery, who had three children of her own, to watch her baby while she went to find her husband's family.

They learned that Grisha, Alex's brother, had not survived the scarlet fever epidemic, but that the rest of the family was safe and living on good, high ground near the Pon. Irina was not married yet. She was a strong girl and worked day and night for all the neighboring Pons that she could to provide for herself and her dying parents.

Irina told her sister-in-law that the Pon had tried to make them move to lower ground. "Papa said he would drown first before he moved. So he let us stay," she reported.

Nadia later told her sister-in-law about the baby and asked if she had a solution to her problem. "Why don't you take it with you?" Irina suggested. "The baby can travel free. Tell Alex you found the orphan."

"No," Nadia shook her head. "He would not believe that story. The baby has the same mark on its cheek as I do." She wrenched her hands in her lap. Her mind and heart were in a state of torture by her indecision. They had traveled too far and now could think of nothing else — Vera must go to America. Irina offered, "Then tell him it is Vera's. She is old enough. Tell him Russian soldiers were responsible. He will understand."

"Oh, no! It would ruin Vera's future," Nadia replied.

"Then it is settled," Irina sat back and folded her arms across her chest announcing this judgment as the only and correct solution. "You must tell him it is mine. Tell him I had a Polish lover Papa would never let me marry and it happened. You know how all the White Russians hate the Poles for taking our land away. He will know I could not keep the baby. I must work. Mama and Papa would starve without me. I will have a letter written to Alex now and tell him how all this happened. It is the answer. Believe me. Mama and Papa cannot read or write. All they did was work in the fields for the Pon. They will never know. They are very old and weary."

Irina was excited and happy to help her sister-in-law whom she knew had endured so much in this poor country with no husband to care for her and her daughter for the past many years. *The poor people of Russia have suffered long enough,* Irina thought to herself. *If families do not help one another in any way they can, who will? The men of this country no longer believe in God, but we women do. The fire in our hearts must blaze to make this a warmer and richer country for the needy. I will send some of this warmth with Nadia and her child. I know God will bless me.*

Nadia and Irina had been neighbors from birth. Shortly after Nadia married Alex, she and Irina had become like sisters. Irina assured her that Alexander would not refuse the baby. She still remembered her brother's fondness for children, their spontaneous laughter when he made clicking and clacking noises, whistles, winks, much facial movement, and jiggling while resting a child on his knees. They always begged for more.

Nadia differed, "No, we must tell Alex the baby is Russian. He too hates the Poles. He would never accept a Polish child, nor support it."

Irina nodded, "It is agreed then, the father was Russian and he was killed in the war. What do you call your child?"

"Ninotchka," she replied. Nadia was about to add "Stephanovna" as is customary in Russia, but she thought it would make the affair worse if Irina knew her lover really was a Polish man. Vera would never reveal their secret; they had suffered too much together. Stephan's mother was Russian but in this country all children belonged to the father and his nationality ruled.

The "ovna" attached to the end of the father's first name relates to a girl child. "Ovitch" at the end of the father's first name relates to a boy child belonging to the father. A wife or husband carries a second name the same way. Nina was a Polish girl child in a Russian family — Nina Stephanovna or, lovingly, Ninotchka.

"Oh, Irina, do you really think so?" asked Nadia, "I would love to take the baby with us. Vera adores the child. Alex will love her too, even more so if he believes she is his sister's child." Nadia felt she was smiling for the first time in an eternity.

"Then take it," Irina insisted. "And the birthmark is nothing. Nearly everyone has one someplace on their body. God chose to put hers on her cheek. Don't let that worry you. I will remind Alex of my birthmark." Irina touched the raised small mark on her neck. "I will tell him you came to say goodbye before you left to join him as he asked you, and I begged you to take my baby with you. I must work twelve hours each day and care for Mama and Papa. I cannot care for a child. This will work. I know it will."

Nadia nodded agreement. She had not dreamt of this good fortune. "God bless you, Irina," Nadia said as she kissed her sister-in-law on both cheeks and then they hugged tightly.

Irina was wishing she were married. She would gladly have accepted the baby, yet she knew after experiencing the loss of her brother, Grisha, how difficult it would be for a mother to part with her newborn baby. It would be as if it had died. Irina did not blame Nadia for turning to another man for affection and wondered why Alexander had waited so long to send for his wife and daughter. She admired Nadia for accepting this decision. Irina knew they would have a better life in the New World.

"Why don't you spend the summer here?" Irina recommended. "The infant is too young to make such a journey."

But Nadia decided, "We will go before winter so we can travel faster."

"All right," Irina agreed, "but let me see the little one. I will walk you to the train station."

Nadia said, "I would like to find out if my two brothers are safe before we go."

"They are ten miles from here. I will take you."

The two brothers were all that was left of Nadia's family. Shortly after Nadia married Alex, her parents died of pneumonia a week apart. She learned her brothers were now married and owned their own land. The reunion between sister and brothers was a joyous one.

Irina informed Sahar and Maxim of her decision to send her fatherless child with Nadia, since the little girl would have an easier life in the rich country. Now the brothers would also write to Alex and be witness to the story that Irina was the mother. The matter was settled. They were bid a safe journey and Godspeed. A scholarly man in the village was paid to write a letter to Alex informing him that three persons would be joining him in the house he was buying. The letter would reach America before they did.

At one of the train stations they saw the bullet-riddled train car the Czar and his family were murdered in. They felt very fortunate to be leaving their hard life in Russia behind. A new life awaited them in America. Nina was now a part of the family.

Alex had to accept her. He loved children—he loved to make them laugh.

They left Grodno and traveled two months to Riga in Latvia, then to Bremen, Germany where they, after a two-month wait, boarded a large vessel named Manhattan (Meim Heim) and arrived to see the Statue of Liberty on 4 July 1923.

Vera's twelfth birthday was 28 July. She just made it at half price ship travel. Nina was six months old and traveled free. Nadia was now thirty-two and felt her life was just beginning. Her husband had a job and a house. Her daughter's dream was coming true. Her love child was with her and not left behind.

Vera had never seen a fireworks display; she saw one now. Ellis Island was closed. No one worked in America on the Fourth of July; it was a celebration. The ship docked three days later. Six weeks of quarantine began when Nina contracted the measles. America had to wait awhile longer.

Vera spent these days looking out a window, wishing there were more fireworks and wondering what awaited them over the tall New York buildings.

America

Chapter One

AN INCESSANT, ALMOST SILENT RAIN HAD COME DOWN from the gray sky since noon. The water rolled off the roof and struck the pavement in the gangway between the close-set houses. The deafening splashes were heard at the two dining room windows, yet the children had hopes that soon the angry, wet clouds would stop releasing the rain.

Four-year-old Daria and three-year-old Olga rode their kiddie cars into the living room and pulled the freshly starched window curtains to one side. They looked out and showed their disappointment by simultaneously remarking, "Oh, heck." Then began chanting, "Rain, rain, go away. We wanna ride on the sidewalk," over and over and over again as they sped through the house, riding the presents they received at Christmas time from their respective godfathers.

The proper name for the toy was tricycle, but in this house, they called them kiddie cars. The girls waited impatiently for clear weather. The screams they released as they rode along and bumped into each other's brightly colored red and white vehicles forced Alex, their father, to refuse further permission to ride the three-wheeled toys inside the house. However, Nadia, their mother, allowed them to while her husband was not at home.

Nina, who had just passed her fifth birthday, was sitting in the dining room close to the black potbelly stove, which heated the house. She was looking at the red velvet dress with white lace collar and cuffs that her godfather gave her for Christmas. Nails protruded from the woodwork of each doorway in the house, affording Alex and the two boarders a place to hang their caps. Nina's dress hung on a hanger on one of these nails by the door that led to the boarders' bedroom. She thought the dress was too beautiful to wear. She had never seen or owned anything so lovely. She just stared at it and felt the material. She wondered how she would look in it; she had not put it on yet.

"I can't see the whole dress if I put it on," she announced when her mother asked if it fit. "I'll wear it even if it doesn't fit," Nina would reply when her sisters happily said they would wear it every day if it fit them.

Nina counted the row of tiny black buttons on the bodice, saying, "Rich man, poor man, beggar man, thief. Doctor, lawyer, merchant," and decided to add the small black bow at the neck to complete the superstitious child's play that predicted the future. These buttons promised she would marry a chief. They never went to parties or had any themselves, so Nina dreamt of the day she would start school, meet rich girls and boys, and perhaps receive an invitation to a party. She was saving the dress for that special day.

Andre Nakov, one of the boarders, was a confirmed Russian bachelor in spite of the fact that he loved children. He was godfather to Olga. When Nina asked who her godfather was, Andre claimed her immediately. Nadia thanked him for the kind gesture. Nina really had no godparents, and was never baptized in church. At birth she received the sacrament from her mother and Nadia knew this would have to suffice her nameless daughter. Vera swore secrecy.

The house Alex bought before his wife, daughter, and Nina came to America was in the town of Winsome, which was bordered by a large lake to the east, a small lake and a corn products factory to the west, oil industries to the south, and a big city to the north. There was very little furniture in the five-room house for the girls to run into with their kiddie cars; beds were more important. The house only had two bedrooms for its many occupants, but the one off the dining room, where the two boarders slept, was large enough to hold two beds. The dining room held a rough textured, maroon davenport with matching chair. The reversible cushions had huge pink and white roses on one side that the two younger girls delighted in exposing. Nadia tried to keep the davenport covered with a large fringed tablecloth. The beige cloth had large yellow roses in the four corners and Nadia wished she had a table to lay it on. It was one of the few items she brought from the old country. But the dining room was not a dining room, it was just a room in the middle of the house where everyone sat around the stove and talked; where everyone would dance when the records were played;

where the children skipped rope, sang, laughed, cried, fought, and slept. There was no room for a table. They ate in the kitchen, never having any company for dinner. They could not afford it and had few friends to invite. But they still called this room the dining room. The chair in the living room was separately covered with an embroidered dresser scarf and sometimes with a small tablecloth.

At night the davenport opened into a bed on which Nadia and her husband slept. Olga had been sleeping with her parents up until that past winter. Nadia never had a baby bed for her children. She kept them close to her as long as they would let her. She loved her girls dearly, and missed their dependence when they were babes in arms.

A large square framed picture of the Blessed Mother holding the Infant Jesus in her very plump, satin-smooth arms hung high on the wall above the davenport. She was clad in a gold brocade robe and He was wearing a red silk cloak. When Alex asked his wife what she would like for her first Christmas present in America, she told him, "Every house suppose to haveit holy picture," in her broken English. He laughed and was quite surprised that Nadia still believed in God after all they had gone through in Russia. She said she wanted nothing else. Her husband did not refuse her. Nadia bowed her head and crossed herself every time she looked at the beautiful, lifelike picture. The eyes in the picture were directed at the onlookers and seemed to follow you until you left the room. The children could not look at the holy figures without lowering their heads or turning away quickly. When the youngsters were doing wrong, Nadia would refer to the Blessed

Mother and warn, "Matka Boska (Mother Boss) no like you if you bad, her sonny was never bad boy."

Four exposed light bulbs hung from a brass light fixture in the middle of the ceiling and were the only source of electric light for the living room. A replica hung in the dining room. The other rooms were not as fortunate; a single bulb hung from a chain and light poured through when the attached string was pulled.

A small, dark table with thick legs and numerous carvings was the only other piece of furniture in the living room. It held the picture of Nadia and Vera that found its way to Alex in America, the picture that made him send for them immediately. In it Vera was holding onto a tall basket filled with flowers in front of her and Nadia beside her. They were beautiful. Alex's passage had brought him through Canada, then much later he entered the United States. Both Alex and Nadia had moved many, many times, which explained the long gaps in their communication for so many years.

Nina, Daria, and Olga occupied the bed that took up one corner of the dining room. They always uncovered themselves at night so it was best that they be close to the stove. Two straight back, wooden chairs stood against the wall behind the stove where the entire household sat or stood while putting on their shoes and stockings. This habit began in the winter time and existed the year round. Even the boarders came out of their room to finish dressing their feet by the stove.

The hardwood floors were bare of rugs except for the large oval rag rug that Nadia made. Rags were not readily discarded that year of 1930. Each cold morning the children would scramble for the woven, warm floor covering. They stood on it while they dressed themselves; it lay to one side of the stove. Their favorite indoor sport was to see who could push who off the rug. The victor would then pound her chest and shout, "I'm king of the mountain."

Their mother was always warning them of getting burned or spilling the coal bucket; in summer her warning changed to, "Watch out, you knock stove over." A darkly varnished four foot tall Victrola stood in another corner of the dining room. The girls could reach the crank, but they weren't tall enough to place the records on the turntable. Alex made a small wooden stool for them to stand on. They were delighted. The Victrola had two shelves on the bottom that held nothing but Russian records. Alex bought the disks before his family joined him in America.

The remaining dining room corner was taken up by a tall, dark stained, wooden clothes cabinet. It almost touched the ceiling, which was ten feet high. Nadia constantly reminded the children not to bump into the camoda, as she addressed it in Russian. It was so tall and narrow that she was afraid it would topple over on them. Each time she told the girls to be careful, Nina and Olga were reminded of the pleasure they found in taking off their shoes and throwing them up on top of the cabinet; they each loved going barefoot and would say they couldn't find them when they were told to put on their shoes. Daria did not like to be without shoes, so every opportunity her sisters had they would toss her shoes up there. If Alex was not at home to retrieve them, they all had to go without shoes until he came home. This task was too strenuous for their mother, and Alex was only five feet six inches in height, so he had to stand on a chair and use a broom to poke around the newspapers that were stored on top until he felt what he was looking for.

The girls would hide under the bed and giggle quietly; if they laughed too loud and aggravated him, they would surely feel the sting of the razor strap on their backsides. The shoes invariably fell between the stacks of papers, and Alex would have to reverse the broom and use the handle to find them. He would start perspiring and before he was able to make the shoes fall to the floor, his angry state found relief only by muttering every profane word and group of words he had learned while he was in the Russian Army.

He would pause to rest his arms, inhale deeply, mop his wet brow and then he would let loose with his favorites: "Yebi tvou mot! Sonofabitch! Sonofabitch!" As he grew angrier he no longer swore, he just blew, "Whew, whew!"

Alex had the habit of repeating his words, either the first or the last spoken, no matter what they were. The girls always asked their mother the meaning of the obscene words their father used. Nadia did not tell them, but they kept right on asking her, hoping one day she would give in. "They just bad words. Matka Boska no like you if you sayit them. You Papa gotit devil in him," was the answer Nadia gave them.

The children were seldom spanked for giving Alex the task of recovering the shoes from the camoda. It was a good excuse for him to find his hidden bottle of whiskey in the basement of the house and have a couple of shots. Nadia was the one who reprimanded the girls for their prank. She wished with all her heart that her husband would not drink.

And on the front porch there was a swing, a swing that was never taken down. It was just a wooden swing that had a back to it and hung on chains from the porch roof, but they would make an attempt to save this item first if the house ever caught on fire, or so Nadia and her daughters always said. If they were not warming themselves by the stove, they were airing themselves on the swing. Before the youngsters took their afternoon naps it was customary for Nadia to join them on the swing and hear their troubles, wishes, answer their questions, and then she would make up a story which usually began, "One time there was a bad little girl . . . mean witch . . . stick . . . cry . . . run away . . . hungry . . . boogey man . . . scared . . . eat her up." The scarier the better while the squeak and motion of the swing closed the children's eyelids.

In winter time this sleepy time procedure was carried out with the help of a large woolen blanket that was used to cover the swing-loving foursome.

Now that Vera was a working girl, she found time to enjoy the swing only on Sundays and late evenings. Alex preferred the back porch for his rest time; it was closer to the basement entrance and his thirst begged satisfaction often for his hidden whiskey. The two boarders joined him there. Much talk went on between them as they looked out on the small backyard that was equally divided between grass and a vegetable garden. They were always comparing the Depression to better times, Russia to America, past to future, Capitalism to Communism. They were indubitably for the latter. Marriage to bachelorhood, having children to being childless, farm life to city life, and deciding whether to smoke or not to smoke, and oh, yes, to drink or not to drink. And did they swear!

"You grow horns pretty soon," Nadia used to say to them. She meant that since they talked like the devil, they would soon look like him.

The bedroom off the living room was too cold for anyone to sleep in winter. It was too far from the stove, but Vera did not mind. She was almost seventeen now and it was the only way she found some privacy in their busy home. Vera cleaned house and cared for the elderly Mrs. Blake who lived next door, and on Saturdays she helped her mother with all the cleaning in their house.

As tired as Vera was by Saturday night, she still went to Dance Palace, which was only six blocks from home. She loved to dance. Although she and her sisters preferred to dance the Russki Kozak, everyone begged Vera to do the Charleston. She was very good at it.

Vera had enrolled in school when she came to America, but it was too hard to take the teasing of being thirteen and in kindergarten. Fortunately, she did not understand her classmates at first, but she could tell by their pointed fingers, giggles, and secret whisperings that they were talking about her. She sulked and cried and thought she would never learn the English language. The teacher did not understand her speech and vice versa. Vera begged her mother to take her back to Russia, she was sorry they came. But slowly, with the help of her father and teacher she learned English during the two semesters of school she attended. During summer vacation Vera went to work for the lady next door and did not want to go back to school. Earning money was more beneficial to her and the family.

When Vera opened the front door and came into the house, Daria and Olga left their kiddie cars and raced to see who could get to her first. Reaching her at the same time, they hugged Vera around her legs and both screeched, "Hi, Vera."

"Hi, kids," she returned. "Hey, don't touch me, I'm all wet." She pushed them away. They ran back to their kiddie cars and hopped on. Vera was big sister and second mother to them. If Nadia was busy — and she always was with cooking, baking, washing clothes, tending the garden, and sewing clothing — then Vera wiped their noses, dried their tears, helped them wash and dress, and combed their hair. Nina was envious of the attention Daria and Olga received from Vera. She never said anything. She was too young to notice that her big sister always turned her head away when Nina spoke to her and that she never looked into Nina's eyes. *I don't need help anyway,* Nina thought to herself. *My sisters want to be babies, I don't.*

Vera took off her wet coat and walked over to the stove. She asked Nina to hang her dress someplace else so that she could hang her wet coat and babushka in its place to dry. Nina did not decline. She hung her dress on one of the knobs on the camoda, sat down on the bed, and continued looking at the beautiful gift that sent her dreamily into the world of princesses, movie stars, ice cream, candy, and cake.

"Isn't Pa home yet?" Vera asked her mother who was sitting on the other chair by the stove, drying her just-washed hair.

"Not yet," replied Nadia as she parted her honey-blonde hair on one side and combed it back. Every time she washed it she was reminded of the old country before the war. All the girls and women in her village washed their hair each Sunday morning before going to church. Many babushkas covered wet heads; it was their custom to attend mass with clean, braided hair.

Now Nadia's two foot long braid lay in a dresser drawer, wrapped in a large crocheted handkerchief.

Occasionally she took the braid out and looked at it and stroked it. She wished she had not had it cut off. The bobbed style she now wore made her feel older. She would wrap the braid around her head and thought she may wear it this way one day when her hair grew long enough to cover her neck and hide the pins that would hold the braid securely.

Or, maybe one of my girls will make use of the braid, she also thought. *It's thick enough to make two. I'll separate it some day if it will match Daria's or Olga's hair. Vera's hair is lighter than mine. She can't wear it. I was crazy for having it cut off. Alex doesn't like it. I don't like it. My girls don't like it. Shingle haircut is for men. Ladies should always have long hair. Matka Boska had long hair. The boarders say it's nice, but I know they don't like it.* Vera had wanted her mother to be in style and not old country looking.

"Did Mrs. Blake pay you today?" Nadia asked her working daughter in Russian. She spoke to her daughters in her mother tongue whenever Alex was not home. He thought it was good for his children to know Russian, but he knew it was more important for his wife to learn English.

Vera answered her, "Yes, Ma, she paid me. Now I can get the shoes I need."

"No tellit you Papa how much you gotit," advised Nadia in her broken English. "He makeit you give him everything."

Alex handled the money in their house. Nadia was too busy to leave the house. Taking care of the children, doing the housework, and the cooking took up all of her time. And then, too, she could not speak English as well as he. He was ten years ahead of her in this respect. He even bought all the groceries at first. His wife had never been to the corner store where he bought all the food on credit. The bill was paid on payday and that was once every two weeks. Sometimes the full amount was not paid since Alex always made sure he had enough money left to supply his hiding places in the basement with half pints of whiskey. He started hiding the liquid habit he acquired while all alone in America. He had more money than he ever had in his life. When he refused his wife the new winter coat she badly needed, she purposely poured a half pint of whiskey down the basement drain right in front of his very eyes. Oh my, did he swear!

"Do we have to wait for Pa? I'm hungry," Vera announced. "Me too," chimed in the three youngsters one after the other.

"You Papa should be home pretty soon. I betcha you he stop by Galuk's. Today payday. He leaveit half the paycheck at the devil saloon," Nadia assumed as she walked into the kitchen. She went to the black and white wood and coal burning stove and poured into plates the boiling hot soup she had made.

Vera took her sisters into the bathroom that was off the kitchen and assisted them in washing their hands. By the time they were finished, the soup was cool enough to be eaten. Nadia and her daughters sat at the kitchen table and had their dinner, knowing how foolish it was to wait for Alex on payday.

Chapter Two

NADIA SAT BY THE KITCHEN WINDOW OVERLOOKING THE back porch, waiting to catch sight of her husband or to hear his footsteps on the stairs. She was sewing Olga's rag doll, which had come apart in a small place at the seams. The children were sleeping. Vera was in her bedroom, waving her bobbed hair. The boarders were working the four to twelve shift at the corn plant in the adjoining small town of Lily. Alex worked in the same factory.

When she heard him at the back door, she went to let him in. He was very late, but she saw that he was not very drunk. Alex was usually gay when he had had a few drinks. He had a routine all his own when in condition and when he had an audience to perform for. First, he would whistle two loud notes, clap his hands, slap one of his raised thighs and then the other using both hands. Then he would go to the Victrola, crank it, and place the needle on the Russki Kozak record. This disk always lay in position to be played.

As the fast tempo of the music began, he would again clap his hands and shout, "You! Ha!" and then did a few steps of his and the family's dance. When he stopped dancing he would roll up one shirtsleeve—he owned nothing but blue cotton work shirts—and display his muscles. The children would feel them and say in amazement, "Gee, Pa!" or "Wow, Pa!" Lastly, he pulled his cap down to his eyebrows and winked at his wife. He was ready to make love to her. Nadia hated his whiskey breath but loved him for his nonsense.

Alex put his muscles on exhibition at every opportunity, rolling up his sleeves or trousers or taking off his shirt for his girls to see them, feel them, as he tightened them to make them move up and down and in and out. Olga and Daria would clamber on his lap to run their hands across his chest. He could defeat any of his Russian men friends at hand clasping, even when he was drunk—especially then. This sport was very popular when Alex was in the Czar's service.

A coin was flipped to decide what side the opponents would push towards. To push to the left side of course was easier for a right-hander. Sometimes they chose to use the left hand after the game was played many times. Elbows were then placed on a table, or any other surface, as they sat or stood. They clasped hands and then pushed towards their side. The loser bought the drinks or paid the wager.

Alex was considered very short and appeared to be thin until he showed his muscles, then people thought only of the strength he must have. When it came to dancing the Kozak, he could do the hardest steps, jump the highest, stamp his foot, shout the loudest, and dance the longest.

Nadia could have kept up with him but she gave him the floor, knowing he loved and deserved the attention for his strenuous performance. His laughing, sky-blue eyes always sparkled and with each smile he made a clicking sound with his mouth and then he would wink.

When he was younger his hair was as blonde as his daughters, but now it was thin and gray with a swept-up wave in front never out of place. He watered his hair so much that his wife teased him by asking if he was growing onions. Alex was a very warm person but he was ready to fight when his Russian temper was riled with the help of liquor.

His swearing was as much a part of him as the gray cap he always wore. It was the closest style he could buy in this country to the type he wore as a young man in Russia. It had a large peak in front. He would even forget to take it off at the table; his wife would knock it off. As for the swearing, all Nadia could do was say, "Aw, shut up, you devil," in a whisper. Nadia never swore.

Tonight Alex was not gay. It had stopped raining so his clothes were just slightly damp. He took off his jacket.

His wife asked, "Where you was?" She did not wait for him to answer. She took his jacket and reached for his cap. She went into the dining room quietly, so as not to waken the sleeping children. She turned a chair around and wrapped the jacket around it, moved it close to the stove, shook the cap free of dampness, and hung it on the nail where Nina's dress and Vera's coat and babushka had previously hung that rainy day. She went back into the kitchen.

"Where you was?" Nadia asked her husband again. He placed his hands on his hips and she thought, Uh-oh, here we go again. A fight. She was glad the children were sleeping. She did not like them to hear Alex swear. She looked at him, waiting for him to answer, and saw that he was pale and his mouth twitched.

"Whatsamatter?" she asked, holding her breath. He stood there, unable to speak, trying to control the anger and sorrow within him, then he sat down by the table.

"You know what, Baba?" he began.

Nadia released her breath. She sat down beside him. "What?" she invited.

He looked at his wife, wondering how she would take the shocking bad news. He said, "I haveit no more job. Today I was fired. Yes, I was fired." This habit of repeating himself was his most outstanding characteristic.

"For what?" Nadia asked as she clutched her heart with both hands.

His voice was full of bitterness as he spoke, yet he spoke softly not to waken anyone. He recounted, "You remember I tellit you how everybody in shop hateit that bastard, Mike, the watchman, because he sucha snitcher?"

"Yes," Nadia answered and nodded. She folded her hands before her on the table.

Alex continued, "Well, today somebody tied piece of wire across steps so he trip and break his goddamn neck. He fallit all right, and he break his glasses, and he getit black and blue. Would be better if he die. That sonofabitch blame me. He say I doit and I was fired. Yes, goddammit, I was fired." Alex still could not believe what had happened to him this day. Knowing

36

he needed a drink and privacy to blow his nose and release a minute's tears, he left his chair and went into the basement.

Nadia remained in the kitchen. She shook her head back and forth and moaned, "Oye, oye, oye, what we doit now?" A few minutes later Alex came back upstairs through the trapdoor in the kitchen floor. Confidently Nadia said, "Maybe you getit job someplace else and no more shift work."

"I dunno. I don't think so, nobody hiring now, nobody," replied Alex. "Giveit me something to eat, Baba." Baba means grandmother, wife, or lady in Russian. "Giveit me something," he repeated.

Nadia went to the stove and filled a heaping dish of hot borscht. It was Alex's favorite soup that consisted of beets, cabbage, potatoes, and on occasion some spare ribs.

Mike, the watchman, had the job of walking around the "shop," as the men called it, to keep an eye on the workers and to report slackers. The long, tapering stick he carried for the purpose of tapping on the shoulder of the accused whom he saw talking, dozing, or taking too much time in wiping their sweat. He did use it and he reported the men, and they hated him for it. "Company man bastard," they called him. The "shop" was the Midwest Corn Products Company in the town of Lily, a mile northwest of Winsome. Alex and the boarders rode the streetcar in winter, loved the walk in summer, and sought a ride in a car on rainy days.

Alex was innocent of the prank that caused the watchman to break his glasses and get bruised, but the guilty kept silent. They had not expected Mike to live to tell about it. Their confession would mean the loss of their job and another would be hard to find; the country was in the throes of a depression. Alex did not know who strung the wire. He was blamed because he worked closest to the scene of the accident. He thought Mike was lucky not to have been pushed into a vat of boiling syrup as the men threatened. Mike should have known the men would get their revenge one day. Too bad Alex was held responsible. How was his family going to get along now? And worst of all, there would be no money for whiskey. They may even lose their house.

Alex was out of work for three months. To earn more money Vera quit working for the lady next door and found employment in a candy factory in the big city north of Winsome. The board money from the two boarders paid for the food, and the earnings Vera gave her father covered the house payments, or rent as they called it, which was $30 a month.

Chapter Three

NADIA WAS STILL A PRETTY WOMAN AT THIRTY-FIVE. HER complexion was smooth and free of wrinkles in spite of all the worry and hard work in her past, in the old country. Her coloring was beautiful. When she stood in the sunlight, her hair glistened with reddish highlights. She washed it in rainwater whenever she could and loved to sit on the back porch and dry it in the sun. The rays would bleach her hair, giving her a halo, but the sunlight also brought out freckles on her face and arms. However, most of the spots disappeared in winter. Her perfectly even, white teeth and blue-green eyes made up the rest of her beauty, but her bosom stayed large after feeding her babies.

When Alex asked Nadia to explain the birthmark on Nina's face—it was on her left cheek, close to her nose, and matched Nadia's own—she replied in Russian, "Oh, lots of people have them. Irina has hers on her neck." She did not look into his eyes when she answered him for fear she would give herself away.

After all they had been through to finally reach America, she did not want her security upset again.

Fortunately, Alex remembered his entire family had a birthmark one place or another. He himself had one on his chin and so did Vera. The faces of Olga and Daria were spared, they had theirs on their chests. She prayed that Alex believed the story. But Alex needed only to remember Irina's letter to confirm the child's origin.

Alex was happy to be reunited with his family and accepted Nina as his own. He would never forget how really poor the poor were in Russia. He agreed the baby would have a better chance here and he knew his parents would never leave their homeland, so Irina had to stay and work and support them. He reflected, Irina will marry some day, and, who knows, maybe she will come here to live and then claim her daughter. But, she had better not marry a Polack. I'll never send her passage if she does.

As far back as Alex could remember he heard his father telling him and the others in their family, "Never bring a Polack home. We White Russians don't like Poland!" Alex wasted no time in telling Vera the same, and he made a resolution to tell Nina, Daria, and Olga before the time came for them to choose a mate. He would die first!

❖ ❖ ❖ ❖

Since Alex had a weakness for liquor and Nadia, during an argument over his wasteful spending, sometimes intimated she would leave him, he became very jealous of her and feared that she would carry out her threat. Therefore, he was glad she stayed in the house as much as she did. When his Russian men friends came to visit, he was pleased that she never interfered in their conversation. She would exchange a few pleasantries and then retire to another room or, if they were sitting on the back porch, she would go into the house to do her sewing, crocheting, or some other of the endless household chores. She would hear bits of their conversation and did not agree with most of it, but she kept silent until the visitors or visitor left.

One of the most frequent callers was a man named Kola (Nicholas in English) Tarasuk, a loud spoken, overbearing Russian who came from Ukrania. His wife and two children joined him in America just two years before Alex's family reunited. Now that the country was in the midst of a depression, they agreed they would have been better off if they had remained in the old country. Now that Mr. Tarasuk was going to have another child in his family, their fifth, Kola was worried about finances. Now that Alex was unemployed, he despised the Capitalists deeply. They admitted the houses and food available in America were by far better than what they had in Russia, but they had to work just as hard here if not harder, what with the "Company Man Bastard" watching over the workers. They believed every "shop" now had a watchman with a "snitcher stick."

Alex and Kola longed for the farm work in Russia. Peasants there learned from early childhood that they had to work hard to survive, and the only weapons forcing them to work were their own hunger pains.

Taxes? What for? Just to line the pockets of the Capitalists. Make everybody equal. One person's needs are as great as the others. Kola would pound the table with his fist, and Alex agreed with every statement his friend made, although Alex pounded the table twice. He received great satisfaction in repeating acts as well as speech. They were

Communists and they were atheists. As they expressed their firm beliefs, Alex's face became flushed, his muscles tightened and he would hear his own throbbing pulse. Kola's voice grew louder and louder and Nadia would look in on them, thinking they were having a battle. Their display of anger was due to the subjects they discussed.

They reached the conclusion that the church was a waste of time. They and all the people they knew in Russia had worked very hard. Their rewards were few. God did not help them get the bread and soup they needed to survive. God only answered the prayers of the rich and made them richer. It was their conviction that everything the poor accomplished was done all by themselves, with their own strength and without prayer.

Alex would flex his elbow, tighten his fist, and feel his own muscles. They remembered the many years their people prayed and prayed hard, day and night. At one time, in all the big cities in Russia there was a church on every block. What good did they do them? They could not eat the candles or the statues. Then the slaves rebelled. The statues were smashed, churches destroyed, their bells were made into bullets, all because the poor were jealous of the rich. The poor were so poor they were starving to death. They were hard-working people and they wanted everybody to be equal. It was the only answer for their vast country. It was the answer for all countries. It was everyone's duty to care for his fellow man. They had a drink to that.

Kola would take his leave, asking Alex to come to the Russian Society meetings and ball. This affair took place every Sunday evening in a large hall. A troupe of Russian dancers performed on stage, food and drink were sold, speeches were made by the officers of the society regarding the advantages of belonging to the group — insurance, Russian dance lessons, and speech classes for the children. Admission was free to the ball where everyone later danced to a five-piece orchestra.

Alex always accepted the invitation by saying, "Maybe I go. Maybe," but he never did join the society or go to their affairs due to the lack of owning a suit, white shirt, or tie. Nadia begged him to buy dress clothes for himself so they could attend the ball, but Alex preferred spending money on liquor for his consumption at home. He thought of the men that would see his pretty wife if he did go there, and he would not risk the chance of losing her.

Kola would not leave the house without saying goodbye to Nadia. He would shake her hand and then kiss her on both cheeks. Alex would offer him one more drink, which Kola never refused. Then Alex would see him to the door, telling him to come for a haircut when he needed one. Cutting hair was something else Alex had learned while in the Russian Army.

After one of these sessions Alex asked his wife, "Why you kissit him? Why?"

"I no kissit him, he kissit me," Nadia corrected him and laughed. "Why? You jealous he no kissit you?"

He was angry. "Yebi tvou mat. Yebi tvou mat," he swore, yet he tried very hard not to laugh with her.

"How many baba you kissit ten years without me?" still smiling, Nadia did not want to let him get the best of her.

Then he replied and smiled, "Lots of 'em. Lots of 'em."

They went on, "You old man, who want to kissit you?"

"Never mind. Never mind." Alex had the last word as he picked up the pint of whiskey he and Kola had been drinking from and looked to see how much was left. He usually managed to save some and seldom exhausted his supply without replenishing it with a full bottle. He pushed the cork down tighter and went into the basement to hide it. His wife would pour it down the drain if she found it.

When he came back upstairs, Nadia asked, "What for you talkit like that? You are in America now."

"Because this country no good," he answered.

"Then why you no go back to old country? You see how good you haveit there. You forget already? No shoes. No bread. You no haveit so much whiskey like you gotit here. Just because you lose job you think this country no good. Go findit job. No drink anymore. You see how good you haveit then."

"Aw, shut up. I lookit for job. Nobody hire now. Nobody. What do lady know 'bout country? You just sit in house with kids. What you knowit?"

"We know lots. We believe in God. He helpit us. If He not helpit us we not be here today, we still be in Russia." Nadia was determined to let him hear all this from her. "You listen too much to your crazy Russki friends. You say you not believe in God, you will see. Just wait when you get sick, you see how fast you will pray, wait. All men not crazy like you. You and your friends jealous of Capitalists because you want to be Capitalist too. Go to work. You be rich too. Russian lady not so crazy like Russian men, we never stop pray. You will go to hell someday." She ended her tirade.

Chapter Four

ALEX WAS SO JEALOUS HE BECAME SUSPICIOUS OF THE boarders, especially of Vasil Kosnakov who was addressed by his last name rather than first, not to confuse him with Alex's brother Vassil who now lived in another state with his wife and two children. Kosnakov was taller and more handsome than Andre, the other boarder who was even shorter than Alex. Andre was so short that his feet did not reach the floor when he sat in a chair; he kept them crossed. Nadia was forever scrubbing the scuff marks he made when shifting and swinging his feet in an attempt to reach the floor.

Kosnakov was Daria's godfather. One day, Kosnakov and Nadia were sitting at the kitchen table talking. Alex was in the basement.

"What you think if I marry your daughter, Vera? You think Alex will let me?" Kosnakov asked her without looking up. He stared at his folded hands on the table.

"I dunno. I don't think so. You twenty years older than our Vera. No, I no think he let you," was Nadia's answer. She knew he liked Vera, but she did not expect this. She was glad at having the excuse of Alex's most probable refusal. She did not want Vera to marry him. He drank. She stressed to Vera that a man who drinks never makes a good husband, even though Kosnakov, for long periods of time, swore off drinking and saved his earnings. Kosnakov was as quiet a person as Vera and his sky-blue eyes matched hers, but his hair was gray; hers was blonde.

Vera was an exceptionally pretty girl. She needed no makeup and wore none. All she had to do was bite her lips and pinch her cheeks to produce all the color she needed to look the picture of health. She was a hard worker, good with children, and was satisfied with the barest of necessities. She was so disappointed in America, her father and their poorness, that she no longer dreamed of riches. She accepted her life and believed that the poor will always be poor because they did not know what to do with wealth. She thought if she was ever lucky enough to marry a rich man she would rather share her abundance with the needy than keep it all for herself. Unbeknownst to her, she was a Communist at heart.

Her mother knew Vera would make a good wife, but she did not know that Vera's majestic unselfishness was due to her inner feelings of guilt.

Nadia asked Kosnakov if Vera had accepted his proposal. He replied that he had not asked her yet. He wanted Nadia's and Alex's approval first. He knew he was too old for Vera, but she reminded him so much of his wife who died of pneumonia during her travel to Siberia when war broke out, that he was helpless in his yearning to recapture his youth and first love by making Vera his bride.

Kosnakov had the habit of interlocking his fingers as if in constant prayer, but he was in complete assent with Alex's belief that prayer never helped him. He decided not to ask Alex for Vera's hand in marriage. Nadia said she would not object if Vera wanted to marry him.

Then Alex came through the trapdoor into the kitchen, Nadia and Kosnakov stopped talking. Alex saw their lowered eyes and nervous expressions and immediately suspected the worst. He accused Kosnakov of trying to induce Nadia to sleep with him. Kosnakov knew it was useless to try and defend himself. Alex had been drinking in the basement and his blood pressure was soaring, his Russian temper and jealousy were out of control.

All Nadia could say was, "Aw, shut up, you devil." She was glad the children were outside playing and were spared this ugly scene.

"Te kurva! Te kurva!" Alex shouted calling her a bad name. He paced the floor swearing. He looked like an angry bull, his nostrils flaring, ready to charge. He clenched and unclenched his fists, daring his veins to burst, and ground his teeth with each tightening of his fists. He took in deep breaths of air and when he exhaled he said, "Whew! Whew!"

He put his hands in the pockets of his pants to keep from striking his wife. Nadia could not make him believe he was mistaken. She was so ashamed of her husband and embarrassed for the boarder that she could not look at Kosnakov. Liquid devils were dancing in Alex's bloodshot eyes and she could not look at him either.

Kosnakov went to his room and then left by the front door. Nadia did not tell Alex what they had been discussing. She knew it would only make matters worse. Alex went into the basement and finished the contents of the bottle he drank from previously. Then he looked in all his hiding places for more. When Nadia heard the basement door slam and saw Alex leave the backyard, she knew he was on his way to Lily Tavern.

Chapter Five

Feodore (Fred in English) Galuk owned the corner tavern in the town of Lily. It was a large frame building, green with white trim, that had living quarters in the rear and rooms for boarders on the second floor. Business was good because the Russian boarders loved alcohol. Only on special occasions did they drink vodka. It was too expensive. They generally drank the cheapest available and a lot of it. Their consumption alone could maintain Feodore's business at a profit, however, most of the adult residents in Lily contributed to making Feodore the richest man in town.

The tavern, or saloon as it was usually called, was two blocks from the Midwest Corn Products Company entrance gate. It was a daily stop for many of the men employed at the plant. Its front and side doors were open from seven in the morning to midnight. Before going to their jobs, the customers went in "to get their machinery oiled and working better" and after work they went in for a "warmer" while waiting for the streetcar that took them into Winsome in one direction and a big city in the other.

"Hello, Alexander Ivanovich Durock," Feodore greeted and raised his hand in salute.

"Hello, Mister, Hello," Alex returned addressing all men as Mister following Russian custom. He climbed up on a bar stool and with one finger pushed his cap back a little. "How my credit?" he asked. "I needit couple shots. I pay you when I go back to work. Pretty soon I go back to work."

"Sure, you credit good. How you family?" asked Feodore, reaching for a glass. He poured Alex a drink.

"Awright . . . my family awright." He took the glass and raised it. "Nasdarovya," he said.

"Nasdarovya, Alex." Alex drank the whiskey and wiped his mouth with his closed fist, first to the left and then to the right. He held out the glass for a refill and repeated his gestures and the words that expressed good luck. He drank his whiskey straight, no wash.

Feodore remembered the news of the day. "Say Alex," he said. "You hearit 'bout Frank Pavlinski wife?" Alex shook his head. "She die in car accident."

"No, I no hearit. By golly, that too bad. Too bad."

Feodore nodded agreement and related, "He bury her today. He lookit for somebody to buy he cow an chickens. He house be for rent. He moveit to Winsome (he pronounced it Vinsome) so he sister could watchit he four kids."

Alex started filling a cigarette paper with loose tobacco. Feodore poured a half a glass of whiskey for himself and set it on the bar, then said, "You know, Alex, that be good place for you family. You kids haveit lotsa room to run an' play over there on White Place."

"Nasdarovya, Nasdarovya," Alex responded when Feodore raised his glass and drank his whiskey. Alex rolled his cigarette and then voiced his opinion of White Place by saying, "Yes, it nice over there. It like farm. I betcha my kids be crazy 'bout that place an my Baba too. She missit old country. It real nice over there."

While Feodore rinsed out the glass he drank from, he suggested, "Why don't you go seeit Mr. Upton (he pronounced it Yupton) at Lily Store? He rent it to you. Three bedroom in that house. Rent only seven dollars month. You could rentit you house in Winsome. You makeit money."

"By golly, maybe you right. I go home tellit my Baba first. I go." Alex pulled his cap down tighter on his head and leaned over closer to Feodore. He spoke softly when he asked, "You gotit half pint give me on credit? I pay you soon . . . pretty soon."

The saloonkeeper nodded once and reached underneath the bar for a half pint of whiskey to accommodate one of his best customers. Alex put the bottle into one of his back pockets and buttoned his jacket. He was ready to leave. Before he slid off the bar stool, he thanked Feodore by saying, "Spasebo, spasebo."

"Okay, Alex. Goodbye." Feodore waved his hand and then began washing out the glass Alex drank from. Adjusting his jacket to conceal the bottle in his pocket, Alex went to the door and said. "Goodbye, goodbye."

Nadia told her husband that Kosnakov packed his belongings and moved out. She also told him he wanted to marry Vera. "No, never" Alex said to that. "Why you no tellit me when he here? Why?"

Nadia replied, "Because he no wanit me to tell you."

"I kill him first. He too old for my Vera, too old." Then Alex sucked in his breath and added, "Sonofabitch! Sonofabitch! Maybe he sleep with her already, maybe?"

"You crazy devil!" said Nadia as she left the kitchen in order to avoid an argument.

Alexander was sorry Kosnakov was gone; he would miss his board money. They needed it. Since Alex was still out of work, he was aware of the possible loss of the house and little food on the table, but Feodore's suggestion of moving to Lily offered a way of keeping the house and supplying an abundance of food. Knowing how much his wife loved farm life, when she came back into the kitchen and sat down across the table from him, Alex asked her, "Baba, how you likeit haveit cow to milk and chickens to giveit eggs? Ha? How you likeit?" He was grinning sheepishly.

"Sure, I likeit, but not here in city," Nadia replied. "You crazy?"

"No, not here. In Lily, in Lily." Alex was now smiling.

They had no trouble finding renters for their house. A Russian couple with two children were happy to be moving in. They would even take the thirty dollar monthly payments directly to the bank and save Alex the trip of coming out to Winsome each month for the money. He could come in once in a while to get the receipts, they told him.

Lily

Chapter One

Lily had a population of exactly ninety-nine people living in twenty-one houses, two shacks, one tavern front building, and a large boarding house. Of these residents, eight families were Russian, three Polish, three Slovak, three Lithuanian, two German, one Irish, and one Swedish. Among the people were one full-blooded American Indian, two gypsies, ten Russian bachelors, and one Irish bachelor. The rest were "I don't knows" and children.

The town was comprised of three sections. The first section upon entering the town was called Red Place. The post office was the smallest in the whole United States and was the first identifying mark to be seen at the entrance to the town where the red, white, and blue flag waved every day. It was a red brick-face building that stood outside the Midwest Corn Products Company front gate.

The postmaster was also watchman at the front gate who let in salesman and the executives. The employees of the plant, however, used the side entrance gate two blocks down the train tracks that ran alongside the plant. Across from the post office was Lily Tavern. In the back of the tavern were the horse stables, and a house where the stable owners lived.

Then came the general store, known as Lily Store. In back of the store was a row of eight houses. The corn plant faced Red Place, Lily Lake was south behind the plant, and a small Forest Preserve boarded the back of the entire town — two huge shadows looming over ninety-nine poor people during the depression, reaching out slowly, affording gloom for the poor intruders who invaded nature's growth with houses, families, animals, and fowl.

White Place was a quarter of a mile around the bend in the main road from Red Place. This section consisted of two rows of framed houses, three in the front row and four in the back row, set wide apart.

The Durock family moved into the last house in the back row at White Place. The entrance to Lily Pad Lake was in front of this section, just across the railroad tracks. The plant fence ended where White Place began and the people of the town had access to the lake there. Old Ivan (John Kozlenko) lived in a shack that was placed on blocks at the lake. He made his living renting boats. Jack Doyle occupied a shack, also on blocks, across the lake on "Irish Island," as the children of the town named it, a small stretch of land completely covered with tall bulrushes and swamp.

An ice house employed a few men and was located by the lake just beyond Old Ivan's boat rental business. This was the beginning of Blue Place. Not too far from the ice house was a small fireworks plant. Across the tracks from these two establishments was a row of three houses. Around the bend in the main road stood a large frame boarding house where all the men who worked at the ice house and fireworks plant lived. Lastly, the Boat Club was at the very end of Lily.

Every night around midnight a freight train with boxcars full of raw corn came into the town from across the lake to the far south. The corn was unloaded at night and during the day the boxcars went back to be refilled.

The main dirt road, big enough for cars to travel on, ran along the one set of tracks, with roads leading off to the three sections. Every kind of tree and weed grew where there was no path or car track. Tall bulrushes grew in all the swampy land and huge sunflowers outshone all the weeds on dry land.

All of Lily was owned by a big shot who lived in the adjoining big city to the north. The people were told no one ever saw him except Mr. Upton who collected the rent at Lily Store. "I betcha he plenty rich to own so much land," the people of Lily said. "I betcha when he buy apples, he buy only cheap, rotten ones. If he old man, I betcha he break tree branch to use for cane. You gotta be stingy to be so rich. He never have to work—I betcha."

Off to one side in Lily Store was Mr. Upton's office. He was the only man in Lily who was addressed as "Mister" except by Alex, who called all men "Mister."

He heard his name mispronounced so often, even the children spoke of him as Mr. Yupton. He was the only person who worked in Lily but did not live there. At first, the rent was paid to him through a barred window at the store. Later, he hired a caretaker to do necessary repairs to the houses and to collect the rent. Mr. Upton cashed checks for the few who did not go to the corner tavern to have them cashed. The store sold meats, groceries, candy, work gloves, thread, tobacco, and school supplies.

Albert, the butcher, left the store Monday through Saturday at 9:00 A.M. in a panel truck to take the grocery orders and then delivered them in the afternoon. The people at Red Place were within walking distance of the store, so his route took him to White Place and Blue Place.

The first and last sections had the better houses. A few were covered with shingles. Each one had a basement and a front and back entrance, and some had bedrooms on the second floor. Of course, the larger families lived in these, but nevertheless, the whole town was poor and looked poor. Every family had its problems; the widow with five children, the widow with three children, and the father or mother who drank. They lived in Lily because rent was cheap and these were hard times. Every house was on the same side of the tracks—the poor side.

White Place was the scantiest section. The houses had no basements. They were two feet off the ground, just enough room for snakes and field mice to nest in. The frame structures never had a second coat of paint. In spring and summer the greens hid the grayness of the houses, but the snow in winter shamed them and begged to be as bright as the whiteness of the season. The face of the sun shone down and wished it could spray rays of paint on White Place that should have been named Gray Place.

The house the Durock family now lived in had a kitchen with a sink, a pantry, a wood burning cook stove, and table and chairs. The plastered walls had been painted white at one time but now looked more gray than white. The previous renters left their old linoleum on the kitchen floor. It had the brightest colors in the room — red and yellow checkerboard — which tempted the girls to play hopscotch on it until their mother stopped them; they could easily fall against the stove. And there was a door leading to a bedroom where Alex and Nadia now slept.

The living room held the davenport (on which the three children slept), the camoda, phonograph, chair, and the stove with the two straight back chairs behind it, the "fighting rug" on the left side of it and the coal bucket on the right side. The colorful picture of Mother and Child was hung in a corner above the davenport where it covered a large crack in the grayish-pink walls.

Two bedrooms were off the living room with the stove in-between the two doorways. Vera had one bedroom and Andre had the other. There were no doors to these rooms so Nadia hung her heavy, maroon brocade cloth across the openings which, during the cold, were pulled to one side at night to let in the heat from the stove. It was almost like the house in Winsome except that they lost a dining room and gained a bedroom, the one in the kitchen. There was only one exit to the house, it was through the kitchen, and there was a small porch outside, but its roof was not strong enough to hold a swing, much to Nadia's regret. She also regretted having the outhouse one hundred feet away from the house and the well was across the road, thirty feet away from the house. But she was thankful that Andre Urkov moved in with them. His board money helped a great deal.

This new residence was closer to his job and Andre felt sorry for the children. He gave them pennies and nickels often. Nadia would tell him the children did not need money, but he said, "That's what godfathers are for." Now that Kosnakov was no longer a boarder, Andre felt he was Daria's godfather, too.

They bought forty chickens from the former tenant, Josey the cow, a hay barn full of hay, and a puppy named Buster, a black and white spotted sausage hound, as the children described him.

Everyone loved the place except Daria, who was afraid of insects, weeds, and the dark. Lily had no electricity. Most of all, she missed the sidewalks of the city; she had to ride her kiddie car on the dirt road now. She also missed the swing. She would not go near the cow or the chickens.

Nina loved to run. "Let Daria ride her ole kiddie car. Come on, let's run," she would say to her little sister. She took Olga with her everywhere. They explored the fields beyond the house until they were hungry, then they ran home craving a slice of the dark crust from Russian Rye bread rubbed with garlic and a little salt, or a slice spread with salted sour cream.

The children went barefoot all summer long. Daria resisted, but her mother insisted, saying, "It good for kids to be barefoot. You be healthy this winter an no getit cold so fast."

Alex made a swing between two trees that stood off the road just around the bend from the outhouse. It was only a board and some rope, but the girls were delighted. Daria would go as far as the swing and no further; she was afraid of snakes too. When duty called to go to the outhouse, they announced, "I'm going to the show!"

Nadia felt as though she was back on the farm in Russia. She loved the sounds of the chickens laying eggs, the rooster's crow at daybreak, and the children's running feet, their laughter and hunger groans, with the barking dog constantly at their feet.

Best of all, she enjoyed the combined sounds of the croaking frogs and chirping crickets. It was music from the earth that lay in weed beds waiting for nightfall to begin the concert. Their shrill "chree, chree" calmed Nadia after a hard day's work and brought a yawn and a stretch to her tired body, telling her it was time to end the day.

Each time she drank the well water or worked in the large vegetable garden or turned on the kerosene lamps, she was reminded of the old country and at these moments felt as though she and Alex had not been apart for twelve years. But she needed only to see Nina to remember the long separation and realize that Lily was a place very far away from Russia.

The cow was Nadia's pet. It was her job to milk her each morning and night and to take her out to graze. Daria did not like Josey's fresh, warm product. She begged her mother to buy cold store milk. She held her nose every time she was forced to drink it. With all the plentiful, practically free, now available foods, Nadia made cheese and butter and baked bread and cottage cheese cakes, and, oh, they had so many eggs to eat.

In early spring Alex took two hundred eggs to the hatchery in Winsome. Then, one hundred seventy chickens were born in the kitchen, all penned in behind the cook stove to keep them warm. The children pulled their chairs as close as they could to the baby fowl and watched them, chins in their hands, and said a hundred "Awes" and "how cutes," until the "peep-peeps" deafened them and their faces hurt from smiling at the "little darlings."

Nadia let the girls pick up one chick apiece. They held them daintily, stroked their cottony backs, then laid them in their laps and let the warmth help them into slumber. They watched the naked eyes close and open and close and open as the heat from the stove came upon the girls as well. The sudden jerks from their weary heads startled the chicks into wakefulness and the whole procedure had to be repeated to calm the helpless creatures who did not ask to be held in the first place. Nina and Olga teased Daria when she participated in this part of farm life.

"Watch out. It's gonna bite ya," Olga joked.

They laughed when Daria released her hold on the chick, letting it drop into her lap, thinking Olga was not joking.

It was Nina's turn, "It's gonna lay an egg right in your lap," she said seriously. Then explained, "Look out! Here it comes!"

Nina and Olga giggled. Daria said, "Oh, shut up, you two." She realized her sisters were making fun of her but could not keep from joining them in laughter. It was the first time Daria made a show of interest in their present surroundings. When the girls' legs became cramped from sitting in one position too long, trying not to disturb their little bundles of slumber, they would return them to the box but continued their watch until the heat from the stove made the girls' faces hot and red. They pushed their chairs farther and farther away and then finally had to leave the room to cool off, only to return shortly. They knew the cute feather babies would soon grow old and ugly only to be looked upon later with favor because of their delectable, edible, parts and the product they yielded that went into making so many of the girls' favorite foods: omelets, breads, meat cakes, cottage cheese cakes, and best of all, open apple cake.

Alex was busy with his ax. He went to the edge of the forest and chopped down trees that went into making a fence around the garden. The yard was already fenced in so Alex set about building six sheds which he joined with the cow barn and the chicken shed, making a long row that would accommodate ducks in one, geese in another, while one would be a feather shed (Nadia saved feathers for the making of pillows and bed coverings called feather ticks). One would house a goat, another a pig, and the first shed closest to the house was Alex's private shed with lock and key.

When Nadia asked, "What for you lockit shandy?" Alex replied, "I no want kids getit my tools and hurt themself." But the girls knew the real reason. This house had no basement so Alex had to make a hiding place.

They bought ducks, geese, a goat, and paid two dollars for a pig. Alex fenced in a pig pen beyond the garden, but the pig dug a hole in the mud under the fence and ran away. The family searched for weeks, but it could not be found. A year later their dog dragged the pig's dead head home from the Forest Preserve. They bought another pig, but they had bad luck with this one too. This pig grabbed a passing chicken and ate it, bones and all. The pig had to be killed because it suffered internal injuries and was bleeding to death.

Alex made a smokehouse a few yards away from the outhouse. A long-lasting fire was made by burning discarded old railroad ties that were found along the main road and railroad tracks. In the evenings the whole family made sausage. It would keep for a year after it was smoked. Some of the meat was sold to neighbors. Everyone at White Place wanted to buy the pig's feet, but those were the first parts that were eaten in a dish Nadia prepared and called studinina. Alex loved it and so did the children, except Daria. She would throw up before she ate it, she said.

They bought three more pigs, hoping the law of averages would allow at least one to survive and grow fat, then be slaughtered in its prime for some special occasion like Christmas, Easter, a christening, or a wedding. There would be hams and roasts and chops and sausages.

Chapter Two

ONE NIGHT ABOUT A MONTH AFTER THEY MOVED IN, ANDRE awakened the family. He knocked on Alex's bedroom door and sounded urgent when he called, "Wake up, Alexander. Hey wake up."

"Uh, whatsa matter? Whatsa matter?" Alex asked when he was startled out of his sleep. He jumped out of bed and hurriedly slipped his pants over the long underwear he always wore winter and summer and to bed, only in summer he wore a pair that had short sleeves. He reached for the flashlight on top of the dresser and opened the door. When he flashed the light into Andre's face, again he asked, "Whatsa matter? Whatsa matter?"

"Somebody shooting," Andre announced.

Nadia came out of the room and they heard a gun shot. Then they heard shattering noises pierce the still night. Nina and Daria awoke. Nadia told them to stay in their beds. They obeyed and hid under the covers.

Olga did not waken. The dream she was having about a beautiful, dancing, singing doll in a pink organdy dress on stage filled with sister dolls in duplicate garments was worth continuing. The artistic beauties went tumbling down and died on the stage floor when Alex stubbed his big toe on the corner of the outstretched davenport and muttered, "Sonofabitch! Sonofabitch!"

Olga joined her sisters in the hideout when another gunshot was heard. Then Vera came out of her room and joined the adults of the household who were looking out of the living room window at the house across the road.

Alex switched off the flashlight and he and Andre looked out into the bright moonlit night and saw a man running away from the neighbor's house.

Vera asked, "What's going on, Pa?"

Alex shrugged his shoulders and answered, "I dunno, maybe robbery . . . maybe."

"Ah, who want to robbit poor people? There nothing in Lily to rob," Nadia said.

A gun went off again. They could hear things breaking.

"It's dishes she throwing down steps," Alex could see. "She is crazy, real crazy."

"There she is with gun," said Andre, astonished.

Then they all began to laugh because Mrs. Dubinski was outside running after someone in her nightgown with a rolling pin in one hand, firing the gun in the air with the other. It was a man that ran into the car that was parked behind the house, slammed the door shut, and sped away. It was the first time they had seen the neighbor lady who lived in the last house in the front row of White Place. They saw Anna, her daughter, going to work every day, but the mother never came out of the house. There she was now, breaking up the porch railing with the rolling pin. Anna came out of the house. Alex opened the window, and they could hear what was going on.

"Ma, stop that. Come on in here. Do you want the people to think you are crazy?" they heard Anna saying.

Mrs. Dubinski grabbed her daughter by the hair and pulled her down the steps. Anna wrenched herself free and ran away. Her mother could not catch her, one leg was shorter than the other and she could not keep up. Anna was out of sight and Mrs. Dubinski went back into the house. She soon came out again, swearing and throwing more dishes down the steps.

"Oye, Oye, Oye," Nadia muttered. "What kind of neighbors we haveit?" She was really frightened.

Andre said, "Maybe she drunk?"

Nadia agreed. Alex just shook his head twice. Alex went out to his shed to get the bottle. He and Andre sat down to have a drink at the kitchen table. Everyone else went back to bed and covered their ears not to hear the crazy, drunken lady.

The next day Alex came home with a gun that he hid in his locked shed. The children were told to never go near the house across the road, and to stay away from Pa's shandy, as they called it.

Alex was glad to have company come over. He could bring out the whiskey and drink all he wanted. Nadia did not like to make a fuss in front of others. Jim Novak came to see Alex the night after the neighbors' antics. They sat in the kitchen. Alex poured two drinks.

"Did you hear that crazy bastard across the road last night?" Jim asked, then raised his glass.

Alex raised his, they drank simultaneously after saying, "Good luck," and "Nasdarovya, Nasdarovya. Oh, you meanit Mrs. Dubinski. How you know . . . how?" Alex raised his eyebrows wondering.

"Yeah, let me tell you. That was me she was shooting at."

"You? Why you?" Alex raised his eyebrows again.

"Yeah, the crazy bastard won't let her daughter marry me. She's afraid if she marries me we won't give her any money for drinks. Anna gives her every cent she earns. The old lady just sits in that house and drinks all day and curses her husband who left her. I'm tellin' ya, she's nuts. Cuckoo." Jim made a curling motion with one finger by his ear. "I hope she shoots herself some day."

"Oh, so that why we never see her. You know, that first time we see her . . . first time." Alex reported.

"She's crazy, I'm tellin ya!" Jim leaned back in the chair and touched his glass.

"Have another drink. Come on, haveit," Alex knew it was time for a refill.

"Sure, thanks. Well I figured you heard us last night so I thought I'd come and apologize. Three times I've gone through this. We keep tellin' her we'll take care of her, but she goes crazy."

Jim was so angry he was perspiring. He wiped his face with his handkerchief, replaced it in his pocket, then raised his shot glass in a silent salute. Alex did the same. Nadia came into the kitchen and placed a pot of water on the stove to make herself some tea. She had just finished the nightly ritual of bedtime spooky story. They could not go off to dreamland until their mother scared them on the path . . . I'm gonna get you . . . bad girls given away to junk man . . . big black bat eat you up . . . little girls lost and hungry . . .

Nadia sat down at the table to wait for the water to boil. Hearing most of the conversation, she said, "Maybe I go to her house and talk to her?"

"No," Jim said, still displaying anger. "She don't trust nobody. She might be so drunk, she will think it's me and she might shoot you. Don't go, I'm tellin' ya. I just want you to know Anna is a good girl, but her mother—Oh, God! The bastard is crazy!"

Nadia thought Jim Novak was the skinniest man she ever saw. Then she remembered how thin Anna was too. She thought, "Too bad, nice skinny couple. Oh well, maybe the mother will drink herself to death, like my Alex, some day soon."

Chapter Three

THE DUROCK FAMILY OWED LILY STORE EIGHTY DOLLARS for groceries. The butcher knew all the men at the corn plant because they ordered sandwiches and coffee from the store at lunch time, which Albert prepared. He wanted to collect on the grocery bill from Alex, so he spoke up for him to his old boss, so Alex got his job back.

Alex was very happy. They would live good now, he told his wife, and he was glad he lived so much closer to the "shop." Now that Alex was back to work, Andre's money was not needed as desperately as it was before. The children were happy to receive a quarter apiece and a bedroom all to themselves at long last, the sofa bed need never be opened again.

Andre moved in with the bachelors upstairs of Lily Tavern. He enjoyed playing cards with the men at night, and need not walk home to White Place on the unlit roads. Payday was every two weeks again. Alex became very drunk at Galuk's when he went there to pay a little something against his bill and to cash his check. When he finally came home Nadia was furious. She had expected this. She was waiting for him outside.

She could see the outline of the two half-pint bottles in his back pockets; he forgot to go to his shed first to put the filled one away; the other one carried the tea he drank at work and was now empty.

He was trying to pull her to him for a kiss when she grabbed the bottle and ran away with it. He did not go after his wife; he just stood there, placed his hands in his pockets and swore. Said, "Whew, whew!" and went into the house and to go to bed.

A couple of days later Alex came home with a watchdog for his private shed. It was a vicious looking police dog; he named her "Topsy." No one could go near her except her master. Alex had to cut a window in the door so the dog could see who was coming in before the door opened; she would bite first and look at the intruder later. The children were told again to stay away from Pa's shandy.

❖ ❖ ❖ ❖

One night shortly after midnight, Alex was on his way home from the 4:00 P.M. to 12:00 P.M. shift when he heard screams coming from the direction of the dumps far to the southwest. He saw Jim Novak and Anna parked in his car alongside her house. Alex went over and called to Jim. They both came out of the car. More shrill screams were heard.

"Come on, Jim. I go getit my gun. Something wrong over there on dumps. Let's go see whatsa matter. Maybe girl's in trouble. I go getit my gun."

Nadia came out of the house. Alex hurried to his shed and came out with his gun and a kerosene lantern. Anna sat down on the porch steps beside Nadia. Vera joined them.

"Come on Alex, let's go," said Jim. "I'm lookin' for a good fight."

"Watch yourself, old man," said Nadia to her husband. Anna and Vera were too frightened to say anything.

The night was hot and sticky and pitch black. It was going to rain. The crickets were playing their field symphony with the frogs as conductors over the uncountable violins. The screaming sopranos were rehearsing high C backstage in their dressing rooms. Mother nature decided to join in with her crashing instruments and created her own audience. The thunder overhead boomed the big bass drum. The wind hurried the dusty people to their seats, lighting their way with lightning flashes. The curtain clouds on stage were drawn back and the clapping rain came down. The midnight marching boxcars coming down the track played the snare drum and the steady ba ra ba boom, ba ra ba boom came closer and closer, stamping over all the other musicians and then two gun shots sounded and the concert was over.

Jim and Alex brought two crying, hysterical, rain-soaked girls into the kitchen and left them to be attended by the women.

"Oh my gosh!" Vera exclaimed.

"Are you all right, girls?" Anna asked.

"We're okay," both girls answered as they sobbed.

"Oye, oye, oye," Nadia moaned.

"Look at my dress," the pretty red-haired girl cried as she looked down at the pale green, wet, dirtied and torn garment. "It's brand new. I just bought it today. Oh, it's ruined, I just know it is. This material should never get wet, it'll shrink."

"Maybe it won't," Vera replied. "Take it off. I'll sew it and try to wash the spots off."

Nadia went into her bedroom and returned with a cigar box that held needles, thread, and assorted buttons, then went to the stove for the kettle of hot water and carried it to the sink, poured some into the pan and mixed cold water into it to cool it off a bit.

"Take yours off too," Anna said to the tall brunette who appeared to be the same age as her friend.

"I don't think it's any use. It's all ripped," she cried. "I saved for a whole month to buy it. I've only had it a week. I'll probably have to throw it away."

"But you can't go home looking like that," Anna told her. "I'll try to fix it a little."

The girls took off their dresses and Anna and Vera sewed and cleaned them as best as they could.

Nadia helped the girls wash the bruises on their faces and backs and applied mercurochrome to their scratched, cut, and bleeding arms. They could not stop crying about their ruined new dresses.

The door leading into the living room had been closed before the victims came in so as not to waken the sleeping children, but their voices were heard, and the youngsters took turns peeking through the key hole.

"What happened to you?" Vera finally asked.

"Oh, it was awful," the brunette began. "They told us to give or get out way out there in no-man's land. We got out and ran. They ran after us. We didn't know where we were, it was so dark, we couldn't see anything. We both fell into a big ditch in the swamps. They found us. We heard the gun go off and they got scared finally and they ran back to the car. They drove off and left us there. We kept screaming and then your men found us."

"Thank God they heard us," the redhead reported with a deep sigh.

"Who were the boys?" Vera asked.

The brunette answered, "Those two Girman boys who live at Blue Place. I know one of them was in jail for stealing, but we didn't think they would do a thing like this."

They had been out for a happy time wearing their new dresses, that's all. The girls put their dresses on and the redhead began to cry again, her crepe dress had shrunken and was skin tight.

Topsy growled as her master tied her closely to the stake in the shed and told her to shut up. Alex and Jim had a couple of drinks inside the private tavern, then went back into the house after they knocked on the door to find out if it was all right to come in now.

"Where do you girls live?" Jim asked them.

"In Winsome," the girls answered together.

"Come on, I'll take you home in my car," Jim offered. Anna went with them. The girls thanked Jim and Alex for their deed. Nadia and Vera told them to take care.

The children scrambled back into bed and talked underneath the covers.

"What happened to 'em?" Olga whispered.

"They were raped," Daria answered.

"Yeah, on the dumps," Nina added.

A couple of months later, the Girman boys, whose father died when they were young and whose mother was an alcoholic, were each given a six-month jail sentence for raping two seventeen-year-old girls.

Chapter Four

THE RESIDENTS OF LILY LEARNED THAT THE SWAMPS and fields were going to be filled in, first with garbage, then it would all be covered with slag. It was a mosquito abatement program. The neighboring cities and towns had been complaining for years. The project began at Lily Pad Lake and worked its way slowly behind Blue Place towards the Forest Preserves. It was five years before the dump area was visible to the people living at White. The trucks were being paid two dollars per load when they dumped their debris. A Mr. Nelson was hired to manage the big undertaking. At first, about ten trucks a day were seen going down the main road. The number increased rapidly. The children made a game of counting the number of trucks seen daily.

Nadia was on the main road one day when she had to step aside to let a dump truck go by. When it passed her, she saw crates of old produce on the truck. The next day she took a stick and a gunny sack and went to the dumps. She brought home lettuce edible enough for the ducks to eat, old bread for the geese, paper wrapping from oranges for the outhouse and a catalog that delighted the children. This would not go into the show until they were through exploring every page, daydreaming about every item. The priceless treasure their mother found was taken to the swing area where they stretched out on the grass and studied every exciting page.

They ooohed and aaahed at all the pretty dresses and pointed to the ones they thought their mother and Vera would look "peachy" in. They picked out high-heeled shoes for Vera and they giggled at the silly looking corsets.

Nina said to this, "How could you run with one of those on?"

"Don't be so stupid," Daria snickered, "You don't run when you're a lady."

The pages of baby necessities made Nina say, "I wish Mama would have a baby."

Olga added, "Be nice if she had a nigger one. I never saw a nigger baby."

"You're nuts!" Daria told her, "If she had a baby we'd never get anything."

When they reached the section with clothes for children their age, they looked them over, chose the outfits they wished they had, went on to the next few pages and turned back to their sizes again.

Knowing they would never own anything as nice as what they saw, they became jealous. The pages of beautiful dresses, coats, hats, and shoes their size were torn out, crumpled almost to shreds and thrown into the bushes. "Spoiled brats! Capitalists!" They said they hated the Sears and Roebuck catalog, but did not throw it away and it did not go to the show.

They searched hurriedly for the toys. When they found the dolls, they went no further. Olga loved dolls and lived in a doll world. She stared at the creatures so long that Nina and Daria gave in and let their baby sister have the catalog all to herself. "Maybe Mama will bring another one home," Nina wished.

Nadia found herself going to the dumps twice a week, then three times a week. When more trucks were seen on the road, she was afraid she would miss something. She went every day. She found an old wagon without wheels. Alex made wheels for it and she no longer had to carry the sacks home; the wagon was heaping full every day. Occasionally she took Nina with her. Daria would not think of going. She would throw up first, she said. Olga begged to go but her mother said she could not keep an eye on two; it was too dangerous to be near the trucks.

Nina came home with broken toys, cigar boxes, bobby pins, barrettes, ribbons, Christmas wrapping paper, catalogs, and magazines. She wondered, as her sisters did, how anyone could throw all these things away. They were seeing most things for the first time. It was Christmas every day. Nina held a stick in her hands all the time, ready to go digging. Mostly, the stick served the purpose of not touching anything her mother told her not to touch. "Dirty, germs. Wash hands when you getit home, wash good."

One summer day Nadia found an old icebox, which she took home and placed under the porch. She went to the ice house with the wagon three times a week. The comrade manager of the frozen water business did not ask payment for the ice. Now Daria could drink milk without holding her nose. If Nadia came home with a doll missing an arm or leg or had none at all, the girls would smash it to bits, making certain no one else could find it good enough to play with. The girls would settle for nothing but a brand new one.

When Nadia opened a cardboard box that came tumbling out of a dumping truck, she was surprised to find it had held a brand new colored doll with ten tiny black braids sticking out in all directions all over her head. A different colored bow was tied on each braid. A green and white striped sunsuit adorned her twelve inch tall brown body. Olga squealed with joy when her mother presented her with the "Pickaninny Baby," as she named it almost immediately.

Nina and Daria were very jealous. Their little sister would not let them touch the new toy and kept it close to her day and night. When their mother was not in sight, they snatched it from her hands and tossed it from one to the other. Olga cried so hard as she ran back and forth trying to recover the mistreated baby and threatened she would tell her father that they had to return it or expect a licking with the dreaded razor strap if Olga snitched. They had never seen any colored children so they were really fascinated by the little doll. Olga could not understand why anyone would want to throw her away. She envied the "nigger kids," as she called them, wished she was one and wondered why their skin should be dark.

"Don't you know, stupid?" Daria said. "They drink chocolate milk."

"What's chocolate milk?" Olga asked.

"Black milk from a black cow, dummy!" informed Nina.

Daria and Nina prayed for a brand new doll for Christmas. When they did not get one, they took their sister's doll while she slept and pulled it apart. The braids were out, she had no more arms or legs, her body was cracked and her suit cut to shreds. They threw the evidence on top of the camoda. If they couldn't have a brand new doll, their sister couldn't have one either, the Capitalist!

They told Olga the next morning the story of the doll-eating dragon they saw come into the house last night. "Just think, it would have eaten us if the doll wasn't here," Daria told her with her fingers crossed behind her back, making it a fib not a lie.

Christmas was a happy time in spite of the fact that they had no tree in the house and no presents, just good things to eat. The Midwest Corn Products Company held a Christmas party on the Sunday before Christmas each year in a large hall that stood apart from the factory in the front. This building was used by the sports club members of the plant. Santa Claus was there to give candy and toys free to all the employees' children. A large, lit, and decorated tree stood in one corner, records played the season's songs, and there was entertainment on stage, a group of youngsters from a dance class in Winsome.

The Durock family celebrated the season according to the old calendar. Christmas was always in January. The Russian men in Lily went to their countrymen's houses carrying a large manger, singing songs and taking offered drinks and money. One man dressed as a horse, a tradition in the old country, and clowned as best as he could under the sack and large horse's head drawn on the sack. The festivities always ended with everyone dancing the Russki Kozak, blessing one another and bidding a Merry Christmas.

❖ ❖ ❖ ❖

Alex gave haircuts to his men friends. Most of them came on Sunday mornings. They still hated the

Capitalists and the church, only now, Alex spit after each subject. He gave the haircuts outdoors, so there was plenty of room to express his contempt with spit. If the children overheard their conversation and asked questions, Alex chased them away. They would run to their mother and ask her to explain. Capitalist was easy, they too were jealous of rich people. But when it came to God, they were full of questions.

"Why don't we go to church, Mama?" asked Nina.

"Because Russian church far away from here, about twenty-five miles. Priest always askit for money. Papa no have money to give. Let priest go to work, like me, your Papa sayit."

"Did you go to school in Russia, Mama?" Daria asked.

Nadia told her children that she went to school a little bit. Alex went for about two years. School was far away. They did not have shoes to walk that far. They taught so much Bible in school that Alex objected. He wanted to read, write, and count. He threw his books at the teacher and quit. He felt the rich people wanted to keep the poor people dumbbells so they could be their slaves. Alex never went to school or church again. Only two people in their village knew how to read and write well. Alex and Nadia knew just a little bit.

She told them their father worked for ten cents a day in the fields in summer and in the forests in winter chopping down trees for firewood for the Pon. The rich were very rich, the poor had nothing. They ate milk soup with barley or dumplings for breakfast, and then cabbage and potatoes for lunch and dinner every day. They made three barrels of cabbage for the winter supply and when they baked bread, they made thirty pound loaves in their huge ovens. Things were

better there now-no more Pon, big revolution, no
more Czar, the State owned everything, everyone was
equal. Daria was astonished and said, "Gee, I'm glad
we weren't born there, I hate cabbage."

"Who is God, Mama?" asked Nina.

"God is God. He makeit you and whole world.
Jesus Christ was God. Jews killit him. They not
believeit he God, but he was; everybody else
believeit," was her mother's response.

"Papa says God doesn't give us anything."

"You have to pray a lot."

"I pray at Christmas for him to bring us store dolls
but he never does."

"Aw, you are not suppose to ask for dolls. You ask
him to keep your belly full and keep sickness away
from you."

"But gee Ma, we never had a store doll and they're
so pretty." Olga thought of nothing else.

"You do not need dolls. Be happy you haveit food
and clothes."

Olga was disappointed. Her sisters gave her their
stocking dolls that Nadia made, but she still was not
satisfied. She would go on dreaming about a new one
with real hair, a beautiful face, fancy dress, and
lifelike. Daria and Nina were sad for Olga.

One of Alex's barber customers was "Orange Art."
The color of his skin matched his orange-red hair. He
came all the way from Winsome on Sundays for a
haircut. He brought Alex a half pint of whiskey in
payment for the service. The contents were always
emptied before he left. They sat on the porch steps and
played the hand clasp game after the haircut. Alex
could have won every time but he was a good sport
and permitted his friend to win a few times. They
drank from the bottle.

When Topsy heard strange voices, she barked and scratched at the door until Alex told her to be quiet, or until she heard the unfamiliar voice or voices no more. During one of these sessions, Topsy would not be still.

"Why you keepit noisy dog like that?" Orange Art asked Alex.

"She my watchdog," Alex answered. "My baba never findit my whiskey now. Nobody go close to my Topsy, she bite. One time my Baba put sand and water in my bottle. Never again. I strain it and drink it anyway. I drink it . . . never again."

"I betcha free haircut she not bite me. I holler good. I betcha she lay down."

"I betcha no," responded Alex.

Orange Art walked over to the shed and yelled loudly, "Hey! Shut up! Lay down!"

Topsy barked unceasingly and kept jumping at the door, trying to free herself of her prison and get her chance to see the person behind the loud, alien voice.

Alex continued sitting on the steps and laughed. "I tellit you she no like nobody but me. You lose."

But Alex's customer would not give up. He opened the window and put his head inside. When he pulled his head back, Alex saw he was bleeding. Topsy had leaped and bit the intruder right on the face.

Alex stopped laughing and ran to his friend. Orange Art said nothing at all. He took one look at Alex, turned his head and spit twice towards Alex's private shed and the now quiet police dog. He walked out of the yard to the well across the road and washed his wounds. Alex began walking towards his friend to help him. He reached the gate when Orange Art shouted to him, "No come close. I punch you right in the nose."

"I sorry she bite you. I tellit you no go," Alex said loudly enough for him to hear. This was the only time Alex had not repeated his words, he was too sorry. Orange Art walked away and continued spitting as he walked down the road. He never came for another haircut. Alex's clipping and shearing business dropped off and he was lonesome for his friends. Apparently the story of the vicious dog incident had been repeated over and over.

One Sunday, when Alex had to drink alone, he became very drunk and went into his shed searching for more hidden bottles of the liquid that kept him company. When he found nothing but his gun, he shot Topsy, wheeled her dead carcass in the wagon to the dumps and dropped her off the embankment among the tin cans, boxes, and rubbish to be buried the next day by more debris.

Chapter Five

Winter in Lily was very hard on a girl who had to rise very early and walk a mile down the uncleaned paths and main road to the streetcar line. Vera still worked in the big city and many a morning hers were the first tracks in the snow. She found herself spending more and more nights with her girlfriend, May, who lived close to the candy factory where they both worked.

One winter Sunday, Vera brought a young man home to dinner and announced she was going to marry him that coming summer. Frank Corban was twenty-five, six feet tall, had black curly hair, and dark blue eyes. He was the handsomest man Vera's sisters had ever seen in their lives. The girls thought Frank should be a movie star. When the time would come for them to start looking for a husband, they too would learn to dance and go to Dance Palace, where their sister met Frank.

The Durock family loved Frank. Every Sunday he came with presents: a pint bottle for Alex, imported hard Russian candy for Nadia, and bubble gum for the girls. After dinner he would take the girls for a ride in the open rumble seat of his car. Sunday used to be just another day, but now they all looked forward to the dress-up day and Frank's surprises and attention. In spite of the fact that Frank was Slovak, Catholic, and poor, Vera's parents approved of him because he was not Polish. Alex said he would have disowned Vera if he was.

Nina found a sled on the dumps. The runners were bent but Alex straightened them. Frank tied the sled to the bumper of his car; Nina and Daria held on tightly as they were pulled out to the lake, screaming at every turn and deliberately trying to upset their ride to go rolling in the snow. Olga was too little for these escapades, and besides, three did not fit on the sled.

For Christmas Frank gave his future sisters-in-law four runner, clamp-on ice skates. Olga fell so many times trying to learn how to skate, she refused to put them on anymore, so Vera would pull her in the sled over the frozen water of Lily Lake. Frank and Vera were very good skaters. When the children went into the car to warm up for awhile, they loved to watch them skate together. They yelled to Frank to show off for them with his figure skating and clapped loudly for him to do more. They attracted so much attention that Frank would wave his hand to the girls and skate away with his fiancée towards the Boat Club where ice-boat races were held.

The fisherman who fished through the ice motioned for them not to come too close to the holes they had chopped in their attempt to catch the fish far beneath with their cornmeal bait. Lily Pad Lake was just as busy in winter as in summer.

One Sunday, after a long cold spell, Frank walked over to say hello to "Old Ivan" and added, "That ice must be so thick, I'll betcha it could hold up a car."

"I betcha no," Old Ivan disagreed shaking his head and blowing on his hands to warm them with the heat of his vapors.

"How much you wanna bet?" Frank smiled, looked at Old Ivan and wondered what size his eyes really were under the very thick glasses he wore. They resembled eggs with large moving pupils waiting for the curtain to close and keep them from popping out.

"I give you dollar," Old Ivan offered.

Vera was on the other side of the lake with Olga in the sled when she saw Frank drive down the embankment and onto the ice. She sucked in her breath as she heard the ice crack and watched the car, a 1930 Ford Roadster, make two complete circles as Frank slammed on the brakes. Everyone there had to help push the small car back up the hill, including Old Ivan; he paid Frank the dollar, but Frank did not take it. Vera was very displeased and asked Frank to promise he would never do a risky thing like that again.

As cold as it was, the children would not miss the thrill of riding in the open rumble seat. They were completely covered with a large blanket when Frank said to Vera, "I'll promise if you'll marry me now."

Vera took instructions and turned Catholic so she could marry Frank in February, just before the Lenten season. She was very happy that she would not have . to walk the paths of Lily anymore. She was going to live in Winsome, and Frank believed a wife's place was at home; she would have to work no longer.

Daria thought her big sister was very lucky; she too could hardly wait to grow up and escape Lily. Nadia was sorry her first daughter was not marrying in the Russian Orthodox church.

"Well, Ma, it's your fault," Vera admonished her mother. "Why didn't you take us to the Russian church if you want us to marry there?" She did not give Nadia a chance to answer and continued, "I'm not turning Catholic, I'm just finally finding time for religion. There's nothing wrong with the Catholics, is there Ma?"

"Well then, you should marry in both churches. We could party for three days like in old country."

"Oh, Ma! Don't be silly. What for? We never support the Russian church and I'm sure the priest would want a lot of money to make up for what you have not given him. And we can't afford to party for three days. You're just dreaming. Besides, the Russian ceremony is too long. We would have to stay for the long mass and then a whole hour more to get married."

"You are right," Nadia relented. "But you would look so nice in Russian wedding dress that I could make for you with lotsa ribbons hanging from crown on your head." Vera was right, she was dreaming.

"Oh, Ma! My white satin dress is beautiful and the lace cap has a long net veil that will trail on the floor. I'll have the florist put hanging ribbons in my bouquet of roses. How's that?" Vera compromised with joy in her heart.

"That be nice," responded Nadia.

Frank looked exceptionally handsome in his white shirt and white tie and dark suit with a large white rose, sprig of fern and one lily-of-the-valley attached together on the lapel. He had to drive to Vera's house that morning to pick up her family and take them to church. The two bridesmaids were already there. "Knuckles," the best man, and John, one of Frank's younger brothers who was to be an usher, were waiting in Knuckle's car to drive the attendants and the bride-to-be. May was maid of honor and Tillie, another girl Vera worked with, were bridesmaids. They both wore light blue satin dresses with matching ribbons in their hair and large bows tied over their right ears. Their bouquets were as large as Vera's, only theirs were pink roses with a great deal of fern and no hanging ribbons.

Nadia was wearing her new wool, fur-trimmed, brown dress with long sleeves, and Alex now owned a suit — his very first in his entire life. But he refused to wear a tie.

"No! Never!" he exclaimed. "It will choke me. I die! No. Never! No."

Vera shouted, "Stay home then!"

"Awright! I stay home then. Awright!"

Vera wished he would stay home. She knew he would probably get very drunk at the reception and she would be ashamed of her father. "But, Pa, how will you look in the wedding picture with no tie on? It's bad enough you won't give me away. Frank's brother has to do it. Now you won't wear a tie!" Shaking his head, he relented, "Then I put in pocket. I wear it for picture. That's all. Then I put it back in pocket."

Alex refused to walk down the isle of a Catholic church. "You think I am crazy? I am Russian! No. Never. Never!" he professed when Vera asked him. "I give you to Frank not to Catholic church. Frank good boy. Church no good. I let you marry him, but I no go in church. No sir. No sir! Never!" Alex would not even button the top button on his white shirt.

Frank asked Alex, "Need some help to button your shirt?"

"You too, huh?" He shook his head and breathed, "Whew. Whew."

"I don't care if you don't." Frank smiled and shook his head.

The next time Frank looked at Alex, the shirt was buttoned, but Vera's father remained in the car to await the end of the hour-long mass and marriage ceremony.

Both families sat with the wedding party for a picture at the Winsome Studio. Everyone was smiling and ready except Nina, who would not hold her head up. The photographer under the black covering had to ask her twice to look up before she finally obeyed. Nina did not smile when he squeezed the shutter. She had been crying all that morning because Daria had a new white dress. Hers was yellow and not new. Daria was flower girl and she was not. Daria wore a strand of pearls. She had none to wear. Daria's ribbon was wider and the bow was bigger than hers. Daria had new, low, white shoes and long white stockings. Her shoes were old, high, and brown, and her long stockings were tan. Nina had red eyes. Daria did not.

Why didn't Vera ask me to be flower girl? Sure, Daria is bigger than me. She's fatter, but I'm older. Vera told me she didn't want me because I'm brunette, and the girls in her wedding party are all blondes. I would spoil it. I hate Daria! I hate 'er! I hate 'er! What's so special about blonde hair? Daria's is straight, at least mine is curly. They could have bought me a new dress. Olga got a new one. I didn't get a new one because Daria's will fit me some day and then I can have hers. Nobody loves me. If only my red velvet dress would have fit. I never got to wear it. Come to think of it, I never even put it on. I'll always save it though. Gee! This is the first party we're going to in all our lives.

These were Nina's thoughts on the morning of the most exciting day for the rest of the family. Daria was thrilled. She found a boyfriend, Peter. He was Frank's nephew and ring bearer for the occasion, and had turned out to be cute. She had wished for days that he would not be fat. She hated fat boys. She was at Peter's side all that day and night.

Olga was still too young to care about being flower girl. She just thought of the pop and candy she knew they would fill up on at the reception.

It was open house at the Corban home that day. The living room rug was rolled up and everyone danced. Knuckles, who constantly cracked his knuckles when he was not playing the accordion, was leader of a three-piece band. A clarinet player and drummer accompanied him in playing the polka, chardash (a Slovak dance) and a few slow, popular tunes.

Alex asked Knuckles to play the Russki Kozak (thank goodness they knew it!) and Daria and Olga joined him in the steps. They called Nina to take part but she still sulked in the kitchen; besides, she was too bashful, there were too many boys there. Frank thought he would be needing a new living room floor once the party was over. The house shook when Alex stamped his feet in his dance.

Two neighborhood Slovak women had prepared all the food that was served buffet style in the large dining room. All the drinks were in the kitchen. Nadia had to keep telling her children to stop drinking pop or they would be sick. If they did not leave soon, she knew her husband would have to be carried home.

Frank drove his in-laws home at midnight and Vera went with them. He helped Alex into bed and waited in the kitchen for his bride while she changed and packed. Nadia started crying when Vera removed her veil.

"What are you crying for, Mama?" Vera asked.

"I suppose to cry. I missit you already. We liveit lots of life together," Nadia answered.

"Oh, Ma, we'll see you all the time."

"Don't cry, Mama," all the other girls said as they went to Nadia and hugged her. They were all crying. They were not crying because Vera was leaving, but because they could not bear to see or hear their mother cry.

Vera laughed and said, "You're silly. Stop or you'll have me crying too." She walked over to them and mussed their hair. They all laughed and kissed Vera goodbye.

"Come to dinner every Sunday," Nadia said to Frank as she shook his hand.

The new bride went to spend her honeymoon night in her father-in-law's house. Vera had no mother-in-law, she passed away many years before while giving birth to her fourth child, a boy who was born a cripple. Johnnie was not in the family wedding picture. He was not able to stand still, his head weaved back and forth, as it had since birth, and one leg was shorter than the other.

The Corban family had a housekeeper, but Vera would now take her place, cooking, washing and cleaning for four men — one who could not tie the high shoes he wore nor button a button. The oldest Corban son was the only one married and not living there. It was a big six-room house and Vera did not know then to how much work she said "I do."

Chapter Six

The closest public school was three miles from Lily. When weather was bad, the children rode the streetcar, and even then they sometimes walked so they could have money to stop at Lily Store for candy. When the Durock girls had no money to spend, they still walked through the store on their way home just to look at the sweets behind the glass case. If Albert would start walking towards them to ask if they wanted to buy something, the girls would leave before he could ask. They shuffled their shoes along the wooden floor of the store as they entered the side door and left by the front door, reluctant to leave.

When Olga started school, her teacher asked what her mother did to her hair to make it so yellow. Olga replied her mother put butter on it every day. The kindergarten teacher told her it was not right to tell a lie and took her by the hand to see her sisters. Nina and Daria confirmed the story, but did not add that the butter was used to oil the hair since it was very dry, not to color it. How dare the battle-ax think their baby sister would fib. Let her figure it out for herself. They would not give her the details. She made Olga cry. From that day on, Olga was nicknamed "Butter."

There were two other girls living at White Place but they always had to hurry home from school to do housework because they had brothers and fathers, but no mothers. The rest of the children were boys and they did not play with girls.

Twenty-two children lived at Red Place but Nadia did not allow her girls to play that far away from home. Nina longed for friends and wished they lived at Red instead. One of the girls was in her class at school, but Martha already had a best girlfriend who lived next door to her, Galina (Gladys in English), who came from the old country just that year with her mother who was now a housekeeper for two single Ukranian men. Galina's father passed away four months before she and her mother arrived in America. He drank so heavily that he could never save enough money to send for his wife and daughter. Thinking his wife might not get his insurance money, he named one of the men he boarded with as beneficiary. Ship-cards were sent to them immediately after the funeral. The new girl was tough, always ready for a fight. She misunderstood things. She did not know the English language yet. Nina stayed away from her.

Daria and Nina were in the same class in school. Their mother waited until Daria was old enough to start school before sending Nina so one could look after the other. Daria persecuted her older sister, calling her a dumbbell for being in the same grade with her, and all the other words that could come to her mind that meant the same thing. Nina withdrew into a shell which her sister broke a hundred times a day with the help of her girlfriend.

Barbara Girman, who lived at Blue Place and was the youngest sister of the boys who had the bad reputation, was in their school class. She and Daria were the best of friends. They were full of secrets and did not let Nina in on any of them.

"Get out, you skinny-blink. Don't walk with us," Daria would sneer to her.

Nina walked far behind them. Occasionally, they turned around to see if she was far enough behind. Nina walked alone. Butter walked with her friend Nanny, who was her age. They walked a few feet behind Nina, they did not want her either. "We don't need a mother," they would say to her. That is the way it was every day going to and from school.

Four of the children living at White Place were the Korosuk boys. They were Russian too. Their names were Vladimer, Ivan, Maxim, and Pavel (Walter, John, Max, and Paul in English) Their dog was always tied to a stake by their chicken shed that stood close to the path where the Durock girls had to pass on their way to school.

One day Nina left for school before Daria did. She wanted to walk in front of her sister for a change. When she looked back, she saw that the Korosuk dog had broken loose and was barking loudly at Daria who had fallen into a puddle of mud. She sat there screaming until Mrs. Korosuk called her noisy canine into the house. Daria dirtied her clothes and books and returned home to join Butter, who had a cold and did not go to school that day.

When Alex came home from the day shift and Daria related her experience, he wondered why she was home and not at school. Knowing Butter was sick, he went to talk to the owners of the beast who had upset his daughter that day and ruined her books. Alex asked if they would be so kind as to keep the animal farther away from the road where it would not bother the children or tie it more securely and closer to its post. Mr. Korosuk said the girls always teased the dog and he refused to put it in another place. It was his policeman and doorbell. Alex knew his girls did not tease the dog. They were deathly afraid of it and simply screamed when the dog would charge at them.

That night someone fed the big black mongrel a piece of meat filled with rat poison. The Korosuks and the Durocks never spoke to one another after that, not even the children. Mr. Korosuk acquired another guard, but this one was taken into a shed before it was time for the children to go to school and before it was time for them to return home. Alex's girls were the love of his life. No one was going to hurt them . . . no one.

Chapter Seven

VERA SERVED AN EARLY DINNER EVERY SUNDAY FOR THE members of her household, but she and Frank would not eat there. They made it a habit of going to Lily for their dinner. Nadia always had more than enough food for everyone. She baked bread, cakes, pies, and killed one or two fowl every Saturday. She made use of practically the entire bird. All the feathers were saved and soup was made from the parts that were not baked. The duck's blood was drained into a pot and neck bones, water, rice, dried raisins, prunes and apricots were added to make blood soup. The adults called it charnina; the children named it "nigger soup."

Nadia was very pleased with her son-in-law when he said he relished the sweet tasting, liquid food. "I'll run away from home before I eat that stuff," Daria would say. She could not sit at the table with them when they ate it.

❖ ❖ ❖ ❖

A year after Vera was married, she and her husband came to Sunday dinner and she stayed for three weeks. Frank, Jr. was born in the bedroom his mother once called her own. He was just as blonde and blue-eyed as Vera, so he was immediately nicknamed, "Whitey." Three months later, Alex cursed as he put on his jacket, buttoned it, and pulled his cap down securely to go out in the rain.

"Where are you going, Pa?" asked Nina.

"I go getit doctor. Mama sick. You kids be nice. I be back right away, right away."

The girls knew it was time for their mother to have her baby. They, like their father, hoped it would be a boy for a change.

Alex had to walk to Lily Tavern to use the telephone. On the way back from his urgent errand, Alex met John Janock, one of the White Place neighbors, and asked him to come over for a drink. Alex needed a man to talk to. Nadia had not seen a doctor at all during her pregnancy. Her husband was worried.

Alex needed the services of a physician for the first time in his life the day he cut his finger while sharpening the sickle. He hurried to Winsome to see about having the wound taken care of. It had needed to be sewn with many stitches. He told Dr. Hope about his wife's condition and asked if he would come to Lily if she needed him. The doctor wanted Alex to bring her in before her time, but Nadia would not go. There was no money to pay for visits to a doctor, and she had needed help from no one when she gave birth to the other children.

"Remember what baba doit in Russia? They haveit baby in fields and they go right back to work," she reminded her husband. Now she had to have help. She could not do it alone. The baby was too big.

"Is the doctor here?" Daria asked her father when he came in the door. "Mama's hollering." Daria had tears in her eyes. Her sisters were whimpering quietly while sitting on the couch and twisting handkerchiefs in their laps.

"No, not yet," Alex answered breathlessly. "He be here pretty soon . . . pretty soon."

He removed his wet cap, hit it against his thigh, and placed it back on his head. It had been raining all day. It was the month of March.

John Janock came into the house to be with his neighbor as he was asked. Alex pulled out a half pint of whiskey from one of his back pockets in his pants and placed it on the table. He then went into the pantry and returned with two shot glasses and filled them. Alex drank two before his friend finished his first and skipped the ritual of the repeated Nasdarovya he was accustomed to saying before each drink. John sat down and was silent.

"I go outside and wait for doctor," Alex announced. "You kids be good now, be good."

He turned to his neighbor and said, "Help yourself all you want, help yourself." Alex pointed to the bottle on the table, turned up the collar on his jacket and pulled his cap down as far as it would go. He turned on the flashlight he took from his pocket and went outside.

Alex was afraid the doctor would not find the way. Lily had no electricity, street signs, or house addresses. When he came out of his shed with a lantern, he heard the crashing thunder and imagined it was the doctor's car smashing into the outhouse, it stood so close to the road just past their house.

Thinking, "Oh no, the doctor passed the house!" the girls knelt on the couch and looked out the window. It was raining very hard. They too feared the good doctor their mother needed so desperately this night could not possibly find the way. Then they saw the wavering light and the headlights of a car. They went off and the good doctor came into the house.

"Get the kids out of here," Dr. Hope ordered. He was as short as Alex and as gray. No one had to tell where the suffering patient was, she could be heard. Nadia was in the first bedroom off the living room. She was saying the Lord's Prayer in her native tongue in between her moans and screams.

"Hey, kids, come here. Go in my room and putit your finger in your ears. And no takeum out till I tellit you, not till I tellit you." This is what Alex ordered. No, he commanded, as he shook his finger at his girls and closed the door after they entered his dark bedroom off the kitchen.

Alex put more wood in the kitchen stove and poked at the fire to make it blaze. He went out of the house and returned with two pails of water. He filled four pots with the well water and John set them on the stove to heat. Alex hung his wet jacket and cap on a nail in the woodwork close to the stove. They sat at the kitchen table and Alex wiped his perspiring face. His hands trembled as he poured whiskey into the two glasses.

"Sonofabitch!" Alex swore. "Lookit what I do to her at her age. Sonofabitch! Sonofabitch!" He downed his drink and poured another.

"Why don't you pray?" John suggested. "Your wife is praying."

"Pray? For what? God no helpit her. She help herself. What can he do? Nothing. Pray? For what?"

"You know you want a son. Why don't you ask Him to make it a healthy son?" John tried again.

"He not makeit son. I doit that myself. No, I no pray. Everything I doit, I doit myself. God no help me or my wife. No. No." Alex shook his head and reached into his shirt pocket for his loose tobacco and papers to make a cigarette.

"Every man to himself," John replied as he shrugged his shoulders. John Janock was Slovak and a Catholic.

The girls obeyed their father and put their fingers as far as they would go in their ears and still they could hear their mother. They cried. Their sobs helped them not to hear her low, moaning wail and piercing screams as well. They cried harder. Nina heard Alex swearing as he paced the kitchen floor and stopped at the stove to poke at the fire, banging the cover as he picked it up with the poker only to have it drop to hear iron hitting more iron noisily. Nina followed suit and muttered a few of her father's favorites in between her sobs, repeating them just the way he always did. She heard these words every day so they were every day swear words.

"I'll never have a baby," Daria announced as she lay on the bed and covered her ears with a pillow. Butter cried herself to sleep. Nina continued crying and swearing, trying to drown out all the other sounds as she looked out the window and placed her forehead up against the cool glass pane. The rain still poured down. It was a long time before she and Daria heard the baby cry in the bedroom right next door.

"Well, Alex, you have your boy and he's a big one," the doctor announced as he came into the kitchen for more hot water.

Alex could not believe what he had just heard. He could not move from the chair he sat in.

"My wife? How my wife?" he managed to ask from his trembling lips.

"She needs plenty of rest. She will be all right," Dr. Hope answered.

"She good strong Russian woman. You know doctor, I waitit twenty years to haveit boy. Yes sir, twenty years. Now I get drunk. By golly, I get drunk!" Alex pounded the table with his closed fist and offered the doctor a drink of whiskey.

"I never touch the stuff," Dr. Hope replied.

The girls went to sleep in their father's bed and Alex and John drank the rest of the night. Alex continued celebrating and missed two days work.

When Vera came to see her mother she brought her scale. The baby weighed nine pounds, ten ounces.

"What are you going to name him?" Vera questioned.

"How about Nickey?" suggested Nina.

"No," Daria disagreed, "Peter is a better name. Please Mama, call him Peter?"

"Okay, Peter," consented Nadia.

"Oh, Daria always gets her way," Nina mumbled. "Just because she still has a crush on Frank's nephew, she has to name our brother after him. I'll never call him Peter. We'll find a nickname for him, you'll see."

The baby boy was christened Peter Alexander in the nearest Russian Orthodox church which was twenty-five miles away. Alex always spoke of the boy he had waited for twenty years as "my sonny." Peter was called Sonny.

Whitey now had an uncle younger than he. Sonny raised the population of Lily to one hundred.

❖ ❖ ❖ ❖

Alex worshipped his son. Every day he told his wife to take good care of him. The girls had their orders too. Before he left the house to go to work, he told them if they did not help their mother, he would give it to them on the backside with the razor strap (a long piece of leather he used to sharpen the straight razor used to shave himself).

The girls were jealous of the attention that was given their baby brother, but were told over and over, "I wait twenty years for my sonny, twenty years." He was Papa's pet. They could not afford to be too jealous because the threat of the razor strap always hung over them.

Alex spent a good deal of his spare time making clacking noises and funny faces at his son. He would wink, pull his cap down close to his eyes, wrinkle his forehead, and then wiggle his cap completely off his head, adding a jerk and an "Oh, Oh" as it fell off behind him. They all loved to see him do this—even Nadia laughed. Alex had so much action in his forehead that his ears moved too. Displaying his muscles was still the girls' favorite and his.

Their merry play would come to an end after they all danced the Kozak. Alex could not keep up with the girls anymore; they already wore out one record of the Russki Kozak and were on their second. Some popular American records were cracked, but they played them anyway. Nina could not understand the principal of the Victrola. She would crank it and play it so long that her imagination would get the best of her. She would reach up into the opening where the sound came from and formed a picture in her child's mind that she was pulling out the minute singing, dancing figures from within, holding them in her palm, commanding them to perform until she closed her hand around them and squashed the tiny people to death. She made the movement so swiftly, she felt they had no time to scream for help or mercy.

Nadia's favorite record was a sad Russian song entitled "Vecher Vecheriya" ("The Night is Getting Darker"). It told a story of a girl named Mary who poisoned herself. No reason was given why she did it. Nadia always sang the lament as she worked around the house. Nina learned the words too. When Alex was not humming or whistling the tune of the Russki Kozak, he was singing "Aay Uhnem" ("Volga Boatman"). Nina soon realized all the Russian songs were either very sad or very gay.

Alex had drinks in him so much of the time that his wife would not let him hold the girls when they were infants. Now, when she tried to keep him away from Sonny, all Alex said was, "Aw, shut up, Baba, he my sonny, mine."

Another hazard was Alex's smoking. He still rolled his own cigarettes, but he started holding them inward, and the smoke was staining the palms of his hands.

Sonny was four months old when his father dropped him off his lap. Sonny cried. Nadia hollered. Alex had became inebriated. Afterward, he never held his son again.

Chapter Eight

SUMMER WAS A HAPPY TIME FOR THE CHILDREN. THERE were so many places to explore in Lily. They awoke with the crow of the rooster and went to sleep when he did. Nadia called her children "my little chickens." They dug for worms in the rich dirt around the garden when their mother wasn't looking, and went fishing in Lily Lake, rarely catching anything big enough to take home. Nevertheless, they ran to the lake with their cans of worms, sticks with string, cork and hook attached, serving as the fishing pole, and high hopes of catching a big turtle that they could sell to a large restaurant in Winsome that made soup with the reptile thought of as a delicacy.

They heard some of the older boys in Lily were paid as much as seventy-five cents for a large one. They enjoyed sitting on the shore, a few yards away from Old Ivan's anchored boats, where there was a huge cluster of water lily plants, and shushed one another when one tried to speak, not to scare the fish away. They sat there and whispered what they would do with the money, usually naming all the candy they would buy in Lily Store behind the untouchable, poor child's dream counter. They were told never to wade barefoot in that area because bloodsuckers would attach themselves to their feet and drink their blood quickly. People wore high boots when they walked out into the water a short distance to catch the fish nesting under the lily pads.

Butter was so elated by the first fish she caught that she decided to keep the sunfish for a pet. The next day she ran to say good morning to it and found that it had jumped out of the coffee can that was to be "Fishy's" new home. Buster was barking at the two cats they had, trying to keep them from eating it for breakfast. Fishy had expired. Butter held a marching, tin-can-drumming funeral up to the top of a small mound of earth by the swing area. She even wrapped Fishy in her best handkerchief before covering it with sand and placed a sunflower three times as large as the dead pet over the grave.

There was a large wild strawberry patch behind the well that was full of garter snakes with greenish skins and long yellow stripes, but that did not stop them from picking the red fruit. They bravely walked in, usually barefoot, carrying sticks in their hands to scare the snakes away. Their screeching voices also let them know the hungry, strawberry-craving children were coming.

Sometimes they found the snakes trying to cross the road to the other side, then they would scream and yell, and stick and brick them to death. They would stretch them across the road and wait for the feedman to come along in his truck to run over what was left of the reptile or reptiles. The youngsters would jump up and down with glee when the truck tires did go over them.

The next day, they would run out of the house to see if the snakes were gone because they believed that when the sun went down, all snakes came to life no matter what! Many times they found them gone and decided to do a better murdering job next time.

No matter where the children went they had a shortcut to getting there. Alex cleared a route to Blue Place especially for his wife to reach the ice house in shorter time and return before the ice melted. He made a bridge of old railroad ties piled high over the biggest barrier on this course, a deep hole filled with water most of the time. The area was cleared so well that the man who sold feed in small quantities began using the shortcut.

The youths shouted the announcement that the feedman was coming long before his old truck was even seen. They heard the rattle of the vehicle with loose fenders covering very thin tires as it bounced over the many holes in the road. The sacks of food that was fed to the fowl and animals lay on a wooden floor with no protection on the sides to keep the cloth bags from falling off and occasionally breaking, spilling the contents into the weeds.

The very tall driver invariably hit his head before alighting through the opening where there once was a door. He jumped down, rubbed the injured area and swore as he tried to retrieve most of the feed, telling "Old Betsy" he would never go this way again. But his pocket watch told him to use the shortcut every time.

The birds had a picnic after the dilapidated conveyance left. The children automatically named this heavily weeded and wooded thoroughfare Feedman's Road. This road was just past their house, past the well, past the outhouse (I mean the show) and around the bend that led to Blue Place.

Daria thought her sisters and Nanny, the boy who lived next door, were fools. Daria was forever washing her hands. She despised everything about Lily. She begged her mother and father to move back to Winsome, but they would not. Her parents loved the farm life they now had. Daria very seldom participated in any of the activities the others found joy in doing. She fought to be first on the swing and remained there most of the day, dreaming of leaving Lily to become a movie star.

Her girlfriend, Barbara, would join her on the swing; she felt the same way about the place she was forced to live in because her mother was an alcoholic. She too wanted to get away from Lily as soon as possible. Only Barbara wanted to be a singer. Daria could not carry a tune, she was always off key. She did not know it herself. Everybody made sure they told her so. So she would listen while her friend sang, "I'll Never Smile Again," over and over and over again.

The shortcut to Lily Pad Lake was called Mosquito Path. To reach this obstacle course they passed the show, turned left, pushed their way through tall thriving bulrushes, covered their heads with their arms, or they would be eaten and blinded for disturbing the millions of sleeping mosquitoes, as they teetered across four railroad ties placed over four deep holes.

They ran through more tall bulrushes, no water here, however, keeping their mouths closed all the time or you know what they could swallow (mosquitoes don't taste good). They reached the main road where they crossed over the railroad tracks and were at the lake, their favorite spot.

❖ ❖ ❖ ❖

Jack Doyle was a tall, muscular man in his middle thirties who lived in a small shack across the lake. He was always in the water so he wore a rubber suit that covered him up to his chest. When he walked on land, he took giant steps even though he was not wearing his rubber shield, raised his legs high, and placed the outstretched legs down carefully, giving the appearance of a man still trudging through water. He raised wild ducks and geese and also rented boats to fisherman who had to walk through a great deal of tall bulrushes and marsh before reaching his place from the Winsome side of the lake. Jack loved living near the water. He went to Alex for his haircuts. "But I never drink that stuff," he would say when Alex offered him a drink. "I drink Irish medicine."

He carried two half pints of his whiskey in his pockets at all times. He did not want to run the risk of running out, perhaps breaking one flask, accidentally spilling one or offering too much to too many friends. He was a perpetual drunk. The color of his skin and hair matched that of the liquor he drank straight from the bottle. His hair felt the snip of scissors and buzz of clippers about four times a year. He shaved on Sundays only, saying, "I talk to the Lord on Sundays only. Water is to wash in."

An abundance of downy hair grew in his ears. A canoe was his favorite means of traveling in the deep water. When the children saw the unbarbered, unshaven, red man in the rubber suit standing up in the easily tipped boat, plowing the water with a paddle as he headed swiftly towards land singing loudly, "Yo ho hum and a bottle of rum," they would holler as they hurried out of his way. "Look out! Here comes the Tippy Canoe Pirate from Irish Island." He would pick up his water transportation and carry it up to high ground holding it up over his head. His purpose in visiting dry civilization was either to replenish his Irish medicine supply or buy groceries, mostly celery sticks, which he crunched continually when he was not drinking or being barbered.

One morning, very early, Jack brought three of his wild geese to Alex in payment for a haircut. Nadia had those old birds in the oven for three days. They refused to be baked and the family, in turn, refused to eat them. Buster took one sniff and backed away.

❖ ❖ ❖ ❖

To get to the Forest Preserve in back of the house, they beat a path through the bulrushes with sticks and running feet. This shortcut they named Bull Path. Not because of bulrushes, but because this path was used when their mother and father took Josey the cow to the bull at a farm in a suburb of the big city. When it rained, the water was too deep for anyone to use their shortcut.

Hobo fires were frequently seen at the edge of the preserve. Nadia tried to discourage the use of Bull Path, but Nina and Olga would tell her they could run faster than bums. They were never without a stick in their hands. They caught frogs with their bare hands in this area, and brought them home to be pan fried in butter and salt. There were times, especially after a rain, when the frogs could be easily seen jumping high, and they were not prepared by carrying a sack; they came home with them in their pockets. And their dog was with them wherever they went. The only other way to reach the Forest Preserve was around Red Place to the bridle path that ran into and around the forest.

Josey gave birth to twins, one a bull. Alex slaughtered the bull when he was one month old. He tied the all-black animal to a fence post and cut his head off with the sickle. Most of the meat was sold to a Russian tavern owner from the big city who also served food in his establishment. He returned a month later and bought the sister calf.

Josey was not the same after her first experience at motherhood. She acquired rheumatism in her feet and the bones were rotted up to her knees. Josey was sold to Mrs. Girman at Blue Place. Nadia was sorry to see her precious pet go. She doubted they could get a cow to replace her; she gave twenty-four quarts of milk in one day. Alex bought another cow from the farm where Josey was sired. This black and white bovine animal, who swished her tail constantly hitting the milker and upsetting the pail in an attempt to rid her body of the biting flies, was named Golzy. Nadia knew there would never be another Josey.

Red Place had a crisscrossed shortcut that led to the store and the corn plant. The colored men working at the Midwest Corn Products Company used this path to go to and from their homes in the big city. The children named it "Nigger Path."

Butcher Road was the name Barbara Girman gave the short stretch leading from the main road to the three houses at Blue Place. Albert the butcher was the only person who ever drove into their section.

Chapter Nine

Vera and Frank did not keep their Sunday dinner dates in Lily as regularly as they did before Whitey was born. They found time to drop in for a short stay now and then. Contagious illnesses occasionally kept the two families apart. Vera was going to have another baby. She was experiencing morning sickness with this child and was content to spend every day at home. Frank thought Vera needed a change of scenery and fresh air to make her feel better, and insisted she accompany him for a short visit to Lily.

The children were out of school for the summer, so Vera asked Daria if she would like to spend the vacation time at her house. Vera dreaded the thought of the large amount of dirty laundry that faced her the next morning and knew Daria would be a big help to her now that she was almost nine.

Daria was delighted to be leaving Lily. When she had packed her clothes into a box, she went out to the car and waited impatiently for Vera to start for home.

Daria could hardly believe she would not have to spend another summer dreaming about living in the city. Nadia thought perhaps absence would make the girls fonder of one another, since they fought constantly.

Nina was happiest of all to see her sister go. She would have the bedroom all to herself and maybe Barbara would be her friend now that Daria would be away. Although at first Nina asked, "Why didn't you choose me to go? I'm older."

Vera answered, "You know Daria hates it here. And Mama needs you to take care of Sonny. You could do a better job of that than Daria could."

"Yeah, I know," Nina resolved, "I don't want to go anyway. There's more room to run out here. She'd make a real sissy out of him. I want my brother to be tough. She's so afraid of the dark she goes number one off the porch rather than go to the show at night. Even then I have to hold the flashlight for her."

Nina thought, *Vera doesn't like me as much as she likes Daria. Anyway, she never looks in my eyes when she talks to me. I wonder why?*

Daria did not return to Lily until it was close to back-to-school time. She had made so many friends in her sister's neighborhood that she came to ask her mother if she could stay on at Vera's. Daria transferred to the Winsome school and never went back to live in Lily again.

Nina was overjoyed. She could continue her role as big sister again with no interference from domineering, particular, nose-up-in-the-air, and don't forget conceited, Daria. Even Nadia admitted the past summer was a very peaceful one from the lack of fights over the swing; who locked Daria in the show, who would walk to the post office. Daria felt there were snakes everywhere, waiting to crawl over her feet, and would not go for the mail. Nina ran all the way there and all the way back, but still tried to get Daria to go. She had nothing else to do. Nina wanted to swim, fish, and explore.

The list of reasons for tears continued; who hid Daria's shoes, making her go barefoot for days, crying and screaming at the screen door as she watched the culprits run away, forcing her to stay in the house? Who would take Daria to the show as she danced and cried, waiting for her mother or father to find the hidden flashlight? Who would wash the dreaded dishes, making the broom decide as they placed hand over hand on it to choose the possessor of the fingers that had no more room at the top? Nina and Butter practiced so much that Daria did not have a chance. Who would peel the potatoes, feed the pigs, chickens, ducks, geese, and goat, fetch the firewood from the woodshed, water from the well, and the cow from the fields, and who would help with the washing and ironing?

Daria assisted her mother with the first chore and the latter, but would not go near anything that grunted, clucked, quacked, hissed, or neighed at her, the goat being the most dreaded. Nadia did most of the work herself, but when Daria left, the others learned that by doing all the small tasks the first thing in the morning, they still had a long day to play. Nina loved her little brother and the responsibility of being his overseer. Sonny was very independent, but Nina had orders from her father that whatever happened to her brother would be her fate too.

Secretly, all the children envied Daria living in the city. They knew she went to the movies every Sunday, and fruit was in a bowl on Vera's kitchen table all of the time. Fruit was just as much a delicacy to them as candy.

The only times they went to the Corban house was on the Fourth of July to see the big parade that went right past the house, stayed for dinner, and went to Winsome park to see the fireworks display at night, and then on Christmas day for dinner and to watch the electric freight train on tracks underneath the large Christmas tree in the living room that they always had. The train belonged to Whitey. Vera's sisters and brother never did believe in Santa Claus, but she would not allow them to tell Whitey and his little sister, May. Vera shook her finger at them when they made an attempt to expose the beautiful myth.

In summer the Durock children, like all the others living in Lily, took their baths in the lake. In winter they washed in a big tub with very little water in it. The well froze over in winter and water had to be purchased at Lily Store. It was a big treat for Nina, Butter, and Sonny to go to Vera's on Christmas Eve, before their whole day visit the following day and have a luxurious bath in the big, steaming, hot-water-filled tub. Nadia did not mind bathing in the tub after the youngsters went to bed at night. Alex showered every day at the plant.

Frank chauffeured the children to and from the washing trip. Daria would snicker at her relations when they walked in the door, "Oh, the dirty pigs are here for their yearly bath. What's the matter? No soap in Lily? You probably feed it to the pigs so you don't have to wash." Daria would say something like this every year.

Nina would reply, "Aw, shut up. We didn't ask to come here."

"You're just jealous cuz you have to wash every day," Butter would add.

Sonny usually came to his sisters defense with, "We wash more than you do cuz we get dirtier than you do."

Barbara Girman, who went to spend a summer with her married sister in the big city, decided to live there from then on and returned to visit her mother only on Christmas Day. Nina thought she and Barbara would probably never be friends because Barbara was just as picayunish as Daria.

❖ ❖ ❖ ❖

Nina, Butter, and Sonny were the best of comrades, realizing one should never be without the other in the hazardous place they lived in. One was not seen without seeing the others not too far behind, and Buster at their feet trying to keep up with their running.

The girls taught their brother to swim before he was three years old. Butter walked with him to the edge of the short pier and pushed him in. Nina was already in the water to rescue him if he needed to be rescued. Sonny swam. They repeated the instruction over and over, watching him splash and kick as he swam short distances with his head under water. Nadia was surprised at her son's accomplishment. Alex was proud of him. His sisters adored him.

❖ ❖ ❖ ❖

The children went mushroom hunting with their mother. The best time for the search was very early in the morning after a rainfall. They all dressed warmly against the dampness in the woods. Boots protected their shoes from the water, mud, soft grass, and fallen leaves. Sonny resisted when his mother attempted to add a babushka to his attire.

Nadia carried a warm scarf in her pocket until they reached the Forest Preserve and insisted that he wear it to keep his head dry from the dripping wet trees above. They carried baskets to place the fungi in and sticks to chase the snakes from underfoot. Nadia was familiar with the plants she hunted so often in her early childhood in Russia and showed her children which ones to pick. Alex was afraid the mushrooms were poisonous and would not let his wife feed them to the children. Nadia enjoyed them tremendously after she washed them thoroughly, placed them into a frying pan, added butter and then checked to see if they were good to eat by adding a dime or an onion. If any of the three items in the pan turned black while cooking, the mushrooms were deadly. When Alex saw Nadia scraping the day's work into the garbage, he demanded that she throw the pan away too.

Fall was the tea picking season. Alex would join them in this search. Coffee was never served in their house. The trees they looked for in the Forest Preserve were called *Lipo Tsveet* in Russian. The same type of tree grew in the old country. It was a short, small-leafed, perennial plant that usually grew in pairs sometimes very close together, sometimes as much as thirty feet apart.

Nadia could smell the tiny fragrant flowers and leaves before anyone could even see them. When either Nadia or Alex located one, the children looked around eagerly for its mate and kept score to see who found the most that day. About three all-day trips were made in order to pick enough to last all year. The children looked forward to spending the days up in the trees in spite of the scratched legs and hands and torn clothing they received in their climbing, tea-picking, monkey acts. The tea was hung in sacks to dry and Nadia would even pin a filled handkerchief corsage to her dress; she loved the smell as well as drinking the delicious brew. It was soon discovered that the two trees that held up the swing Alex had made for the children were *Lepo Tsveet* trees. They were told to be very careful not to break their treasured branches.

Chapter Ten

MATCHES FASCINATED SONNY. HE LOVED TO STRIKE THE short, slender piece of wood, to watch the flame as long as the heat allowed, blow out the light and blink his eyes a few times before lighting another. Alex allowed his precious Sonny to perform this arsonous function while in his presence only. One hot day in July, Sonny could not wait for his father to come home from work to begin his daily, enchanting act. He ran out of the house with the small box he had taken from the shelf above the stove, and lit one of its contents. When he held the match too long, he burned his delicate, four-year-old fingers and dropped the red-hot torch that it seemed to be at that moment. It so happened that he was standing outside the haybarn door, and the town's first fire started.

Nina and Butter were on the swing around the bend and could not see the burning hay from where they were. Nadia was in the house. She heard Albert drive up in the panel truck with the groceries she had ordered that morning and decided to go out on the porch to save him the trouble of coming in. One wall of the barn was blazing. Albert ran to the fire with a bucket of water from the well and ran back for more. There was only one bucket at the well. Nadia ran to her feather shed to get another, and joined Albert in the desperate attempt to save the haybarn. They knew they needed help. As they ran back and forth from the well to the burning structure, Nadia screamed and Albert yelled for help, hoping the neighbors would hear.

Nina and Butter came running with Buster behind them. Nadia would not let her girls go near the fire. They stood on Feedman's Road and watched the flames eat the dry wood. Smoke poured from the door that was now ajar. The wood turned blacker and blacker as the fire crawled higher and higher on the front wall. Mr. and Mrs. Costello, who lived next door, came to help, and brought two buckets. Mr. Costello was barefoot and just wore pants. Nanny Costello joined the girls at their vigil. Nadia held the water bucket lower to the ground each time she ran back to the inferno. The load was getting heavier and the girls heard their mother swear for the first time when the bucket spilled, making her return for a refill and wasting precious time.

Albert jumped into the truck that was parked alongside the house and returned with more neighbors, Alex and the fire department. The heat was so intense and the gray smoke billowed skyward from the dry grass inside the barn that was completely ablaze. Alex went into the row of sheds a few feet away from the barn, and released all the fowl. The chickens, ducks and geese ran to the road. The pigs ran into the fields.

Golzy was out grazing. Alex ran to untie the goat who was close to the house on the other side of all the excitement. There was nothing more for him to do. Alex stood in the road, holding the rope that was tied around the goat's neck, and watched the whole row of sheds burn to the ground. He could not swear—there were too many children around—so he just blew, "Whew. Whew."

Three pieces of fire equipment pumped the well dry and had to make connections to the lake to pour water on the house. Everyone was sure the heat would ignite it also. The frame building steamed when the water struck. There was no insurance on anything, of course.

The firemen would not allow Nadia to go into her home. She wanted to save the pillows and feather ticks she had worked so hard to make. Nadia decided to look for her children. "Deh yeah Sonny?" she asked her girls in Russian. "Where is Sonny?"

"I don't know, Ma. We haven't seen him," Nina replied. "We thought he was home with you."

"Lookit for him," she ordered.

They searched the entire area of White Place. Sonny could not be found. When they returned to the scene of the holocaust and reported their unsuccessful results, Nadia told them to look again and joined in the hunt. The fire was out. The house was out of danger. The fire department began putting all their apparatus away. The search for Sonny continued. His mother was crying and shouting for him. His sisters cried and screamed frantically for him. They ran through the fields in panic, not knowing where else to look. "If he burned in the fire," Nina thought, "Papa will burn me too."

There he stood, hands on hips, on the porch of the wet house, as if to ask what the commotion was all about. One of the fireman found him under the bed, knowing children hide when they have done something wrong or they are frightened.

"Deh ti buh?" Nadia asked where he was as she took his hand and led him down the steps.

"Hiding under the bed," he replied, wrenching his hands away from his mother.

"Poh chamuh?" she asked in Russian. "What for?"

"I didn't want to get a lickin'."

"There he is," yelled Nina when she saw her little brother. She ran to him and hugged and kissed him. "I'm glad you're safe. Where were you? We looked all over for you."

"I was hiding."

"So, there you are, you little snot!" Butter angered as she approached Sonny, "You're gonna get it this time."

Alex was too busy to reprimand his son that day. He was glad every living thing was safe. The livestock and fowl had to be attended to first. The cow, goat, and pigs were tied to the fence close to the house that did not burn. Golzy was covered with a blanket to keep the mosquitoes and flies off her. The chickens spent the night on the fence. The ducks and geese hid underneath the porch. Buster kept watch over everything.

Chapter Eleven

THE DAY AFTER THE ESTIMATED TWO HUNDRED DOLLAR loss, the children went frog hunting around Bull Path. Their nets consisted of cheesecloth sewn around a piece of wire that was attached to a stick. Sonny was very good at catching the leaping things bare-handed. He announced, "Gotcha, Bugeyes," as he cupped his little hands over a squirming, slimy prisoner. A cigar box held them captive until Nanny's pocket knife was used to sever their eatable parts. The remainder was tossed into the bushes or weeds, and ordered to grow back bigger legs by the time they were captured again. They caught quite a few large ones and Nina sent Sonny home to get a frying pan and some butter, salt, and matches. Butter gathered firewood as Nina and Nanny skinned the frog legs. Sonny returned with the ordered items and lit a match to the materials that would cook their lunch — dried twigs and bulrushes.

Alex saw the smoke rising from the fire they had made in a shallow ditch off Feedman's Road across from the swing. Alex ground his teeth in anger and swore as he hurried to the scene. He picked up a stick, shook it high in the air over his head, and yelled, "I teachit you how to make fire! I teachit you!" He stamped out the fire and threw the pan into the weeds with all his might. The contents of the flying utensil appeared to come to life as if searching for their rightful parts which were waiting in the weeds below. The lunch scattered in all directions and the hungry cooks did the same.

They had never seen their father that furious. They ran as fast as their youthful limbs would carry them to escape the shaking stick and raging intruder. Butter ran down Feedman's Road toward Blue Place. Nina ran down Mosquito Path to the lake. Nanny took off for the fields, then headed for home and stayed there. Sonny ran into the house looking for his mother. When she did not answer his calls, he went back outside and hid behind the well until he saw his father break the stick in half over his raised thigh before entering his private shed. Then Sonny ran to the lake to join his sister. Butter soon became a member of the runaway twosome sitting on the pier, dangling their feet in the water, trying to decide what their next move would be.

They knew the razor strap was waiting to make them sing a crying tale of woe if they ever went home. Nina expected to get the worst beating. She thought, "I should have known better than to start a fire today after the big one we had yesterday." Alex always told her she was responsible for the actions of her sister and brother. He relied on her older years and sagacity to keep them out of trouble and danger.

When the sun went down, they decided to go home, hoping the tyrant had calmed down, or forgotten the incident or possibly was not even at home. They had not eaten anything since very early that morning, and their stomachs were eager for nourishment. A slice of their favorite dark Russian rye bread with butter, or one of the other spreads they liked so much, would appease their hunger and obliterate the pains. Nina and Butter hid behind the well and watched their brave brother enter the yard. They heard the screen door slam, knowing he had gone into the house, listened for his cries, but heard none.

"Papa wouldn't hit his little pet anyway," said Butter. "Sonny's little apple never felt that damn razor strap yet."

"Maybe he isn't home?" Nina hoped.

"Huh, as mad as he was? Don't worry, he's waiting for us."

"Well, I'm not going in, I get blamed for everything you kids do wrong. We made a fire before to fry our own frog legs and he never hollered."

"I'm hungry."

"So am I."

"Let's go get it over with."

"You go first."

Butter left her sister and went into the house. When Nina heard her screams and cries, she firmly resolved to stay where she was. "I won't go in," she said out loud. "I'll stay here all night."

The female mosquitoes left the strawberry patch in search of human flesh and Nina had to leave her hiding place to escape the stinging, buzzing, persistent insects who feasted on her young blood. When she saw the lights go out in the house, assuming everyone had gone to sleep, Nina waited awhile, then walked to the window of the bedroom which Butter and Sonny shared. Realizing how close her father's bedroom was to theirs, she decided against her plan of tapping on the screen to receive attention from Butter.

Papa has big ears, Nina thought, as well as muscles. He'll hear me for sure. Wishing her sister was sleeping in her room tonight instead, she walked to the back of the house and called softly underneath the open window, "Hey, Butt, are ya in there?"

Finally, Butter snapped, "Whaddya want?"

"Sssh, don't wake anybody," Nina whispered. "Take the screen out. I'll climb in."

Butter pushed on the screen and reported, "It's nailed on, stupid."

Remembering something Nina said, "The one in the living room is loose. Go take it out."

Butter assisted Nina in her climb through the window and went back to bed. Nina did not remove her clothes. She covered herself with the thin blanket and wished they had not been heard by the ruler of their domain who had the just power to punish severely. When she had climbed into the house Butter had whispered, "You're gonna get it too. He said he'd give it to ya no matter what time you got home."

Nina was trying to fall asleep in spite of the emptiness in her abdomen when her father came into the room. Knowing she was going to get it, Nina decided to go under the bed and let him think she was not at home. There were no lights in the room so he could not see her under the bed as he poked with the broom handle after not being able to use the razor strap. He managed to poke her a few times as she curled up into a ball and kept moving from one corner to the other against the wall as far as she could go.

Alex started to perspire from bending down so much that he gave up and even left the broom in the room. Nina spent the night sleeping under the bed and cried herself to sleep.

"My kids never touchit match again . . . Never . . . no sir, never." Alex announced after the chastisement had been completed. He hung the razor strap on a nail by the kitchen door and went out to his shed to have a drink to his proclamation.

❖ ❖ ❖ ❖

The hay Alex cut in the fields beyond Feedman's Road was ready to be brought in, but there was no barn to store it in and no time to make one; quarters for the occupants of the burned out sheds were more important. The hay was piled where the barn once stood. It would be exposed to the weather that winter. Everyone helped carry in the hay and made a mountainous heap.

Alex ran from the field with a pitchfork full at a time. He tossed the dry grass on the pile and went back for more. The children carried it in their arms. Nadia used the wagon. It was a hard three days' work, but when the job was done, the children had the pleasure of climbing the very top to pack it down. When they reached the peak, they would pound their chests and shout "Aahuuhaah," the way they saw Tarzan do it in the movies.

Buster joined them in playing hide and seek in the big stack. The trip back to earth was a wonderful slide. The children limped on sore feet for days after this event. They refused to wear shoes and the closely-cut fields were like acres of thorns. Their throats were sore from the screaming they did to chase the snakes away as they ran with the bundles. Buster rested quietly after three days of continuous barking and chasing after his playful masters.

Alex worked very hard rebuilding the sheds and a new haybarn. He did not know then that he would be rebuilding them soon again.

Chapter Twelve

A MAN WALKED THE ROADS AND PATHS OF LILY ONCE A month carrying a heavy valise. The one suit he owned was black, crease free, shiny all over, and had sun-faded shoulders. Long underwear absorbed the moisture from his huge body in summer; but in winter he would doff the undergarments and needed only his regular clothing for warmth, no coat ever covered the fatigued suit. His white shirt was always soaked with perspiration and looked gray, but the handkerchief he used to wipe his wet face was so pure white in contrast that it projected like a thousand dollar bill protruding from a large opened garbage can, filled with nothing but potato peelings. The blue and white polka dot tie he consistently wore was never askew.

He used his battered black hat with a wide brim to brush off a tree stump, a log, or a porch-step before he sat down gingerly and breathlessly to rest his weary body.

"Oh, Lord, be kind," he would groan each time he made preparation to sit down, placing the hat in the spot he chose to set his large frame, looking back a few times, being certain he did not miss sitting on the hat. This habitual procedure discouraged the residents of Lily from buying his wares. Getting up was even a longer process. He would extend his arm as far as he could; if it be a porch railing he was reaching for, the timbers would creak and loosen from their nailed positions as he pulled up his fortyish years of two hundred fifty pounds and asked again, "Oh, Lord, be kind."

He required five minutes to dust off his hat, straighten it and wipe the inside with his immaculate handkerchief before adjusting it to one side on his head and turning the brim up in front. Before taking his leave, he said nearly a hundred goodbyes, good-lucks and God bless yous and, had to pat the cheek of everyone present, be it man, woman, or child.

He sold shoe laces, socks, stockings, pins, paper, pencils, envelopes, thread, needles, snaps, buttons, ribbons, bottle openers, handkerchiefs, razor blades, neckties, gloves, and so on. A cardboard separation at the bottom of the large, black leather case held lipstick, rouge, powder, creams, nail polish, and small bottles of toilet water that only three women in Lily purchased and consumed.

Nina and Butter waited anxiously for him to expose the last layer. He let them look and smell the articles they wished their mother would employ and dreamed of growing up to begin painting and perfuming themselves. Nadia felt sorry for him. Many times, knowing she needed nothing of what he had for sale, she asked him to come into the yard and sit down on the porch steps. Each time she inquired if he was hungry, his reply was always the same, "Bless you. A drink of water, please." Nadia would enter the house and return with a glass of water, or milk and a piece of bread and butter or cheese cakes. He never imposed. He would get permission first before opening his large suitcase.

One day, after a torrent of rain had fallen on the town of Lily, Nina, Butter, and Sonny were playing in the mud alongside the house. Nina was using a stick to write numbers in her spot and made long division problems to solve. Butter drew pictures of clowns in her lined-off area. Sonny was making mud cakes. Nina looked up and saw the salesman coming down Feedman's Road from Blue Place. He always walked along the main road to the last section first, then made all his stops on the way back. When sighted, Nina would announce, "Here comes the 'Walking Dime Store Man.'" No one in Lily knew his name; no one asked.

"Let's throw mud pies at 'im," Sonny suggested with a big grin on his tanned little face. "I don't like it when he pats my cheek."

"I don't like it when he pats Mama's," Butter offered. "Pretty soon he'll be trying to kiss 'er. Maybe if we're mean to 'im, he won't bother Mama anymore."

Nina disagreed, "You better not throw mud pies at 'im. I'll be the one to get a lickin'. He's a poor old man. Leave him alone."

"If he's so poor, why is he so fat?" Butter asked. "He must eat pretty good."

Nina responded, "I heard him telling Mama he has a hard time losing weight because his trouble is in his glands. He eats only once a day." Then she exclaimed,

"Oh, my gosh." She stood up and pointed down the road, "Look what happened!"

The corpulent man slipped on the soft, sticky earth and was sitting in the middle of the road, close to the show. He looked up into the sunny heavens and beseeched, "Oh, Lord, be kind." He placed his one hand on the suitcase beside him, steadied himself and was on his feet. But the bag opened from his pressure and the "dime store" spilled out into the mud puddle. Being so fat, he could not stoop to pick up the articles he had for sale. He sat down again and began picking up the dirtied items. He saw the children and called to them, "Help me, kids. Won't you, please?"

"Come on, let's go," Nina announced, and ran to the man in distress.

Sonny remarked, "Good for 'im. That's what he gets for patting everybody's cheeks."

"We better go and help," Butter decided. She and Sonny walked to the troubled area.

The fat man sat in the mud as his assistants handed him the wares which he wiped with his immaculate handkerchief before placing them in the store. When the job was done the three children made a human chain. Nina gave him her hand and pulled him up along with the others behind her. Their good deed was rewarded by a penny apiece and an accepted pat on the cheek.

He used his hat to wipe the muddied bag and went down the road away from White Place, holding the soiled handkerchief, hat and dime store in one hand. He lifted his head high as he walked and implored over and over again, "Oh, Lord, be kind."

The children stood in the road and observed his lopsided trudge and the unclean suit that looked more black now that the shiny fabric was wet and covered with mire.

The Korosuk's new dog leaped for the salesman as he approached the chicken shed. The canine pulled the stake out of the ground, ran in circles, and barked and growled loudly. The peddler swung his valise completely around to ward off the mongrel. The shoelaces, socks, stockings, pins, paper, pencils, envelopes, thread, needles, snaps, buttons, ribbons, bottle openers, handkerchiefs, razor blades, gloves, and neck ties spilled onto the ground all around him when the big case opened. The bottom layer of perfumed articles was tied securely and were spared the embarrassment of revealing themselves in such an undignified way.

The Korosuk boys called off their dog and stood in their yard and laughed at the sight before them. The salesman looked for a dry spot in the road and laid his bag down. Looking at the other two grimy items he still held in his hand, he tucked the handkerchief inside the soiled, rumpled hat and placed it lightly on his head. He sat down in the muddy road and began to cry. He began shuffling along on his large posterior area picking up the once-again dirtied dime store that was his only livelihood. He did not call to the laughing boys for help and the Durock children would not go to help. They were not allowed to go that close to the Korosuk's property and they were afraid the dog would get loose again or be released.

Sonny sadly said, "Gee, that's too bad."

Butter sympathized, "Poor old guy."

Nina added, "Sure must be rough to have only one arm. Oh, Lord, be kind."

Another peddler came to Lily. Except this one sold fruits and vegetables in summer, drove a truck, always wore a gray, denim apron over his clothes, and was the shortest man Nadia ever saw. Nadia grew her own vegetables so she occasionally bought fruit from "Shorty." Bananas were a treat for her children. The salesman, peddler and feedman were the only outsiders who traveled the roads of Lily regularly, not to mention the dump trucks and the people who belonged to the Boat Club, usually driving out there on Sundays, but they used the main road only.

Most of the Lily residents left their relatives in the old country, so they had very few visitors. The children envied having aunts, uncles, cousins, and grandparents. They would give up candy to have just one.

Nina and Butter marveled at the boy they saw stealing apples from the peddler's truck. They knew if they tried it they would surely be caught. But Thomas Costello was never caught. The Durock girls became his friends the day he stole two apples for them. After Shorty left and the apples were eaten, they went to call on the generous boy who lived next door. When they approached the gate and inhaled deeply, getting ready to shout, "Oh, Tommy," they saw him stretched out on the ground, drinking water from the duck pond in the middle of his yard. They did not call out his name. Instead, they exhaled, looked at one another and guffawed as loudly as two girls could. He got up and sauntered over to the laughing girls and asked, "What's so funny?"

"You are," Butter answered, still laughing.

"How stupid," Nina's turn. "Drinking water from the duck pond."

"Why not?" Tommy replied. "If it's good enough for the ducks, it's good enough for me. You eat ducks don't ya?" He released the rope that held the big gate closed and began swinging on the gate.

"Sure we eat ducks, but the clean parts." Nina answered.

Butter asked, "What does dirty water taste like?" She wrinkled up her nose.

He returned, "Like water. But it ain't dirty. I push the grass away."

"Oh my gosh," Nina said in surprise. "But the ducks probably go number one and number two in the water, stupid!"

"No they don't." Tommy shook his head. "I watch them all the time and—"

"Thomas, don't swing on the gate," Mrs. Costello shouted from the kitchen window.

"Wanna swing on our gate?" Butter asked him.

Nina offered, "Come on," and started running towards their rented property.

Their new friend sauntered far behind, dragging his feet, and adding more gum to the wad he already had in his mouth. Nanny, the black and white goat, was tied to a stake with a long rope alongside the house. When the children were walking past the grazing area the goat charged and almost pulled the post out of the ground.

Tommy was so frightened that he lost his gum to the ants on the ground and ran back home. It was the first time they ever saw him run. The girls laughed at him again and immediately decided to give Tommy the nickname of "Nanny." The girls had seen very little of the boy next door before this. He played alone most of the time. He seldom played with the other two boys living in White Place who were his age. Nanny was too fat and could not keep up with them. Then too, he wore knickers and the boys teased him.

The girls did not care. They were glad to have a playmate. The boys called him "sissy" for playing with the girls. Nanny would play alone for a few days but would join the girls again. Later on, the two families thought perhaps they would be in-laws if Butter and Nanny were to marry. They were a year apart in age.

Every Saturday morning, the driver of a shiny, new automobile opened the Costello's large gate and drove into the yard and parked. Then he opened the trunk of the car and unloaded sacks containing something quite heavy. He never lifted them. They were dragged into the chicken shed. The sacks were a mystery. Nina and Butter imagined the worst—dead bodies.

The girls questioned Nanny, but his response was, "I don't know."

"Whaddya mean, you don't know?" interrogated Nina. "You live there don't ya?"

Nanny's answer was, "I don't care what's in the sacks. I know it's not candy."

"Oh, that's all you care about is feeding your fat face with candy," snickered Butter. His pockets were always filled with candy, pennies, and bubble gum. If the girls would not let him have his way in their pursuit of fun and choice of games, he would bribe them with his extended handful of sweets.

Nina continued her query, still trying to solve the enigma concerning the next door neighbors. She asked, "Where do you get all that money for candy?"

"I have a piggy bank full all the time. I get some from the people that come over and my dad gives me some."

Butter gave him a shove and said, "He's your pa, not your dad." She was jealous they did not address their father as dad.

"He is too my dad," Nanny rebutted.

"He's your pa!"

"He is not!"

"He is too!"

Butter ended the controversy when she placed her hands on her hips, clenched her teeth and took a step closer to Nanny. Then she stamped on his toes remarking, "I said he's your pa!"

Nanny went home limping and crying but was out playing with his only friends within the hour.

Mrs. Costello was a friendly, robust woman with a perpetual smile. She drove the only car in White Place and was the sole woman in that section who wore makeup. She rouged her cheeks to match her wavy red hair, but did nothing to enhance her pale eyebrows and lashes. She gave the appearance of a big roasting chicken strutting to her car, going to see her boyfriend in the big city who was favored to win the cockfight that day and every day. Bernice Costello's face was completely pock-marked. The Durock children secretly called her "Holey Face." Nanny never knew.

Saturday was a very busy day at the Costello house. Cars drove up and men and women from Red, White, and Blue went in and out all day—another mystery. Why was their home so popular on Saturdays? Before these goings on, hardly anyone came to White Place.

Chapter Thirteen

A NEW ROADWAY WAS MADE FOR THE DUMP TRUCKS coming from the big city. They came in on an angle in back of the houses at Red Place and in front of White and in back of Blue. This road was made completely of a material called slag. It was almost white in color and was a coarse, hard waste from ore, discarded by the steel mills. It compacted easily. It was good for a road bed.

Small fires had started spontaneously on the dumps. Slag was hauled in to snuff them out. The new road was very busy. A truck went by every fifteen minutes raising a cloud of dust as it sped to its destination. The empty trucks hurried back for more slag and raised a white cloud that settled on all the plants in Lily. Various nauseating odors permeated the dumping region. A southeasterly wind would carry the smoke and smells of the burning garbage towards White Place.

The Durock family opened their bedroom windows at night just long enough to hear the chree, chree summer lullaby sung by the crickets. The songsters lulled the household to sleep, but the stench was so bad the windows couldn't stay open.

❖ ❖ ❖ ❖

Nadia took "her little chickens" for their daily treasure hunt on the dumps. They now found scrap iron, which they sold to the junk man who frequented the dumps regularly. One time it amounted to five dollars. They found pennies, nickels, and dimes so many times that they had dreams of finding a great deal of money one day soon. Nadia found a gold-plated wedding band that fit her ring finger. She lost her and her husband's copper wedding bands years ago. Alex had paid twenty-five cents for them in Russia. She wore this newly found treasure the rest of her life. Honest.

Nina and Butter shared their dreams and aspirations with Nanny. Sonny was never too far off. He lived in the world of small boys—sticks, stones, dirt, running, jumping, and climbing. The longest time he sat still was when he joined the others in the quest for four-leaf clovers in the small area around the swing. Finding one meant good luck. They spent hours in that region looking at catalogs and magazines that city people tired of and tossed into their refuse cans much to the joy of the fortune hunters.

The girls still wanted to become movie stars. They wanted desperately to achieve their goal before their sister Daria did. Nanny wanted to be a policeman. "Everybody likes a policeman," he would announce. "Or maybe I'll be a fireman."

Their dreamy thoughts were interrupted one bright, sunny day when a car stopped in front of them. They could hardly believe it. A car, and by their private swing. Holy Cow! A young woman put her arm out of the window and asked, "Did any of you kids find an old purse on the dumps?"

"No," they all replied, shaking their heads.

"It's a big black, cloth bag with small, different colored beads sewn around the top of it."

The children shook their heads again.

"Well, if you do find it, I'll give a reward of fifty dollars. There's three hundred dollars in the lining of it."

"Gee whiz," exclaimed Nina as she stepped closer to the car.

Nanny said, "Let's go look for it. What're we waiting for?"

Butter and Sonny said, "Come on."

Nina asked, "How come you threw it away?"

The young man behind the wheel answered, "She was packing her things and got careless. We're getting married this Saturday. That was our honeymoon money."

"We saved a whole year for it," informed the pretty, blonde bride-to-be.

"Gee, that's too bad. We'll go look for it. When did they pick up your garbage?" questioned Nina.

The young man replied, "Yesterday."

"It might be buried deep by now," Nina said. "but we'll look."

"You kids want a ride over there?" the girl offered.

"We'll get there faster than your car can," Nina advised. "We'll run down our shortcut."

Nina pointed towards Feedman's Road. "But you better not go that way. It rained yesterday and you might get stuck. We'll see you on the dumps."

Everyone from Red, White, and Blue learned of the young people's plight. Adults who used to say, "I go dig on dumps when roses flower in December," were now seen digging earnestly. They even brought their lunch to spend the day. Children from Red Place never went any further than the lake. Now, they all raced on their bicycles to see who would be the first one there in the morning.

Mrs. Korosuk went regularly to look for lettuce for her ducks, but when she asked her boys to go along, they answered they'd eat a worm first. Now, they were the last to leave. The mosquitoes told everyone when to go home. Many trees were minus branches. Every person carried a stick in his or her hand. Some carried two and three. In case one broke during their diligent efforts, no time was lost in getting another.

Lily Store sold their complete stock of gloves. Neighbors looked at one another suspiciously, wishing bad luck to everyone but themselves, and sucked in their breath when they saw someone who found an old purse.

The losers of the small fortune did not participate in the digging. They either sat in the car and held hands or walked around. They were depending on veracity and charity, hoping the reward would satisfy the finder. The compassionate searchers wondered if the sad couple who were now spending their honeymoon on the dumps, would ever see their money again. The odds were great. Most of the people in Lily had not seen that much money at any time in all their lives.

"What will you do with the fifty dollars, Butter?" asked Nina.

"Whaddya think? I'll buy every doll in the store."

Sonny responded with, "I'll get ten baseballs and a glove."

"An' me?" Nadia chimed in. "I getit pump inside house."

Nanny's turn, "I'll buy enough candy and gum to last all of us a whole year or two."

"I wouldn't know what to do with that much money," dreamily spoke Nina. "I'd put it away for awhile and think about it. If I didn't, I'd probably spend it all at once and then be sorry later. This way I'd be sure."

Even Alex let them know what he would do with it. "An' me? I saveit money to have enough to send for Irina some day."

The hunt for the purse went on for ten days. Gradually, everyone gave up. No one would ever know if the money was still buried or if someone's dreams came true with more than fifty dollars. It was finally assumed that the dump truck driver found it. Some adults said, "I go to dumps again when it snow in July." Some young people said, "I'll eat a dirty, rotten apple before I go there again."

The dumps attracted youngsters from the neighboring cities who went seeking buried treasure. They were usually boys who had hitched a ride on the back of a garbage truck. They very seldom tried to hop a returning ride. The large vehicles traveled too fast when empty and bounced over the now bumpy road to the extent of throwing off the unlawful passengers. And then too, the dust screen prohibited vision. Now that the new road was in, a few garbage trucks from the big city had permission to dump in Lily.

Nevertheless, more trucks filled with slag rather than garbage came in from the north.

Three, thirsty, slag-eating boys came to the well and asked Nadia for a drink of water. Nadia had been washing clothes that day—by hand, of course—and had already made her eleventh trip across the road to the well. Her arms were extremely enervated. As she was lifting the heavy, water-filled pail, she dropped it back into the well. What she saw made her even more weak.

"Oh, you crazy boy," she exclaimed to one of the boys who looked not more than ten years old. "Take that outta you mouth. No. I no giveit you drink water."

Reluctantly, the youngster took the baby garter snake out of his mouth and placed it in the pocket of his blue jeans along with three brothers or sisters already in there. He put his hand in his shirt pocket and revealed two more infant reptiles. He held them in his hand awhile, then returned them to their new, warm nest over his heart.

Nadia gave the boys a drink of water and had to have one herself; she felt sick. She held onto the wooden sides of the well and spoke to her rippling reflection, "See, city boys worse than farm kids."

She spat on the ground and went back to her laundry. She stopped before she reached the gate to switch the load to the other hand, feeling the weight of the pail filled almost to the top with water, and noticed the calluses on both hands that looked as though they belonged to a hard-working man.

One day Nina stood and stared at the girl she saw sitting in Mr. Nelson's parked car on the dumps. She had never seen a prettier girl. The fair-haired girl left the car, said something to the dump manager, and they walked to the car together and drove away.

Nina came out of her trance and asked, "Who was that, Mama?"

"Who?"

"That beautiful girl with Mr. Nelson."

"Oh, she he daughter. She old like you." Meaning they were the same age.

"Did you see her pretty dress? Where do they live?"

Nadia pointed towards the Forest Preserve. "Over there."

Nina could not see the house. The next day Nina asked, "Who wants to go with me?"

"Where ya goin'?" Butter inquired nonchalantly as she swung higher and higher on the swing.

"To see where the Princess of the Dumps lives," Nina responded just as coolly.

Butter stopped swinging and asked, "What? Who? Where?"

Nina began to laugh. "I thought that would floor ya," she said with glee.

"Who are you talkin' about?" Butter was very interested now.

"The dump manager's daughter. Is she ever pretty! I saw her yesterday and you should have seen the dress she had on." Nina spoke excitedly. "It was yellow and had a scoop neckline with little white flowers all around the top. And her hair. It's so blonde, it's almost white. I don't know her name so I call her the Princess of the Dumps. I'd sure like to be her friend. I'll bet she has everything. Betcha her father doesn't drink. She wouldn't have such a pretty dress if he did."

"Where does she live?" Butter was really interested.

"Come on, I'll show you. Mama showed me where."

"G'bye," they both called to Sonny and Nanny. "See ya next Christmas." They crossed over the dumps and followed the course Mr. Nelson had made with his car. The bulrushes were so tall all around them that they felt like Jack had planted millions of beanstalks here. They kept looking back to make sure the giant was not coming after them. They could not get close to the house. Two dogs barked and they had to run. They had caught a glimpse of the house that was surrounded by tall trees and their curiosity was satisfied. However, they had planned on calling for the girl even though they did not know her name. They decided they would just call out "hello." They ran through the bulrushes until they reached the dumps.

"Oh well," Nina said breathlessly and shrugged her shoulders, then held her nose. The area they were in was in great disfavor of anyone requiring fresh air. Still holding her nose, Nina went on to add, "Maybe we'll bump into her sometime."

What they saw was a two story structure that was made of cement blocks. It looked like a castle to them. They had never seen anything like it. It was from a picture book.

That night Nina's thoughts kept her awake. She wished the dogs had not been there. But then, every castle has to have knights guarding the grounds. *I wish we could have met the girl. I wonder what her mother is like, if she has one. I'll bet they have real nice furniture inside. Gee, the outside looks great, just like pictures on calendars. All those trees all around the house really make the place look nice. I wish I was an only child. No I don't either, I love Mama and Butter and Sonny . . . and Papa too. If only he didn't drink so much of that fire-water, we'd have more money. Then, maybe, I wouldn't have to wear Daria's hand-me-downs. I'm older, but she's bigger. I meant fatter. Gee, that was a pretty dress the Princess had on. Oh well, I'll get a job one of these days and I'll buy my own. That Daria thinks she's somethin'. Huh, she should see the Princess with that long white-blonde hair of hers. What does Daria have that I don't. A stuck-up nose and blonde hair. Everybody likes blonde hair better. But mine isn't too dark; the sun lightens mine in summer. At least mine is curly. Daria has straight hair. And who likes kids that think they're something they aren't.*

"Oh, go to sleep, you Lily dope," Nina said out loud, speaking to herself. This was a habit she acquired when she had things to say that she would never say to anyone. "Who notices you out here in the sticks anyway."

She put her thumb in her mouth and went to sleep.

Chapter Fourteen

FIRE ENGINE SIRENS AWAKENED THE WHOLE TOWN THAT night at midnight. Nadia would not let the children leave the house. The destruction they recently experienced was still fresh in her mind. The safest place for them at a time like this was right at her side. They stood on the porch and saw people with flashlights running along the main road by the railroad tracks.

Alex ran down Mosquito Path with the neighbors to see what was burning at the lake. He returned a short time later with the news that the ice house had burned to the ground. There was so much straw covering the ice, that the old frame building burned rapidly. The four horses that pulled the ice wagon into Winsome and Lily on their daily delivery route perished in the blaze.

The Winsome Coal Company added the town of Lily to its ice route. They made deliveries twice a week; an ice card was placed in the window telling how many pounds were requested. The ice house was never rebuilt.

Nadia no longer had to walk for ice. There was talk that soon electricity was coming to Lily. This meant refrigerators could be had to keep things cold. No more ice would be needed and more and more people in Winsome could afford refrigerators.

"I think, maybe, insurance money burn down ice house," was the talk. The children had wished the fireworks building would have caught on fire instead; it would be a big Fourth of July.

The total loss forced the men who had worked there to seek new jobs. They all moved to Winsome where they found employment. The first floor of the large two-story boarding house they had lived in was converted into a tavern. A large area on the premises was cleared. Weeds were cut as close to the ground as a sickle would permit. Trees were sawed, but their stumps were left protruding to serve as a resting place for the people who would come there.

❖ ❖ ❖ ❖

Every Sunday afternoon from July to the first week in September before the children all went back to school, a picnic was held. Counters were set up outside to sell beer, whiskey, pop, ice cream, and candy. Russian sausage sandwiches with a lot of mustard seeds in the meat, and sometimes caraway seeds, were sold inside the tavern. A few picnic tables stood off to one side. A dance platform was built high off the ground, giving the youngest children a place to hide behind the square pillars underneath. A railing protected the dancers from falling off. Two sets of stairs on opposite sides made it convenient to enter and exit.

The young people never used the steps. It was much faster to jump down. The boys went over the railing and the girls went under it. A four-piece band occupied the extended, raised niche on one side of the dance floor.

Artum (Arthur in English) Sorenuk was a likable, musically inclined Russian who lived with his wife, daughter, and three sons at Red Place. He was proprietor, violinist, and leader of the band. A clarinet, drums, and an accordion accompanied him in playing Russian, Polish, and Slovak music. Occasionally, they slipped in an American piece, but very few danced to this type of arrangement. Old-country music was by far preferred. There was much hand clapping, foot stomping, whistling, and shouting when the adults began the vigorous steps of the Russki Kozak. When the adults tired, the children took possession of the floor and money was thrown to them when the music stopped. They ran to the concessions to spend their easily earned change.

Mrs. Sorenuk was a beautiful woman. She also had a forceful voice that led her compatriots in singing all the Russian songs she knew so well. She could hold her liquor as well as some men, yet looked very feminine and gay in the Ukranian blouses she wore. Her tall stature and coal black hair and big brown eyes against her white complexion and delicately rouged cheeks and lips made her stand out above all the women in Lily. She treasured the gaily colored and intricately stitched shirtwaist with three-quarter length sleeves that she brought from the old country.

Everyone said it was unfortunate that her daughter, Martha, did not have any of her mother's attributes. The boys and Martha had all the aspects of their father, even in the respect that they loved musical instruments. The boys were not old enough to study music yet, but Martha already began violin lessons. The Durock girls outshone Martha in dancing the Kozak, but she was extremely light on her feet when doing the Polka.

Nina waited anxiously for Martha to choose her as her partner in the dance. Tears were displayed openly when the adults gathered at the picnic tables, spoke of the past, and read recently-received letters from relatives.

Everyone there had left loved ones in Russia and the neighboring countries. Letters were far and few between. They all longed for a reunion. The disconsolate group would wipe their tears (men too), blow their noses, helplessly shrug their shoulders, and then change their mood into a rollicking, laughing, singing assemblage. They gulped their sorrows down with a drink and Julia Sorenuk would lead them into song. Some of the songs were gay but most were very sad ballads. The cheerful music from the platform called them all to come and dance.

All kinds of races were held in the cleared area in front of the boarding house (they still called the building by its former purpose). There were various races for children and adults. The prizes were tickets for refreshments. Nina was the fastest runner in Lily. Butter was second. They even beat the boys to the finish line in the mixed race. Everyone in Lily looked forward to the Sunday picnics. The sounds of the music and laughter carried over the dumps and echoed off the Forest Preserve. Voices carried the news into Winsome the fun to be had at the picnics.

At one of the Sunday picnics, Nina saw Daria standing at the pop booth with two of her girlfriends from Winsome. Nina waved to her sister, but Daria turned her head and did not return the salutation. Nina spoke to Butter who stood beside her, eating an ice cream cone.

"There's highfalutin Daria," smirked Nina. "She didn't even wave. I'll bet she didn't tell her girlfriends she has sisters. Let's go." They walked up to Daria and stood behind her. Nina bumped against her and asked, "What's the matter? Don't you know your own sisters anymore?"

"Go on. You're not my sisters, you dump pigs. Go away and leave me alone. I don't even know you!" Daria sneered, put her nose up and turned her head away.

"Why you sonofabitch!" swore Nina. "You get out of here. Not us. What did you come here for then?" She knew she did not like Daria and vice versa, but now, the rejection of their relationship turned her emotions into hatred.

Butter shoved Daria and retaliated, "Who do you think you are? Miss Bizitz?"

Daria regained her footing and stepped back towards Butter. She held her ground and said, "Aw, shut up, you dirty pig! Go to the dumps."

The two girlfriends walked away from the scene as the girls began mincing words. They watched from a short distance, but could not hear what was said.

Nina stood very close to Daria, daring her to touch her, wishing she would give her reason to strike back. She said indignantly, "Listen you, if you're too good for Lily, what did you come here for?"

"To show off. What do you think? You don't know what city people look like," Daria grinned and walked away from her sisters. When she reached her friends, she said, "Come on girls, let's get out of this place."

She turned her head and looked back at Nina and Butter. "I can smell the dumps," she loudly stated, enough for them to hear her. "Whew," she added, as she held her nose and walked away.

"Who were they?" one of the girls asked.

"Oh, just a couple of tramps," Daria replied, "who are just jealous of city slickers and don't want us intruding."

"Gee," said the other girl, "did you hear that skinny one swear?" She raised her eyebrows as far as they could go.

"Yes, isn't it awful? They probably hear it all the time in this place and think nothing of it," Daria guiltily related, knowing her father used those words almost in every sentence.

"I thought I heard her call you sister," one of the girls remarked.

"Naw, you heard wrong. She just called me that because she didn't know my name. I don't have any sisters." Daria shook her head and held it high as they walked out the gate, lips pursed tightly, seething with discomfort.

Nina tried to hold back the tears, her mouth quivered. She and Butter watched Daria and her friends until they could see them no more.

"Don't let her bother you," advised Butter. "Come on, let's go get some pop. I don't know how she can stand to be away from Mama and Papa." Butter thought Daria was the most selfish girl ever.

"I hate 'er. I really do," Nina mourned as she blew her nose. "I was glad to see her, and then she treats us like that. Why, we haven't seen her since Christmas. Why does she think she's so much better than us?"

"Eh," Butter waved her hand, "the heck with her. I'll bet she'll never come here again. Let's go get some pop."

"You go. I'm going home. See ya later." Nina was almost in tears again, not understanding her sister Daria.

Butter ran to the pop concession. Nina walked slowly home, no need to run today. She could still see Daria and the girls far ahead. She knew that by running, as she was accustomed to, she would overtake them in no time at all. The less she saw of Daria, the happier she was, she decided. Daria never attended another picnic.

❖ ❖ ❖ ❖

Nina was almost thirteen and still sucked her thumb. Nadia tried every method to stop the habit that was making her daughter's front teeth protrude. She thought a bandage full of mustard would cure her, but nothing worked. The thumb was clean and in her mouth every morning when she awoke.

Daria's words had made a lasting impression on Nina's tender susceptibilities. She cried very hard that night. Her blocked nose rendered the impossibility of practicing her sucking habit. She searched her pillow for a dry spot, then turned over and looked out of the screened window. Finally, the sound of the crickets chirping calmed her.

She stared into the star-filled sky and spoke to herself. "I'll show that Daria some day. Let her be a movie star. Who cares. I hate 'er. I hate 'er. I hate 'er. Oh, why did she have to come to the picnic today? She spoiled everything. I figured she didn't tell any of her friends that her family lives out here. She is ashamed of us. It isn't as bad here as she thinks it is. She's just too uppity and we're just poor people.

"But why did she come out here? She should have known we'd be there. Like she said, just to show off and make us jealous. I'll do something big someday, maybe write a book about Lily. I'll bet there isn't a place like it on the map. I really think I'd like to be a schoolteacher. Gee, Miss Hayfield is a wonderful teacher. She knows I live way out here and she doesn't treat me any different than she does the city kids. I always know my lessons.

"Martha? Well, there's no hope for her. She'll just make it in school. Her first love is the violin. Who knows? She may be great some day. Her brothers love music just as much as she does. They could make a lot of money as a band."

Nina tried to suck her thumb, but she could not breathe, her nose was still blocked. She reached for a handkerchief and said out loud, "Why does Mama always have to crochet all the hankies? I'd love to blow my nose in a plain one just once."

She blew her nose and moved to place her thumb into her mouth. She decided not to, looked up at the stars again and said, "I'd better stop sucking my thumb or I won't be as pretty as Daria; buck teeth don't make a pretty smile. Gee, Daria has beautiful teeth and so does Butter and Sonny, just like Mama. Maybe I wouldn't have sucked my thumb all these years if I had someone to curl up with in bed. Nobody loves me. Butter is okay, but she just laughs things off. I'll find somebody some day that will have me for a friend and won't care where I live or what I live in.

"Everybody says it's more important how you live and who lives in it. We have a lot of fun here in Lily. I can't help it that we live here and I can't help it that they started dumping out here. Mama and Papa love this place. If only Papa didn't drink. But, it's been such a long habit that he can't stop. He must have been pretty lonesome without Mama and Vera for ten years, and worried about her and Vera all alone in such a big country like Russia. Gee, I should be glad we weren't born there."

The midnight train blew its lonesome whistle and the clickety-clack of the wheels on the tracks said, go to sleep, go to sleep, go to sleep. Nina made the sign of the cross, touching the right shoulder first, then the left, the way her mother taught her, explaining the Catholics cross themselves just the opposite. She did not know the words to say, Nadia whispered them so fast in Russian that the children never learned prayers.

Nina tucked both hands underneath her hips and asked, "Please God, don't let me find my thumb in my mouth when I wake up." Her prayers were answered. She never sucked her thumb again.

Chapter Fifteen

THE NEXT DAY WAS A VERY HOT AUGUST DAY. THE wind was blowing from the southwest and brought with it the smell of the dumps. To prevent the task of holding their noses, Nina, Butter and Sonny decided to go swimming. Water lilies with their huge green pads were seen everywhere along the shore, making the name, Lily Pad Lake, quite suitable. The white flowers with their yellow faces in the center hid from the sunlight. They opened their delicate petals at night to watch the frogs that hopped from pad to pad and felt the water snakes slithering by as they swam in between. If motorboats did not travel in the middle of the narrow lake, the entire body of water would be completely covered with the plants and their huge, flat, floating accompaniments. Old Ivan, and Jack Doyle kept their section clear of foliage not to discourage boating. Even the children helped by throwing seaweed onto the shore. They did this with a quick jump and a heave. They dreaded touching the soft mud at the bottom of the lake.

When the escapees reached their watery destination, a big turtle was on shore trying frantically to turn back on its legs and get free of Nanny's poking stick. They gathered around the action and Nina cringed, "What an ugly bastard. Let's kill it. You can take it to the restaurant in Winsome and get some money, Nanny." They all agreed and went looking for a weapon. As Nina was about to pick up a brick, she pointed to an animal drinking water in the lake and exclaimed, "Hey, Nanny, isn't that your cow?"

"Sure it is. What's it doing here?" wondered Nanny.

"Drinking water, naturally, stupid. Or did she come to go for a swim with you?" Butter asked jokingly.

"Aw, go drown yourself," returned Nanny. "Come on, let's chase her home. I'll bet my mother will give us all a nickel." He already had a stick in his hand so he went into the water to drive the cow out. Nina picked up a stick and waited on shore to help him guide the animal onto the path. Buster ran to the shoreline and his barking confused the cow. She did not know whether they wanted her to stay in the lake or come out.

Sonny called out, "Hey, what about the turtle?"

Butter suggested, "You stay here and watch it till we get back!"

Shaking his head he replied, "Oh, no. I want a nickel too."

"Then let's put it in that old boat over there." Butter pointed to a half sunken boat that Old Ivan gave up hope of ever fixing, and added, "We'll kill it when we get back."

"Good idea," Sonny agreed.

He pushed the kicking, snapping marine reptile onto a board, dumped it into the boat with a big splash, and ran to join the others in their pursuit of money to spend on candy or one of its other sweet affiliations.

Buster obeyed instantly when Nina called him to come to her and the cow came out of the water with great effort and reluctance. Then Nina ordered, "Keep her on the path, Buster, chase her home." He complied with zest, knowing the pat on the head and the "Good dog, Buster," he would receive later would make him complacent until the next adventure.

The barking dog and the shouting children brought Mrs. Costello out of the house onto the porch. "Open the gate, Ma, open the gate," shouted Nanny. The confused aggregation she witnessed made her hurry through the yard to open the gate. Being the easy-going person she was, she very seldom moved with more than the normal speed. Her heavy brazierless breasts bounced as she ran. The day was too hot to wear undergarments.

She then looked with surprise and asked, "Oh my goodness! Where's her calf?"

"Calf?" they all asked reciprocally and in unison, and looked at one another.

"She was in the lake, Ma," her son reported.

"Can't you see she's not fat anymore?" questioned Mrs. Costello and pointed to the cow who had stopped to get a drink of water from the duck pond in the middle of the yard.

"She had her calf someplace. We better go look for it. I'll give you kids each a nickel," she offered, "if you help."

They accepted with vigorous nods and smiles, "Okay!"

The dumps were searched first, then the fields, and then back to the lake. Sonny looked to see if the turtle was waiting to be killed; it was not. They ran all that day calling, "Here Bossy, here Bossy." They wasted no time in naming the young cow they had not yet seen. The mother of the new born calf was called Bessie.

The calf was not found that day. The youngsters reported to Mrs. Costello, waited for payment for a hot day's work, and wished they had gone swimming instead.

"I'll pay you kids a nickel a day," Mrs. Costello offered again, "until we find that calf. It has to be around here someplace. Tomorrow we'll search the Forest Preserve. Okay?" She waited for an answer.

They all acknowledged with a short nod and a breathless, "Okay."

If there was snow on the ground now, thought Sonny, *I'd eat it.*

Butter thought, *I'm goin' home to chip a piece of ice.*

Nina wished for rain.

Nanny said, "I'll bet I lost a pound today. Let's go for a swim before the mosquitoes start to bite."

Mrs. Costello said, "Bessie had that calf on such a hot day she must have been awful thirsty. She probably left the calf and went looking for water." Mrs. Costello was tired too. She did not like the sun. It made an uncountable number of freckles come out on her arms and the pock marks on her face were enough marks for one person to contend with. The children closed their hands tightly over their nickels and ran to the lake to cool off.

The next day was just as hot as the day before. To the enjoyment of the Durock children, who very seldom had the pleasure of riding in a car, Mrs. Costello drove them to their destination. The bridle path did not permit an automobile to trespass very far. The car was parked and locked at the entrance of the woods. They were glad they all packed lunches. The entire day was spent in the Forest Preserve. The shade in the grove of trees made it a cool search. They made up signals to call out every few minutes deciding on descriptive nicknames for identification. The name calling was heard throughout the woods.

"Hey, Skinny, where are ya?"

Nina shouted her reply to Nanny, "Over here, Fatso."

"Where's Mother?" hollered Sonny.

"Here I am, Shorty," Butter shouted.

"And here's me," Mrs. Costello called out, never too far away from the young group.

Nina kept a closeful watch on her brother. Papa will lose me, Nina thought, if Sonny gets lost.

The calf was not found that day either. Buster was glad to see his masters upon their return. He missed this excursion. Mrs. Costello did not like dogs; one bit her when she was a child. The third day, Mrs. Costello had the idea that perhaps the mother would lead them to her calf. She tied a long rope around the cow's neck and followed her lead down Bull Path. The cow led them directly to her baby, who was in a hollow at the edge of the Forest Preserve.

Mrs. Costello was very happy. The cow licked her calf. The children were sorry the search was over — a nickel a day would buy a lot of ice cream and pop at the Sunday picnic.

After having seen so much of Bernice Costello the past three days, Nanny's playmates felt free to enter the neighbor's yard and play for a change. They usually called for him at the gate and played nearer their own house which gave them better access to the swing area, fields, dumps, paths, and quick journey to the lake.

Mrs. Costello announced she was driving into Winsome and her son would have to go with her. Nanny did not want to accompany his mother. He felt proud to have his friends in his yard at long last. They were too busy watching the ducks wash themselves in the cement bottom pond in the center of the yard. Buster sadly waited outside the gate for them.

"Don't go away from the house, then," Bernice ordered. "I'll be back in a little while." She never before left the door of the house open and her only son home alone. Her husband was working the day shift at the corn plant this week.

Nanny promised he would not leave the yard and ran as fast as his stoutness allowed, holding both hands on his pants pockets to make sure the treasured, sweet contents would not escape and opened the big gate. Buster thought he was being invited in. "No, no Buster, you can't come in. Stay outside," he commanded. He waved to his mother as she backed the car out of the yard and drove off.

He fastened the rope around the post that held the gate closed and told Buster to lay down. He could not come in, he would bother the ducks. Then he pulled a package of bubble gum from its hiding place and walked lazily back to his friends who now were sitting on the porch steps in the shade. It was cooler there.

What an opportunity to see the inside of their house, Nina thought suddenly. They have been in two houses in all their young lives, their own and their sister Vera's. "Got any candy?" Nina asked Nanny when he sat down on the bottom step. He searched his pockets and found only one piece of bubble gum. "I'll go get some," he said. "Make way." He rose and they all moved over to let him pass.

"Let us come in too," Nina stated rather than asked.

He did not refuse. He said, "Come on." And motioned for them to follow.

At last! They were going to see the inside of a third house. They were more excited than the time they entered the movie house in Winsome for the first time.

As they went up the porch steps, Nina thought it was too good to be true. *He'll change his mind in a second and not let us in, I'll betcha.* She wondered what her brother and sister thought at this moment and how they felt. She looked at Butter, grinned, touched her fingers together as if to clap and then formed words with her mouth which her sister read as, "Oh Boy. Goody, goody." She took Butter's extended hand and they entered the house. Sonny was already inside — he followed behind Nanny.

Nina was almost afraid to look around when they were inside the kitchen. Butter still held on to her hand and started to back away. Nina pulled her in two more steps. Butter was afraid. This was all too exciting. Sonny was already in the living room with Nanny where he had his stash of sweets.

Why it's no better than what we have, Nina was thinking as she found courage to raise her eyes a little and looked around. She was disappointed. She did not know what she had expected to find, but certainly something better than what she now saw. She always thought her family was the poorest one in material possessions in all of Lily. *I better stop being jealous of people until I know more about them.*

I wonder why there's so many chairs in here? Only three people live here. She pointed to the shelf over the sink and exclaimed, "Sonofabitch! What's that?"

"Bottles of poison," Nanny replied nonchalantly, as he walked into another bedroom in his search for candy. He had it hidden in all different places.

"Bottles of firewater, you mean," corrected Nina. "What's that swimming around inside? Looks like snakes? Sure it is. What the heck for?" she questioned in alarm and held on tighter to her sister's hand.

"Let's get out of here," whispered Butter. She was afraid of what else they might find.

"Hey, Nanny," called out Nina. "Does your mother make that stuff?"

"What stuff?" he asked when he came into the kitchen carrying a box of candy bars.

"The whiskey."

"Naw, she just sells it to the people that come here. A man from the big city makes it. He brings it here every Saturday. Then my father uses pliers to take out the tongues of the garter snakes and puts them in the bottles. They flavor it or something. My mother says it's poison medicine. I don't know."

He conveyed the feeling that he could care less. He passed out the candy bars. He had found the good stuff, he had never before shared big candy bars with anyone. He kept them for himself. Today his friends were closer than ever before. He was happy.

One mystery was solved. *Our neighbor's house is a tavern,* Nina learned. *That's why all the chairs. That's why so many people come here on Saturdays, to get fresh whiskey. Oh, oh, one thing more. The sacks,* she remembered. *If I don't find out now, I might not get another chance. I better take it now,* she thought. "Hey, Nanny, what's in those sacks that man drags into your chicken shandy?"

"Oh, that's the corn that the man makes the whiskey out of. My mother feeds it to the chickens. Does it ever stink."

Nina turned her head to avoid looking at the snake-whiskey and noticed a piggy bank on the kitchen table. *I'll bet it's loaded,* she thought. Pointing to the bank, she asked, "Is this yours?"

"Yeah, it's my candy money. My mother leaves it where all the customers can see it. They keep it filled for me." Nanny grinned slightly, he felt like it was Christmas every day, now that he had friends. Having friends was better than having candy.

Butter finally relaxed a little and suggested, "Let's open it and see how much you've got." She walked over to the bank after releasing her sister's hand, picked it up and shook it. "You don't need all that. You're too fat anyway. How about splitting it with us, we're your only friends, aren't we? Come on, open it, then we can all go to the store and buy penny candy, all kinds." Her eyes were like saucers, seeing before her the goodies at Lily Store.

Nanny took the bank away from her and said, "I don't know. My mother will holler."

Nina said, "It's your money isn't it? You can do whatever you want with it." She turned and left the house.

"Come on, Sonny, we won't play with him then," Butter decided. "Let him keep his old money." She reached for her brother, grabbed his shirt sleeve and pulled him outside.

Nanny followed them onto the porch still holding the bank. He heaved a big sigh and surrendered. "Oh, okay," He reached into his pocket for the key. They sat down on the porch steps while he opened the treasury. It contained pennies, nickels, dimes, and two quarters.

"You keep all the big ones, Nanny, they're worth more," bluffed Nina. "I'll take the smallest ones." She picked up all the dimes, gave Nanny the two quarters and all the nickels. Sonny and Butter took all the pennies.

"Let's go to Lily Store," Butter excitedly proposed and ran to the gate.

Nina caught up with her and whispered, "Boy, is he stupid."

They dashed to tell their mother they were going to the store. When she did not answer their calls, they left without her knowing, figuring they would be back in no time at all, and they would run all the way there and back.

Nanny put his nickels and quarters in one pocket, jingled them, ran his fingers through them and walked to the gate his friends had left open and swung on it.

"Hey, Nanny! Are you coming?" Butter shouted as they ran down Feedman's Road.

"No, can't," he answered. "I promised my mother I wouldn't leave the yard." He wished he could go with them, but then, he did not relish trying to keep up with them. *They run too fast for me*, he remembered, *even Buster has a hard time keeping up with them.*

Nina, Butter, and Sonny never had as much money in all their lives, and now, they never had as much candy in all their lives. They each had a sack filled with bubble gum, different colored jawbreakers, tootsie rolls, bull's-eyes, watermelon slices, caramels, fudge, maltesers, jelly beans and small boxes of salted and chocolate covered peanuts. They did not spend all the money, some was saved to spend at the Sunday picnic. They held the sack of goodies tightly as they ran back towards their allotted play area. They stopped running when they reached Feedman's Road. Instead of turning down it, they went to the lake for a swim. Buster was the first to jump in.

When they went home at dinner time, they learned their mother had been informed of the deceitful piece of mischief her youngsters performed at the neighbors home that afternoon. Nadia tried to make them return what was left, but they were afraid and ashamed to face Mrs. Costello who had been so kind and generous to them lately. Nadia collected what was left of the money and candy and returned it herself.

Nanny received a slap in the face from his mother for allowing his playmates to take advantage of him and was told, "You cannot leave the yard or play with the next door kids for a whole week! And a dime is more than a nickel! Ten pennies makes a dime and only five make a nickel! Do you understand?" This gentle woman had a parched throat from shouting and needed a drink. She poured one.

Nadia never spanked "her little chickens." She gave that unpleasant task to her husband. He was notified when he came home from work. Nina was the only one who felt the sting of the razor strap. She was responsible for her brothers and sisters conduct. She should have known better than to think she could get away with a prank like that. Why, it was stealing!

There was still another mystery Nina had to solve at Mrs. Costellos. She pondered, why do all those people climb the ladder into the haystack on

Saturdays? What do they do up there? I wonder what's up there? More whiskey?

That week proved to be quite an eventful, money-wise week for the children. They lost money by letting the seventy-five cent turtle escape into the lake, earned money, indirectly stole money, spent some, and returned some. As a result the consequences taught them, never throw a turtle into water if you have intentions of killing it later. Money does not come by easily, you have to sweat for it. You never get away with stealing. If you eat too much candy all in one day, you may not taste or even see any again for maybe a half a year. And, it's more fun keeping friends than losing them.

The tumultuous week ended that Sunday with even more turbulence. On the last day they learned liquor breeds irrationalism. The children's interpretation, "Never trust a sonofabitchen drunk!"

The reason behind all that goes like this; Nanny and Nina were confined to their houses that Sunday. Their sentences for the piggy bank incident had not been served yet. Butter and Sonny had to go to the picnic alone. They returned a short time later and Butter was shouting, "Mama, Mama. Look what I found."

"Oye, oye, oye." Nadia moaned and then smiled.

"There's thirteen of 'em!"

"Deh ti nazlah?" Nadia spoke in Russian asking where she found them.

"I found them on the main road. Look at 'em, aren't they cute?"

"Papa never let you keepit. Who feedit so many."

"Who the heck would want to get rid of these darlings?"

"Yes, they cute."

"Hey, Skinny," she hollered to Nina. "Come see what I found."

She heard Butter calling her and came out of the house. When she saw the thirteen German Police puppies all in one cardboard box, she said, "Aw, how cute," and went to join in the petting and cuddling.

"Can't I keep at least three . . . or two . . . or maybe one, Mama?"

"I not know. You askit Papa. He pickit eggs in chicken shandy now. I haf to go back in house and watchit meat on stove." Nadia left the cooing cluster and went into the house. Just then, Jack Doyle walked into the yard. He was badly in need of a shave, haircut, and black coffee. He was highly intoxicated.

"Well, well, what have we here?" he asked. When he stooped and reached for a puppy, he fell down on the ground and the young dog whined when it flew in the air and hit the ground.

"Hey!" exclaimed Nina.

"Hey. Watch that," added Butter.

"Yeah, watch what you're doin'," Sonny advised. "They're just babies."

Jack kneeled on the ground and picked up the puppy he had dropped, "You have to cut their tails off. They've got to be short. Where's the ax? I'll do it for ya," he offered drunkenly.

"Don't you dare," Nina admonished.

"You leave my babies alone," insisted Butter.

"You touch 'em and I'll kill ya," Sonny threatened.

"It doesn't hurt 'em. Here, I'll show ya. I don't need an ax," Jack announced. "If I can bite celery all day long, I can sure as hell bite off a little dog's tail."

He took one fierce bite and a little stub was left. He spat. He put it back in the box and picked up another.

175

He said, "See. I told ya it doesn't hurt 'em. They just yipe a little." He proceeded in biting the other tails off.

The children gasped and looked at one another, then stood up and placed their hands on their chests, attempting to soothe their hearts that pained them so much at that moment. They were so shocked they knew not what to say or do. They could hardly believe what they were witnessing.

There kneeled the Big Red Pirate from Irish Island, biting and spitting and biting and spitting, giving the appearance of a giant with an enormous appetite who had encountered thirteen bunches of grapes lying in a box, tasting the bitter fruit hungrily, finding them too distasteful to swallow, but hoping the next, or the next, or the next would be sweet enough to eat. The violent unexpected biting made the green newborn grapes whine, some yipped, and some barked.

The children finally found words. Nina screamed, "Mama! Mama! Come here!" Butter yelled, "Papa! Papa! Hurry! He's crazy! He's hurting my puppies!"

Sonny ran over to Jack as he was about to conclude the thirteenth operation. He jumped on Jack's back and pounded him with his tiny fists. "Leave them alone! You leave them alone you old drunk! You damn crazy pirate! Leave them alone!" Sonny screamed and began to cry.

Jack stood up and dropped the last puppy, its tail was spared. When the airborne relative landed on top of the brothers and sisters in the box, the tailless menagerie cried out in their minute voices and moved over to make room for their sibling.

Sonny still clung and beat the huge back and shoulders of the surgeon who had used nothing but his strong Irish teeth as instruments. Jack reached behind and grasped the legs of the small infuriated boy. He pulled Sonny off his back, held him upside down and shook him.

Sonny hollered, "Help. Help!" The girls were screaming hysterically. Buster barked, ran to the drunken beast, who was forcing his little master to yell, "Help! Help!" leaped and bit the Red Pirate on the arm.

Jack swore at Buster, "You goddamned mutt!" and dropped the helpless, crying, frightened, beseeching youth whose plea for help had been answered by his faithful dog.

Sonny hit the ground head first. Nadia came out of the house, hurried down the steps and ran to her son who lay in the yard. Alex came out of the chicken shed holding a basket brimming full with eggs. He had witnessed the latter part of the rowdy, savage, ferocious action and injustice.

Alex hastened, still holding the basket of eggs and ordered, "Git out! Git out! You crazy drunk! Git out! Git out!"

Jack stood there, held his arm and looked at the wound. When Alex came near him, he took the container out of Alex's hands, held it high over Alex's head and tipped the basket, spilling the fresh, still warm, roundish objects onto Alex's hair, ears, face, arms, and clothing.

Four dozen eggs were lost and would never see the intestinal tract of the Durock family. Jack threw the basket down on the ground with great force. The woven strips of wood cracked, ricocheted, hit the porch, and bounced back in front of him.

He stepped over it and strode out of the yard swearing, "Goddamn, sonofabitchin outfit!" over and over and over. Then he spat, took another stride and spat, took a stride and spat, took a stride and spat. He stopped at the well to wash his wounded arm.

Alex stood there speechless. The moist mass dripped off his outstretched arms. He watched the crazed drunk until he disappeared in the bulrushes on Mosquito Path. Then he sucked in his breath and whistled, "Whew, whew." He felt the bump on his son's head, told his wife to take him into the house and went to the well to wash himself.

By the time the children came out of the house looking for the little animals Butter intended to mother, they were gone. She cried, "Where's my puppies?"

"They never give us trouble again, they dead. One dog enough. Buster is good dog."

Butter cried for days. But, the lack of ownership of one of these playthings caused her to turn her attentions to substitutes — fish, cats, dogs, baby chicks, ducks, geese, birds — anything that could serve as a pet, that she could cuddle in her arms and mother. She longed to have something living that she could call her very own. If she found a wounded bird, she tried to nurse it back to health. She wished Buster was a female so there would be a litter.

Her mother would not let her hold the two cats they had because they came in contact with mice much too often. She wished the fowl remained small and fuzzy much longer than they did. She desired greatly to grow up quickly and become a mother or a nurse. She no longer wished to become a movie star.

"Oh, once in awhile I still think I'd like to be one," Butter would say. "But I'm only dreaming." She still had a love for dolls. A long time ago she was given a second nickname — Mother.

The children played close to home that week. They went no further than the swing area. Butter sulked about her loss. She grieved, "Gee whiz, why did Papa have to drown all of 'em? The poor little things. I never saw such cute puppies. He should have kept the one with the tail. Maybe I'd had one of 'em now if that damn drunk didn't come over. He spoiled everything. Now for sure I'll never have my own dog. Buster loves Sonny best of all. When I get married I'm gonna have a house full of dogs and cats, a couple of canaries, goldfish, and kids too. Lots of 'em. And when they ask for pets, I'll let 'em have all they want."

That Saturday, Nina was anxious to relate all the happenings to Nanny, thinking the event would take his mind off the prank they had played on him a week ago. His punishment time was up that day. When he did not come out to play with them, they went to call for him.

He reported, "I'm goin fishin'."

Sonny said, "We'll go with ya."

"I don't think Mama will let us go," expressed Nina. "She doesn't want us to go near The Red Pirate."

"Eh, he's across the lake. If we see him, we'll run," Sonny said.

"What are ya afraid of him for?" asked Nanny.

Nina and Sonny told him the story. Butter did not participate. She swung on the gate when Nanny stopped swinging to hear the tale. She knew she would cry if she mentioned the word puppy.

Alex was giving Joe Turkov a haircut that morning. He was one of the neighbors who lived at Blue Place. He was the most handsome man in Lily. He was from Turkey. Nadia liked him and vice versa. When the barbering was finished, they went to the

Costello's for drinks as Alex's payment for the haircut. Nadia went next door with them. She had just finished making open faced cottage cheese cakes and was taking one to Mrs. Costello. She always said, "They tasteit best when they warm." When her children saw her entering the gate, they asked if it was all right to go fishing. She did not refuse. "Just be careful when you seeit Jack. You runit home fast," she advised.

Nadia very seldom drank, she called it poison. But her husband persuaded her to have one that day. Alex had three. Then they went home together.

It was a good day for fishing. It had rained the night before. Worms were plentiful. The children had no trouble finding them in Mrs. Costello's garden. Nina stopped digging and looked up just in time to see Mr. Turkov and "Crazy Catherine" entering the hayloft. Then two by two, six more people climbed the ladder and went into the hayloft that was above the cow barn.

Now's our chance to see what goes on up there, Nina thought. She didn't think they played hide and seek like they did. "They're all up there now. Let's sneak up the ladder and take a peek," Nina intimated. She was the curious suggester. She put down her can of worms and said, "Come on, I'll go first. Sonny, you stay and watch the worms."

Butter and Nanny followed Nina quietly up the ladder. Nina reached the closed door of the hayloft, opened it a head's width and looked in. No one saw the young face at the door. Nina thought, *Thank goodness the door didn't squeak.* Almost immediately, she motioned for her sister and Nanny to go back down. They ran to join Sonny in the garden.

"What did you see?" Butter asked anxiously. "Come on, tell us."

"Never mind. Find out for yourself. I'm not gonna tell ya," she refused.

"Aw, they're all drunk, that's all," believed Nanny.

Sonny started running and hollered, "Let's go fishin'."

What a fat, stupid kid Nanny is, thought Nina. *He doesn't even know what goes on in his own backyard and he doesn't care as long as he has candy and money.* Nina said, "I don't feel like goin' fishin'. You go without me. I'm goin' on the swing," Nina reported. The others ran down Mosquito Path.

Nina talked out loud to the trees and the sky as she swung on the swing, "Am I ever glad they didn't see me. How will I ever be able to look those people in their eyes again? That's what I get for being so nosy. If whiskey does that to you, I will never drink or marry a man that drinks. Oh my gosh I can't believe what I just saw! How could they? That Crazy Catherine was lovin' up that handsome Mr. Turkov. I wonder if his wife knows what he does on Saturdays?

"And Mr. Costello had his hand up Mrs. Buzack's dress. Mr. Buzack was in another corner with Mrs. Costello drinking out of the same bottle and her big boobs were exposed. Old Ivan and Mrs. Girman were naked and a little covered with hay. And those other people aren't even married and he had his hand inside her dress feelin' her tits. Another man was on top of a woman pumpin' away.

"Ye gads! What a crazy place this is. I'm glad Mama never goes there. I wonder if Papa does? It's that poison they drink that makes them do those crazy things. I'll never tell anybody what I saw today.

181

That'll teach me to mind my own damn business. Sonofabitch! I wish I could erase it all from my mind. I'll never be the same. Mysteries are more fun when they're just mysteries."

Nina stayed on the swing until she had nothing more to say to the surroundings, then ran down Mosquito Path to join the others at the lake.

That night Butter climbed into bed with Nina. She wanted to be in on her sister's secret.

"Honest?" Butter expressed in amazement.

Chapter Sixteen

LITHUANIAN LOUIE OR LUGAN LOUIE AS HE WAS CALLED by all the neighbors, lived in the first house in the front row at White Place. He had four grown children, three boys and a girl, who were working. When he began drinking heavily, his wife left him. The children married as soon as they could and left him too. He drank so much that he lost his job. He was given whiskey payment for the hay he cut in the fields for the Costello's one summer. But, that winter, he went to the poorhouse, the neighbors said. The house he had lived in remained empty. Work was picking up all over the country, and then too, the dumps discouraged people from moving to Lily.

In White Place, no one other than the Durock, Costello, and Korosuk families kept animals and fowl. There were two cows at Red and two at Blue. All the other residents in these two sections raised chickens and ducks. There were five dogs at Red, two at White, and three at Blue.

The Korosuk family occupied the second house in the front row at White. Their dog was kept inside the shed at all times now, but the parents and their four boys still did not speak to the Durocks. Two apple trees stood across the road from their shed, which Mrs. Korosuk claimed as her own. The numerous blossoms were beautiful in spring. Nina and Butter loved to pinch off a few of the tiny flowers to take to their teachers in school.

Mrs. Korosuk caught the girls stealing one day. They each had taken one little branch. She chased them, shook a stick in her hand at them, and yelled a Russian word over and over. The girls were hearing this word for the first time. They thought they had heard every swear word there was but they hadn't heard this one. It stuck in their minds. They ran as fast as they could until they reached the main road.

Nina looked back and returned, "Eh, you're a kurva yourself!" Her sister agreed. "Those trees don't belong to her," Nina stated.

From that morning on Mrs. Korosuk guarded the trees. She stood by the shed, tightened the white babushka she was never without, folded her arms and watched them as they passed by. "Kurva" she muttered again and again each time. The girls pretended they did not see or hear her.

After they had passed the trees, and it was safe, they both said in a low voice, "Eh, you're one yourself."

Curious Nina asked her mother, "Mama, what does kurva mean?"

"Oye, oye, oye! Where you hear it that?"

"Mrs. Korosuk calls us that."

"She old witch. You no lisen to her."

"What does it mean?"

"Never mind. It bad word and you never sayit."

When weather was bad in summer and winter, Mrs. Korosuk could be seen at the kitchen window or sometimes standing outside on her porch, watching and muttering. The girls became so accustomed to the watchful eyes, they never missed saying, "Eh, you're one yourself!" as they walked by, or ran by, and even nicknamed the woman, "Eh, you're one yourself."

❖ ❖ ❖ ❖

The Janock family lived next door to the Costello's in the second house in the back row. Mrs. Janock passed away after giving birth to Helen, the youngest and only girl. Helen had four brothers. She had no time for play. She did all the cooking, cleaning, washing, and ironing for the family. In late evening Helen would come out on the porch to rest. All the children at White Place were jealous of Helen. She earned a dime a day delivering the newspaper to "Indian Joe" who lived next door to her in the last house in the front row.

Nina wished Helen would move away so she could have her job and get to see the inside of Indian Joe's house. Everyone knew he had a radio, the only one in White. It was a crystal set. Helen also earned a nickel a day every time Catherine, Indian Joe's live-in housekeeper, called her to go for a half pint of whiskey at the Costellos.

It was a very short walk, but "Crazy Catherine," as the children called her, was always too drunk to walk straight. Her employer gave her enough money to buy just a half pint each day. Catherine had a large family at one time, a husband who left her for the reason that she drank too much, and five children who married and left her too. She then took the job of housekeeper to an Indian. A real Indian.

Very little was known about Indian Joe, not even his last name. No one asked him and very few people said anything more to him than "Nice day" or "Bad day."

The children at White said, "Indians don't have a last name." They never spoke to him. They said, "He talks Indian talk anyway." They were frightened of him. He never went anyplace but to work. He would come out of his house occasionally to watch the children at their play. He would stare and stare and stare and the youths would say, "Let's git out of here, he gives me the willies."

Indian Joe was very tall, very thin, had prominent, high cheekbones, wore a cap pulled down very tightly on his head and smoked a corncob pipe constantly, even on his job as watchman at the corn plant.

Nina wished he would bend over to tie his shoes one day. She imagined his cap would fall off and she would see his long braid all rolled up on top of his head come tumbling out. All the other kids thought he had a snake in there.

Her thoughts went on, *I'll betcha that Crazy Catherine is really his wife. But he's so quiet, how can he stand her mumbling to herself all the time and shuffling cards all the time telling fortunes. Well, Anyway, I'll betcha she sleeps with 'im. Gee! The crazy people in this place. I wish we'd stayed in the city so we could go to the movies more often.*

❖ ❖ ❖ ❖

Nina spoke excitedly when she came home from school one day. "Mama, policemen took Helen away from school today."

"Poh chamuh?" Nadia gasped asking why.

"I don't know. The kids said she was bleeding."

At first, Helen was afraid to say anything. She just covered her face with her hands and cried. Her tears matched those of the crying windows. It was raining very hard. The small room was spotless and smelled of antiseptics. A tall scale stood on one side of the room, a desk was in front of the windows, and a small spotlessly clean basin was underneath the medicine chest. After the nurse had washed the blood off of Helen, she asked her to sit down in one of the four chairs that lined another wall. The school nurse opened the door that led to the hall and told the principal it was all right to come in now. She sat down beside her patient and asked, "Who did this to you?" Helen could not answer, she just cried harder.

"You must tell us," said the nurse. "The boy must be punished. Why didn't you run away?"

"Here, dry your eyes." The nurse laid some tissue in Helen's lap.

Helen blew her nose and finally spoke, "I didn't wanna run away. They gave me money."

"They?" the nurse was startled and sat up straight in her chair. "You mean there were more than one?"

Helen wiped her eyes and hid her face again, then answered, "Sure, there was four of 'em."

"Oh, my Lord," the nurse looked up at her employer, then asked Helen, "Why did you let them? Didn't you know they could hurt you?"

Helen started crying again and in a little while replied, "They gave me money, candy bars, and one gave me a dime," she sobbed. "I got fifty cents one time."

The principal could hardly believe what this fourteen-year-old girl had just said. He asked, "Who were they?"

Helen blew hers nose again and answered, "I won't tell. I never have any money for candy or anything. We're poor. All I do is go to school and keep the house, the cooking and laundry and ironing and—" She squeezed the wet tissues in her hand and looked down at her lap.

The nurse put her arm around the young girl and said, "But, Helen, don't you know it's bad to do this thing? Don't you know that is how girls get babies?"

"Nobody tells me anything," Helen stated flatly. "I don't have a mother."

"Dear God," the principal exclaimed. "Nurse, you better tell her everything."

"Not now. I think we better take her to a doctor."

The school nurse went with Helen and the two policemen who had arrived to see a doctor in Winsome. Helen was thoroughly informed of the facts of life before she left the doctor's office. Then the police questioned her, but she refused to reveal the names of the persons who had harmed her. The nurse and policeman took Helen home and told her father, Mr. Janock, to keep closer watch on his innocent young girl.

Nadia never told her girls what really happened to Helen. She was one of the unfortunates who lived in Lily. It remained an adult Lily secret. Nadia explained to her girls, "She was sick, that's all. She gotit her time like you girls getit pretty soon." She started to tell her girls the facts of life.

Nina interrupted her, "Oh, Ma, we know all that. What do you think we are, dummies?" Their mother shut up and grinned, glad that she had smart kids.

❖ ❖ ❖ ❖

Mr. Janock loved the water. He was seen swimming and floating on his back for hours in the middle of Lily Pad Lake, even at night. He loved to fish too, even in winter. But, Helen did not like the tedious task of cleaning the fish her father caught. She would prepare them, but would not eat them.

One hot, sticky evening in August, Nadia sprayed the screen door to get rid of the numerous insects that clung and tried to squeeze through the mesh and get to the light in the kitchen. As warm as it was, she still tied a babushka around her head to keep the bugs out of her hair before she went outside. It was a Russian female custom to keep the hair clean with these coverings and then too, they believed the Blessed Mother always covered Her head with cloth. When Nadia came out of the outhouse, I mean the show, she met Mr. Janock on the road. They stopped to talk.

"Hello, Mister," she pronounced it Meester.

"Hello, Misses," he pronounced it Meeses.

"Where you go on sucha hot night?"

"Too hot to drink, so I go to lake to cool off."

"That water takeit you some day," Nadia said jokingly.

He shook his head and said, "Jesus walked on water. I could too."

Nadia laughed, "Ha, ha, you think some? You watchit youself, Meester."

"Yes, I watch myself."

Nadia pulled her babushka down closer to her forehead, then rubbed her arms to prevent insect bites "Too many mosquitoes tonight," she said. "They getit you up on Mosquito Path before you getit to lake."

"Oh, no, my blood too old an' my skin too tough. They no want me," he smiled.

"Keepit you mouth closed when you on path, or you be eatit them. I have to go tellit my Sonny spooky story so he go sleep. Watchit youself, Meester."

"Okay, Misses," he waved and headed for the shortcut to the lake.

It was almost twelve o'clock when Nadia and Alex heard the sirens, woke, and went out on the porch. They saw the lights of vehicles and small flickering lights of flashlights on the main road.

"Somethin' happen at lake. I go see," announced Alex.

"I go too. I betcha it John Janock," guessed Nadia. "I tellit him he drown someday. Oye, oye, oye."

Alex went back into the house to get his cap and a newspaper to cover his head. Nadia threw her scarf around her head, but did not tie it, she would cover her mouth with it before they reached Mosquito Path.

Mr. Janock was cut in half under the wheels of the midnight freight train in a hurry trying to beat the train across. Helen mourned her father, but enjoyed her freedom after he died. Her brothers were seldom home so there was no one to watch over her. She stayed out after dark with the boys and girls at Red Place and she was often seen in the city with older boys.

"Something bad happen to that girl on dark Lily roads. I no want you kids playit with Helen, she wild now," Nadia told her girls.

A short time later, Helen was sick in school again. This time the doctor told her she was going to have a baby. She was taken home and her brothers did not allow her to even leave the house. The town of Lily waited for the birth of the infant, and perhaps through the characteristics of the child they would learn the

identity of the father and kill him. Helen did not know
who the father was.

Chapter Seventeen

ARTUM SORENUK WAS ROBBED OF HIS SUNDAY RECEIPTS and was left to die on the picnic grounds with an ice pick in his chest while his establishment burned to the ground. The talk at Galuk's corner tavern was that any number of Julia Sorenuk's admirers could have done this horrible thing to get her husband out of the way.

The robbery, murder, and arson mystery was never solved. Everyone in Lily was sorry there would be no more picnics at Blue Place and they would also miss hearing Julia sing the Russian songs she knew and sang so well.

Alex said, "Sunday just another day in Lily again." He reached in his pocket for his cigarette papers. "Dumps getit too close. Pretty soon we all have to move, I betcha. Pretty soon."

Feodore Galuk filled Alex's glass and said, "Maybe you right, Alexander."

The slag that now covered most of the fields at Blue Place restrained the growth of the grass that remained and left very little for the cows to graze on. The wind blew the powdery substance in every direction and settled on the three houses.

Vacate notices were served to the residents. One by one the families left. The houses were torn down. The dumps consumed Blue Place.

❖ ❖ ❖ ❖

Lily was to have electricity. The first modern convenience raised the rent for each house from seven dollars a month to twenty dollars a month. The high voltage towers were coming in on an angle from the big city. The Durocks, Costellos, and Janocks learned that one of these large current electrical suppliers would rest in their backyards.

Gypsy Joe gave notice to these families. They all had to move. The three houses were going to be torn down. The others would remain, they would not inhibit progress. It was almost a pity to bring this brighter light into the homes of this poor place. These small magic bulbs were going to embarrass the cracks in the plaster, old wallpaper, and sparse furnishings, and would not flatter the deeply lined face of the alcoholic and the tired look of an over-worked woman, but would reflect into the eyes of old and young and reveal the dreamy look of a child's wishful thinking for more material possessions and the faraway look of a woman reminiscing, "If only I had not done such and such. If only I would have married the other one. If only this would happen. If only I did not start drinking. If . . . If . . . If . . ."

This new supply of light would suspend from the ceilings of two main rooms in each house. The children would delight in pulling the chain, but their masters would shake a finger and say, "No, no, you waste whole penny when you click off and on."

Jim Novak moved in as a boarder in the Dubinski house to help pay increased expenses. The "ole lady," as Jim called her, became accustomed to having him around. He was very good to her. She had more money for whiskey than she ever had before. She finally consented to let Jim marry her daughter. The entire town congratulated Jim heartily for winning the long battle; Anna was worth fighting for and waiting for, she was a good girl.

The Costello family was moving to a city fifteen miles away. Nanny went to say goodbye to his playmates. He shifted his weight from one fat leg to the other, then kissed Butter on the cheek very quickly and said, "We'll get married some day. You'll see." His face was flushed. He tucked his fat hands inside his sweet-filled pockets and took one last look towards the swing area and the fields and secret paths, trying to fix the treasured places in his mind, knowing he would never forget the fun-filled years he had spent there.

Butter gave him a shove and responded, "Aw, go on, you're too fat for me."

He turned and ran to the waiting car, still holding his hands in his pockets. He sat in the back seat and started to cry. As they passed the Korosuk's chicken shed, out of acquired, imitated habit, he said, "Eh, you're one yourself." Then he looked out of the back window, but it was too late to wave to his childhood friends, they were out of sight.

The four Janock boys and their sister, Helen, moved into the house that Lithuanian Louie had lived in. It had remained empty ever since he went to the poorhouse. Everyone in Lily was glad they were not leaving. They anxiously awaited the arrival of Helen's baby.

"Gypsy Joe," or "Lily Joe," as he was called, was the caretaker of all the houses in Lily. He mended a broken step, added a nail to a loose porch railing and replaced a broken window, but he never touched a paint brush to any of the buildings. He also collected the rent which he turned over to Mr. Upton at Lily Store. Gypsy Joe called on Alex and his family to find out when they were going to move.

"I would like to stay," Alex told him. "My wife no wanit move. It close to my job, the kids haveit lotsa fun here, lotsa room to run. Maybe there another house for us to move to here in Lily . . . maybe?"

"I don't know. Why don't you go see Mr. Upton?" suggested Gypsy Joe.

"Take me there now, will you please? Please." They drove off together in his pickup truck. Alex came home and told the family the good news. They did not have to leave Lily. The house would be moved instead, they all shouted a bunch of "Hurrays" and clapped their hands until they hurt.

The house was placed on blocks and moved by truck to a spot two hundred yards north. Their house was now the first one in the front row at White Place. It stood apart from the others. A small cluster of trees made their house invisible to the others.

The Durock family was very happy about their new location. There was plenty of grass for the cow and more room for the animals and fowl than they had at the old place, as they now called it. Alex worked very hard tearing down the newly built sheds and haybarn, and rebuilt them all on the new place. His son-in-law, Frank, came to help. The sheds were built in an inverted L shape to save making a lot of fence. His private shed was the first one by the house. Next to that was the shed for the geese, one for the goat, a feather shed, wood shed, and the cow next to the haybarn. The big gate connected to the pig shed and pen that was on the other side of the yard.

Nadia's garden was all fenced in beyond the gate and in back of the shed that was occupied by six pigs. The outhouse, sorry, I mean the show, was much closer to the house this time. It stood in front of the pig pen. The smokehouse was set up a short distance beyond the big haybarn. A small area in front of the house was fenced in. The fowl enjoyed the grass in this spot, however, the chickens and ducks were housed underneath the house.

In the moving process, Alex thought it was a good idea to leave the large blocks of wood under the house to make it higher off the ground. It was a place for snakes and rats and mice to hide in as well. Frequently the household was awakened at night by the noises the ducks and chickens made as they scattered from one corner to another trying to elude the unpleasant visitors.

Alex set traps everywhere. The rats came from the dumps. Slag covered the garbage as soon as it was unloaded so the rodents had to look elsewhere for food. Nadia was on her way to the garden one day when she saw seventeen rats sitting in a line along the pig pen fence. She gasped and then thought, "If I haveit gun right now, this be shooting place like in park in Winsome on Fourth of July." She threw a stick at them and they scattered.

Eleven mice were caught in one night. They came into the house through the hole under the sink that Alex forgot to cover. The children could not sleep for fear all the mice were not caught. Nina crawled in bed with her brother and sister.

When Alex dug for a well alongside the house, he drilled a hole under the sink to install a pump. His wife was very happy at the thought of having water inside the house. However, the water was not fit for drinking; the entire family suffered intestinal upset. Alex dug another well in back of the house. Nadia lost hope of ever having a pump. The mechanical parts had been very expensive and Alex had worked hard for weeks to install the apparatus.

The disappointment was so great that he refused to remove the machine. "No, I no takeit out pump. No . . . never." He shook his head and walked to his shed to have a drink to his refusal. The pump was covered with a gunny sack and tied with a rope. It stood as a monument to Alex's sweat.

Chapter Eighteen

Alex had to clear a section filled with weeds to make a road for Albert to turn off the main road and take their grocery order. The youngsters soon found a name for it—Lovers Lane. Now that their new location was so much closer to Red Place, the Durock children were allowed to go there to play. They had no playmates at White Place now that Nanny was gone and they still did not speak to the Korosuk family. Now that they were the first house at White and not the last, they no longer passed the dreaded, beautiful, apple trees.

No more being called a whore (that's what kurva means in Russian). Nina and Butter became very good friends with Martha and Galina. Sonny played with Martha's brothers. In summer they played games with their new-found friends under the two street lamps that lighted the road in front of the houses there.

On the way home, shortly after dark, they were used to seeing parked cars on their new road.

Henceforth, it was named Lovers Lane. The cars were easily hidden by the tall weeds on either side. On very dark nights they had no fear of being seen so they merely ran past the cars, but on bright moonlit nights, they crept past the cars on their hands and knees. Sonny was still short enough not to be seen. He was so brave that he even whistled as he walked by.

One night after they had passed the cars, Butter said, "We oughta charge 'em for parking on our road."

"Shut up! They'll hear us," Nina whispered.

They ran onto the high slag road and Butter wondered, "Why do they open the doors? I almost whacked my head on their sticking out feet. Crazy lovers! I'll bet the mosquitoes eat 'em alive. What do they want to park there for?"

"It's a good place to hide and make love," Nina wisely answered.

"Yeah," Butter responded, "Goddamn crazy lovers. I'll puke first before I sleep with a man or let 'em get on top o' me."

❖ ❖ ❖ ❖

Picnics were held every Sunday in summer in the Forest Preserve. Sections were cleared and different denominations roped off their areas. This place was named Jones Grove. However, the Lily children did not enjoy these picnics as much as they did when they were held at Blue Place. There were too many people. The children felt self-conscious to dance with so many strange, watchful eyes looking at them. At Blue Place everybody knew everybody. They only looked forward to seeing their godfathers who always gave them money. When they were given a dime, they would ask their mother if they could spend the rest of the afternoon at the movie house in Winsome. They usually ran all the way.

Every Sunday Butter wondered why Nina received more money from Andre than she did. "Probably because I'm older," was the only reason she could think of.

Sonny's godfather was Kola Tarasuk, Alex's friend from Winsome. He paid more attention to Nina than he did to his godson and Nina wondered why he called her Nina Tarasova Bulba. When the other children heard him call her this, they teased her for days by calling her Bulba (potatoes in English).

Nina began spending a good deal of her time at Lily Pad Lake. Old Ivan came for a haircut early one morning and asked her if she would take care of his boat business while he went to the city on business. It became a habit. Old Ivan found someone he could trust and his business excuses took him as far as Red Place to the beautiful Julia Sorenuk who set up a tavern in her house. She took in boarders, sold whiskey cheaper than Mr. Galuk at his corner tavern, and let the men play cards until any hour. She did not marry any of her admirers; Artum was the only husband her heart had room for. Old Ivan was not very old. He walked hunched over, always looked at the ground, and was called the old hermit who lives alone at the lake, thus the nickname Old Ivan.

His wife and child never did unite with him in America. She divorced him, waited seven years and married another man in Russia. She and the child died two years after she married and everyone said, "Old Ivan look at ground all of time like he lookit on his wife and baby grave."

Old Ivan was enjoying his freedom from the lake. He was drinking very heavily. Nina was paid fifty cents a day. If she managed to give her employer no change, he gave her a dollar, but not often. Colored people arrived very early in the morning to fish for carp and bullheads. Nadia was afraid for her pretty daughter to be alone at the lake, so Butter went with her to share the fifty cents or dollar.

Their fair skin was exposed to so much sun that their faces and arms were covered with freckles. They cut out clippings in magazines and sent for ten cent jars of freckle-removing cream. Nothing worked, they had to wait for winter when most of them disappeared by themselves. To pass the time waiting for boat rental customers, they fished and swam in Lily Pad Lake.

The half-sunken boat had not yet been repaired. They used it to hold the bullheads they caught until they could sell them to the colored people. When they went swimming off the boat pier, they soon had to touch bottom and the soft, oozing mud made them return to shore where they read magazines and looked at catalogs they had previously found on the dumps. They sent for ten cent samples of lipsticks, which they applied away from home. Nadia would not let them spoil their youthful beauty with makeup.

Mrs. Sorenuk was the only Russian woman they knew who used artificial coloring, but she would not let her daughter wear any. Nina informed her sister, "Martha told me she can't wear any makeup or go out with boys until she's twenty years old," as she looked into a small cracked mirror she found on the dumps and applied some lipstick.

Butter added, "Yeah, and she told Sasha, Misha, and Kola (Alex, Michael, and Nicholas in English) that they can't smoke until they're twenty-one."

Nina turned her face to her sister and asked, "Like the color?"

"Oh, too pink. I like a deep red."

"Same here."

Nina picked up a leaf, went to the edge of the lake, washed it and wiped off the lipstick with the leaf. She could not use her handkerchief, or her mother would surely know.

Sonny went to the post office for the mail every day now that his sisters were working. They paid him not to tell their mother about the lipstick when it arrived in the mail.

Nina joined her sister again and said, "Russians sure are strict with their kids. I guess the mothers don't want their kids to be bad like their fathers."

"You know, I think Indian Joe is the only one in Lily that doesn't drink. All the rest are alcoholics."

"How do you know Indian Joe never drinks?"

"Papa said, and he oughta know, he works with him."

❖ ❖ ❖ ❖

The short road that led from the house to the slag road was named Billy Goat Road. The goat was tied to a very long rope so that she could graze on both sides of the road. The children had to run as fast as they could past Billy before she went after them. This was the same goat they had at the old place but they missed their friend Nanny so much that they could not bear to say his name. Therefore, the goat's name was changed to Billy and the road was named Billy Goat Road.

A lone tree stood close to the slag road and off to one side of Billy Goat Road. Alex tied the swing to this tree. Nina and Butter still did all their dreaming while swinging on the swing. Sometimes they took turns, but most of the time one sat while the other stood and pumped on the one board.

"Think I'll ever be a movie star?" asked Butter. She was really asking the Sunday sky as she looked up, but her sister Nina answered her.

"Sure, you look enough like Shirley Temple to be her double. I thought you wanted to be a nurse?"

"I wanna be both, but I think I wanna be a movie star first. What are you gonna be?"

"A writer," replied Nina without hesitation.

"A writer? Are you kiddin'? You hafta go to college to do that and besides, what're ya gonna write about?"

"Lily. And I'm gonna name my book, 'Red, White, and Blue Lily.'"

"Sounds like a Fourth of July flower."

"That's just what this place is. Every day is Fourth of July for us. We have fun here, so many crazy things happen here. That's the firecrackers, and the characters that live here are the parade. They're always drunk and always celebrating their freedom from the old country. Oh, and one thing more, all of Lily is the picnic grounds."

"What's the story gonna be about?"

"I don't know yet. But it'll come to me some day when I'm older."

"Yeah, if we ever get out of here. Ma and Pa like it here too much to ever move. They feel like they're in Russia."

"What's the matter, don't you like it here anymore?" Nina was surprised. Butter never before mentioned wanting to leave Lily.

"Sure, I like it here. We're used to it. This is home. But when we get older, we could never go out with boys if we live here. City boys would be scared stiff to walk down these dark roads."

Ah, ha, Nina thought, *my baby sister is growing up. I guess I feel the same way, but never had anyone to say it to.*

Nina stopped the swing and said, "Your turn to sit and my turn to pump." They changed places.

Butter said, "I'll bet Daria thinks she'll be a movie star some day."

Nina responded with, "Huh! She thinks she's one already! That hotsy totsy pants! I hate 'er!" Butter was quiet for a long while allowing Nina to think further. *The dumps will catch up to us some day, I'll betcha, and we'll have to move back to Winsome. Then Daria will probably come back to live with us. That old bossy-ossy. She was always trying to tell us what to do. My mother is my boss, not her. I'll never go to live there if she comes to live with us. I'll run away.*

Butter glanced around to see that her brother was not close by and then said, "Hey, Skinny, you know what?"

"No. What?"

"I caught Irene doin' you-know-what with her own cousin when we were playin' post office on Nigger Path. It was my turn an' they were in the weeds so long that I went to get 'em, an that's when I saw 'em. Yuck!"

"Honest? Oh, my God! She probably doesn't even know that's how you get babies. I'll have to tell her. Don't you ever do anything bad," Nina insisted firmly.

"Don't worry, I'm not nuts. I just kiss on the cheek when we play post office or spin the bottle. I see a lot of bad things. There's Anna who never wears any underpants and when she sees one of the bachelors from Red, she lifts her skirt to show 'em and then they go into the bushes. She gets two dollars, the kids say. Yuck! An some of the guys are really old."

Nina now knew her sister was getting an early education in sex. "You just let 'em know we're good girls and they'll never try anything. Look at what happened to Helen. Her life is ruined. She never comes out of the house now. That must be awful. But I'd be ashamed to show my face too. I wonder who the father is?"

A car went by and slag dust blew in their direction. They stopped swinging and covered their eyes.

Nina couldn't believe her eyes when she opened them. "That was Iris, the Princess of the Dumps. I'll bet she'll be a movie star some day with that beautiful hair of hers. Naw, her father never lets her out of his sight. He's probably afraid the men will go after her and make her bad like Helen."

They started swinging again. Nina went on, "I wish we could get to know her. I sure would like to see that castle she lives in. It's beautiful on the outside, it has to be twice as nice on the inside. Too bad she doesn't go to our school."

Another car went by. They moved to protect their faces again.

"Did you see who that was?" Butter asked, very surprised.

"No, I wasn't looking," replied her sister as she shook her hair to get rid of the slag dust. "Who was it?"

"Our dear sister, Daria, and she was with a new boyfriend. I never saw this one before. They are probably going to the Boat Club. Come on."

Butter stopped the swing. "Let's go there and let him know she has a family living on the dumps. That oughta fix 'er."

Nina responded with, "No, we better not. It's too hot and too far to walk. The heck with her. If she's ashamed of us, let's be ashamed of her and give her the same treatment. She's not our sister anymore either."

They resumed swinging. Butter spoke, "I've seen her go by lots of times on her way to the Boat Club with no one else but Joe. She always turned her head when she went past our house. You know, I heard Vera telling Mama that Daria is crazy about Joe, but he's going to be a missionary."

"Good for him! That'll show Daria she can't have everything she wants. That's her punishment for being so ashamed of us. I'm older than her and I don't go out with boys yet. She sure started early. But that's cuz she lives in the city and we live way out here. I hope she gets married right away so we can get rid of her. The only time she comes here is when she wants something."

"I wanna get married some day and have lots of kids," dreamily Butter relented.

"I wanna get married too, but I'll tell you one thing, I'll never marry a man that drinks. Especially not a Russian. Even Mama tells me that. All the Russians we know sure like their whiskey. And I wonder why Papa always tells us not to marry Polacks? I'll have to ask him."

"I won't marry a drunk either. We wouldn't have to live here if Papa didn't drink. He's not too bad though. At least he does most of his drinking at home. Mama just has trouble with him when she can't wake him up to go to work for the twelve to eight shift. He's a lot of fun when he's drunk, wiggling his cap off the way he does. I don't think anybody can do that."

Nina's turn, "Well, we shouldn't blame Papa so much. He was real poor in Russia. When he came here and made so much money, he didn't know what to do with it, so he celebrated."

"Yeah," Butter laughed, "he's been celebrating ever since."

Nina laughed too. Then she remembered something, "Hey, Butt, the kids at Red named their street Fourth Avenue and gave themselves addresses. The post office man didn't care, all our mail just goes to one place and we pick it up. Why don't we do the same thing? We've never had a house or street address. How about calling the slag road 5th Avenue?"

"Sure, good idea."

"What about the number?"

"How about 1234. After all there were four sections at one time, counting the picnic grounds and boarding house."

"That's it! 1234 5th Avenue." Nina was so excited. She would now have an address in her English class when they wrote letters to students in Hawaii, where her teacher knew another teacher. Whoopee!

They heard their mother calling, "Ninotchka. Olgutchka. Come eat." They ran down Billy Goat Road with the gander leading his ladies in chase after the two girls and Billy just stood there, chewing, watching the flight of the hissing geese and the screaming girls. They reached the gate and fastened it just in time, the gander came very close.

"I hate that ole gander," Nina professed, huffing and puffing, trying to get her breath. "He's always after me. He's just like Billy. He doesn't like the red ribbon I wear in my hair."

No one was allowed to speak at the table while eating. The children received a sock on the forehead with a spoon if they did. Alex's father practiced the custom in Russia, so Alex imitated the discipline in America. You see, there was too much snickering, jostling, punching, tongue-sticking-out going on with the kids, and under the table kicking, that this solved the problem and a peaceful dinner was enjoyed.

After dinner Nadia started washing dishes. She excused her girls from this chore when they habitually complained. They did all the ironing and cleaning and helped with some of the outside chores, so Nadia did not mind doing the one job they despised. Besides, it was very dangerous for them to carry a kettle of steaming water from the stove to the sink on the other side of the kitchen.

The girls ran back to the swing. Sonny took his slingshot and went out to shoot crows that were sitting on the electric lines along the now 5th Avenue. Alex spoke to his wife, "Well, Baba, we liveit good life here in Lily in depression. No, Baba?"

"Yes, we livit good here, but lookit you nose, it blue from alcohol. If you stopit drink, we could live better. Maybe pay off our house in Winsome and moveit there when kids get bigger. They likeit here now, but they no likeit when girls start haveit boyfriends, you see."

"Whatsa matter with this place? We not haveit chicken every Sunday and so much butter and cheese and eggs if we go to city. How about ducks and geese we eat? You will missit your blood soup. Lookit good Christmas we haveit every year. We kill pig and make sausage."

Alex killed a pig with an ice pick through the heart. The children were told to close their ears. He believed the pig would die much faster if the squeals were not heard by anyone. Even Nadia put her fingers in her ears during this long, tortuous ordeal for the pig. There are many layers of fat to go through before reaching the heart. It took at least twenty minutes for a pig to die.

Alex continued with his list of advantages in Lily, "How about you garden? You haveit everything. Potatoes, carrots, lettuce, beets, beans, radish, onions, tomatoes, even watermelon. This place like farm."

Nadia agreed. He continued, "My Sonny gotit goat's milk and you know how kids likeit you cheese cakes."

"Sure, but you think it nice for Daria to live with Vera alla time? We not even know our own daughter and she not knowit us."

"That's awright. Vera needit her."

"No, it not right!"

Alex responded, "Lookit how much money you make sellit milk to people at Red." Nadia had the only cow in Lily now. "I let you keepit money. An no forget this Saturday that nigger, he name Boy, he come to buy eggs and cheese. He wantit two brick cheese so haveit cheese ready." Nadia added salt, cream, and vanilla to cottage cheese. It was then pressed between boards to form the mass and was allowed to dry slightly.

"No let him come in house when he come — the kids!"

"Why not? Yebi tvou mat? Why not?" Alex was angry. "I work with him every day. He clean. He takeit shower every day. I let you keep he money too. Yebi tvou mat! Yebi tvou mat!"

Alex swore saying, "Fuck your mother!" He said it twice. He then went outside and unlocked his private shed. He looked for one of his bottles and had a few swallows.

The corn plant employed a large number of colored men. Alex was friends with anyone that wanted to be his friend. He saw no reason why a Negro could not come to his house to buy the delicious cheeses his wife made, and they could not consume all the eggs their hens laid. Nadia never had any contact with Negroes. She knew they lived in the big city and heard that everyone had to lock their doors at night. The people in Lily never locked their doors.

When Boy came with his wife and twelve-year-old son that Saturday, Nadia did not refuse them entrance into the house. She was surprised to see the neatly dressed people with very proper manners and could not comprehend why they laughed so heartily. The young lad stood up when he was introduced to the girls and they made conversation easily.

Nina began by asking, "What school do you go to? What's your favorite subject?" And on and on. When the boy said he envied their life in Lily, they took him on tour of the outside and told him how much they envied the kids that lived in the city.

After Alex and Boy had had a few drinks and the ladies had tea and cheese cake, they took their leave saying, "We'll be back for more cheese and eggs." They drove off in their modest car.

"Gee, that's the first time I saw a nigger," said Sonny.

"That's the closest I've ever been to one and the first time ever spoke to one. That boy is a little gentleman," stated Nina.

Butter thought, "What an odd first name his father has. Boy. And did you hear Papa calling him Mr. Boy like he does everybody else? Too bad they didn't have a baby. I think nigger babies are the cutest things. I always look for them in the cars when we walk to school."

Alex spoke to his wife after they left. "Well, what I tellit you, Baba? What I tellit you? They nice people. No? Well?"

"Yes," Nadia agreed, "they nice people but they silly. What for they laughit so much for nothing?"

"Yebi tvou mat! Yebi tvou mat!" he swore and went into his shed. Fuck your mother is what he said. He said it twice. That night Nadia locked the door for the first time since they moved to Lily. She locked it every night.

❖ ❖ ❖ ❖

The next day Sonny announced that Buster was missing.

"Oh, he'll come home," Butter said, "he always does."

"Maybe that nigger came and stole him. Boy, I'll never talk to another one!" Sonny declared. "Remember how he petted him. If Buster comes home I'll give 'im a bath and really scrub the spots where he touched him."

Nina said, "Don't be silly, Buster would never let anybody steal him."

"Well, help me look for him then," Sonny retorted.

Butter assured, "Don't worry, he'll come home."

Sonny heard him whining with pain on the evening of the second day after he was missing.

"Papa! Papa!" cried Sonny. "Come see Buster. He's all chewed up."

Buster lay close to the house. He was covered with wounds. Sonny could not look any more at his treasured pet. He turned his face away and cried very hard and loud, trying to drown the painful sounds the dog was making. He screamed when he saw his father come out of his private shed with a gun.

"No! No! Don't kill 'im! Please don't kill 'im!" Sonny pleaded. "I love 'im. Pa, I really love 'im."

Alex put his arm around his son, trying to console him and said, "Aw, Sonny, I have to. He die slow if I no killit him. He was in fight with big dogs on the dumps, I betcha. It too bad. I getit you a better one, Sonny."

"I don't want another dog! There couldn't be another dog like Buster!" He wrenched free of his father's arm and ran up to the house. He leaned his head against the wood, covered his face with his hands, knowing he would soon hear a gunshot. He placed his fingers in his ears and sobbed very hard.

Alex went to Buster in back of the house and put him out of his misery. He wondered how the dog ever managed to get home with the mangled throat he had.

When the girls heard the gunshot, they left the swing and came running. Sonny would not let his sisters come near him.

"You wouldn't help me look for 'im! Now he's dead!" he screamed. He ran to the swing saying, "Oh, Bus, what am I gonna do without ya? What am I gonna do without ya?"

Alex covered the carcass with sacks and tied them securely. He placed him into a wheelbarrow and Sonny and the girls lowered the body gently into the grave they had dug in the fields just beyond the swing. They all cried as they covered him and made a large mound. Sonny placed a flag into the earth and they all knelt in prayer.

"Oh, Bus, I hope you're in dog heaven," Sonny prayed. "I'll never get another dog. There isn't one to take your place."

Butter prayed, "I'll never forget how you obeyed. I know you would have come all the way to school to get us, but we told you to wait by the swing. You wouldn't even cross the slag road—I mean 5th Avenue—when you saw us coming."

"Remember," Nina said out loud, "how he always carried a book home for us. If he got a heavy one and he dropped it, he had tears in his eyes, he felt so bad. Then when we didn't run home and he got there way ahead of us, he wouldn't even put the book down on the porch. He waited until we got to the door and he was so happy to come into the house and put it on a chair. He really loved us."

"And we loved him," Sonny and Butter said in unison. Sonny recalled, "Remember the time he bit the Red Pirate?"

"Yeah," acknowledged Butter, "He understood everything we said to 'im. He was the best friend we ever had."

"Gee, how can we ever forget that? We never had to worry as long as Buster was with us," Nina knew. "We'll sure miss 'im." Nina stood up and Butter followed her in the direction of the swing. Sonny stayed.

Butter remarked when she caught up to her sister, "Gee, he was saving that flag for the Fourth of July parade in Winsome."

Nina responded with, "Well, Sonny found the flag on the dumps and Buster met his death on the dumps, so that's where the flag belongs."

Sadly Butter said, "Maybe Bus won't mind if he takes it off the grave for that one day. I'll tell Sonny. He can put it back when he gets home."

Sonny felt remorse. He cried himself to sleep that night with his sisters on either side of him. They, too, had cried themselves to sleep. Alex and Nadia had tried to console them, but to no avail. Their first relative was buried that evening. They had experienced their first trip to a cemetery. The little fish didn't count, as it had only been with them one day.

The big day came, but Sonny went to see the parade empty handed. Alex obtained another dog, but the children would not claim it. Knowing he had to have a watch dog, Alex made himself its master and kept it in his private shed. He let it out to run in the fields every day. He became attached to his dog, talked to it, and knew how his children felt about the loss of Buster. He asked them again and again if they wanted a dog, but they refused. They saw Buster in their dreams and held him dear in their memories. There was no more room in their hearts for another dog. Alex felt that his son had to have a pet, so he surprised him with a present of six rabbits. Sonny was pleased.

Chapter Nineteen

EVERY NIGHT A LONG, SLOW MOVING FREIGHT TRAIN pulled boxcars filled with raw corn into the Midwest Corn Products Company yard. Each morning the empty cars came out of the yard, and were switched onto the track that would lead them back from whence they came for more corn. However, some of these cars still had some corn in them. Seepage was allowed between the wood lining of the inside walls that had broken, split, or had large knots that fell out. Nadia was given permission by Paul, the engineer, to go into these cars when they stopped, and remove what corn she could. This corn retrieving act was an unlawful offense. Nadia was trespassing on railroad property.

Paul reminded Nadia of Stephan, the love she had had in Russia and the father of Nina. She had only to look into Nina's eyes to remember Stephan, but now that she saw the same twinkling, green eyes in Paul, her heart was in turmoil. She found Paul exciting after all the past years of hard work, seclusion in Lily, and a drinking husband who squandered so much of his paycheck for his own consumption and left none for small luxuries for her and the children. There were times when Nadia wished she had remained in Russia. When Vera started school and could not understand the teacher and her classmates and vice versa. The days when Alex drank too much. The time he pushed her very hard when she tried to wake him to go to work, she had hurt her back against the dresser. And now that she knew Paul, she prayed for Stephan's soul.

In spite of her occasional secret yearnings, she loved Alex and her children and resolved, "God sendit me here and I have to like it." But Nadia was weak and human and did not resist the attention given her by Paul. She was still an attractive woman at forty. Her coloring had enhanced by her outdoor life in Lily. Her hair was still blonde with no trace of gray in it.

Paul had an opportunity to leave the train engine when he waited to receive the signal that it was time to go into the yard and fetch the partially empty boxcars. Nadia joined him in this spot on the main road. Day by day Paul edged her farther off the road. They had worn a small amount of surface between two huge bushes. They conversed. Paul told her his life story and she returned hers.

He flattered her, he kissed her, and one day told her, "Don't wear a brazier tomorrow. It will be easier to find you. And I still say this one is bigger than the other one." He squeezed her left breast and laughed.

"You devil," she exclaimed with a smile. When the fireman on the engine whistled, Paul reluctantly went back to work and Nadia waited for the boxcars to come out.

Each day, Tom, the switchman, told her which car had the most corn left in it. He would boost her into the car and she would quickly dig out the corn. A stick and a small broom assisted in the theft and a sack held the yellow grain until she fed it to the chickens. She carried the quarter-full sack over her shoulder and wondered what Alex would do if he discovered her infidelity. The relationship had not gone as far as grounds for divorce, but Alex's quick, hot-tempered, judgment would condemn her without question or explanation.

"So what if he find out?" she thought. "He kissit lotsa baba when he is drunk. And it was all right when we all go up to Costello hay barn with different man and baba. And how do I knowit what he do before I come to America? Maybe Alex drink lots and die, then I marry Paul. He says his wife leaveit him long time ago so he is free. If he not marry me, I will live with him. Lots of baba do this. Kola Tarasuk never marry his baba and they haveit five kids. Galina mama liveit with her boarder at Red. And lookit Julia Sorenuk, she runit saloon in her house. She haveit lots sweethearts. She be rich if she stay single. Paul makeit lots money on engineer job. He say he haveit nice house in big city and he gotit no kids. We see what happen. We see."

It was not long before her free corn expedition came to the notice of others. One of the women from Red Place saw Nadia alight from a boxcar and spread the word to the neighbors. The next day, four women from Red Place were waiting to climb into the cars and search for the grain that would fatten their chickens too. The freight cars did not stand still very long. The women had to work very fast. They had to be careful when more and more cars coupled; the jerk felled them and many slivers were begot as they reached for the wooden sides and floor to steady themselves. As the long line of boxcars moved along, they soon reached the plant's side entrance, and the women had to stop digging and sweeping to prevent being caught by the watchman at the gate. Nadia still received information and an occasional helping hand from Tom and went home carrying more corn than the others.

A jealous woman reported that corn was being stolen with the help of a switchman on duty. The informer warned her neighbors to stay away that day, but no one warned Nadia. Two railroad detectives were hiding in the bushes along the road and approached her when she had evidence in her hand. Luckily, Tom had not assisted her into the car or he would have lost his job.

When Alex came home from work at four o'clock, his dinner was not ready. He called to his children who were catching butterflies in the fields. They came running. "Deh yeah Mama, kids?" he asked where their mother was. "She always home this time. Dinner not ready. Go look for her, kids. Go ahead, go look for her."

"Maybe she went to Red to sell milk and butter." Sonny guessed.

"We'll find her Pa," Nina assured. "Come on. I'll race ya up to the swing."

They ran. Nina won the race. She always did. Sonny was second. Butter was putting on weight and "Ball" was added to her nickname. When they reached the main road, Tom called them and said he wanted to see their father right away. The urgency in his voice told them something was wrong. They asked no questions and ran all the way home. Alex went to the police station in Winsome and learned that his wife was in the county courthouse fifty miles away. He went to Frank, his son-in-law, to take him there. He paid the twenty dollar fine and Nadia was released.

She could see from her porch that the women from Red were still going for corn. Visions of larger eggs and more contented hens and roosters soon made her rejoin the neighbors in supplying the noisy fowl with the excellent nourishment.

There were so many women in the game now that they had to devise a system to know whose car was whose. They each had their own markers. It was either a handkerchief, or a rag tied around a rock, a small broom, or a brightly colored piece of cloth tied to the end of a stick. They ran after the moving cars and tossed their marker into the partly or completely opened door. They continued running and looked for their identifying sign. Many times they missed their first choice. If they tossed too hard, and the opposite door was also open, the tag dropped to the ground. If they had foresight and brought more than one means of claiming possession, they soon had a boxcar to call their own; otherwise, they had to search for one that was not occupied.

The women were grateful to the engineer, fireman, and switchman for permitting them to trespass. They began bringing them edible, home-baked delicacies. Each one had her own special recipe. Paul asked for Nadia's. He wanted her to go away with him. She refused.

"My kids need me. We just be sweethearts."

"Sweethearts see more of each other than we do. Meet me tonight by the lake."

"Oh, no. Alex will killit us both if he find out. He no likeit secret."

"He won't find out. He's working tonight."

"How you know he work tonight?"

"I see him going and coming. I know which shift he's working."

"Awright then. By lake. Nine o'clock. After I tellit my Sonny spooky story so he sleep."

"Look for my car."

Later that evening, Nadia announced, "Kids, I go out for while. You listen radio little bit then go to sleep. I be back in little while. Come lockit door."

Nina went to the screened door and asked, "Where are you going Ma?" She noticed that her mother was wearing lipstick for the first time in her life.

"Someplace. I be back right away," she said, but could not meet her daughter's eyes.

"I know, you're going to see Paul. That's why you have lipstick on. I've seen you talking to him. If Papa finds out, we'll have big trouble."

"He nicer than you Papa. Maybe he be your new Papa some day."

"We don't want a new one. Maybe Pa drinks, but he's still our father."

"Lockum door," she said and went down the steps. Nadia walked as far as 5th Avenue and turned back. She removed her makeup with her handkerchief and decided, "My kids needit me. Paul no haveit kids. Maybe he wants only me an not my kids. I no want makeit trouble for my kids. In Russia I only haveit Vera and I left Stephan. Now I have three kids and they needit me more than Paul need me."

222

Nina said nothing to her mother when she unhooked the door to let her in. Nadia began patching Sonny's pants. Nina was ironing clothes. Butter sat listening to the Saturday night barn dance on the radio and waited to put away the ironed clothing. Nina wondered if her sister was cognizant of her mother's love affair. She had said nothing to Butter of her own knowledge. The less they knew, the better the chances of Alex never discovering. She knew there would be a big fight and her mother would surely leave. She also knew she would never leave her father. He was her father in spite of his drinking. But she dreaded the thought of her mother ever going away. Nina was content with her family just as it was. She glanced into the kitchen and saw her mother wiping her quiet tears.

Nadia thought, Some day, maybe, I tell Nina Papa not her Papa.

The next day Nadia did not go for corn. When she did, two days later, she asked Nina to go with her.

Tom the switchman loved children. He wished he had a dozen of his own. He had none. He gave Nina a nickel that day. The next day, Butter went along, she wanted a nickel too. Sonny complained because he was not allowed to go. He was too short to climb into the boxcars and his mother feared the slivers would get into his young, tender hands.

Paul was angry and jealous of the attention Tom was showering on his former sweetheart and her young. Paul notified the proper authorities and Nadia was caught again. The other women ran away, but Nadia had to wait for Butter and Nina to get out of another boxcar. The seizure meant another twenty dollar fine, and if she were caught for the third time, one hundred fifty dollars would have to be paid.

Nadia wondered who had done the reporting this time. All the other women were there that day and no one knew the detectives were waiting. Nadia felt very unfortunate about the two heavy fines imposed on her. Forty dollars would have bought enough corn to feed the chickens for two years.

Paul had not meant for Mrs. Durock to be the sole captive. In fact, he had told the detectives not to take anyone into custody, but to chase them away for their own safety. When the officers recognized Nadia as the same woman who had promised never to trespass again, they had no choice but to arrest her. Paul's intentions were for Nadia to see no more of Tom; he was carried away with jealousy and could not forget the night they had planned their tryst. Paul had waited until midnight. The mosquitoes were fierce. He smoked a pack of cigarettes and his throat was parched. It was pitch dark when he finally headed home, so no one saw how mad he got when one of his tires blew out.

Tom discovered that Paul had been the informer and told Nadia. She never went for corn again and regretted having befriended such a jealous man when he himself knew Tom was happily married. Any conversation she had had with Tom was never without her girls being close by and involved in the small talk.

Chapter Twenty

WHEN ALEX WENT TO WINSOME TO COLLECT THE BANK receipts from the tenants, he found a letter from Russia had arrived at their former address. He waited until he reached home to read it. It was from Irina. She wrote that she was married to a fine, hardworking Russian, and they had two children, both girls. They were well but her parents were dead. They had passed away a month apart. Living conditions were good, but her children needed clothes. She asked about their welfare but did not single out Nina.

Nadia decided she would prepare a package and send it to them. She would first have to inquire if Americans were allowed to mail packages to Russia. Their equality plan may not permit one family to have more than another. The entire country may have to share the contents. Nadia thought she would make the attempt, at least Irina would get part of it.

Alex and Nadia shared the painful loss of his parents. They cried and Alex went to his shed and drank a half pint of whiskey. The next day Alex was very sick. He did not want his wife to call a doctor, but she knew he needed one. Her husband had never been sick before. The children stood outside his bedroom door and cried. They heard their father swear and moan. Then he was praying, "Please God, help me. Please. Please, help me."

Nina smiled and hugged her crying brother to her. "He'll be all right Sonny, don't cry. He prayed. Did you hear him? He prayed," she said, "just like Mama always said he would if he ever got sick. God won't let him die. He just wants to teach him a lesson not to drink so much."

"Sonny. Sonny," Alex beckoned. Sonny answered his call and went into the sick room.

Alex instructed, "Be good boy allatime. Allatime. Never drink when you get big. It poison. It killit you inside fast. Real fast. Take care of you Mama and girls. You be boss now."

"Don't talk like that Pa, you'll be all right." He was patting his father's hand and sniffling.

"No, I think I go now. I think I go." Alex was trying to keep his eyes open, they were fluttering and he was breathing heavily.

"Oh, Pa, you can't!" Sonny kneeled beside the bed, hugged his father and cried.

"No cry, Sonny. No cry, okay. I get well for you, for you Sonny."

"Sure ya will." He kissed his father and said, "I'll go see if the doctor came. You pray, Pa, God will help you."

Sonny left the room. He walked to the kitchen table and sat down. "I'll never drink! Never! Never! Never!" he proclaimed. He crossed his arms on the table, laid his head down and cried. "He thinks he's gonna die. Oh, he can't, he just can't."

Nina and Butter whimpered and sniffled and wiped their eyes and blew their noses as they still stood beside the door, thinking their father would call them in next. Nina said, "I wish we knew how to pray. I don't even know who God is." She blew her nose and decided to find out some day.

Nadia waited for Dr. Hope on the main road. Their house had been moved and he did not know their new location. Dr. Hope told Alex it was his heart. Alex was ordered to rest and to let up on his drinking if he wanted to live any longer. One small drink each day is all the doctor allowed. He also told him not to smoke too much and not to do any strenuous work. "You punished your body long enough," Dr. Hope admonished.

Alex confined his liquor consumption to two or three small glasses a day. His fingers were not steady enough to roll his own cigarettes anymore. He began smoking store bought Marvels and longed for the Mahorka cigarettes he used to smoke in the old country. There were no more fights when Nadia raised him to go to work for what was called the graveyard shift, and he even began kissing his wife goodbye before leaving for work.

Nadia was pleased and thought, *Too bad he not getit sick long time ago.*

Chapter Twenty One

NINA CUT A PIECE OF CHEESE CAKE FOR HERSELF AND asked her mother, "Want some, Ma?"

"No. I already have piece with tea. Have glass milk, Vera, Olga, Nina. Nina." Nadia shook her head back and forth after saying Vera, Olga, and then nodded when she said Nina.

"Oh, Ma, don't you know our names yet?" Nina laughed.

"Yes, I knowit. It habit," Nadia laughed too.

"You should have had only one kid, then you wouldn't have any trouble."

"No makeit fun of me," Nadia smiled and blushed, she felt a little senseless. She still had the habitual characteristic of naming one or two or three or even four of her girls' names before saying the one she meant to say first. Sonny was the only one she had no problem addressing. They all teased her and they all laughed each time. When she spoke to or of her husband she had a different name for him, dgeed (man, grandfather, and father), stari dgeed (old man), Batko (another word for father), Papa, Pa, Alex, Alexander, Alexander Ivanovitch, Sasha, muzik (husband) and even, "Hey Durock!" (Hey crazy, dumbbell or stupid in Russian).

Nina went to the icebox and returned to the table with a bottle of milk. As she poured, she said, "We saw that man who has a hole in his head today again. He took off his hat to Butter and me when we were on the swing. He smiled and said hello. Gee, he has small eyes. This is the fourth Sunday in a row that we saw him walking down 5th Avenue. I wonder who he is."

"I don't know," said Nadia.

"I guess he walks down to the lake. He wears a white shirt and a tie, and his suit looks like it cost a lot of money." This was a most unusual sight in manner of dress in Lily. "But I wonder why he has a hole in his forehead. It can't be a bullet hole, can it?" Nina started to drink the milk she had poured, but had to stop midway to laugh at what her mother answered.

"You silly, he be dead if it bullet hole. No," Nadia shook her head and laughed with her daughter. "It something else, maybe sickness."

"I wish we could find out where he comes from and why he walks out here. He always walks holding his hands behind him like he's thinking and doesn't care where he's going. I'll show you, like this." Nina stood up, gulped her milk, finishing it, and demonstrated the man's walk.

"I've never seen anybody walk like that or as slow. He stops once in a while and looks around, then he puts his hands in front of him and stands real straight," Nina demonstrated again. "Not like Old Ivan, he stays hunched over. Seems to me like this man likes the ground, and the sky, but when he looks around here I think he sees something else because there's nothing out here to see. Know what I mean, Ma?"

"You think too much, dotchka (daughter). Allatime you look like you seeit something else too. Even when you little girl you always serious. It not good to be that way, you hurt yourself to think too much. It pretty hard to figure out life an' people."

"I don't have any friends, Ma. Martha just wants to play her violin and the other girls just want to play games. I don't have anybody to talk to. I talk to the sky and the stars and birds and trees and I even make up people who are with me and are talking to me. I'm jealous of the city kids in school, they're always so happy and I'm afraid of real people because I think they don't like me. I get all tongue tied and say the wrong things so I keep quiet. The kids try to make me laugh so they can see my eyes close up, so I try not to even smile. How come my eyes are so different from the rest of us?"

"Oh, lotsa brother an sister lookit different. You eyes nice an you lookit better when you smile than when you haveit long face."

Nadia knew then and there she could never tell her sensitive daughter her true bastard identity. She would search very thoroughly for all the answers and be hurt to no end. Her inferiority complex was great enough as it was. No, she would spare her this one great hurt of human weakness her mother experienced to make conditions as they were.

Nadia continued naming Nina's more pleasing attributes, "You have very pretty hair, nice an' wavy, an' you gotit beauty mark on cheek like mine. Not everybody gotit beauty mark on face. That mean God touch you with special mark, but you too skinny. You runit too much. You have to walk like lady, then boys have time to lookit on you."

"Boys, huh! Who's gonna notice me out here? Daria's been going steady already. She thinks we're pigs because we live out here. You don't know it, Ma, but she hasn't even told anybody she has a family. She's ashamed of us because we live so close to the dumps."

"Aw, dumps far away from here. This nice place."

"We saw her at a picnic one time and she said we weren't even her sisters. She probably tells everybody she's an orphan and Vera is her aunt or something. I really don't know what she tells them and I don't care. She should be ashamed of herself. Why don't we move back to Winsome, Ma?"

"I don't think so. Papa likeit here. He used to this place, an' me too."

"Nobody understands me or even cares," ended the most lengthy conversation she had ever had with her mother. Nina walked out of the house not stopping to catch the screen door as it banged, opened again, and then stayed shut after two flies had gone in.

❖ ❖ ❖ ❖

The following Sunday the bent and sometimes gaunt stranger who fascinated Nina and aroused her curiosity to the point that she imagined he must own Lily, was seen again. Nadia and Alex were sitting on the porch steps watching the pigs loll in the mud in their pen when the gentleman waved to them. They returned the warm, neighborly salutation.

"Who that man?" Alex asked his wife.

"I don't know. He not from Lily. He walk to lake on Sundays."

He waved to them again the next Sunday. On his way back from the lake he turned off 5th Avenue to Billy Goat Road and stopped at the gate to talk to Alex. Nadia came out of the house to join them. She was just as anxious as Nina to learn who the stranger was. After they said their hellos and talked about the weather, the animals, and fowl, Nadia asked, "Where you comeit from?"

He smiled and answered, "Oh, I come and I go, no place. I like it here, it's peaceful and poor, like I was once, yet rich because you look happy, your children look happy. I live in the big city where six days a week everybody is in a hurry going someplace and trying to make money. On Sundays the city is ugly and dead. Here it looks peaceful. I ride the streetcar to the end of the line and then I walk to the end of the line here. This place is the end of the world and the beginning."

He turned up the palm of one hand and directed his deep-set, sky blue eyes, at the surroundings, then glanced at his hand as though all of Lily had shrunk to miniature scale and the town rested in his extended palm. Then quickly, with the bat of his eyes, he returned to the present, still smiling and added, "Where are the children?"

"They go to show in city, seeit cowboy movie, Hopalong Cassidy," Alex answered. "My Sonny crazy about him. They never miss listen to he story on radio too."

Mr. Barton was no longer a stranger and he no longer walked to the end of the world. Each Sunday he went no farther than 1234 5th Avenue, Lily, Indiana. The visiting days were filled with conversation and each one brought him closer to the family until he was in the house and spending as much as three and four hours talking to anyone who was home. Nina monopolized most of his time. She cared not to go to the picnics in Jones Grove or to the movies in Winsome anymore. She waited for the Sunday visitor who philosophized on life's eccentricities. Butter could not understand why her sister was so interested in what the elderly gentleman from the big city had to say. It was too deep for her. She ran to join the girls at Red Place.

Samuel Barton was a short man, a little taller than Alex, but had the same build, except that he lacked Alex's muscles. He was the same age as Alex, and had the same amount of gray hair. He found Nina to be an avid listener to the lessons he had learned the hard way, all alone and penniless in a vast city where greed mixed with hard work were the only means of survival for him.

He's my teacher, Nina thought. *I've learned more from him this summer than I could learn in all my school years. Nobody talks the way he does, he's so wise. I think he knows everything there is to know about life. He appreciates everything. He can pick up a blade of grass and analyze and theorize on the thin, green subject until it leads to a multitude of subjects that would make a throat dry and a mind tired from umpteen hours of speech. He doesn't carry a watch, he tells the time of day by the sun.*

"What is time" he says, "but a piece of machinery to tell man when to sleep and when to eat, but it does not tell you when to die or how to live. I can now come and go as I please. But," he says, "Never put off for tomorrow what you can do today." And, "Life is very short, reach out and grab all that you can from it. The early bird catches the worm. Know where you are going, and get there before someone else does. Know what you want to do and do it." Then he says, "Mind your father and mother for they are wise in years and in experience. Set a goal for yourself, aim high, but never let dark days cloud your mind. Let bygones be bygones and never live in the past." And lastly, "Never let anyone tell you they are better than you, for we are all equal—same body, same eyes, and same mind. Think! The mind is a marvelous gift!" I used to live for the far future, but he tells me that every day is important and to make the most of it.

Nina asked him about his boyhood, he answered, "Very hard, very hard. We were poor, I was poor. You wouldn't believe it. But that's the past, let's not talk about the past, the future is more important, much more important."

Now I know why he comes here. We are poor, and we remind him of himself when he was young and poor. He must have lived in a place like this somewhere, maybe in the old country, I won't ask because he doesn't want to talk about it. That's why he looks around when he walks out here. He probably sees his own town or village or maybe just his house in a place like this. He stops to remember where he played and where he cried, and where his mother comforted him. Now he is rich and successful, but he will never forget his struggle to get to the top and find a place for himself, Nina said to herself.

"May I ask what happened to your forehead?" Nina inquired when she finally had the courage and thought she could bear the unanswered question no longer.

Mr. Barton covered the deep scar with his fingers and answered, "That was a sinus infection. I had an operation when I was young. I suffered a great deal."

"I'm sorry. I hope you didn't mind my asking? I was curious and just couldn't understand it," Nina humbly said.

"That's perfectly all right." Mr. Barton smiled. "A curious mind is a healthy one. You learn by asking. Never be afraid to ask. Knowledge is power!" he spoke very softly but forcefully.

Nina was grateful he did not think her impudent. "I'll remember that, thank you."

"And you must know this," he pointed a finger, and went on, "a mountain of knowledge is waiting for you in books. Read everything you can. You will learn something new every day of your life. You may not think you can apply everything you read to everyday life, but, slowly, in a lifetime, you will. Store in your mind all that you can, and apply it."

Nina listened and smiled and knew she would remember his words all her life. She felt that she too had a deep scar in her forehead from trying to absorb all the philosophies and proverbs she had heard all that summer. Nina felt pity for Mr. Barton the day he entered the house for the first time; he had to remove his hat. He wore his hat low to cover the scar, and when he removed the hat, he continuously rubbed the area to hide it, or turned his head. When he looked at a person, his small eyes appeared to look deep into the subject, analyzing the person's innermost secrets.

Nina learned he was sole owner of a five-story corner building in the big city that housed his publishing company. Two floors were rented to a bindery that worked in connection with his book printing firm. As wealthy as he was, he lived alone at the YMCA two blocks from his shop, as he called it. He gave up his sweetheart to a man who could give her more at the time and himself never married.

Mr. Barton never paid a visit empty handed. He never gave the children money, but he brought delicacies they had never seen or tasted or knew existed—marshmallow-stuffed dried fruits, assorted nuts, oranges as big as grapefruit, apples that appeared to be two in one, large clusters of sweet grapes, huge watery pears, imported hard candies and assorted filled chocolates. He gave Sonny a book entitled How To Play Baseball (Sonny's main interest). Butter received a harmonica, and Nina treasured and read and reread her gift of *One Hundred and One Famous Poems.*

Butter did not care to learn to play her instrument, so she asked Nina to trade her scrapbook of movie star pictures for the harmonica. "You don't want to be a movie star anyway," Butter said.

Nina gladly made the exchange and learned to play by ear quite well.

Sonny teased his sister, "Who ever heard of a girl playing a harmonica?"

Mr. Barton's visits ceased when cold weather set in. Nina was busy with school homework, but on Sundays she found time to miss her philosopher friend. She found herself applying his proverbs to her school work. These questions arose, "Why am I studying Algebra? What good will it do a girl when she finishes school?" Then she remembered what Mr. Barton had said to her, "All your life you will be faced with problems only you can solve." Then she knew, school gives me one kind of problem, and life will give me others to solve after school and all my days.

The entire family was happy to see Mr. Barton on Russian Christmas. He arrived with bags of goodies but had no time to see Nina alone. The days were short and the dark Lily roads were fearful for a man in expensive clothes.

When he took his leave, Nina asked, "Mama, how come he never eats with us, he only has tea?"

"Because him Zyd. He eatit different kind food. He Mama Russian but he Papa Jew."

Chapter Twenty Two

FIFTH AVENUE WAS BUSIER THAN EVER. A TRUCK WENT BY every fifteen minutes, raising a white cloud of shiny ore dust as it sped to its destination. The increased speed of the empty trucks hurrying back for more slag made even a larger screen that settled on all the plants in Lily. Only the heartiest weeds and trees sprang up through the granulated cinders, daring the unasked and unwanted material to thwart Mother Nature.

Nadia told her son, "Makeit sure you cover you eyes when truck go by." And she told her girls, "Wearit babushka allatime." There were more trucks hauling slag now than garbage. On hot, windy days the residents of Lily could taste the slag in the air. Nadia had to take Golzy close to the Forest Preserve to graze and Alex went there to cut hay.

The day the hay was ready to be stored in the barn, Daria came with Vera and Frank and the three children they now had. Frank hired a trailer to drive into the fields and hauled the dry grass in. The distance was too great to do the work completely manually and with great exertion as they had done when they lived at the old place.

Nina was ironing clothes in the living room when Daria and Vera unexpectedly walked into the house. Butter was out in the fields helping her father and was not there to help Nina put the ironed articles away, as she usually did. Piles of clothes lay everywhere on the couch and chairs, making the room appear disorderly and unkempt.

"Gee look at the pig pen," Daria sneered.

"What the hell do you want here, hotsy totsy?" Nina sneered in return.

"What the hell do you care?" was Daria's snickering reply.

"Nah, nah, nah!" returned Nina.

Vera stepped in with, "All right girls, don't fight. We have some clothes for you, Nina."

"What, her old things?" she questioned. "Who wants to wear her rags? That's all I get is hand-me-downs. Most of her things don't even fit me, she's so fat! Butter gets most of 'em and I have to go to school looking like the last rose of summer. Why can't we get new clothes for a change? She gets everything. The only time she knows her family is when she wants money for new clothes."

Nina was hurt, angry, and about to cry. It was Daria's turn to be sassy with, "Nah, nah, nah."

Nina stopped ironing and went to her bedroom. She drew the drapes across the door and lay on the bed and sobbed. "Why does she have to come here at all?" she whispered into her pillow. "Every time I see her, I hate her even more. When she comes here the place is always a mess. Why doesn't she come here on Sundays when people are supposed to visit, then the house is always tidy. We live here, it's not a picture to look at, or a museum to just walk around in. We don't have any closets to store things in. That camoda holds practically everything."

Daria was in high school now. To escape some of the workload in Vera's busy house, Daria went to summer school, and was a year ahead of Nina in classes. Alex figured since he did not have to feed Daria, the least he could do was to give her all the money she asked for to spend on clothes, shoes, and books. His other three children were given only the bare necessities, which of course made them envious of Daria.

What made the situation worse was what Alex said when they complained: "Daria live in city, she needit nice clothes. You live in Lily, you not needit nice clothes."

At fifteen Daria was an attractive girl, a little too heavy, but she would slim down in the next few years. Her honey-blonde hair hung loosely over her shoulders. It was combed straight back on top and held fast by a large barrette in back of her head. The orange-red lipstick she wore made her white teeth look whiter. Her nose was slightly tilted and she carried herself erectly. She was popular in school and had dates for all the dances far in advance. Her best girlfriend, Janet, was the only one who knew Daria's family lived in Lily and she never revealed the secret. Nina, Butter, and Sonny did not attend the same school that Daria did, so it was easy for her to stick to her tall story. She was certain she would not be as popular if her friends knew her family lived in an old house near the dumps. Daria never used the word "dead" in her explanation. She would say, "I don't have any parents. I'm an only child and I live with my aunt," and quickly change the subject.

Janet was also the only person who knew Daria was heartbroken when Joe went away to be a missionary in China. He was her first love and she would always hold him dear. The attention she received from other boys did not give her time to mourn him long, but her tears soaked her pillow many a night after Joe left. He had tried to explain that he was going because he had the call, and not mainly that his father wished his only son to be a priest.

Joe had incited in Daria the strong desire to be his wife and the mother of his children, and made her give up the lifetime aspiration of wanting to be a movie star. Now she was more determined than ever before to fulfill the glamorous, exciting, fortune-paying ambition.

Nina left her room when she heard the laughter that was coming from the haybarn. She walked through the kitchen without looking or saying one word to Daria, Vera, or her mother. Sonny, Butter, and Vera's children were packing down the hay.

Nina started a game of hide and seek in the dry grass. She hid in one corner and covered herself completely with straw. When she felt something cool, slimy, and wiggly around her legs, she screamed, "Eeek, a snake" and ran out of the barn.

Sonny finished packing down the hay all by himself. He was afraid of nothing. Nina was proud of her brother, and felt she had accomplished her desire to make her brother a fearless toughie, but realized she must be changing into a lady since she was finally afraid of snakes.

Nadia had insisted that Vera and her family stay for dinner. Frank had been of great assistance to Alex that day. When the work was done, Alex's pounding heart told him not to go into his private shed for whiskey. He was grateful that Frank had refused the offered drink, or he would have found the temptation too great to resist having one himself. After dinner, Daria received the moneys she came for, and sighed a sigh of relief knowing she would not have to come to Lily for another year.

❖ ❖ ❖ ❖

The next day, Vera was in her kitchen peeling apples to make pies. Daria sat at the table removing the core, and sliced the fruit into a large bowl. Daria asked, "Why do Nina and I always get into it? Come to think of it, I can't remember a day going by that we didn't fight over something."

Vera replied, "It's probably because you are so close in age. And then, you two don't like the same things."

"How can they stand it living out there? I'll bet Nina never had a boy ask her for a date yet."

"Probably not, but they won't live there too much longer, the dumps are getting pretty close."

Shaking her head, Daria replied, "They'll never leave there. The dumps will probably be all around them and they'll still stay because they're so used to the place. My gosh, they've been there almost ten years. I couldn't bear the thought of any of my friends finding out that my folks live out there. I'd die."

"Oh, Daria, you're too particular! They're still your family no matter where they live."

"Family! Huh! An alcoholic for a father and sisters that I just fight with. Ma should have left him a long time ago."

"Oh," Vera smiled, "she had her chance, but didn't take it."

"What do you mean? When?" Daria was surprised and stopped her chore.

Vera went on peeling apples and did not look at Daria. Vera laughed and said. "Oh, never mind, it's a secret."

"Oh, come on, you can tell me," Daria whispered. Vera turned somber and replied, "No, it's better it stays a secret for Mama's sake."

Daria was indignant. "Fine friend you are! You get my curiosity aroused, and then you drop it. Aw, that's not fair. Cut up the apples yourself!" Daria put the knife down on the table and went into the bathroom to comb her hair. She was not satisfied with dropping the subject the way they had, she returned shortly to prod her big sister with more questions.

"I'll bet it has to do with Nina. Come on, tell me," said Daria when she sat down at the table.

Vera finally looked up at Daria and said, "No, I won't. And what makes you think it concerns Nina?"

"When I looked in the mirror, I remembered Nina's eyes and how different they are from ours. The rest of us look alike, but her eyes are so green, and they even slant a little when she smiles, which I see very seldom because we're always fighting, and they close shut if she laughs hard. Her hair is darker than ours, too."

Vera shook her head. "I'm not talking. You can think anything you like."

"I'll solve this myself then. I'll bet she's not even our sister, that's why she and I always fight. I felt there was something missing between us. Don't tell me she was born in Russia?" exclaimed Daria at her own accusations. "I'll bet she was." She waited for

Vera to answer, but she just went on peeling apples, and did not look at the interrogator.

Daria answered her own questions, "No, she's not in the picture that you and Mama had taken before you came here. Mama wouldn't do a thing like that anyway. What year did you come here?"

"Mama says 1922, or was it '23? I don't even remember myself, and you can think what you like, I'm not talking I said."

Vera kept her eyes on the work she was doing and still could not look into Daria's eyes; she felt she would surely reveal the truth if she did. She also knew that was the reason why she could never meet Nina's glances without turning away quickly. Vera regretted having mentioned anything to arouse Daria's suspicions. She had carried the secret so long and did not even tell Frank, her husband. Alex never spoke of Nina as anything other than his own daughter, and he knew there was no chance of Irina coming to America now that she was married and had two children. Nina was so sensitive, she may even kill herself if she found out she was born illegitimately.

Chapter Twenty Three

IT WAS WINTER. THE TIME WAS MIDNIGHT. SNOWFLAKES mingled with the gray smoke that rose from the chimneys atop the white roofs announcing the town lived, but it slept. Lights shone brightly at every window of only one of these bleak houses at White Place that should have been named Gray Place. Running feet and a hasty knock summoned lights from a neighbor; and then a light shone in a third house. Alex arose to rake the coals and add more wood to the stove to keep his house warm. A shot rang through the cold, still night and echoed off the Forest Preserve.

Alex was startled. "Yebi tvou mat!" he swore. "Scto to? (What's that?) I hearit gun. Sure. I hearit gun!"

He sucked in his breath and reached for his cap that hung on a nail by the door and went out on the porch wearing only his long underwear. He pulled his cap down tightly and exclaimed, "Oye, oye, oye," when he saw the fire and heard excited voices.

Returning to the house, he roused his wife, "Baba! Baba! Wake up! Wake up! Big fire!" The children had heard the gunshot and looked out of a bedroom window at the house that was burning. Everyone hurriedly donned warm clothing and ran to the disaster scene. At first Alex insisted the youngsters remain at home, but he was too anxious to reach the fire to argue further. Every resident of White Place was there.

"Alex! Go get your gun!" Jim Novak ordered.

Alex did not ask questions. He could tell by the violent movements, commanding, swearing male voices that something was drastically wrong other than just a house on fire. He quickly returned with his gun loaded and ready to shoot.

"Give it here," Jim insisted, as he took the weapon from Alex's hand, and ran to the one entrance of the burning house.

Nadia approached Alex saying, "Stay here. Your heart, remember?"

They stood and watched and listened, trying to grasp what was happening. The neighbors backed away into the fields, teeth chattering, families huddled together, clutching their wraps. The women and girls tied their babushkas tighter and closer to their faces. The men and boys tucked their cold hands into their pockets. Alex removed his cap, took the ear flaps out, and put it back securely on his head, then pulled his collar up.

Jim ran to the small groups and commanded, "Make a circle, everybody! Around the house!" The people obeyed and stretched out to a makeshift circle. Jim yelled further, "All the women and children stay in back! You men and boys get on the sides! Don't let him get away. Watch yourselves now! Don't get hurt! And not too close!"

He ran back to where the four Janock boys stood holding guns pointed at the door of the burning house. Again everyone obeyed and took the positions Jim had ordered. The sides and the roof of the house were aflame. The melting snow on the roof prevented rapid spreading. The odor of kerosene permeated the fresh, crisp air. The black smoke dirtied the clean snow, and the heat melted it.

The Durocks asked questions of the Korosuks and vice versa. Mrs. Dubinski shifted her weight from her crippled leg to the other one, and held her daughter's hand. Anna listened to the inquiries passing back and forth that no one could answer just then, "What's wrong? Why do the Janocks have guns? How did the fire start? Who set it? Why? Where is the fire department? Did anybody go to call them? Why are we making a circle? Why don't they want him to get away? Oh, here comes Crazy Catherine, let's ask her, maybe she knows."

"Sure, I know," she answered as she weaved towards the women, kicking up the light snow as she walked. No one had ever seen her sober. "I could have told this stinkin' town a long time ago, but you all call me crazy." She made a sweeping gesture with her hand, and struck her chest. "I drink! So I drink! So what?"

She stopped and looked at all the anxious awestricken faces. Her coat blew open exposing the flannel nightshirt she wore underneath. She pounded her chest again and said, "At least I don't have bastard babies!"

She was shouting now. She laughed, "I could have told you she'd have an Indian baby. Sure! That sonofabitch is the father of Helen's baby! Ah, ha, ha! Ah, ha, ha! Yeah!" She looked into the old and young faces and announced nodding her head, "She had a bastard Indian! Ah, ha, ha! Ah, ha, ha!" She did not turn her back from the shocked audience, but pointed to the blazing house. "He gave her all the money she asked for. But me? He only gave me enough for a half pint a day. I hope they burn 'em!"

And that is just what the men did. When Indian Joe tried to leave his house, the Janock boys, Helen's brothers, fired into the air and ordered him to go back inside. When they heard glass breaking, they ran to the windows and fired in the air again, allowing no escape. The roof fell in. The neighbors broke the circle and stepped back, he would not escape now. The people damned him, spat on the snow, and watched the house burn to the last ash.

Then the women reached for the snow covered tree branches, broke them, and chased Crazy Catherine out of Lily for allowing a terrible thing like this to happen to an innocent girl who was not quite sixteen.

Indian Joe was between fifty and sixty years old. The Winsome Fire Department was notified that an old man had not escaped his burning house in time and perished in the blaze as the neighbors slept. And, oh yes, the Durock and Korosuk families had spoken to one another for the first time in ten years.

Chapter Twenty Four

NINA WAS IN LOVE FOR THE FIRST TIME. SHE HAD HAD crushes that lasted a day or two or a week at the most, but never had experienced anything like this. She could not eat, sleep, or concentrate on her homework. She was in her first year of high school and the homework was heavy.

Alex turned out the lights at nine o'clock, and Nina had to use a candle to finish her studies. She really did not mind, she felt completely alone with the small flickering light and quiet atmosphere, giving her time to think of the new event in her life. It all began when she was in the school library doing some history reference after school when something inside told her to look up just then.

He was walking out of the large room, and their eyes met. She felt that a bolt of lightning had struck her. She had never before seen such deep brown, sparkling eyes. She nudged her girlfriend, Martha, who sat beside her, and whispered, "Did you see what I just saw? He's nice."

"Yeah, I saw him looking at you," Martha said. "There's nothing to him. He's just as skinny as you are."

Still whispering, Nina said, "I wonder who he is?" Her heart pounded and she felt she was choking with the excitement that went through her. She could not concentrate on the report she had to give in front of class the next day. She did not dare ask anyone for his name, the girls would tease her and know she was stuck on him, and then he would find out.

Martha laughed at her when Nina told her of the dreams she had of him. "You're silly," Martha laughed, "you don't even know his name."

From then on Nina kept her thoughts to herself, and her dreams, and her feelings. He was something she felt so deeply and treasured greatly, she did not want anyone laughing at her and spoiling everything. She liked the excitement of being in love. It made her feel joyous. She was content in seeing him in the halls at school and to pass him on the sidewalk on the way home from school.

I like his serious face, it's like mine. And those eyes, I feel they can see right through me, is what she told herself.

She did not learn his name until she saw it listed with his classmates' pictures in the yearbook. He was a year ahead of her. *He must be Polish,* she thought. *His name sounds like a Polish name. Papa would never let me go out with a Polish boy. Wouldn't you know I'd have to go and fall in love with a Polack. I wonder what Papa has against the Poles? I've heard it all my life, but I never thought to ask why. Who wants to marry a Russian*

anyway; they're all drunks. I'll never marry a man that
drinks. Look at the life Mama has had with Pa.

"Ma, why don't the Russians like the Polacks?" she
asked her mother after dinner.

"Oh, that because we liveit in White Russia and
Polish people takeit our land away from us a long
time ago. Poland say our land belong to them. Russian
people no want our land belong to Poland. They sayit
Russians in White Russia are Polish, but we say no. It
like Croatians no likeit Serbians an' Americans no
likeit Indians an' black people. It nothing. Don't listen
to your Papa. God makeit all people good."

Is that all there is to it, Nina thought. *Oh well, he*
probably doesn't even know I exist anyway. Her dreams
continued. Summer vacation came and Nina could
hardly wait for school to begin again.

Nina and Butter were sitting on the porch steps
when they saw Frank's car turn off 5th Avenue onto
Billy Goat Road. Vera was driving and Daria was the
only other occupant of the car.

Nina said, "Oh, oh, here comes Daria with Vera. I
wonder what she wants now? It's too early for back-
to-school money."

"I hope she's coming to tell us she's getting
married, then we won't have to put up with her
anymore, and maybe get some new clothes ourselves
for a change," Butter wished.

"Move over for her highfalutin highness," sneered
Nina when Daria approached the steps.

"Move, you dirty slobs," Daria sneered back.

Butter dared, "Make us."

"Now, now, girls," intervened Vera. She walked
up the stairs with Daria behind her. Nina and Butter
moved over for Vera. Daria was given a shove when
she walked by. They stuck their tongues out at Daria,

and she returned the disrespectful gesture. Daria had entered a beauty contest in Winsome, and came to ask for money to buy a new bathing suit to wear at the big event.

"What makes you think you can win a beauty contest?" Nina asked.

Daria replied, "Never mind, you never could with that silly, old fashioned hairdo of yours."

"What's the matter with my hairdo?" Nina asked. She placed both hands on her waist and decided, *Just let her come near me, I'll slap her.*

"What can you expect from a hick out in the sticks?" Daria answered.

Alex came into the house and Nina did not want to feel the razor strap in front of Daria. She went to her room. She lay on the bed, and looked out the window and talked to the clear, blue, July sky, "She gets everything. All she has to do is ask for it. No wonder she won't tell anybody we're her sisters, look at our clothes compared to hers. Why, I was wearing a snowsuit with ski pants when Daria was wearing a fur-trimmed coat. Now she has a fur coat, a Persian lamb at that. It just isn't fair! It just isn't fair, blue, blue sky, is it?"

❖ ❖ ❖ ❖

Alex and Nadia were entering a movie house for the first time. Nina, Butter and Sonny were with them. Vera and her family sat across the isle. Daria was the first to come out on stage. She received loud applause. The boys in attendance gave her a whistling ovation. Nina did not clap for her sister the first time she came on stage. She could not move, she was awed by the breathtaking appearance Daria made in her blue and white bathing suit. But she did clap for her second and final appearance. Daria won first prize.

She now held the title of "Miss Winsome of 1940" and had taken the first step in embarking on the career she had dreamed of. Her prize was a two-year scholarship to a modeling agency in the big city, which she would utilize after graduation from school next year.

Nina changed her hairstyle. She did not pin it back anymore. She let it fall close around her face, made a wave on top, and pinned one side with a barrette. It was very becoming. She told her reflection in the mirrors, "If Daria is my sister, I could at least look a little bit like her. My hair is prettier than hers anyway. I have natural waves on top and on the sides. I hope he notices me now. But I need clothes. Wish I could get a job before I go back to school. But it's too far to go to Winsome. Mama won't let me. And what could I do here in Lily? Mama won't let me work for Old Ivan anymore. Ever since Butter and I told her we saw Jack Doyle coming out of his shack in the morning with two girls who probably must have spent the night with him, she won't let us go there anymore."

❖ ❖ ❖ ❖

Nina went to the post office for the mail one Saturday morning. Lucille Brecker approached her and asked if she would baby-sit for her that evening. Nina said she would be happy to.

The Breckers lived upstairs of the second house at Red Place. They had two children, a girl of two and a two-month-old boy. Nina had a steady job every Saturday night. When Mr. and Mrs. Brecker did not return home together, Nina conceived that they each went their separate ways to seek Saturday night entertainment. At first, Nina did not question why a man and a wife would do such a thing. After all, she had seen and heard of the immoral happenings in Lily, anything was possible. Nina was mainly interested in the money she was making to buy the clothes she needed so desperately.

Richard had to notice her that coming school year. She was going to burst from anxiety, she thought. There were times she almost told Butter she had found the man she wanted to marry one day, but decided against it. She knew her sister would tease her by calling her Mrs. Lawsky instead of Skinny, so she decided to remain quiet.

The Breckers were staying out later and later. Lucille was a tall redhead, and her husband was a tall blonde. She wore a great deal of makeup. She was colorless without it. She tweezed her eyebrows completely off and made her own pencil lines. Mr. Brecker was very handsome, and Nina could not understand why they did not get along.

If I had two babies, she thought, and the man I loved, I would not care for another thing. We are so lucky to have such a good mother. She could have run off with Paul, I know, but her first concern was for her kids.

Nadia questioned Nina, "Why you comeit home so late?" She was concerned for her safety in the dark. "Where do Lucille and Bill go?"

"I don't know, Ma. I have to wait till they get back. I can't leave the kids alone. They never come home together, and they're always drunk. How could a man and wife do such a thing? And their kids are so cute. Last Saturday the baby had a cold, and they still went out. I can't see it." Nina shook her head. "And there weren't enough clean diapers for him. He was soaked when I put him to bed. You didn't do that to us, did you, Ma?"

"No, never. My kids always come first. But you know, Lucille no love her husband. She have to marry him. She was three months pregnant."

"Oh, my gosh! But how could a woman sleep with a man if she doesn't love him, Ma?"

"That life. Some people weak, some people strong. Some girls thinkit that lotsa fun. Then they spoil whole life for themself an' for kids too."

"I just can't see it," Nina could hardly stop from shaking her head.

One rainy night it was four o'clock in the morning before Bill Brecker came home. Lucille was still out. Nina had fallen asleep with the baby in her lap and the girl huddled next to her in the rocking chair. The baby had a cough and wakened from his sleep crying for milk. There was no milk in the house, so Nina rocked him to sleep. His cries awoke the little girl and she wanted to be rocked too. When Bill picked up his sleeping daughter, she wakened and refused to go to bed; she wanted to continue sleeping next to Nina in the rocker. Her cries woke the baby, who wanted milk.

Bill swore when he found none. Lucille walked in, she was drunk. They began to argue. Nina ran all the way home in the rain and caught a bad cold. She never went to baby-sit for them again. She thought if they did not have a baby sitter, they would stay home with the babies where they belonged. They had paid her twenty-five cents a night, then they each gave her a quarter, not knowing if the other one had paid since they returned separately.

Lucille could get no one from Lily to take Nina's place. Bill told the patrons at Lily Tavern that his wife was stepping out with other men, so he enjoyed the sport too. They began their evening's gaiety there, then each went his and her own way. The word was spread, and none of the other girls at Red Place were allowed to baby-sit for the Breckers, thinking as Nina thought, that the couple would be forced to stay home. But Lucille hired two girls who lived in the big city to work for her.

Lucille came to see Nina one day, and informed her as they sat alone on the porch steps, "Can you imagine what those girls did? They left my babies alone at five o'clock in the morning, and went home, that's what they did."

"Gee, they should never have done that," Nina offered.

"Well, my husband got home first and now he's taking me to court to take the babies away from me. He's going to try to prove I'm an unfit mother. Can you imagine?" Lucille waited for Nina's opinion.

"Gee, that's too bad," was all Nina could think to say.

"I know he'll ask you to be a witness. He'll want you to say I'm a bad mother. You wouldn't want me to lose my babies, would you?"

"No, I wouldn't. Babies need their mother more than their father." Nina was trying to imagine what kind of life she would have had without her mother.

"I knew I could count on you, Nina. You're a good girl. I like you. I knew I shouldn't have asked those girls to come. You would never have left my babies like that. I can count on you not to let me down then?"

"Sure," Nina nodded, then shook her head, "I won't let you down."

Mr. Brecker came the next day, and Nina agreed with him that his wife was not a very good mother.

She would go to court on Friday and tell the judge about the time there was no milk for the crying baby, and that Mrs. Brecker was usually the last one to come home, and that she always came home drunk.

The other baby sitters were afraid to testify. They knew they did wrong by leaving the two babies. Bill thought Nina's testimony would be sufficient, so he did not insist that the two girls go to court.

When the judge asked Nina if she thought Mrs. Brecker was an unfit mother, Nina did not tell him the truth. This was the first time she had been in a courthouse and a courtroom, seen a judge, a Bible, and swore on one. She was excited over the importance of the scene, yet all she could think about was the two children whom she rocked, fed, hushed their cries, told the little girl stories, and sang to both of them. They need a mother, no matter what. Mrs. Brecker kept the children, and she and her husband promised to be better husband and wife and parents.

Nina stayed in her chair until everyone had left the room. Then she walked into the adjoining room, knocked on the door, and told the matron on duty, without looking at her, that she had lied. The matron took her in to see the judge, and she repeated the story. He told her he was aware that she had not told the truth. "That was the wrong thing for you to do," he said.

"I know, but I just couldn't help myself," she cried, "babies belong with their mother."

"I believe that too. It will be all right. It all turned out for the best. You don't have to feel badly anymore. Thank you for telling me the truth."

A big sigh of relief came from Nina as she left and joined the Breckers who took her home and told her they were happy to have the family together and understood how she felt. She was a good girl.

Nina did not have the nice clothes she had planned, but Daria brought her her clothes, and they would have to do for that school year. Butter got some of Nina's hand-me-downs and some of Daria's fatter clothes that did not fit Skinny.

Chapter Twenty Five

RICHARD NOTICED HER. HE SENT HER A NOTE ONE DAY when they were in the library that read, "Why do you stare at me?" Nina was too hurt to send a reply. She was afraid she would write the wrong words. How do you tell a person you don't even know that you like what you see. The boy is to make the first move in that department. She was embarrassed.

She thought, *I should write, "I'm sorry it's so noticeable, but you are a magnet and I'm a helpless piece of steel with a melted heart." But I won't. If I write that I like what I see, he may think I am a big flirt. And I'm not. I really can't understand why I've chosen him. Why do you, when you're in a store looking at a counter filled with candy and only a penny to spend, pick one kind that other kids would never have picked. He's for me, that's all. It's usually called love at first sight. Now, why did he have to write that? Here's a room full of boys and girls, as I lift my eyes from my book, all I see is him, no one else. I just would like to get to know him, like him and hope that he likes me, that's all. Oh, God! If this study period doesn't end soon I think I'm going to cry right here.*

She choked back the tears and did not lift her eyes from the book. When the bell rang, she waited until everyone left the room to avoid meeting his eyes, which she would surely find no matter how large the crowd.

After school Nina stayed on the swing by herself a very long time, and repeated her thoughts, hopes, dreams, desires, and misgivings to the birds, the trees, and then the sky. She was up with the candle until eleven o'clock doing her homework. Alex blew out the light and ordered her to bed. She sobbed in her pillow and then prayed to meet the new day in school with strength and wisdom.

A few days later another note was passed to her in the library. It said, "Dear Nina. Do you go out with boys?" Her answer was, "No, never." No more notes were passed between them, only glances, all that school year.

Her reason for answering, "No, never," was that she never wanted Richard to know where she lived and what she lived in. Nina tortured herself with her thoughts. She still looked for him around every corner and at every opening door.

Nina was secretary of her class that year. There was to be a dance, and the class sponsor thought her presence to take notes would be advisable. She went there alone, and danced with a few boys. One asked to walk her home. She refused at first, then relented, telling Howard he could walk her part of the way.

"You don't know where I live," Nina said when they left the school.

"Oh, yes I do," smiled Howard.

Oh, my God! How could he? Nobody knows where I live. I wouldn't tell anybody. Nina held her breath.

He continued, "You live in Lily. 1234 5th Avenue. You told me once." He was always smiling. He was short, even shorter than her father, and would probably never grow any taller than what he was then, she observed.

Nina released her breath, then asked, "Oh, but you don't know how to get there, do you?" and held her breath again, waiting for his answer.

"I went fishing at the lake one Saturday, and I looked, but there were no street signs or addresses on the houses."

Nina laughed, "Spook town. Only we can see them, they hang from sky hooks." She was relieved that he had never seen the house she lived in.

Howard laughed too, then asked, "You're going to let me take you all the way home, aren't you? It isn't nice for me to take you just halfway."

"Nope."

"Why not? You don't have to be ashamed of where you live. It isn't important where you live, it's who lives there."

"Now you make me feel bad." Nina put her head down. It was the first time she had ever talked with anyone regarding where she lived.

"You're a nice girl, you're an A student and secretary of the class, you're always giving reports for extra credits, you're conscientious. How do you like that word?" he laughed.

Nina laughed with him, then said, "Thank you, but you don't understand. We live way out there, and—"

He interrupted, "So you're poor, so what? We're not so rich."

"But you would get lost way out there on the dark roads and paths."

"How about yourself? Aren't you afraid?"

"No, I'm used to it." This was not the truth. Nina had never been out this late on a school night before. When she used to baby-sit, they drove her home, except for the one rainy night when she ran all the way home without stopping. Butter was with her every other time they were out after dark. It was a very dark night.

When they reached the post office, Nina insisted that Howard turn back. She thanked him, waved goodbye and walked on. She turned back and looked to see if he was following her. He was going home to Winsome. She saw him stepping over the equipment that lay on the sidewalk. The streetcar tracks were being torn out to make way for progress. Buses were to come into play.

Nina did not cross the tracks to the main road right after the post office, but walked along the corn plant fence where there was light. She thought she would cross over to the main road when she reached the entrance gate to the plant.

The midnight train was early that night. Boxcars blocked the gate crossing. There were boxcars as far as she could see. The cars were too numerous to be driven into the plant all at once. They were parked on the outside track while the engine switched them two, three, and four at a time inside the plant where their contents were unloaded.

She continued walking along the fence, hoping there would soon be a break in the boxcars. When she saw none and could not hear the engine banging into the cars, she assumed the engine must be inside the yard.

Lovers Lane, the crossover to 5th Avenue and home, was close ahead. She knew she had three alternatives, either going all the way back to the post office to cross over, walking ahead (it was too dark to run) until she passed the beginning of the long line of cars, and that was up to the entrance of the lake or take the risk of going underneath the boxcars to reach the main road and then home on the run, if possible, down Lovers Lane.

She chose the latter. She crouched down and went under the first set of wheels. It was slow moving. Then she was under the middle of the boxcar, again slow moving. Then she was under the second and last set of wheels when she heard brrrraabaaboom as the engine connected with the cars and started to move.

Nina got out from under just in time. She made the sign of the cross, looked up into the dark sky, saw one bright star twinkling and thanked God for letting her live. Then she started running. She cried out loud, "I will never go out with a boy as long as we live in Lily."

❖   ❖   ❖   ❖

Nina studied hard trying to gain respect and friendship from teachers and students by being on the honor roll at school. Mr. Barton's voice kept telling her she was just as good as anyone else, and she should be herself. Her inferiority complex left her when she was in school, but when she returned to Lily, she retreated into her world filled with dreams of returned affection from Richard one day when they would leave Lily to live in the city.

I don't have a chance as long as we live here, she thought. *He lives in the city, and he must have a lot of girlfriends. I hope he never finds out where I live. What's*

*the use, he doesn't care anyway since I turned him down. I
know he would like me if he got to know me, and I know I
would like him, we have the same depth in our eyes. Next
year, maybe. In the meantime, I'll see him in my dreams.*

Nina continued her search for Richard
everywhere. She spent the summer thinking about
him everyday. She sat on the swing and imagined him
standing by the tree, not caring where she lived.

Nina was going on seventeen now, and was
determined to become Richard's friend that
approaching school year. Again, she realized she had
to have some new clothes. She had to find a job.

An outdoor roller skating rink came to her rescue.
The elongated structure with canvas top was set up at
the edge of the big city and at the entrance of 5th
Avenue. Records played organ music over a loud
sound system. Mr. Adams hired Nina as evening
cashier. She would also sell pop and candy bars. Nina
had asked for a job at the right time; his six-year-old
daughter was down with the chicken pox. Mrs.
Adams, who cashiered, had to stay home and care for
her. Mr. Adams could not handle the turntable, watch
the skaters, attend the cash register, and sell
refreshments by himself.

Nina found the work to be wonderful fun. She met
a hundred boys and girls, smiled more than she had in
her life and lost some of her inferiority complex. She
had Wednesday nights off. She spent that time
skating. Mr. Adams presented her with a pair of white
shoe skates. "She is good for business," he thought.
"She attracts the boys and the boys attract other girls.
Very nice girl. Very pretty. The cash register balances
too."

After weeks of refusal, Nina finally accepted a ride
home after work from Bob Holly, a tall, blonde,

handsome boy who lived in the big city and drove his own car. Later that evening Nina changed her mind, and told Bob she preferred walking home. Richard was skating at the rink. Nina could hardly believe it was really him when she saw him standing in line to buy a ticket. They exchanged smiles and hellos. He had come with two other boys who were soon asked to leave the floor, their money refunded, for acting roughly while skating. Richard left with his friends.

Nina was filled with questions, and was carried away with imagination. *Did Richard know I work here? Did he really come to see me? Maybe he'll be waiting for me when I get through working? Maybe he found out where I live? Maybe he does think about me as much as I think about him?*

Bob was disappointed when Nina told him she would rather walk home. He said, "I'll try again tomorrow, and the next day, and the night after that, until you say yes."

"We'll see," she returned with a smile. It was a lonely walk down 5th Avenue. Richard was not waiting. She sat on the swing thinking he would come. It was midnight when she gave up hope. The crickets' symphony did not put her to sleep that night. She spoke to the millions of star and cried herself to sleep.

Alex asked Nina for part of her small weekly salary. It was nice to have one of his children working. It was about time. "You work," he told her. "I needit money. What for you needit school? You only get married some day."

Alex refused to let his daughter go back to school. She spent what little money she had left on clothes. She did not have enough to buy books and a winter coat. She outgrew and wore out the snowsuit jacket she had worn for three winters. Alex would pay her way no longer.

Nina was disconsolate. It was a big mistake going to work. "Now Papa is spoiled. I might as well draw an X through my career, fat chance I have now. Daria never had to go to work. She always got what she asked for. It just is not fair."

She went on working. The roller rink closed a month after school started. Mr. Adams took his outdoor rink to a warmer climate. Nina took a job working evenings at the Red Duck Diner. The small restaurant stood across the road from where the roller rink had spent the summer. Nina began seeing Bob Holly on her evenings off, but with each goodnight kiss, she closed her eyes, and wished it was Richard instead.

Each time the door of the restaurant opened, she was relieved not to see Richard's face. *I'd die if he knew I worked here,* she thought. *I wonder if he knows I'm not in school? I was sure we would have been friends this year. This is his last year in school. I wonder who he'll take to the prom? I hope he misses me as much as I miss him. I know I don't even know him. I've only spoken to him to say hello, but I feel something down deep inside that it hurts and I can't forget him.*

Chapter Twenty Six

DARIA FINISHED HIGH SCHOOL AND WAS WORKING IN the big city as a secretary to a bank executive. Her workday was very long. She rode a commuter train to and from, and it was a forty-five minute ride one way. On Saturdays she went to modeling school, her prize for winning the beauty contest. Daria now had little time to help Vera with the housework, and that increased since Frank's father took to his bed after he was pensioned, and remained there. He even refused to feed himself. He just felt useless and wanted to die. It was hard enough caring for her crippled brother-in-law whom Vera had to dress, and now the father-in-law was worse than a baby — at least they wore diapers. Vera became very irritable, her duties were confining. She was envious of the freedom Daria had and chose to argue with her sister over slight matters as an outlet.

One morning after one of their disputes, Daria was too upset to go to work. Instead of taking the train to work, she rode the bus to Lily. She convinced her parents to move to Winsome. If they had not agreed with her plan, Daria had made up her mind to set out on her own. She could not remain at Vera's any longer. It was a constant battle. She felt sorry for her sister with the numerous tasks, but Daria now had a new and exciting life of her own to live.

That day, Nina, Butter, and Sonny were not at home and missed the opportunity of heckling Daria. Nadia did not tell them of Daria's visit. She knew how they always fought, and thought it would be best if they believed it was her and her husband's decision to move back to the city. Nadia also remembered Nina saying she would never move to Winsome if Daria came to live with them. She and Alex agreed; we will move first, and then tell them Daria will live with us. It will be better that way, no trouble.

The tenants who lived in their house in Winsome were given a month's notice to move out. The Durock family was moving back to the civilization where there was running hot and cold water, a bathtub, inside toilet, telephone, street lights, sidewalks, paved streets, house numbers, and street signs.

Alex told his youngsters it was best they move before they received notice to move from Lily. The slag was everywhere. Huge piles were dumped in the fields waiting for the bulldozer to level them off.

All the animals and fowl were sold. Nadia knew Golzy was happy to be leaving Lily, the flies were as large as cockroaches, as they flourished on the dumps, then came to take their naps on Golzy's large frame.

One Saturday, a few days before they were to move, Nina and Butter walked to Winsome to look over the house they were going to live in. They walked down the alley and entered the back yard.

They had not been this close to the house in ten years. On their occasional walks to the movie on Sundays in summer, they caught a glimpse of the house, and boasted to the friends who were with them, "That's our house over there." They would point to the city house they could not remember ever having lived in. When Nina turned the knob on the back door, she was surprised to find the door unlocked. She turned to Butter and said, "Maybe Papa's here? Good, now we can see what the inside looks like."

"Hi," said Daria from her crouched position on the floor. She was scrubbing the kitchen.

"Sonofabitch! What the hell are you doing here?" asked Nina, amazed at finding Daria in the house.

"What does it look like? I'm going to live here, and we're not going to live like pigs like you do in Lily. I'll show you how people live in the city," answered Daria.

Butter placed her hands on her hips, and returned, "We don't live like pigs! We clean house all the time! You try to live in a small house with no closets and only one dresser. Then you'd see how neat you could be, you old fancy pants!"

"Nah! Nah! Nah!" Daria snickered.

"Who said you could come here and live with us?" Nina asked. "Vera still needs your help."

"I asked Ma and Pa to move here," Daria replied. "Vera can get herself another slave. Why don't you go there to live?" She looked up at Nina. "You don't belong here anyway."

"Oh, yeah! I belong here more than you do. You don't even claim us as your family. Why should you now?" Nina was very nervous. She tightened her grasp on her arms and dug her nails into her own flesh.

"Listen!" Daria put the scrub brush into the pail and stood up. "You should be glad my father supported you all these years."

"Yeah? He spent more money on you than he did on any of us."

"That's all right. I'm his daughter. You're not."

"What the hell do you mean by that?" Nina held her breath. She could feel her mouth twitching.

"Just what I said," Daria smiled and reached down for the scrub brush. She knelt on the floor and went back to her task. Nina placed both hands on her hips and walked over to Daria.

She repeated deliberately, "What did you mean by that? I oughta slap your mean, ugly face."

"Just you try it," dared Daria without looking up.

Nina gave Daria a nudge with her knee, and said very slowly again, "I said, what did you mean by that?"

"Watch who you're shoving," exclaimed Daria. "Get out of here. I said you don't belong here." She stood up still holding the brush in her hand, and faced Nina.

Butter had been on tour of the other rooms. She returned to the kitchen when she heard the raised voices, and interrupted, "Cut it out you two. That's all you do is fight!"

"She says I'm not Pa's daughter," reported Nina as she turned to look at Butter.

"You're not!" Daria announced with a smile, then sneered. "You're just a bastard cousin!"

Nina was stunned. She could not move or speak. She looked at Daria and wished she had the strength to swing her arm, and slap Daria across the mouth erasing the words that had just come out of the self-satisfied face. Then Nina practically whispered,

272

"That's a dirty lie. You hate me so much, you made that up to make me feel bad, didn't you?"

"Oh, yeah? It's true. It's been a secret all these years, but your cat eyes told the story. You're so stupid, you should have guessed it when you looked in a mirror. And you're nothing but a Polack! Papa's sister is your real mother, and a Polish soldier she never married is your father. So there. What are ya gonna do about it?" she related and questioned.

Nina stood there and began to tremble. She felt faint.

Butter stepped over to Nina and took her arm. "Don't believe a word she says," Butter said. "She's nothing but a bossy ole trouble maker." She looked at Daria and continued, "You take back what you said or I'll pull your hair out, you ole fancy pants!"

"I will not! It's true! Vera told me so." Daria responded very indignantly. Nina began to cry. She wrenched free of Butter's grasp on her arm and went out of the house. She hurried down the porch stairs and began to run. She was blinded by her tears and had to stop running. She walked and then began running again until she reached the house in Lily. No one was home when she packed a few belongings into the cardboard suitcase she had found on the dumps, then ran to the lake. It was noon. The lake was deserted. Fishing is best in the mornings.

She put her suitcase down beside a tree on top of the bank, and sat down on a log. She covered her face with her hands and sobbed until her head ached. Then she looked out on the lake and spoke to the water lilies, "I can't believe it." She shook her head. "I just can't believe it." She blew her nose and wiped her eyes. "I'm not Russian, I'm Polish! Irina is my mother? But I thought I look like Mama a little. I have her birthmark." She felt her cheek and rubbed the raised mark. "But maybe Irina has one too or maybe my real father? And I was born in the old country? Why did Mama bring me here? Why didn't my real mother keep me? She probably wasn't allowed to marry a Polack. But what's the difference, if she loved him? I always knew my eyes were different from the rest of the family, but, like Mama said, lots of brothers and sisters don't look alike. That Daria! Why did she have to find out? She just couldn't resist telling me. I hate her! I hate her! Why did Vera have to tell her? Why didn't they tell me a long time ago? I would have understood, and I would have been grateful to Mama for bringing me here. And I would have loved Pa for supporting me. And maybe I wouldn't have griped so much about wearing old clothes, and having to quit school. What will I do now? Where will I go? Nobody loves me. I've always felt all alone. No wonder I got blamed for everything Sonny and Butter did. I always got the most lickings. What am I going to do? Daria will never let me forget I don't belong. I'll never go to Winsome. Why, I'd have to share her bedroom with her; that would be impossible. Oh, my God! Help me!"

She felt dizzy. She held on to the log and inhaled deeply. "I can't believe this has happened to me. It's bad enough I lost Richard, and my career, and now my family. Like everybody says, things happen for the best. Richard could never have come to our house anyway. Papa would never have let me go out with a Polish boy. But I would have been his friend no matter what. I'm so sorry I put so much importance on where we lived. I wish I had a real friend, a real heart to heart friend." She put her head down and cried very hard.

After awhile Nina lifted her head and looked out at the lake trying to find the closed flowers among the numerous green lily pads. She spoke to the plants in the water. "I'm like you, lily in the lake, only the pads surrounding you should be red, white, and blue like this town." Then very slowly she rhymed:

> "I'm the flower in the middle
> who hides from the light.
> Oh lily, it will always be night.
> If I go home, Daria and I will fight.
> The sun will never be bright.
> Your leaves are my family,
> They used to surround me.
> But now they are gone,
> And I do not await the dawn.
> So, tell me dear lily,
> What am I to do?
> I cannot go home
> So, I must stay with you."

She sat there and stared into the lake. A dark cloud hid the sun. It was going to rain. She looked up at the sky and said, "Almost every tragedy happens in this town on a rainy or snowy day. Oh, God, please show me the way. Tell me what to do. I wish I was dead. I can't take it anymore, it hurts too much. I've had an ache deep inside of me so long that I can't bear to feel it any longer. Should I jump in the lake? I hate to die that way. I don't like the mud at the bottom. But what should I do? I don't know. I just do not know."

She looked down at the grass at her feet, reached down for a few blades. She pulled them up, held them in her palm, then blew at them, and watched them scatter. She put her head in her lap, covered her face with her trembling hands, and cried uncontrollably.

Chapter Twenty Seven

"HELLO. ARE YOU ALL RIGHT?" SHE HEARD A VOICE ask. Nina looked up to see who was being so kind to her in her time of need. It was Iris Nelson, the girl with the beautiful hair, the Princess of the Dumps.

"Oh, I'm okay," answered Nina. She covered her face again.

"You aren't sick, are you?" Iris asked further.

"No," Nina moved her head from side to side. "I just have a problem I'm trying to solve."

"Maybe I can help. It always makes a person feel better to talk about a problem than to keep it all inside." Iris sat down on the log beside her.

"I guess you're right. I just don't know what to do. My family is moving to Winsome and I don't want to go there. My sister, Daria, and I are always fighting and it'll be just miserable. She's been living in Winsome with my older sister for a long time, but now she's going to move in with us. I knew this would happen one day and now it's here. I always said I'd never go there to live if she came back with us."

She thought, *I can't tell her the rest, I just can't. I can hardly believe it myself yet.*

When she looked at Iris, never having been this close to her, Nina concluded, *Why she's not as pretty as I thought she was. She has lots of freckles and deep set eyes. She looks as though she never smiles. It's that white-blonde hair of hers that stands out so much.*

"Gee," Iris began, "that's too bad. I'd give anything to live in Winsome and I wish I had a sister; I'd never fight with her. I've been so lonesome living way out in no-man's-land. I don't have any friends. The kids in school don't even know where I live. I'd never tell them."

"I've been the same way. We were pretty happy living here as kids, but it's no place for a girl when she grows up. But I just can't go to Winsome now."

"Why don't you come and stay with us. I know my mother won't object and I'd be more than glad to have you."

"Do you really think she won't mind?"

"I know she won't. Come on, let's go ask her," Iris stood up. She was overjoyed to have a possible friend, and right in her own house, every day. *Wow!* Nina walked over to the suitcase and picked it up. *Gee, this is too good to be true, she was thinking. I'm finally going to know Iris after all these years.*

Iris said. "It'll be wonderful to have someone to go to school with. Do you think you'd like to transfer to my school?"

"I don't go to school anymore. I spoiled my father by going to work. He got so used to me bringing money home that he made me go on working."

"Oh, heck."

"Oh, heck is right. I sure miss school. I'm a waitress at the Red Duck Diner. I don't make much money but the tips are good. Sometimes I get over two dollars in tips in one night. I work steady nights and I get one night off a week, and I get to eat there."

"I'll bet it's hard work."

"No, not too bad. But the times when the midnight girl doesn't show up, I have to work till morning. Then it's rough. But it's pretty quiet then and I even get to doze off at the counter usually around 4:00 A.M." They walked off together, down the main road, across the dumps, and down the path that led to the house at the edge of the Forest Preserve. Iris told the two barking dogs to be quiet.

"You know," Nina began, "my sister and I walked over here one time. We wanted to make friends with you. We saw your house, but the dogs frightened us away."

Walking up the house, their conversation went like this, "You should have called me."

"We didn't know your name then."

"Gee, I'd have given anything to have a friend. My mother has been my only friend."

"You should have come to our house. We saw you drive by with your father."

"I thought of it lots of times."

"We've called you 'The Princess of the Dumps' because of your beautiful hair."

"I wish it was black."

"Oh, don't be silly, everybody prefers blondes."

"I still wish it was black."

"Your house has always been 'The Castle on the Dumps.' It is a very nice house. The nicest one in Lily or even in Winsome."

"Huh, you'll change your mind when you get inside," finished Iris as they got up to the door.

Mrs. Nelson was a very soft-spoken, stout woman with a mass of wavy, gray hair, and very tanned skin. Mr. Nelson was tall and thin and had thin wisps of gray hair. His skin was very tanned also, due to outdoor supervisory work he did on the dumps. Iris talked to her mother in the kitchen while Nina stood close to the door. She was too conscious of her swollen eyes to look at or talk to Mr. and Mrs. Nelson just then. She had said hello, nice to meet you, and then lowered her eyes to the floor.

"Sure, she can stay," Mrs. Nelson told her daughter. "Take her upstairs."

"Gee, your mother is nice," Nina said as they walked up the curved staircase to the attic.

"Mom's okay, but I'm not talking to my father. That's my bed over there by the windows."

Iris pointed to one side of the attic. Two beds stood on the other side of the room underneath two windows. The entire attic was not separated by any walls or doors. The pitched roof ceiling was very high in the middle of the room, so a path was permitted only in the middle to walk from one side to the other; the east and west walls were completely filled with storage boxes piled up to the ceiling.

"Your mother and father sleep over there?" asked Nina as she nodded and looked towards the two beds.

"They undress downstairs. Pop stays out most of the night playing cards and betting the horses at Lily Tavern. He won't bother us. Then he's up before it's even light to go to the dumps every morning, except on Sundays, of course, then he doesn't come home at all." Iris handed her some hangers to hang up the few clothes Nina had brought. The other things she left in her suitcase.

Mrs. Nelson called to them. They went downstairs to eat. Nina told Mrs. Nelson the same story she had told Iris. Mrs. Nelson sympathized, shook her head, and said, almost in a whisper, "Well, that's too bad. If I were your mother, I would take Daria in hand. I would not allow her to call you names and I do not like fighting. I believe people should keep quiet if they have nothing nice to say to each other."

"Thank you for understanding," Nina graciously said, "I really appreciate your help right now. I didn't know what to do until Iris came along and saved the day. I'll have to write to my mother and tell her where I am."

"That's a good idea," Mrs. Nelson agreed. Iris went into the living room for paper and pen. She gave her a stamp and envelope too. "I'll mail it on my way to school Monday." Iris offered.

"That will be swell. Thank you very much," Nina obliged. She sat down in a chair in the living room and wrote on a book that she placed in her lap. Iris played some records on the Victrola. Nina saw her open a dresser drawer that revealed its contents to be filled with records. Nina finally had time to look around the room. There were stacks of everything, everywhere. Two old couches stood back to back in the middle of the living room. Odd chairs lined one entire wall. Two gray cats slept underneath two of the chairs. There were stacks of newspapers in one corner. Boxes and sacks bulged from underneath, between, on top of, and in every corner and available space.

Two chests of drawers stood together. They were minus some knobs, and some could not close. A bookcase was filled with broken knickknacks, and the glass on the door was cracked. An opened sewing machine stood under a window. Stacks of magazines lay on the floor beside it. Three calendars hung on one wall and four on another. Nina looked into the kitchen and saw three more calendars in that room.

Why, this is the dumps! Nina realized. *They must save everything they find. But, I never saw them digging on the dumps. And we thought this was a castle? Our house was a castle compared to this. What a mess! The kitchen looked clean but the living room was dusty, all the treasures were dusty. I'm so disappointed. Now I know what Iris meant when she said, "Huh, you'll change your mind when you see the inside." But, I'm not sorry I'm here! They're being so nice to me. I would probably have killed myself if Iris hadn't come along. She looked at the French windows that lined two walls in the living room that overlooked the dumps and thought, It's those windows that make this house so beautiful on the outside. But, they're dirty, or is it the frosted glass that makes them look that way?*

One of the cats awoke and stealthily walked around Nina's legs, she raised them. The cat looked up at her and meowed. Suddenly, Nina was reminded of Daria and all that had happened that day. She tried to cry quietly. Her tears dropped onto the letter and blurred her vision. She fumbled in her small red purse for a handkerchief and hurt a finger on the sharp edge of a bobby pin.

She folded the paper that had, "Dear Mama, I am at the Castle on the Dumps with Iris" written on it and put it in her purse. She laid the stamp and envelope on a chair and decided not to write home. *Let them worry about me,* she thought. Iris turned off the phonograph and the girls went upstairs.

"I'm not going to work tonight. I look awful and I have a headache," Nina reported to Iris as they undressed.

"You'll feel better tomorrow. Do you want an aspirin?" asked Iris.

"No, thanks. I'll be all right. You have been so kind. I don't know what I would have done without you." Nina climbed into bed nearest the window and up against the wall.

"I have a problem too," Iris said as she lay down beside Nina. "I told you I'm not talking to my father. I haven't talked to him in three weeks."

"Why not? What happened?" asked Nina forgetting her own troubles for the moment. Iris placed her hands behind her head. Nina did the same. Iris spoke, "Well, I want to go to college and be a schoolteacher some day. I'm in my last year of high school. I hate to leave my mother, but then, she won't miss me too much. She has the dumps as her hobby. She goes there real early in the morning, every morning, with her wagon and brings home everything. You should see some of the junk in those old trunks." She pointed to the six trunks that lined one wall; two were smaller than the others and lay on top. Iris went on, "But, I can't go to college. My father won't let me. You'd never guess what he wants me to be. Guess?"

"I don't know," Nina said. "Probably he wants you to go to work and get married as soon as possible so he doesn't have to support you, like my father told me."

"Huh, I wish that was it. He wants me to be a whore."

Nina exclaimed, "Oh, no." She looked at Iris and saw she was whimpering. Nina looked away. Iris was never without a handkerchief. She carried three in her purse at all times. One was tucked into her brazier and in every pocket she had in her clothing. There were two under the pillows and one lay on top of the light blanket. She placed it there after she climbed into bed. She carried one in her hand at all times. She used the latter to wipe her tears, then reached for the one on the blanket to blow her nose into. Then she sighed and said, "Whores make a lot of money. My father thinks that's all women are good for."

"I can't believe it!" Nina was shocked. She remembered what she and Butter had always said about Iris, "Her father protects her from men. She never goes anyplace alone." Then Nina asked, "How could he even think such a horrible thing?"

"He always took me with him to the taverns he went to. He made me sit and wait for him while he got drunk. I used to drink pop and watch all the women play up to him just to get him to buy them drinks. He used to tell me he hated it, but I knew better. He loved it. He told me not long ago that he used to take me along just so the men could see me. Then, when he thought I was ready, he was going to sell me to them."

"Oh, my God!"

"My mother told me not to pay any attention to him. So I don't even talk to him. I can't wait to finish school and get out of here. I'll bet I've cried more than anybody in the world. I have a handkerchief mania. If I didn't have one close by, I think I'd never stop crying."

She reached under her pillow and pulled out a clean one. She unfolded it and looked at it. "These are the only things that make me stop crying. I get them all wet and then feel sorry for the pretty things and then I stop. My mother sews all my clothes and saves all the scraps to make hankeys for me. I have hundreds of 'em."

"Gee, I thought I had a problem," sighed Nina heavily.

Iris continued, "I'm pretty good at shorthand and typing. I guess I can get an office job. I'll never be a whore. I hate men. My father has a lot of kids by other women. My mother doesn't know. I'll never tell her. Lots of times I wanted to, so she could leave him, but she likes it here. He bets on the horses to support his bastard kids. He used to boast about it to me whenever I told him I wished I had a brother or sister. He'd laugh and say, you have lots of brothers and sisters.

"I even wished he'd bring one of them home, but then I decided I'd probably hate the bastard anyway." Iris left the bed. She reached under the bed for two pans that she placed on the floor where the rain was leaking through the roof. She climbed back into bed, turned on her side and went to sleep. She snored.

Nina could not sleep. She was sorry she had not taken the aspirin, her head ached and her eyes quivered when she closed them. She also regretted not knowing what to say to Iris after she narrated her story. When Iris mentioned the word bastard, Nina was reminded of her own case.

I'm so glad I didn't tell her my whole story, she thought. *I wonder what Iris would think? What a crazy mixed up world this is. I wonder if Papa knows I'm Polish? I don't think he would have raised me if he knew. I miss Mama and Butter and Sonny. I wonder if they're worried about me? They would never guess where I am. Why did Daria have to move in with them? Why couldn't she have stayed at Vera's? She needs Daria more now than ever with Grampa Corban bedridden. When I asked Ma and Pa to move back to Winsome after I told them about almost being run over by the train wheels, they wouldn't do it, but the minute Daria asked them to, they did. She's their favorite. Nobody loves me. Why didn't my real mother keep me? I wish I was with Richard right now instead. I'll think of him even if I never see him again. There's something about him that makes me want to touch him. I'd be happy just to hold his hand all my life. He wouldn't even have to kiss me if he didn't want to.*

Nina began crying again, softly, so as not to waken Iris. Mrs. Nelson came up to bed. Nina heard Mr. Nelson start the motor of his car and drive away.

Nina dozed. She awakened and felt something crawling on her lips. Bugs! They were on her face and in her hair. She felt them on her legs and arms. She saw them on the top of the blanket-bedbugs and spiders and beetles and mosquitoes and flies and every kind of bug that breeds in dampness. She looked at the screened window. There was a hole in the screen where the mosquitoes were coming in out of the rain. She looked over at Iris. The bugs were crawling all over her face, and around her open mouth as she still snored.

Nina covered her mouth with her hands to keep from crying out. Iris did not stir. *She's used to it,* thought Nina. The rain found another place to leak through and dripped onto Iris' face. She covered her head with the blanket, turned onto her side and still slept. Nina did not sleep all that night. She wanted desperately to get out of bed, but she did not want to offend Iris and her mother by letting them know she could not stand the bugs. Besides, she was by the wall and would have to climb over Iris to leave the bed, surely to wake her. She lay there quietly rubbing her face, arms, legs, and body and shook her hair to keep the insects off her all night long. She watched the rain drip onto the blanket. It was the longest night of her life.

Her headache was worse the next day. She did not go to the restaurant. She thought of the long walk at midnight on 5th Avenue and across the dumps and she knew she could not work there while she lived here. The only solution was to look for a daytime job in the big city on the other side of the Forest Preserve.

The next night was the same as the first, Nina could not sleep. *They'll eat me alive*, she thought in horror as she lay there beside the sleeping Iris and rubbed, and patted, and turned, and squirmed, and shuddered, and cried. The bugs were alive; she wished she was dead.

The third day Butter was at the door asking for Nina. They walked into the Forest Preserve together.

"Oh, Butter! What am I going to do? I haven't slept in two days. That place is full of bugs. Butt, where am I going to go? Gee, I miss you and Ma and Sonny," Nina said to her sister as they sat down on a tree stump. "How is everybody? Does Ma like it in Winsome? Is Daria bossing everybody around?"

"Oh, that Daria. I hate her! Mama slapped her face," Butter happily reported.

"It's about time somebody did. Gee, come to think of it, Mama never laid a hand on any of us."

"She's wonderful. And she's your real mother too." Butter smiled and hugged her sister.

"What?"

"Sure," Butter stated matter-of-factly. "Vera just told Daria that story to keep her from pestering her any more after she slipped and said there was a family secret. You see, that story about you being a cousin is for Papa's sake, so he wouldn't kill Ma and you.

287

You're Polish though. Mama left your father in Russia and had you on the way. Daria promised Vera she'd never tell, but you know her hateful mouth, anything to get back at us."

"Oh. I hate 'er!" She clenched her teeth and her fists. "Well, when I came home and told Mama what Daria said, and Mama saw your things were gone, she and I took the bus and went to Vera's. That's when Mama slapped Daria and told her the truth. Even Vera bawled her out for spilling the beans, the wrong beans. But, Papa better not find out or he'll shoot you and Mama. He thinks his sister is your real mother and your father was a Russian soldier who was killed in the war before Irina could marry him, and, don't worry he will never know. He doesn't even know we all had a fight. He just thinks you don't want to come to Winsome because of Daria and you fighting all the time. Sonny doesn't know anything, so we don't have to worry about him, and Daria knows I'll kill 'er if she hurts my mother in any way."

"Oh, Butter, I can't believe it!" Nina sighed and smiled. "I'm so glad Mama is my mother. Why I look more like her than any of you," she touched the beauty mark on her cheek, "except for my hair and eyes, they must be his. I don't care if he is Polish. So what? The Russians aren't any better than anyone else. God made all of us. But I can't go home. Daria and I will fight and she will tell Pa for sure, just to get even. I know her."

"Uh, uh," she shook her head. "Pa said if there is any fighting he will send Daria back to Vera's, or else chase you both out. Mama wants you to come home."

"How did you know I was here?"

"I saw the Red Pirate. He told me he saw you and Iris from across the lake."

"Oh."

"I thought maybe you jumped in. I know what a softy you are." Butter grinned at her.

"I thought of it, but now I'm glad I didn't, or I'd never have known the truth."

"And what do you want to waste your time thinking about Richard for?" Butter looked at her and saw her surprised expression. "Oh, I know about him. You were always calling his name in your sleep, so I asked Martha who he was. You are so pretty, even prettier than Daria. You can have anybody you want. He is not worth it if he doesn't even know you are alive."

Nina looked down at her hands in her lap and said, "I can't help myself."

"Well, come on, get your things. Let's go home. I missed school today just to look for ya."

"Oh, Butt, I love ya!" Nina sprang to her feet and pulled her sister by the hand. They ran to the house with the dogs barking and the chickens in the yard scattering. Nina felt young and lighthearted once again. She felt as though it had been years since she had ran so joyously with her sister.

"Mrs. Nelson, thank you for everything, but I am going home," announced Nina.

"Well, that's fine. I knew you would. And don't let Daria bother you, just ignore her."

"I'll try. Thank you again. I'm very glad to have known you. You are wonderful and so is your daughter."

"Oh, it was nothing. Iris will be sorry to find out you are gone. Why don't you wait a little while? She'll be home from school soon. I think it would be a good idea for her to go home with you to let your mother know you have been in good hands."

"All right, we'll wait for her. Better still, we'll go and meet her at the bus stop and go to Winsome from there. Okay?"

"Sure."

"I'll go upstairs and get my things."

Nina walked away from the town where she had spent her childhood. She turned around a number of times to fix in her mind all the memories she would have of Lily, thinking she would never see the place again, not knowing she would return again one day next spring.

Chapter Twenty Eight

NINA WAS UNHAPPY. SHE LONGED FOR THE contentment the family had shared in Lily, and wished she was still in school. Daria and she carried on a silent truce. They neither spoke nor even dared to look at one another. They slept in the same bed, but did not so much as touch each other. At the dinner table, one time, Nina caught sight of Daria's trembling hand holding a fork and quickly looked to see if her own hand was doing the same; it was. Daria very seldom finished all the food on her plate and was always the first to retire from the table. Nina was relieved when she left so she could enjoy the remainder of her meal. The tension between them was sensed by the rest of the family.

Nadia missed the animals they had had in Lily. There was not as much work for her to do in Winsome. She found time to crochet, knit, sew, reminisce, visit with neighbors, and sit on the swing. She was grateful that Nina did not ask questions about her real father. She thought, *My Nina good girl. She understands life better than any girl her age because she seeit lots of life in Lily. But, sometimes she live in different world. I hope she be strong and find lots happiness some day.* She was sorry she had not told Nina the long kept secret the day she had the opportunity, and spared her the hurt Daria inflicted upon her.

Sonny was happiest of all to be living in the city. He was closer to the movie house now and needed only to ask his father to receive all the spending money he wanted. He did not miss a single picture that played. Sonny was a boy any father, mother, and sister would be proud of. He was kind, considerate, and lovable. He ran errands for his family unquestionably. He even went to the drugstore for Kotex for his sisters. He loved them.

At fourteen he still kissed his father. Although, in the presence of his boyfriends, he was not demonstrative. He fought any lad who called him Sonny. He demanded to be called Peter from now on, but never objected to Nina calling him Sonny when they were alone. He would never forget all they went through together in Lily.

Nina protected him, mothered him, and toughened him. He remembered, *She saved me from drowning in Lily Pad Lake one time and I saved her one time. I probably wouldn't be here now if it wasn't for her guidance. Mama was always so busy, but we all survived Lily.*

One would think that Sonny would turn out to be a spoiled child what with all the attention he received from his family, but it was quite the contrary. He appreciated everything that was done for him. He was so thankful for the friends he had that he would not do anything to belittle them.

Nina asked him why his grades were not better in
school when he came from a family of girls who were
A students—except Daria, she looked at the boys too
much. His answer was that he too could be an A
student but none of his buddies were, and a top report
card was not worth the loss of friendship. He wanted
to be equal and not above.

"Why, that's Communism!" Nina said.

Sonny would grow no taller than his father and he
already sported muscles just like his. He was tiny but
mighty, his friends would say. He participated in all
the sports in school, excelled in all of them, but he
waited for the day he could play professional baseball.

Butter found work after school and all day on
Saturdays, and reported her desire to quit school. She
was envious of the girls who had nice clothes and
wanted to make more money to buy her own. Nadia
insisted she go on with her schooling, but Alex agreed
it was more important to earn money. Butter did not
enter high school.

Nina did not want to go on with restaurant work.
She knew she would one day meet her school friends
from Winsome and did not wish to face them and
have to answer questions. After she talked to Mr.
Barton on the telephone, she packed her belongings
and told her mother she was going to work for him
and live in the big city. She stood by the window
waiting for the taxi that was charging three dollars to
drive her to his place of business. Her mother
pleaded, "Don't go. Stay home."

"It's better this way, Ma. I can't stand it here with
Daria. I'm a nervous wreck just waiting for her to start
something and tell Papa everything some day."

"No, she no makeit trouble no more." Nadia was
shaking her head.

"I know her better than you do, Mama. Besides, I can't find work around here. I need a lot of money. I don't want to work in a restaurant or a store. You have to have a high school diploma for office work. Mr. Barton is a good man. I'll learn a lot from him." Nadia began to cry. "Don't cry, Mama. I don't want to go away, but I have to. If it doesn't work out, I'll come back home. I'll call you up once in a while."

"Takeit good care of yourself then an' no go out with bad boys."

"Don't worry. I won't go out with anybody. I'll just work and save my money so I can go back to school some day." She heard the taxi blow its horn.

"Why you takeit taxi? Too much money," her mother asked when she looked out the window.

"I don't know how to get there. I would get lost if I took a bus or the train. Bye, Mama."

She kissed her mother. "Goodbye, dotchka," her mother said.

"Tell Butter and Sonny I said goodbye. And Papa too." She left the house and did not look back for fear she would change her mind and stay home.

While she rode in the cab, she decided, *I won't tell Mr. Barton all our family troubles. He considers us as being a happy, contented family. I will tell him I could not find work around here because no one will hire me without a high school diploma. I would be ashamed to tell him the truth, and I wouldn't want him to think less of Mama or Papa. I think he in turn would be ashamed of me to know I let Daria upset my whole life. I thought I had learned so much from him by all his wise teachings, but I haven't applied anything of what he told me. Maybe if Daria had known Mr. Barton, she would respect us more and be a little kinder instead of thinking of herself.*

Mr. Barton put her to work immediately. Her small, dark office where she kept ink records was located in a corner off the press room. The noise of the presses drowned her sobs.

What am I doing here so far from home? she asked herself. I'm lonesome for everybody already. I will never make it. But anything is better than chancing an argument with Daria. I just know she was waiting to tell Papa everything. She is the one who should be living away from home; she intends to some day anyway. Dear God, please give me the strength to face these days. I need time to get used to this life. Everything has changed so quickly. I can hardly believe this has all happened to me.

She cried for two days and two nights.

❖ ❖ ❖ ❖

After Mr. Barton and Nina had dinner together that first day, they walked to the YMCA where he made arrangements for a room for her on the ninth floor. Two floors were for women only. It rained again on this tragic night, her first night alone in a big city thirty miles away from home. A strong wind accompanied this storm to make it worse than any of the others she had experienced in Lily. Nina had never been on the ninth floor of any building before this, and now that she had to sleep there and call this room her home, the swaying building frightened her close to hysteria. The wind howled like a dog who sensed death. The flashes of lightning interrupted the steady blinking of the neon sign that was trying to sell gasoline that night.

A light tapping on the door and a voice announcing it was 7:00 A.M. awakened her to face another day away from home. She could hardly believe she had actually slept. Her eyes were swollen, she dared not look at anyone in the main floor coffee shop where she had tea and a donut. This day was harder than the first. The rain continued and so did her tears. It was one of the longest days of her life.

She stood at one of the third floor windows and decided to end it all. Her life was full of tortures now. She could bear them no longer. One of the men from the press room office approached her and announced there was a telephone call for her.

"Butter. Oh, Butter. It's so good to hear your voice," She spoke to her sister on the phone as she held one finger in the other ear to enable her to hear above the roar of the presses. "I miss you all terribly." She thought, *I can go on now. Somebody loves me. Somebody cares enough to take the time and spend the money to find out if I am alive.*

"How's the job?" her sister asked.

"Oh, so-so." Then she told her all about her first fearful night in the big city and the dark, noisy, dismal old building she now worked in.

"Why don't you come home? You don't belong there," her sister asked.

"I can't. I'm here now, so I have to give it a try. Mr. Barton is very kind and I'm going to enroll in the Smith Commercial High School this Saturday. He suggested that I finish school, so I'm to go nights and all day on Saturdays. I'll get used to it. How is everybody?"

Butter answered with, "We're all okay."

"Do you miss me?" another question from Nina.

Answer, "Sure I do, and so does Sonny and Mama. You shouldn't have gone. Now Daria is happy to have the bedroom all to herself."

"I had to leave, Butt, you know that."

"Bob Holly called you last night. I gave him your number. He said he would call you."

"That will be real nice. I am so lonesome. I work in a little office all by myself. The work is easy. I keep an account of all the ink they use in the press room."

"I still think you should come back home."

"I will if I don't make out. You take good care of things at home now, and call me again, will you?"

"Sure. And you take care of yourself too. Bye, Sis."

It was the very first time she did not call her Skinny.

"Bye, Butt, I love ya."

Nina went back to work with a smile on her face. Bob telephoned that afternoon and begged her to come back home. He really liked her and could have cared less where they came from nor how they lived. He was a happy, carefree young man. She was pretty and he enjoyed just looking at her and wanted to be with her.

She was troubled again and cried herself to sleep that night too. She dreamed of Richard and awoke to a bright, but cool, sunny day. Mr. Barton was waiting for her in the lobby to breakfast with her. She found no time for tears in the next eight months that followed.

Nina worked, went to school, and ate most of her meals with Mr. Barton. Saturday evenings they went to the movies, theaters, and concerts. Sundays they visited the museums, art institute, shopped, and took in lectures. They looked for a different restaurant to dine in every Sunday. They traveled the city by streetcar in search of Chinese, Italian, Russian, Bohemian and, sometimes, American cuisine. And they walked and they talked.

Occasionally, Butter drove out on a Sunday with Bob Holly to see Nina and the three of them took in a movie. Each time they tried to convince her it was best to go back home. She refused. She thought the life she was now leading was a good experience for a softy from the sticks and from the other side of the tracks.

She shared a large bathroom with a dozen girls who came from all parts of the world to live on their own. Some liked it; some did not. Nina had no time to befriend anyone in particular either in school or at the hotel. She was learning independence. She had turned into a young lady who no longer ran or walked hunched the way she did in Lily. The sidewalks of the big city looked cold. The only beauty she found in the immense city was in the blue sky above the very tall buildings.

One Saturday night, while attending a movie, Nina froze in her seat when she saw Mr. Barton's arm around the back of her chair. Then he placed his hand on her shoulder. She did not take her eyes off the screen, yet, did not see the picture or hear any sound other than the beat of her strong pulse.

What is this? she wondered. *Have I led this man, this elderly gentleman whom I wish was my real father, this lonely, rich, self-made person to believe I could be his sweetheart? Oh, Lord, help me not to hurt him. I love Richard. I respect and worship Mr. Barton. He has helped me more than any other living being. Should I be unselfish this time and grant him affection? I owe him so much. How can I repay him? He tips his hat and we shake hands each night when we part. I take that hand because I am grateful for his time and his wise teachings. But, I am a mere child and an ignorant one at that; what could I offer him but a listening ear to his philosophies. I can add nothing to them. I am only filled with questions which he answers so brilliantly. Something tells me to wait and look for Richard. I can love no other. Even if I never see Richard again, I will*

*dream and feel his arms around me all my life. Yet, I could
never explain to Mr. Barton that I am in love with a boy I
don't even know. He may laugh at me the way Martha and
Butter did. No, Richard is my secret, my prayer for the
future. I can show devotion to no other.*

After the movie they stopped for tea.

"Did you enjoy the movie?" asked Mr. Barton
when they were seated at a Chinese restaurant.

"Yes, good or bad, I enjoy every movie we see."
She met his glance for the first time since the display
of affection. Quickly, she picked up her teacup, but it
was too hot to drink, she set it down. Her hand
trembled.

He placed his hand on hers and asked, "My dear
child, do I dare hope that you will be my companion?"

"I am that already," she replied without looking at
him. She stared into her steaming cup of tea.

He went on, "I can give you anything you ask, just
name it. Be my friend. I'm not asking you to be my
wife. That would be too much to hope for. I want you
only to be at my side for the rest of my days. I did not
realize how lonely I was until you came to me. I don't
want you to go away."

"But—"

He interrupted. "No, please, let me finish before
you give me your answer. Do you know what I am
asking?" He squeezed her hand tightly.

"Yes," she nodded, "I understand."

"My work and my building have been my whole
life. It has been a bleak existence, but I have my health
and work is the seed of life. I could have retired years
ago, but to what? With no one. I could not live if I
could not work. Now, with you, we could travel
around the world, see sights you would never know
existed and return here to live in separate rooms, and

enjoy the theaters, movies and dinners just as we have. I will give you anything."

"Oh, Mr. Barton, I am grateful to you for everything, but you will always be Mr. Barton. I'm nobody. I feel that you feel sorry for me. I needed pity from someone and you gave it to me. But, now, you have made me strong and I feel I have a mind of my own at last. You have made me walk with my head high. I am proud that you think of me so highly. But I am a different person from the girl you knew in Lily."

"Your innocence has always been precious to me. Am I asking too much?"

"I could do what you ask. We could go on like this. But it would not be fair to you because I would only be showing gratitude to a man I feel is my father. I have been searching for love, real love, for a long time. I have so much love stored in me that I wish to share with a man one day, but that man is not you. I am sorry, but that's how it is. Now I'm being very selfish, but please try to understand."

"I do. And I was selfish in asking. Forgive me. We won't talk about it ever again."

He released her hand and they both drank their tea. They walked to the hotel in silence, shook hands, he tipped his hat, they both smiled and said goodnight in the elevator before he left her to exit to his room on the fourth floor. She did not get off on the ninth floor. She rode the elevator down to the lobby and telephoned Bob Holly. She was packed and ready when Bob came for her the next morning. She left a note for Mr. Barton at the desk saying she was going home to Winsome, and would come into the city to see him again very soon.

Chapter Twenty Nine

NINA WENT HOME WITH THE KNOWLEDGE OF operating a telephone switchboard. When Mr. Barton's office girl joined the WACS, Mr. Barton took Nina under his wing and taught her the fundamentals of the switchboard. She caught on quickly. She also learned to type and keep books, but she preferred, above all else, the job of servicing telephone calls. Every voice she talked to she formed a vivid picture in her mind of how that person looked—short, tall, fat, thin.

I'll bet he sits with his feet propped up all the time. I know he wears glasses, she wears a lot of makeup and colors her gray hair. Oh, he thinks he's big stuff! He never waits until I locate Mr. Barton. "Call me back," he says. I'll bet he's as bald as Humpty Dumpty. I'll bet he buttons and unbuttons his coat constantly. He's a finger tapper. She looks in the mirror every chance she gets. Oh, it's that gum chewer. I'll bet she has halitosis. And so on and so on.

The work fascinated her. Many times in meeting the voices, her conclusions were absolutely correct. The times she was mistaken, she thought she had better put a stop to her prying hallucinations.

She went to the telephone company in Winsome, and asked for employment. Two girls were hired that day. She was one of them. Her steady 1:00 P.M. to 10:00 P.M. working hours made it possible for her to avoid Daria.

The house was very peaceful in the morning hours. She felt she had made the right decision in coming back home and severing the now painful relationship with Mr. Barton. Had she stayed, there was a possibility of an affirmative answer out of gratitude and sympathy. Her thoughts of Richard were stronger and brought her home. She was reading a book at the dining room table when she heard Alex come in the back door. Nadia was having a cup of tea. She poured some for her husband.

Nina overheard their conversation, "I haveit lotsa news, Baba, lotsa news." Alex announced. He slurped some of the hot brew.

"What now?" his wife asked.

"Helen baby adopted by judge family in big city, an' Helen go to live in his house to be housekeeper. That nice, no? Real nice." He answered his own question and nodded. Nadia agreed.

"An that Irene who live at Red Place, she same age like our Olga. She have to getit married. Some older boy in big city. That too bad, too bad, no?"

"Oye, oye, oye," moaned Nadia.

Alex went on, "We lucky our kids good. They lucky nothing bad happen to them when we liveit in Lily, real lucky."

"Our kids smart. I tellit them everything."

Hearing this Nina thought, *Well, that's a break for Helen. But, poor Irene. I'll bet her folks feel worse than she does. She thought sleeping with boys was a sport no worse than kissing. I told her that's how you get babies, didn't I? Sure I did. I told her and Martha and Sophie one day when we were walking home from school. Martha knew, but the others didn't. I wonder how Martha feels knowing she can't date boys until she's twenty? She'll probably marry the first one that asks her. I'll bet her three brothers smoke secretly already. If Mrs. Sorenuk wasn't so strict with them they wouldn't be so tempted. You tell kids they can't have something and they want it worse. Papa told us, "Go ahead. smoke. If you wanit to be crazy and dirty you lungs, but no askit me for money to buy cigarettes. Go to work. Go ahead an smoke."*

We all tried it at the lake in Lily, even Sonny. It was horrible. The taste was awful and we got dizzy. Daria smokes and Pa thinks nothing of it. He said, "As long as my girls no bringit home babies with no fathers. Smoking not so bad. Not so bad."

Alex had more news, "You know what happen to Chiban? Gypsy Joe. Lily Joe. Man who care for Lily houses?"

"Schto?" Nadia asked. "What?"

"He house burn down in middle of night. He dog wake him up and they run outside. He haveit twenty thousand dollars in house. He go back inside to get money an' he stove explode. Goodbye Joe. He burn with house. No more Lily Joe. Goodbye."

"Oye, oye, oye," Nadia pressed her hands over her heart. "So many fires in Lily. Horses die in ice house. Mr. Sorenuk die and he saloon burn. Indian Joe die hard. An now Chiban. Oye, oye, oye. Die Boza (good God) our house no burn, or, goodbye Sonny too."

"Yes, we lucky. Real lucky. You know what, Baba?"

"Schto topero?" Nadia asked. "What?"

"We moveit out at right time. Now everybody have to move out. Superhighway go through Lily pretty soon. They dump slag on whole town. No more Lily on United States map. No more. No more Lily. That why they dumpit so many years. For big road from New York to Chicago. No stop. Too bad Lily in way. Nice place for kids and animals long time ago. Long time."

❖ ❖ ❖ ❖

Daria persecuted her sister. Nina was never over far enough in bed. Many a night Nina slept on the couch not to disturb her sister. When Nina came home from work shortly after 10:00 P.M. she enjoyed reading before going to bed. Daria needed a full ten hours sleep in order to feel wide awake in the morning. She went to bed early on the nights she had no date. Most of her boyfriends, and she had many, were in the service. World War II was in its third year. Occasionally, the boys came home on leave, or she and her girlfriend, Janet, went to the USO in the big city to find entertainment. They both smoked and they both drank beer.

Daria took first choice in everything; the top three drawers in their bedroom dresser held her clothes; Nina had the bottom two. Daria had a great deal of clothes. She needed the entire closet. Nina had to spend some of the money she was saving for the next rainy day, and bought a wardrobe cabinet that was kept in the dining room for her clothes. Daria would not even let her use the mirror in the bedroom. To apply her makeup and comb her hair, Nina had to use the mirror in the bathroom, or the mirror that was on one door of her wardrobe cabinet. Nina kept her distance to avoid Daria's criticism.

"Get out of here, you dirty pig," Daria would say to her. "Don't come near me! Go on back to the dumps! You're full of bugs!"

Nina would retaliate like this, "What makes you think you're so much better than us? We came out of the same place. You know goddamn well we never had bugs in our house. Can't you ever forget we lived in Lily?"

"No, I'll never forget it. How did you think I felt not being able to tell my friends I had a family. I was too ashamed."

"You're nuts! Lily was heaven when we were kids. Sure, I was ashamed of the place when I got older, but that was silly too. I was told lots of times, it's not where you live that's important; it's who lives there. Why, there're houses in the city that are worse than what we lived in. I'll bet there're a lot of kids that wished they could live on a small farm like we did. And besides, why do you take it out on me? Why don't you take it out on Ma and Pa? They're the ones that moved there. Afraid of the razor strap?"

"Oh, yeah? Nobody's going to lay a hand on me! Least of all an alcoholic!"

"Oh, Daria, Pa's not so bad, and you know it. He gave you anything you asked for. Why, you had a fur coat when you were sixteen years old, you sonofabitch!" Daria smiled and stuck her tongue out at her. Nina continued, "He never slept in the streets like I saw men do in the big city. And we were never on welfare. Pa did most of his drinking at home. He never bothered anyone. The worst of it was that he kept most of the money for himself. He didn't spend all of it on drinks; he just held on to it so that he would always have money when he needed it. I know what your trouble was. You were always so high-and-mighty, you probably wished you didn't have foreign born parents. And you still do, don't ya?"

"Sure I do. That's because I have seen how the better half lives."

"But you can't change Ma and Pa. Besides, you should thank them for bringing you into the world. And, if Vera didn't take you to live at her house, you would have lived in Lily too."

"Oh, no, I wouldn't have. I'd have run away a long time ago."

"Yeah? And where would you have gone? To a whorehouse?"

"That's where you belong, you bastard! Why the hell did you come back home?"

"You shut your sonofabitchin' mouth! If you're so ashamed of us, why don't you move out?"

"Maybe I will some day when I save enough money."

"If you ever breathe a word to Pa about Ma and me, I'll kill ya! And Butter will help me. I'm not thinking of myself, it's my mother. She could have done worse."

"Naw, that's the worst a woman can do," expressed Daria hostilely.

"That's what you think! I saw and heard plenty in my time. Mama's first thought was of us. We would have never survived the Depression if we hadn't moved to Lily. We ate real good, and we had a roof over our heads. We would probably have lost this house if we hadn't moved. We have a lot to be thankful for. How would you have liked being born in Russia? What if Mama hadn't come here? Mama didn't tell you, but she told me that Pa was so used to being free of obligations that he didn't want Ma to come here. That's why she was in Russia as long as she was. It was Pa's brother and his wife who kept after him to send for Ma and Vera. Then when Mama sent a nice picture of herself and Vera, he was reminded how nice Ma was, and he sent for her.

"There was a man in Lily who was tricked into sending for his wife and daughter. He boarded with Mrs. Sorenuk. She used to rob his pockets when he was drunk and slept. He too liked his freedom and his liquor. Then, she told him how much money she had saved of his and took him to the bank. She said she was going to open a savings account for him, but what he signed was a ship-card for his wife and daughter, and they came here without him knowing it.

"And, there was a woman who waited years and years for her husband to send for her and her daughter. He died and then they came here on his insurance money. Yeah, you don't know what could have been. You should be grateful instead of being so uppity and selfish." This was the longest she and Daria ever spoke.

"Don't think you're so smart! If I tell Pa it'll be what you and Ma deserve."

"Don't you ever try it! I wonder what you would have done if you were in her shoes? I thank God that she brought me here. She really took a chance. And, God bless Irina for what she did, claiming me the way she did. You would never do that for anybody, would you?"

"Why should I? People make their own beds and they should lie in them."

"Ah, ha! Why don't you practice what you preach? This is your bed, lie in it." Nina had her, she thought.

"Oh, no, I didn't make it. I have no choice right now, but pretty soon I will. And believe you me, I'll be choosy!"

"Nobody should be that choosy. You want to be better than anyone else, that's why you want to be a movie star. Where's your heart? Do you mean to tell me if you loved a poor man, and he was an alcoholic, you wouldn't marry him? I'll bet you would."

"The hell I would!"

"Well, I believe in following the heart no matter what. A person could be happy under any circumstances. It's all what they themselves make it. You're looking for something perfect, but you're no prize. You're too selfish!"

"All right, so I'm selfish. I wouldn't be any other way. If I don't take care of myself, no one else will."

"You don't give people a chance. You're too bitter and unforgiving. Now I know what's eating you."

"Yeah, smarty, what?"

"That first boyfriend of yours who went away to be a missionary. He turned you down, so you're blaming us."

"Never mind. How do you know about him?"

"Word gets around. If you wanted him so bad, why didn't you sleep with him and have his baby? Then you would have had him."

"Shut your dirty mouth!"

"Oh, Daria, don't tell me you didn't think of it? You're selfish enough. But, he must have been a good boy if he wanted to be a priest. I'll bet if you saw him now, and you still cared for him as much, you wouldn't say no if he asked you to go to bed. Yeah, even a priest. I've read plenty of books. If it can happen to other people, it can happen to you. You just think about it awhile and then you will be able to forgive Mama for what she did. Daria, when you love a man, you will do anything he asks. But, I believe you really have to love him hard."

"You talk like a gal who's had a lot of experience. How many guys did you say yes to?"

"If I said none, you wouldn't believe me, and if I said I did it once or twice, you wouldn't believe me, You'd think I said yes a hundred times. So don't ask such stupid questions."

"Oh, my, you think you're so smart!"

"No, I don't. I try to understand people and their weaknesses; you do not. You're as hard as nails. But I would like to be there when you see Joe sometime. I'd give anything to know what you would be thinking then, or what you have thought already. I'll bet you would have given anything to keep him. Vera told us how much you cried when he went away. Why hide it? That's life."

"All right, so I loved him, and I lost. Now I think about myself. What am I supposed to do? Be a nun?"

"Be what you want to be, but don't step on others and try to hurt them because you were hurt."

"Listen, you, I'll do what I like, and I don't need any advice from you, you bastard!" Their words usually led to slaps, punches, shoves, kicks, or hair pulling until Nadia or Alex stopped them. Daria would always lock the bedroom door, and could not be reached to be reprimanded. Nina had to do her crying openly. She had no room to lock herself in if the bathroom was occupied.

Chapter Thirty

BOB HOLLY DROVE TO WINSOME PARK WITH NINA ON one of their date nights. He turned off the motor of the car and warned, "Prepare yourself for the longest goodbye kiss in history."

Nina placed her hands on his chest to stop his advance and asked, "Why? Where are you going?"

"Into the army. I received my 'Greetings' letter from Uncle Sam today." He pulled her to him, and kissed her until her lips hurt and head ached from his hold. He kissed her softly, then hard, crushing her in his grasp. He released his grip when she moaned, but continued kissing her. He breathed hard and fast as he hugged her to him, and whispered, "Please let me. Please. I won't hurt you. Honest, I won't."

"No, never! Please let me go." She pushed him away, and pressed her fingers to her bruised lips.

Bob hugged her to him again and said, "I'm sorry. I just love you so much. I want you to be mine. I'm afraid when I go away you'll find someone else. You're so pretty, anybody would want you."

"I'll be here when you get back."

"Then let's get married before I go. I don't want to get married yet, but I will just to keep you for myself. What do you say, honey?"

"Oh, Bob, you've been so good to me." She kissed his cheek. "I would like to get married just to get away from Daria, but this isn't the time for anyone to be getting married. You're going away to war, and you should be free from worry. It wouldn't be right for you to marry now. You will have lots of time when you get back. And, not only that, there is someone else I want to marry."

He released her, placed his hands on the steering wheel and looked out of the window.

She continued, "I never told you or anyone, but it's only fair that I tell you now. He went to the same school I did. I never got to know him, but something tells me he is the only one for me. Please don't think I'm silly."

"No, I don't think you're silly. I loved you the first time I laid eyes on you, and I didn't know you then."

"I've always been very fond of you, Bob, and grateful to you for disregarding the fact that I lived in Lily. But something keeps telling me to wait for the day this boy and I will meet. It may never happen because we got off to a bad start in school, but I have to wait for him. I didn't think I could ever tell anybody about him. I'm sorry, but that's the way it is."

Bob looked out at the lake and Nina knew she had broken his heart. *It's better to tell him now that he's going away,* she thought. *He will have time to forget me. He's so handsome. I'm sure he will find someone else right away. I may be sorry I'm letting him go because I could really learn to love Bob if it wasn't for Richard. I must be crazy. What if Richard is already married? And here I am turning down an escape from Daria, and refusing Bob who says I'm his first real love, and who I know would be very good to me. But, it wouldn't be fair to be in his arms all my life and still dream of someone else. I know that's how it would be.*

She reached for one of his hands and kissed it. She said, "I'm really sorry, Bob."

He looked at her and smiled, "Oh, that's all right. I wasn't sure you'd have me. You can't say I didn't try."

"You have been wonderful." She took his face in her hands, and kissed him on the lips. He did not respond. She opened her eyes and looked at him. She said, "Please don't be mad at me. We'll always be friends. I'll write to you. Who knows what the future holds. I may still end up being your wife. You might be sorry, I have cold feet." She laughed.

He smiled. "I'd love to warm them. Anytime. You just say when. I'll never give up. It took me a long time to get you to go out with me, but I finally won. I'll keep asking you to marry me. Maybe I'll win again." He kissed her hands, her eyes, her nose, her cheeks, and her lips for a very, very long time. Then he cupped her face with his hands and said, "How will I ever be able to leave you? You mean so much to me. I'll never love anyone else."

"Sure you will. You're just used to me. You're so handsome, all the girls will be after you, you'll see."

"I don't want another girl," he said as he hugged her. "I just want you. I don't care if I am second fiddle. I'll make you love me. Who is this joker who doesn't even know you want him?"

"Nobody you know. It wouldn't do any good to tell you his name. I'm even sorry I told you. I didn't mean to hurt you."

"Oh, honey, I love you. I love you."

"I love you, too."

"Then be mine, please. Say yes. I'll make you forget all about this guy."

"I have tried. I can't."

He kissed her again. Then he buried his face in her long hair and cried, "Oh, darling, I couldn't live without you. I want you more than I've wanted anything in my whole life." She felt his wet tears on her neck when he kissed it.

"Oh, honey," she said, "don't make it so hard. This doesn't have to be goodbye. I'll see you again before you leave. When do you have to go?"

"Next Friday," he announced.

"Well, that's a long way off yet."

"Uh, uh. I couldn't go through this again. This is goodbye until I get back from the army." He looked at her and said, "I hope you see this guy real soon. If he isn't all that you want him to be, will you let me know? I'll come running." He smiled, showing his perfect, white teeth.

"Oh, thank you for understanding. You're great," she smiled with him.

"You can thank me by kissing me," he said as his arms encircled her. He kissed her for such a long time that she felt their lips were glued for life. She tried to push him away, but he would not let her go. One of his hands held her head. With the other hand, he picked her up off the seat and sat her in his lap. The kiss continued. He caressed her thigh and slowly moved up to her hips, her waist, her back. And she could feel his hard muscle where she sat. She did not resist his hold. She ran her fingers through his hair and continued kissing him.

Oh God, tell me I'm not being bad. It is so wonderful to be loved and wanted she thought. Should I be unselfish this one time, and say yes? I tell Daria she's selfish but I'm no different. I hurt Mr. Barton by refusing security, money, travel, and adoration. Now I'm saying no to Bob. It's so much easier to say yes. Negative reasons only produce hurts that require a great deal of time to heal. This is what a girl looks for – a man to tell her she's pretty, and that he loves her, and wants her, and can't live without her. These are a girl's weakness. This is how a girl gets into trouble. I could give in and share this passion with Bob, but what happens when it's all over? How do you feel then? Ashamed? Yes, I believe so. And Bob would like me less. I'm sure. Or else, I'd have to marry him. I can't. I'm only feeling sorry for Bob right now because I've hurt him. I should never have told him about Richard. Oh, if I don't find you pretty soon, I won't be a virgin, or else I'll marry somebody just not to hurt them. But, this is wrong. Love at its highest is for married people only. I'll never forgive myself. I wouldn't be able to look at myself in the mirror. Now I know how this happens to other girls. You close your eyes and you forget everything except your selfish desire to be wanted, loved, and needed. It is so easy to forget about tomorrow, but I mustn't. I've lived for the day to see Richard. Oh, Bob, if only you were he.

She opened her eyes and begged. "Please, no, don't." She shook her head free. "This isn't what you want, or me either. We would lose respect for one another. We mustn't spoil our beautiful friendship. It's not worth it, is it? Really? Ask yourself. You don't want a girl who loves someone else. Do you?"

"I'm just thinking I'll never see you again."

"I know you love me. You don't have to prove it."

"But I want you to love me."

"Well, this isn't the way. Only time will tell. Not now. Please take me home. Please."

"If that's what you want; you're the boss."

It was 10:30 when she entered the house and heard the telephone ringing.

"Hello beautiful, this is Don. I hope you don't mind me calling you this late, but I know you don't get off work until ten o'clock."

"Today was my day off. I have to whisper because my sleepyhead sister is already in bed, and all hell will break loose if I wake her. She needs ten hours sleep every night."

Daria did wake. She came out of the bedroom. "Give me that!" she ordered as she grabbed the receiver from Nina's hand. She said into the phone, "What do you want to call her for? She's nothing but garbage from the dumps!" and slammed the receiver down, breaking the connection.

"You didn't have to do that. Why did you do that?" Nina asked. She stood up, hands on hips and faced Daria.

"I'm trying to sleep, and no bastard is going to keep me from sleeping!"

"But it's all right for you to get calls at any hour. Nobody complains." Nina started to cry.

"That's all right; I pay for the phone."

"I pay for all the calls I make. I'd never do a thing like that to you. How could you be so mean? What makes you think you can get away with treating me like this? How do you think I feel now?"

"Oh, who cares."

Nina slapped Daria in the face and she in turn pushed her. Nina's head hit the woodwork of the dining room archway, which rendered her unconscious. Daria ran to her room laughing and locked herself in. Alex came running out of his room and went for the razor strap in the kitchen.

Nadia and Butter attended to Nina. Alex pounded on Daria's door, but she would not open it. Nina came to and resumed crying. Her head hurt. Butter ran for a cold, wet towel.

"Why can't she leave me alone?" Nina cried. "What did I ever do to her?"

Nadia asked, "Why she do this?"

"I was whispering on the phone to Don and she came out and grabbed it from me and hung it up. I slapped her and she pushed me."

"You all right?" Alex asked.

"I'm okay," Nina answered, holding the cold cloth to her head. "But what will Don think? He'll think we're all crazy!"

Alex said, "Whatso matter with my girls? Always fighting. Always." He walked back into the kitchen and hung the razor strap on the bathroom door, then went into the basement to get a drink. Nadia helped Nina off the floor into a chair. Butter assisted with the cloth.

Nina cried, "Oh, she's awful! I hate 'er! I hate 'er! Who does she think she is that she can insult me like that? How can I live here, Mama, and take all this from her? I'll bet she wasn't even sleeping yet. Oh, what's the use? I guess I'll just have to go away again. For good."

Nadia patted her hand and said, "I talk to her tomorrow. I tell her leave you alone."

"Wait till she's on the phone, I'll make so much noise she won't be able to hear a word," said Butter. "Don't you dare go away again; let her go."

"I just can't stand it anymore. Insults. Insults. That's all I hear from her," sobbed Nina.

"Go to sleep, dotchka. You feelit better. I talk to her tomorrow," Nadia said.

"She is a pill!" said Butter. "Don't pay any attention to her. I wish she'd move out."

Everyone went to bed. Nina was going to spend the night on the couch. She could not sleep. She went to her wardrobe cabinet and took out her diary. Then she went into the living room and turned on the softest light. As she sat there in a chair she listened for the rain.

Why isn't it raining? she thought. *It should be storming tonight of all nights. It will start pretty soon. I know it will.* She cried. *I can't take this anymore from Daria. Some day she's going to tell Papa about me, and that will be the end of Mama and me. That must not happen. But I can't go away again. Where will I go? I can't marry Bob. I don't love him enough. And Mr. Barton is like a father to me. I can't marry him. If I can't have Richard, I don't want anybody. But he probably wouldn't want me if he knew what goes on in this house. I don't have a chance.*

She went to her cabinet and found what she was looking for. Then she went to the kitchen sink and swallowed eight sleeping pills. Her hands trembled and her mouth quivered as she drank water after each pill. She felt as though they were stuck in her throat. She drank more water. Then she went back into the living room and began writing in her diary.

She wrote, "Dear Diary, I don't want to live anymore. God forgive Daria for being so mean and teach her unselfishness. I'm not strong enough to go on and face the problems that are too big for me to handle. I don't want to hurt anyone anymore. Daria, we were happy in Lily. Our childhood was glorious without you. Butter, if you ever see Richard Lawski, tell him that with all my heart I am sorry I gave up my chance of ever getting to know him. I love you Butter, Ma, Pa and Sonny. Goodbye everybody."

In back of the diary she found the two notes Richard had written to her in school. They were wrapped in a white chiffon handkerchief that had "Forget Me Not" sewn in one corner. She placed one hand on the last written page of the diary that lay in her lap, and in the other hand she held the notes that read, "Why do you stare at me?" and "Do you ever go out with boys?"

She closed her eyes and rested her head on the back of the chair. She whispered, "Please, God, take me to heaven. I know you love me."

❖ ❖ ❖ ❖

The next day there was complete silence in the Durock house. Alex and Daria were having lunch in the kitchen. Alex slurped his soup noisily, and Daria became very nervous. "Sonofabitch!" she swore. "Do you have to eat like a pig?" She threw her spoon onto the table. It fell with a clatter to the floor. She pushed her chair back and hastily left the room. Alex stood up and went for his razor strap.

Daria ran to her bedroom. The key dropped to the floor. She could not lock the door fast enough. Her father pushed the door open and grabbed her wrist. He pulled her out of the room and raised the strap, ready to swing. Daria lowered her head and covered it with her free arm.

Alex announced, "I teachit you how to swear at me! My kids never swear at me! Nina never swear at me! Never! Never!" He swung the strap. It hit Daria across the back. She screamed and sat down in a chair that was in back of her. Alex still held her wrist.

Alex asked, "Whatsa matter with you? What kind girl you are? Lookit what you do to my Nina! She good girl! You hateit her! She hateit you! Whatsa matter with you?"

Sonny had been in the bathroom all this time. He now stood in the dining room watching his angered father, and listening. Daria answered Alex, "She didn't hate me that much. Only one thing makes a girl commit suicide. She was probably pregnant! Why don't you find out? None of the girls from Lily were any good!"

"You crazy! My Nina good. Always good!"

"She wasn't your Nina!" shouted Daria. "She was a bastard! And she wasn't your sister's child! She was Mama's by a Polish man! Yeah! She was a Polack! So there!"

Alex released his hold on her wrist, and slapped her very hard across the face with his hand. "What you sayit? What?" asked Alex as he stepped back.

Daria cried out, "It's true!" She stood up and added, "And no father of mine is going to hit me! I'm getting out of here!" She went to her room and locked the door behind her.

Alex went into the kitchen, sat down in a chair and exclaimed, "Whew! Whew!" He touched his heart, then went into the basement.

Chapter Thirty One

NINA OPENED HER EYES. THE ROOM WAS SPINNING. SHE could not raise her head. She was very weak. "Where am I?" she asked the blurry figure she saw standing beside the bed. A nurse answered her, "You're going to be all right." She smiled and patted her patient's arm. "You had us all scared for a long while last night. You just rest. The doctor will be in to see you soon."

Nina covered her face with the sheet and began to cry. She realized, *I didn't die! I didn't die! I'm still alive! Why didn't I die? I don't want to live. It would have been much better.* She sobbed. She went back to sleep. She heard someone calling her name.

"Nina. Nina."

She opened her eyes. "Oh, hello, doctor."

"How do you feel?" he asked as he checked her pulse.

"Weak and dizzy," she replied.

"Why did you want to do a thing like that for? A pretty, young girl like you. You have everything to live for."

"My sister."

"I know about your sister. You shouldn't let her bother you. How many did you take?"

"I think eight. I dropped two on the floor, I was shaking so much."

"Where did you get them?"

"From a boy who works in a drugstore."

"Do you have any more?"

"No, doctor, that's all I had."

"You know, if they had worked, that boy would be in a great deal of trouble by now. You won't do that again, will you?"

"No, doctor, I won't."

"You just rest. You'll be all right." He patted her hand and tucked it under the sheet. He pulled the blanket closer to her face. "Are you cold?" he asked.

"Not very," she answered.

"You were an icicle when they brought you in. You rest, I'll see you a little later."

"Thank you, doctor."

"Oh, your sister, Olga, is here. Would you like to see her?"

"All right."

"I'll send her in."

"Hi, Sis," Butter came in smiling and greeted her.

"Hi, Butt," she returned weakly. "How did I get here?"

"I couldn't let my favorite sister die. I got up to see if you were all right. I know what a softy you are. Then I read your diary and then I found two pills on the floor. Where did you get the pills?" she whispered so that the other patients in the four-bed ward could not hear her.

"From Chuck. You know him; you had a crush on him. He had a pocket full at the roller rink a long time ago. I was saving them for a rainy day."

"But it didn't rain that day," Butter smiled. "You don't have any more do you?"

"No, that's all I had." She started to cry. "Why did they have to save me? I'll never go back to live in that house with her again. Where will I go now?"

"Forget about that now. Everything will be all right. Just rest. I'll see you tomorrow. I have to go. The doctor told me not to stay too long."

Butter leaned over the bed and kissed her sister. Butter said, "Now don't cry anymore. That will only make you feel worse. I said everything will be all right. Bye. I'll see you tomorrow."

Butter left the hospital room and talked to the doctor in the corridor. He told her if conditions did not change in their home, Nina may try it again.

"She's a sensitive girl," Dr. Hope reasoned.

Butter was the only visitor Nina had all that week. On the seventh day Nadia came with Vera in the car to take her home. Daria had left for California to try to get into the movies. Nina would not have to put up with her persecutions any longer.

Vera left Nina and her mother off in front of the house, and drove home to her numerous chores. Sonny greeted his sister with a kiss at the front door. Nadia went into the kitchen and started preparing dinner. Nina was glad to see her brother.

Gee, she thought, *I can't ever remember fighting with him. He is so sweet. I feel as though I'm entering this house for the first time. I can't believe that Daria won't be with us anymore. I hope she makes good in California, then for sure she won't come back. She doesn't belong here with us anyway. Ever since I can remember, she was always above us. How foolish to try to be something you aren't. Oh, well, I was ashamed of Lily too, when I got older, but I still loved my folks. She probably does too, but didn't know how to show it. She was too busy trying to better herself and us. She got spoiled living at Vera's and seeing people who had more than she did. We lived around people who had no more than us, and even less.*

Nina sat down on the couch in the living room. Sonny sat down beside her. He asked, "How are ya?"

"Okay," she said and nodded affirmative. "How about you?"

"Oh, we were pretty worried about you."

"Well, you don't have to worry any more. I'll be okay. Why did Daria leave?"

"Well, she and Pa had an argument."

"About me and what I did?" She turned her head away from Sonny. She looked at her hands in her lap.

"No," he answered slowly, "that didn't start it." Sonny crossed his legs and made an attempt to crack his knuckles. He cracked one on one hand and gave up. He looked at his sister and said, "Daria doesn't even know you're all right."

"Oh, my gosh!" she exclaimed. "How come?"

"She didn't ask and we didn't tell her."

Nina shook her head and said, "You should have told her."

"Eh, nuts to her!" Sonny made a waving gesture. "She only cares about herself, and she doesn't care who she hurts as long as she gets what she wants. She always has been unfair. I never put my two cents in when you used to fight, especially when we lived in Lily, but I thought it was terrible the way she treated you. I always thought she was jealous of you because you are prettier than her. Oh, Daria is pretty, but there's no love in her for anybody but herself."

Nina added, "She aimed too high too fast. She hated Lily even when she was a little kid. But I'll never forgive her for being ashamed of Ma and Pa."

"Yeah, same here," Sonny agreed, "and I found out why she always called you bastard."

"Oh, you know? How did you find out? Oh, my God! She didn't tell Papa did she?"

"Wait a minute. Not so fast. It is a long story," Sonny went on. "Let me tell ya."

"What happened?" Nina was in suspense.

"Well, Butter was at the hospital with you the next day and Mama went to Vera's to tell her all about what happened. Mama was going to ask Vera to take Daria back to live with her. I was washing up for lunch when I heard Daria swear at Pa."

"Oh, my gosh! How could she? At her own father?"

"Well, you know the noise Pa makes when he's eating soup."

"Yes, I know. I can hardly stand it myself, but maybe when I'm old I won't care how I eat soup either."

"I guess Daria couldn't stand it, that's why she swore at him. Pa was mad. He got the strap and went after her. He said no daughter of his was going to swear at him. He said none of us swore at him."

"Hmm, we wouldn't dare. We'd be black and blue for weeks," Nina knew.

"Well, he hit her with the strap. He sure hollered and blamed her for what you did. She said it wasn't her fault you did what you did. She said only one thing makes a girl do a thing like that." Sonny could

not bring himself to say the words, "commit suicide."
"She thought you were going to have a baby."

"Oh, my gosh! How can she think such a thing? What's the matter with her?" Nina started to cry. "I guess she wished it was that way so she could condemn me even more. Oh, why does she have to hate me so much? I can't help the way I was born. I'm sure I'm not the only one in the world. You don't hate me now that you know, do you Sonny?"

"No, I don't. Why should I? You have been wonderful to me and everybody. I don't know what I would have done without you and Butter in Lily. We sure had good times together. A brother couldn't ask for better sisters and mother and father. Sure, Papa drank, but so did all the other men in Lily. What else did they have to do, but work? And, as long as he liked it, I didn't care. We all crave something more than anything else. With me, it's baseball. With Papa it was liquor. It must have made him relax from all his hard work and problems."

"Oh, Sonny, I'm so glad you understand. I always knew you were a good boy. I wish Daria could have heard you say that."

"I'm glad she's gone. She gave you nothing but trouble. Well, to get on with what happened that day. After she said what she did about you, Papa slapped her. She went to her room and packed her things and left the next day."

Nina asked, "Then she didn't tell Pa about me not being his daughter, I mean, Irina's child, no, no, no. I mean that Mama is my Mama but that I have a different father?"

"No, she didn't," Sonny lied. "Butter told me the whole story after you went to the hospital in an ambulance. She said that was one of the reasons why Daria hated you so much."

Nina said, "I'm glad she's gone. It's too bad it happened this way. I'll bet Pa feels bad now. It's terrible when a family can't get along."

Sonny put one arm around his crying sister, and said, "I have something worse to tell you." Nina held her breath.

What could be worse, she thought, *than what's already happened?*

"Papa is gone."

"Gone? You mean he's—"

Sonny nodded and started to cry.

"Oh, no! No. No. No!" Nina cried out.

Nadia knew from the sounds that carried into the kitchen that Sonny had informed his sister that Alex was dead. Nadia's tears blinded her. She sat down at the table and joined in the sobbing from the other room.

"How? When?" Nina asked.

Sonny answered, "He had a heart attack when he went into the basement. Daria left and I had a baseball game to go to. Mama found him when she came home."

Nina hugged her brother and they both cried. Sonny thought, *She will never know the rest and neither will Mama. I'll never tell anyone that Papa knew Nina wasn't his sister's child, that she was Mama's by a Polish man. I guess the shock was too much for his weak heart but he should never have drank after the doctor told him not to. Daria doesn't know Nina is alive and doesn't know that Papa is dead. I hope she never comes back.*

"May I use your bike?" Nina asked her brother after they finished their dinner.

Sonny consented, "Sure, go ahead." He heard someone calling his name at the front door. He was walking through the dining room when he remembered, "Hey, you know what? Johnny Mostil, a scout for the White Sox farm teams, promised he would sign me up to play baseball as soon as I'm out of school."

"Gee, that's great! I knew you were good," Nina affirmed.

Sonny smiled and made a muscle the way his father always did. He went out the door to join his friends on the front porch swing.

Nadia announced she was going to walk to Vera's house and visit for awhile.

"Where's Butter?" Nina asked.

"She work late tonight. Tonight store open up to nine clock," Nadia answered.

"I'll be back before dark, Mama," Nina told her.

"Where you go? You still weak, no?"

"I'm okay, Ma. I'll take it easy on the bike."

"Where you go?" her mother repeated.

"To Lily."

"What for? There nothing there now."

"I just want to see the place. It's been a long time since I have been there."

"Ah, stay home."

"I won't be gone long."

"Then takeit easy an' stop an' rest little bit."

"I will, Ma."

Nina went to her wardrobe cabinet and found her slacks. She headed for Daria's bedroom, but changed her mind; she went into the bathroom instead, and changed clothes. Inwardly, she blamed Daria for her father's death. She could not bring herself to mention

328

the accusation openly. She wondered if the family held her partly responsible.

Nadia told her, "It was time for Papa to go, that's all."

But, Nina thought, *if I hadn't done what I did, Daria and Pa probably wouldn't have argued. Yet, Daria started it by swearing at Pa. God forgive me and Papa. Please forgive me if I'm to blame. I would rather it was me that died instead of Papa. I wish Butter had told me he was gone. In a way, I'm glad she didn't tell me when I was in the hospital. I don't think I could have stayed there. I certainly was weak. I needed rest. It would have been awful to know then, in the hospital, all alone without my family close by and Papa gone. Thank you, God, for sparing me the grief I would have suffered then. I certainly would have blamed myself. But, I know Mama and Sonny and Butter don't blame me. I couldn't live if they did.*

She rode out to Lily on her brother's bicycle. She chose to walk when she reached Red Place. She pushed the bike along and her memories were filled with the past. The post office still stood. The flag was flying atop the federal building. There were boxcars parked on the tracks that she crossed remembering the night she came close to death under the wheels of the train when she crossed underneath them. Two cars were parked by Lily Tavern.

Out loud, she spoke, "Well Papa, you won't see your friends in there anymore." Walking along the main road, she realized they had never named the road. She stopped. "Oh, my goodness. You never had a name!" she exclaimed with surprise and realization. She smiled and talked to the road. "Why you should have been the first one to be named. We sure goofed. The very idea of being called just the main road all those years when you were surrounded by such fancy names as 4th Avenue and 5th Avenue," she laughed. "Just like downtown. You would think this was New York.

"Let's see," she tried to remember. "What did we call the paths? There was Nigger Path and Lovers Lane. Mosquito Path and then there was Feedman's Road and Butcher Road. Oh, and Bull Path and Billy Goat Road, before that it was Nanny Goat Road. We had this whole place to ourselves to name and run and explore and enjoy. But, how did we not name you? I better do that right now.

"Let me think. First Avenue? No. There is no 2nd or 3rd Avenues to go with 4th and 5th. We should have called you Lily Road or Red, White, and Blue Road because you led to all three sections. I know." She snapped her fingers and smiled, "Fourth of July Road! That's your name! Howddya like that? The barababoom of the boxcars are like fireworks every day and the fireworks plant is at the very end of Lily. Wait till I tell Sonny and Butter." She took a deep breath, sighed, and walked on.

She went past the horse riding stables, but heard nothing and saw no one. She walked past Lily Store. It needed a coat of paint, but she noticed that the two doors, the front entrance and the side entrance, were boarded and a "No Trespassing" sign was posted at the front door. She looked at the row of houses at Red Place. All the doors, except one house, stood open, and some of the windows were broken. She looked around and saw no sign of life. "I guess you're waiting to be torn down," she spoke to the houses. "Gee, this looks like a ghost town you see in the movies." She then rode the bicycle past the Midwest Corn Company entrance gate, straight down Fourth of July Road to Lovers Lane, until she reached the slag road called 5th Avenue, as they had named it. She jumped off the bike and was surprised to see the house they once lived in was the only one still standing in White Place. She walked, pushing the bike along Billy Goat Road. A huge pile of slag lay in the middle of the road. She walked around it. She saw that all the sheds were torn down except the first one close to the house—Pa's shandy.

She felt very close to him at that moment. She knew then her reason for coming out to Lily. "I wasn't there for your funeral, Papa," she said as she looked at the shed, "so I've come to the funeral now." Tears welled in her eyes. She leaned the bicycle against the outhouse—I mean, the show—and walked up the porch steps. Every board squeaked and each one was cracked. She almost fell as one loose board came up when she stepped on it. She held on to the railing when she walked on the porch.

Nina stood in the open doorway. She felt the slag under her shoes. She walked into the kitchen. She looked down at the floor, which was covered with slag. A piece of paper lay on the floor close to the door that led to the bedroom that Alex and Nadia occupied when they lived there. She looked into the room and remembered the time they had held their fingers in their ears the night Sonny was born. She picked up the paper and read the vacate notice. A smile came to her lips. She said, "Sorry, we beat you to it." She laid the notice in the same spot she had found it in, and looked around the house.

"I wonder if anybody lived in here after we left?" she expressed her wonderment out loud. "I doubt it, but it could be. Poor old house. But, we loved you when we lived here. You and this place gave Mama and Papa the feeling they were back in Russia and that made them happy, and they were happy because we kids were happy here. And, because Daria hated you and all of Lily so much, she left us and that made me happy. I am sorry I was ashamed of you at one time."

She looked at the huge cracks and holes in the plaster. "I was punished for my feelings towards you and Lily when I turned down Richard. I've regretted it for a very long time. If I hadn't been so foolish in putting so much importance on where I lived and what I lived in, I wouldn't have shed so many tears. Come to think of it, if he lived here and I lived in the city, that would never have made a difference. If only I could have realized that then. Most of the hurt that people experience is due to their inflictions. Oh, if only I could relive the past, I would have done this one thing oppositely. Please house, don't punish me too much longer. Forgive me now."

She stood in the doorway that led to the living room and glanced into the bedroom that was once hers, then pictured the holy picture of Madonna and Child that had hung there.

She turned and left the house to keep from crying. She stood on the porch and all she could see were a few trees, all the rest was slag. She walked carefully down the steps, jumped over the loose board and noticed the pump that still stood covered with the burlap sack. She walked over to it and brushed off the slag covering it and patted it saying,

"Oh, how you made Papa sweat! Then your water wasn't any good; we all got sick, and Mama was so disappointed that she couldn't have water inside the house."

She patted it again and lowered her head when she passed Pa's shandy on her way to the well in back of the house. She stopped and remembered the time

Buster came home to die behind the house. "Good ole Bus," she said. "You have a deep grave now with all that slag on top of you. I hope the flag is still on your grave. You were the best dog in the world."

She went to the well and looked in. She could not see the water for all the debris in it. Turning, she noticed the small gate that closed off the yard from Alex's shed to the house was off its hinges and lay on the ground. She walked over to it and picked it up. She tried to make it stand up, but could not. She laid it down and once more lowered her head as she walked past Pa's shandy.

"Bye, Papa," she said. Tears came to her eyes. She bit her bottom lip, then made the sign of the cross and said, "Bye, Papa," again. She picked up the bicycle, took one more glance at the old house and drove off down Billy Goat Road, walked around the slag pile. When she reached 5th Avenue she stopped and looked at the large tree that once held their swing.

"Oh, the dreaming I used to do under you," she said. "Keep growing. Don't let them bury you or cut you down." She looked at the position of the sun and knew she still had some time before darkness fell. She rode the bicycle down 5th Avenue to the lake; seeing the log she had sat on one tragic day, she laid the bicycle down against it, and walked to the edge of the water. She looked out at the water lilies and their pads that filled the shores.

"Hello."

Nina turned to see who was greeting her. It was Iris Nelson standing on the steps of Old Ivan's shack. "Hello," returned Nina. "What are you doing here?" She walked over to her.

"I live here, believe it or not," Iris responded.

"You do?" Nina was surprised. "What happened to the castle? I mean your house."

"That was torn down some time ago. My father still manages the dumping of the slag, so he didn't want to leave. He bought this boat place."

"What happened to Old Ivan?"

"Oh, he lived at Red for awhile at Mrs. Sorenuk's house, then he passed away."

"Aw, that's too bad. Poor old guy." Nina sympathized, then remembered her own loss. "I just lost my father last week."

"Oh, gee, that's too bad. You have my sympathy." Iris offered.

"Thank you."

"But, what are you doing here? The last I heard about you, you were living away from home."

"I was, but I have been back home for quite awhile. I came out here today because something told me to come. Don't think I'm silly, but I came to say goodbye to my father here. Do you know our house is the only one left at White?"

"Yes, I know. My father said they're going to start tearing it down tomorrow or the next."

"See there, I did pick the right day to come here. And, do you know my father's private shed is still standing too? I couldn't believe it when I saw it. I couldn't go inside though; we were never allowed to go in there, the chicken feed barrels hid my father's fire water in half pints at all times." Iris was smiling. "And, do you know what I found inside the house? A notice telling the people to vacate. Say, maybe you know. Did anyone live in our house after we moved out?"

"You mean you don't know?"

Nina shook her head and waited anxiously for Iris's information.

"Helen lived there with her Indian baby. Her brothers couldn't stand to look at the boy so they set her up in your house."

"Oh, for goodness sake! Well, I hope Helen's happy in her new home. You know where she is now, don't you? The judge and his wife adopted him and she lives with them."

"Yes," Iris knew, "that was a good break for her."

"What have you been doing with yourself, Iris?"

"Oh, nothing much. Let's sit down someplace."

"How about that big log?" Nina pointed to it. "Remember? That's where I first met you."

"I remember. I found my first girlfriend that day. Too bad you left so soon." They walked to the log and sat down. Iris reported, "I've finished school, but it's too far to travel to the city to work. My father could drive me in his car, but I still don't speak to him."

Nina looked at Iris and could hardly believe what she was saying; how could anyone not speak to their father for years? She asked Iris, "You mean he still wants you to be a you-know-what?"

Iris nodded her head, and started to cry. She said, "That sonofabitch! I hate him!"

Nina put her arm around her and admonished, "Oh, honey, no you don't, not really."

"Oh, yes I do," asserted Iris. "My grandfather made him marry my mother because she was pregnant with me. He never wanted to be tied down. My mother says her father threatened him with a gun and made him marry her. He thinks no man or woman should ever get married. That's why he wants me to be a whore. And I hate him! My mother is so easygoing, she doesn't let anything bother her. She just laughs off the things he says. I think she really loves him, but then she loves everything. She never raises her voice above a whisper. She is wonderful to me. But I don't know how she can stand him."

Nina interjected, "He must love her too, or he would not have stayed with you all this time."

"Yeah, but he doesn't love me. I'm the reason for his being tied down." Iris was sad, tears came down her face.

"He's not so tied down if he goes out and does things with other women," Nina explained. "Don't cry, you'll get a headache. There's better days to come. Just pray real hard. Good things happen to good people. You will see. You'll meet somebody some day who will take you away from here."

Iris wiped the tears away and looked out at the lake. Nina removed her arm from around her friend and looked at the water lilies, which were everywhere. Iris said, "Oh, I've thought of leaving every day since we moved here, but I just can't leave my mother. Her life would be so empty without me. My father is away so much. She is getting old and hasn't been feeling well lately. I work evenings taking care of the Brecker kids. Lucille and her husband get drunk every night. They haven't moved from Red yet. They will pretty soon, everyone else has. Then I don't know what I'll do. I hate it here. Mom and I sleep in that trailer in back of the shack."

Iris nodded in the direction of the small, green trailer that stood high off the ground, and was supported by railroad ties. Tall weeds surrounded the area and two young trees were growing on either side of the door. Nina wondered if Mrs. Nelson still had her precious trunks, remembering Mrs. Nelson showed her some of the treasures she was saving that would be antiques one day, especially the comic books.

Iris then added, " My dad sleeps in the shack and my mother cooks in there. Say," she looked at Nina and touched her arm, "how are you and your sister? What's her name?"

"You mean Daria?"

"Yeah, how are you two getting along?"

"We never got along," Nina said solemnly. "That's why I moved away before. But that didn't work out in the end. I worked for an old family friend and I got in one more year of school. I have one more year to go, but I don't think I'll finish. I have to work. Well, getting back to the man I worked for. We met him in Lily. He owns a publishing company downtown. He was wonderful to me. I learned so much from him about how to appreciate the little things in life. We went everywhere together. I didn't even visit home once in all the time I was there. I was so busy. I used to call home once in a while, and Butter called me now and then. I had a boyfriend who came once in a while; we went to a movie together. But, he's in the army now."

"What's Butter doing?"

"She quit school and went to work in a supermarket. She's getting fat. She can sit down and eat a whole thirty-nine cent cake by herself. She's making up for the sweets we didn't have in Lily. She has a boyfriend; he's in the navy."

Iris grinned remembering, "She is a good egg. I like her. She was always laughing. I wish I had you two for sisters."

"Oh, thank you, and we would love to have you."

"Does Butter still like dolls?"

337

"Oh, you will laugh," Nina smiled. "She bought a little pickaninny baby doll that has braids wound and tied in a circle on each side of its head. She sleeps with it and says she's going to get married as soon as she can and have lots of babies, and buy them all kinds of dolls."

Iris laughed, "What if she has all boys?"

"Ha, ha, I guess she never thought of that. I'll have to tell her."

"Well, get back to your story. Why did you come back home?"

"I never told anyone, not even my mother. Promise you won't say anything to anyone?"

"Cross my heart and hope to die," Iris crossed her heart and raised her hand in front of her.

"Well, mind you, this man is old enough to be my father, and that's how I felt about him. I worshipped him. I thought I'd do anything he asked to repay him for helping me out when he did, but I turned him down when it came to affection."

"Honest? He proposed?"

Nina shook her head. "He said I didn't have to be his wife — not really — you know what I mean. He said I could have anything I wanted."

"Gee, I'd marry anybody just to get out of here."

"Uh, uh, don't say that. When you're married, you're married for a long time. You're just thinking of tomorrow. You've got to think farther than that, and imagine yourself and how things would be years ahead. Another important thing to help you choose a partner is if you can say, 'Yes, I can sleep with this man, and think I'd be in heaven to have his arms around me all my life,' then go ahead and marry him. I couldn't say yes to that so I said no to Mr. Barton and came home."

"You gave up a good deal. I don't think I could
have turned that proposition down. Haven't you
regretted your decision a little bit?"

"I'm only sorry for him. He was lonely, but that
was my fault because I befriended him. He would
have been all right if I hadn't come along. He's been
busy making money, and he turned down his
sweetheart when he was poor and a doctor offered her
more at the time than he could. I still see Mr. Barton
once in a while. We have dinner and go to a movie.
Bob Holly proposed marriage, but I turned him
down."

"Gee, you're a popular girl."

"Oh, not very. There's one thing I want more than
anything else." Nina thought of her Richard dream.

"What's that?"

"Oh, I'll tell you about that some other time, not
now. Daria and my father had a big fight before he
died. Daria moved away. She said she was going to
California to get into the movies, as always was her
dream."

"She did?" Iris was surprised to hear of yet
another girl who left home.

"Yes, she did. Say," Nina suddenly thought, "why
don't you come and live with us? We have plenty of
room for you. You can sleep in my bed with me now
that Daria is gone. You can find all kinds of work in
Winsome. I'd love to have you. I work at the
telephone company. I have funny hours—one in the
afternoon to ten at night. But I get two days off a
week. We could have lots of fun together. Butter
would be tickled pink. You can pal with her when I'm
working. And, you won't be too far from your mother.
You could come to see her often. Do you have a bike?"

"Sure."

"Well then, you could ride out here in no time. Whaddya say? You helped me out one time. Now it's my turn to help you out."

Iris thought, "Gee, that would be great!"

"Go ask your mother."

Iris was excited. "Okay," she said and ran to the shack.

Before she went inside, Nina yelled to her, "Hey, let me use one of your boats for a couple of minutes."

"Sure, go ahead," Iris hollered.

Nina removed her shoes and chose a rowboat. She picked up the small anchor and put it in the boat, then rowed slowly along the shore. When she reached the largest flower she could see, she reached down into the water and pulled up the thick stem. Then she pulled up three floating leaves and laid them in the bottom of the boat and said, "Yes, siree, you should be, red, white, and blue. I'm going to drop you into the well on my way home. You will be the flowers I never bought for Papa. And when I go to the cemetery, I'll get some lilies at a flower shop and plant them on his grave." She looked up into the sky and said, "I know you're up there with God, Papa. Thank you for bringing me up as your own daughter. I will always think about you as my father and never ask who my real father was." She rowed back to shore.

Mrs. Nelson consented to let her daughter live with the Durocks. Iris packed a few things and said she would come back for the rest if Mrs. Durock agreed to the arrangement, and if she found suitable employment. The girls rode their bicycles down 5th Avenue, and Iris waited for Nina on the slag road while she went to ceremoniously drop the water lily and the three leaves into the well in back of the house where they once lived. Nina was choked with emotion. She patted the covered pump once again, and said, "Bye, Papa." Then she looked at the house, and said, "Goodbye house. I haven't been happy since I left you."

❖ ❖ ❖ ❖

Iris had no trouble finding work as a secretary in a real estate and insurance office. The girls enjoyed one another's companionship, and shared their hopes and dreams, and prayed for the war to end and for the boys to come home. However, Nina kept her secret love of Richard to herself. Iris knew from the faraway look in Nina's eyes that she pined for someone. Iris asked Butter if her reasoning was correct. Butter told Iris about Richard, and about what happened the night she tried to end it all.

Iris mentioned nothing to her friend, knowing how a girl could suffer in her quest for happiness. She, too, speculated suicide many times. When she walked along the railroad tracks before reaching the path that led to her house in the Forest Preserve, she had wished a train would unexpectedly sweep over her and stop her endless tears. Iris spent many hours looking into the lake, and contemplated a push from someone behind into the muddy waters. She thought it took more fortitude to die by one's own effort, than to live, and respected Nina for her courage. Butter did not tell Iris that Nina was a half-sister. That would remain a family secret.

Iris missed her mother a great deal. She went to see her every Sunday without fail. One day, Iris announced she was getting married and asked Nina to go to Lily Pad Lake with her; she was going to tell her mother. Nina and Butter had enjoyed Iris's friendship for seven weeks. Iris moved to a town six miles away to live with her husband who was twenty years older than she. Before Iris left, she said with downcast eyes, "Anything is better than going back to Lily. I miss my mother so much; I just know I would be going back there to stay with her, if I wasn't getting married. I just can't take it anymore."

Nadia wished Iris lots of happiness. Iris acknowledged, "Thank you, Mrs. Durock. Thank you for everything."

Butter said, "I hope you have lots of little ones real quick."

"I'll name my first girl after you," Iris proffered.

"You better not," ejaculated Butter. "She will leave home with a name like Olga," Butter grimaced. "Or else she'll change it as soon as she can."

"Well, then, I'll call her Butter!" Iris suggested.

"That's better," smiled Butter. She winked at Iris. Everybody laughed.

Nina kissed Iris and hugged her hard. She offered, "I hope you will be very happy."

"I'll try," Iris returned, unsmiling.

Sonny shook her hand and said, "Goodbye. Good luck."

Chapter Thirty Two

WHEN NINA CAME HOME FROM THE HOSPITAL, SHE rested at home for a week before going back to work at the telephone company. She read a book entitled *A Tree Grows in Brooklyn* by Betty Smith. The book took her mind off the past for a few days. She read the last page, closed the book and thought of the night she tried to say goodbye to life. *I felt so tired of enduring tortures of the heart. I tormented myself with yearning for love for such a long time. Papa spoiled my chance of ever getting to know Richard by making me quit school. I know we would have been friends that year. I really don't blame Papa though; we were so poor.*

I've been jealous of Daria all my life; everything came easy for her. Maybe Daria isn't as tough and self assured as she appears to be. She has shed a few tears also, I am certain, over the loss of her first love. I wonder where Richard is now? He's probably in the war.

Nina closed her eyes, folded her hands on top of the book and prayed, *Please God, take care of him and all the boys. Watch over him. Don't let him get hurt. Bring him home safely. Send him to me. Please, God.*

Again, she remembered the night she had taken the sleeping pills. *I was telling myself I would never have the love I wanted. Then, all of a sudden, when I closed my eyes, I remembered what Mama told me one day when I was a little girl and got a licking with the razor strap from Papa for cutting Butter's hair. We called her Olga then. I cried so hard. When Mama came to see me, I said, "Nobody loves me." Mama answered, "Sure, we love you, but we no likeit you when you bad. But God loveit you allatime. He loveit all little kids." Then as I sat in the chair, about to write in my diary, I tried to picture God.*

All I knew of God was that he made everything, He loved little children, and He was a statue in churches. I pictured one of those statues. His arms were extended in front of Him, He called to me to come to Him, and He said, "I love you. Come to me," very slowly and softly over and over again. Then He drifted away, and I couldn't see Him anymore. Then I opened my eyes, and went for the pills. I took them because I was going to Him who loved me. But, He didn't take me. Maybe He meant something else? Anyway, I'm still here, and I better go to work and pay Mama for the hospital bill and doctor too.

She put the book away in the bookcase and went to the telephone to find out if her job was still waiting for her. Nina went back to work.

After Iris left, Nina became very good friends with Jean Collins, the girl who had been hired the same day Nina was. They both had the same working hours.

Jean was Catholic. World War II was still on so there were very few young men for them to spend time with. One Sunday morning, Jean telephoned and asked Nina if she would like to meet her at church, attend service, and then come to dinner at her house.

"But I wouldn't know what to do in church. I've never been inside one," Nina confessed to Jean on the telephone.

"You just do what I do, and pray, that's all," explained Jean.

"Well, all right," Nina accepted, "but make sure you're outside waiting for me because I won't go in without you."

"Okay, I'll see you there a little before eleven." Jean could sense her friend's anxiety.

Nina said "Bye," before she was ready to hang up the phone, and Jean said, "Hey, wait a minute."

"What?" was what she heard her friend reply. "Don't forget to wear a hat."

"Do I have to?"

"Sure."

"Why."

"It's customary."

"Okay." Nina hung up the receiver and dressed carefully for her first attendance in a church. As Nina and Jean walked up the steps of the largest Catholic church in Winsome, Nina proposed in a whisper, "Let's sit way in back."

Jean smiled and answered, "I always do. The church looks bigger from the back and you feel God's presence more so." Jean entered the vestibule. Nina followed.

Fear and reverence overwhelmed Nina. She closed her eyes for a moment and thanked God for bringing her into His church. She saw Jean fingering her rosaries and wondered what they were for. She had never seen them before this. She heard others tinkling against the pews, and wished she had a pair in her hands. Her inquisitive mind was searching for answers. *Who is God? Where is He? How can He hear all*

*these people's prayers? When Catholics cross themselves,
why do they touch the left shoulder first, and why do the
Russian Orthodox touch the right shoulder first? What do
you say when you cross yourself? Why do women wear hats
and the men do not? Why is Jesus on the cross? How did
God make us? Where do we go when we die? What is a
soul?*

She prayed, *Please God, forgive me for being so
ignorant. It is not of my choosing. Religion has been a great
mystery to me. Help me to find the answers to my
questions.*

Nina went to church with Jean every Sunday. It
was something to do, and someplace to go. Nina
asked her tall, red-haired friend questions. Jean tried
to answer them. Jean recommended, "Why don't you
get an instruction book from the church? I can't
answer all your questions. I was taught all that when
I was a child. I've forgotten so much of it."

Nina reflected, "But I would have to talk to a
priest, and I wouldn't know how to talk to one. They
are so holy looking."

"Don't be silly," Jean laughed.

That evening Nina had a date with Don Marino,
the young man who had phoned Nina the night Daria
had snatched the telephone from her hand, and said,
"What do you want to call her for? She's nothing but
garbage from the dumps," and hung up.

Don had telephoned again the next day and Butter
explained the rude incident as one sleepy-headed,
nervous sister who did not like to be disturbed by
telephone calls at 10:30 at night. Don now had an
extended leave from the draft. His father was ill and
Don was managing the ambulance service he and his
father operated. Don was Catholic. Nina badgered
him with questions about religions.

346

Don offered, "I'll take you to our priest. He's real nice. You will like him. You don't have to become a Catholic if you don't want to. Just tell him you want to find out what the Catholic religion teaches. If you like it, he'll help you."

Don made an appointment for Nina on her day off to see Father Nicholas at St. Dominic's Church in the big city north of Winsome. Don dropped her off at the rectory; he would be back for her in an hour.

Nina went for catechism instructions for almost a year. Father Nicholas was very kind and gave her as much of his time as he could. Nina was a likable, sincere, and serious minded girl. Father Nicholas had not had such an avid pupil in all his life as a priest. He had compassion and pride for this girl who had the courage to admit to herself, and to him, that she knew nothing of where she came from, where she was going, and why. Father Nicholas asked his student if anyone in her family attended church.

"Yes, Father," Nina answered, "my mother now goes every Sunday to a new Greek Catholic church that isn't too far from our house. She says it's almost like the Russian Orthodox church; they cross themselves the same way she does, holding the thumb and first two fingers together and crossing to the right first."

"Why doesn't she go to a Russian Orthodox church?"

"The closest one is about thirty miles away and that's too far for her to go."

"I understand," Father nodded assent. "What does she say about you coming here?"

"She doesn't mind. She is easygoing. She knows it's her fault for not taking the time to teach religion to her children. She was always busy, Father. We lived on a small farm during the Depression and she had animals and chickens and ducks and geese to feed. We didn't have plumbing and she worked pretty hard all the time. She said if it makes me happy to come here, she won't stop me. Any religion is better than none, she says. I think my father would have objected if he was living; he was an atheist."

"He was bluffing. Everyone knows He is up there above us." Father glanced heavenward and leaned back in the chair he sat in behind the desk.

"My mother always said we shouldn't listen to him or believe anything he said about God. She knew he would pray if he ever got sick, and he did. Father, it was the first time in his life that he was ever so sick. My mother went for the doctor and I heard him ask God to help him."

"See there. Then he was not an unbeliever. You know that now."

"Yes, Father, my mother never stopped believing. She said my father prayed so much as a boy that even when there was a storm at night his parents would waken the entire family, and they would pray on their knees until the storm subsided. But the poor were so poor in Russia before the revolution that they sometimes didn't have enough to eat.

"Can you imagine? There was a family living close to my father's land that had nine children, and they had only one pair of shoes in the house. I guess they took turns wearing them. Maybe they just looked at them and kept them as an ornament the way I did with my first party dress."

"Did you do that?" Father smiled.

Nina laughed with him, "Yes, I did. Please don't think I'm bragging, but I have quite a memory. I can still remember the hours I spent looking at it. I believe

I was only five years old then. I never wore the dress. I gave it to my oldest sister's little girl."

"You must have been very poor to treasure a little party dress."

"We were, Father, but we had a very happy childhood in Lily. Do you know where that is?"

"No, I don't."

"Well, it isn't even on the map. The town has vanished now. A highway is going through there. Everyone had to move. Everyone that lived there was poor."

Father Nicholas offered, "Russia is still a poor country. But, don't let anyone kid you, everyone believes."

"I'll remember that, Father. You know, my father worked very hard in Russia for less than ten cents a day. The poor were slaves and their prayers weren't answered. My mother said that is what turned my father and many others against religion. All the Russian men we knew said they didn't believe, but all the Russian women believed."

"Just remember what I said," Father emphasized, "everyone believes."

"I will, Father."

"Tell me, do you have an ambition? Besides getting married, of course."

"Do you think I could be a nun, Father?"

"My dear child," he unhesitatingly answered and shook his head, "you are much too worldly."

"Someone else said that to me. I would much rather be a priest. Too bad I'm not a man."

Father laughed and asked, "And why do you think you would like to be a priest?"

"Well, Father, I find people very interesting. I'd like to spend my whole life just talking to people, and finding out their problems and their life story. A priest gets to meet the public more so than a nun. I wish I could be a nun, but I think I'd find it much too confining."

"And what makes you think a priest's life is not confining?"

"Is it Father?"

"I can only speak for myself. I haven't seen my mother and father and four brothers and two sisters in twelve years. I long to see them, but I can't. It hasn't been easy for me."

"Gee, I'm sorry, Father. I never thought to think of that."

"Now, tell me, what would you really like to do or be?"

"Well, Father, I call myself a digger. When I have a question, I can't rest until it is answered. That's why I'm here now. I dwell on the past, present, and future. I'm a dreamer and I talk to myself. I keep things to myself, yet, I want the whole world as my audience. I said I'd like to talk to people and find out everything about them, but I'm really afraid of people. I believe the only way I can reach people is by writing to them. Father, I have the material for a book, but I lack the education to write it."

"Nonsense." Father sat up straight in his chair and said, "Why, the bestseller this month was written by a fourteen-year-old girl and in very simple form. You could do it."

"If I hadn't quit school, maybe I could have done it one day, but there's no hope now. I have to work. It would be much easier to give the material to someone and let them write it."

Father Nicholas took his hands out of his cassock for the first time since their visit began. He shook a finger at her and directed, "Don't you do that. Listen to me, you can do anything if you try hard enough, and want to badly enough."

"I'll try to remember that. Thank you, Father."

He adjusted his glasses and returned his hands into the black outer garment. He said, "Let's get on with our lesson. Any questions today?"

"Oh, yes. I have a list of them, Father." Nina reached into her purse. She remembered something and started to laugh. She said, "May I tell you something, Father, that will prove how ignorant I am?" Father Nicholas nodded once. "I just learned the meaning of the second commandment," Nina went on, "'Thou shalt not take the name of the Lord, thy God, in vain.' It means not to swear. But, I thought it meant that when a woman has a child and she and her husband are searching in vain for a name for that child, she and he shouldn't name her or him Jesus Christ or God. How's that for stupidity?"

Father smiled and said, "Not at all, my dear, at least you are taking the time to learn. There are millions who don't even know there are ten commandments."

At her first visit she was presented with a paperback book entitled, *Father Smith Instructs Jackson* by The Most Rev. John F. Noll, D.D. At each visit, Father Nicholas gave her a "Convert Instruction Card." All twenty-five were covered by questions and answers. When they had finished with the lesson, Father Nicholas asked her what she thought of the Catholic religion.

She replied, "All my questions have been answered. I'm satisfied. I believe. I don't feel so all alone anymore now that I know God is up there watching over all of us. I had so many fears before and questions. My goodness, I thought there were no answers to the questions I had. I believed they were just mysteries that no one could answer. I remember giving a report in school in front of class on the theory of evolution. I talked the whole forty-five minute period. I really don't know if I believed all that I reported; they were mostly facts from books. But I do remember one thing that stood out in my mind above all else. The beginning — there was no explanation for the very beginning. If we derived from monkeys, how did they get here, and how did the earth get here? I must have known that God was the beginning. Now I know God made everything. I really believe, Father."

"Do you want to be a Catholic?"

"Please, I'm sure I do."

❖ ❖ ❖ ❖

Jean Collins stood beside Nina as she received the Sacrament of Baptism. Jean was her godmother. Jean also stood beside her when she walked to the altar with a candle in one hand, placed the other hand on the Bible, and made the Profession of Faith.

Nina meditated, "I will remember this day in my life as long as I live. This is what He meant when He said, 'Come to me.'"

Father Nicholas shook her hand, and said,

"Congratulations and welcome to the Catholic church. God bless you" He knew he was going to miss her. He really enjoyed the visits with this deep thinking child. She reminded him of himself as a poor, questioning young lad.

Nina had a lump in her throat. She swallowed and managed to say a weak, "Thank you, Father." He told her she could now go to confession on Saturday and receive her first holy communion along with all the other communicants at mass that Sunday.

She was very nervous when she went to the rail for fear she would not do the right thing. Don was with her that Sunday. He was now in the U.S. Army, but he was home on leave. He smiled at her when she returned to her seat.

Six months later she asked one of Don's sisters to be her sponsor at Confirmation. Nina was a Catholic. After the ceremony, Father Nicholas singled her out and presented her with a gift—a *Bible*, the New Testament. It bore an inscription: "To Nina from Father Nicholas, OFM 1944."

Chapter Thirty Three

WITH THE ENCOURAGEMENT NINA RECEIVED FROM Father Nicholas, she decided to pursue her ambition. Knowing the first step was to acquire a high school diploma, she went back to the school she had attended as a child and young girl and enrolled in morning classes. This arrangement offered her the opportunity to continue working at the telephone company. The attempt was futile. She felt uncomfortable with the younger classmates in spite of the fact that the teachers and principal accepted her and praised her for the foresight in realizing the importance of completing her education and furthering it with college.

The greatest obstacle in her pursuit was her endearing thoughts of Richard. She associated him with the hallways and could not bring herself to enter the library. Her vivid memory brought him into the school each day. She tried very hard to shake her feelings, telling herself to put him out of her mind for just one school year, then she could go on to another school where there would be no painful memories. The harder she tried to forget him, the more he came back to her. She said his name a hundred times a day. She would have given anything for time to turn back and for Richard to be in school with her again.

Each day she found it harder to attend classes. The poignant memory of him made her heartsick. He was everywhere around each corner, at every opening door, at the top of every staircase, in front of her, at her side, and in the very air she breathed. He was running to her, pushing his way through the youngsters in the halls. When the halls were very congested, he soared in the air above the students to reach her. His arms enveloped her, they were ropes around her body, squeezing tightly, there was no urge to escape, she tried desperately to swallow the lump in her throat and to breath for him. She discontinued her classes.

Nina changed jobs thinking if she worked steady days she could go to another school evenings. She was hired as a switchboard operator in the office of a toy factory in an adjoining city five miles east of Winsome, and paid to attend evening classes in shorthand, typing and advanced English in a business college in that city.

One night, after classes, Don was waiting for her in his car. He was home on a ten day furlough. Nina was surprised and happy to see him. She was grateful to him for helping her find her religion.

If it had not been for Don, she thought, *the questions I had may never have been answered and religion would have remained a mystery. I know the Dear Lord had a hand in this. He guided both of us to Father Nicholas.*

After the preliminary exchanged hello, kiss, how are you? and what are you doing here? Don asked, "Where would you like to go?"

She suggested, "It's too late to go anywhere. Let's just park in front of my house and talk."

"Okay," Don was agreeable.

They drove off. Nina looked at Don, and to her he was the neatest, handsomest soldier she had ever seen. Don was tall, good looking, and had a soft-spoken voice. He was always joking and Nina was just the opposite, she was always serious. Don was good for her.

When they reached the house, they saw Butter and Scott Montgomery, her sailor boyfriend, sitting on the front porch swing, hand in hand. Butter and Scott came to the car. Scott saluted and Butter shouted greetings. "Hi, Don, hi, Sis." They leaned against the car and Butter asked, "How would you two like to be our witnesses? We're getting married." Butter looked radiantly happy. She put her arm around Scott's waist and his encircled hers.

Nina was amazed at the news. Her mouth dropped open, then she asked, "Honest? When?"

Scott replied, "Saturday." Butter grinned and nodded affirmatively.

"Did Mama say you could?" Nina inquired. "You're not even seventeen yet."

"Sure," answered Butter. "And I'm going with him wherever he'll be stationed."

"I can't believe it. My baby sister is getting married, boohoo," lamented Nina.

"Well, will you stand up for us?" asked Butter.

"Why of course." Nina answered. She smiled broadly.

"How about you, Don, will you still be here Saturday?" asked Butter.

Don nodded. "I have nine days left," he said. "Are you getting married in church?"

"We're gonna look for a Justice of the Peace," Scott answered.

"Well, good luck to you both. Sure, I'll be a witness," Don accepted. He offered his hand to Scott. "Congratulations." They shook hands heartily.

Scott acknowledged, "Thanks."

"How about me, don't I get a kiss?" Butter piped in. She put her head through the open window and turned her cheek. Don kissed it.

Nina moved closer to Don and said to Butter, "Gee, Butt, I wish you all the happiness in the world."

Don turned to Nina and said, "Let's make it a double wedding."

"What, a proposal?" laughed Nina. "And in front of my sister and brother-in-law to be."

Don laughed and said, "I'm serious." Smiling, he added, "I probably wouldn't have the nerve to ask in private."

Everyone laughed. Nina mussed Don's black curly hair. Still laughing, Don said, "Look." He reached into his breast pocket. "I have the ring right here." He opened the small case and exposed the diamond engagement ring and wedding band set. Nina was astonished. She was speechless.

Butter exclaimed, "Oh, my gosh. He isn't kidding." She looked at Scott and offered, "We better leave them alone, maybe she'll say yes." Scott and Butter went into the house.

Nina stared at the rings, and said finally, "Oh, Don, they're beautiful."

"Well, what do you say?" he asked, hopefully. Nina did not answer.

Don put his arms around Nina and kissed her softly, sweetly, the way he always did. Nina gave him a short, crushing hug after he kissed her, and said, "Oh, Don, I love you for asking me. Promise you'll ask again after the war."

"Then it's no?"

"I said after the war. Okay?" She looked pleadingly into his big brown eyes.

"Okay, you win." He looked down at the rings, snapped the case shut and returned it to his jacket pocket. He put his arms around her again, and stated, "I'll keep asking you until you say yes. You know I would do anything for you. I worship the ground you walk on."

Nina bit her bottom lip, and humbly lowered her head. Then she looked at Don, and said, "Thank you, dear Don." They kissed.

Nina thought, *Now this is who I should marry. Oh, if this were only Richard, I wouldn't hesitate, war or no war. I'm sure if I married you, Don, I would still go on dreaming of Richard all my life. Give me time. Richard must be in the service now too. The end of the war will tell the story. I've lost Bob already; I haven't heard from him in a long time. I can't lose you too, Don. I won't tell you about Richard. I'll wait a little longer. I can't hurt you too. I must see Richard somehow, somewhere, sometime.*

❖   ❖   ❖   ❖

That Saturday Olga Durock took the name of Mrs. Scott Louis Montgomery. Nadia held a buffet style open house for the family and closest friends of the bride and groom. Butter looked very sweet in her light blue suit with white accessories. She was wearing her first white orchid. She smiled radiantly at her tall, slim, fair-haired, blue-eyed husband in navy dress blues. Butter was very happy, and her sister was happy for her.

How wonderful it must be to marry the man you first chose and loved above all else, Nina was thinking. *I pray that I will follow in her footsteps. Everybody loves Scott; Sonny thinks he is the greatest thing that happened, and now there will be another man in the family. I wonder where Daria is? How unfortunate she missed seeing Butter on this, the happiest day of her life. Papa would have been proud to see his youngest daughter married to such a fine young man as Scott.*

Nina closed her eyes for a moment, and meditated, *I hope you are watching us right now, Papa. We miss you.* When she opened her eyes she was looking at the suit she was wearing. She quickly covered her mouth not to let her gasp be heard, and questioned by the persons attending the occasion. *What is the matter with me? I'm wearing a black suit to my sister's wedding. It's the one I bought after Papa left us. I won't say anything. Maybe no one noticed. Butter is the main attraction today. I didn't even realize. How ignorant of me. Well, anyway, I wasn't a bridesmaid, I was only a witness. If it was improper, I am sure Don would have noticed it right away and told me so. Maybe everybody will think I am still mourning Papa.*

Butter had a three-day honeymoon in the eight room, beautiful house her in-laws lived in and owned in the big city. Scott left for overseas duty, and promised he would send for his wife as soon as his missions as tail gunner on a navy plane were completed and he returned to the States to serve the remainder of the ten years he had signed up for. Scott was an only child. Butter chose to live in her in-laws house to keep Mr. and Mrs. Montgomery company while their son was fighting the war. The day after Scott left, Don took off for parts unknown.

❖ ❖ ❖ ❖

Nadia listened to the Polish news announcer on the radio broadcast the reports of the war.

The language is somewhat like Russian and there was no Russian radio station. The fighting was very heavy in all sections. With each tragic event, Nadia moaned, "Oye, oye, oye," and thanked God her son was not old enough to be in the war. She missed her husband a great deal. She no longer made the large kettle of Alex's favorite Russian soups. Nina and Sonny preferred the American style of cooking. The one Russian dish she still prepared was halupke, also known as pigs in the blanket, stuffed cabbage, cabbage rolls, or just plain pigs.

She had no regrets for the life she had had with Alex. She had loved the twelve years they had spent in Lily. Yes, Alex was an alcoholic, but he enjoyed his drinks. She forgave him his weakness for liquor, realizing she too had experienced a weakness by having a child by a man other than her husband. She did not blame Daria for Alex's death. He had a weak heart, and if their argument had not taken place, then the continued daily drinks would have taken him one day. So be it. It was the way of the Lord. Nadia was resolute.

Sonny was her baby and always would be. She now lived for him, waiting for him to come running home from school, preparing his favorite steak dinner that gave him energy to play his sports, and she watched him grow to look exactly like his father. Sonny even had the same muscles Alex had and made the same gestures with them every time he went out the door.

Nadia spent a good deal of her spare time at Vera's house; it was only a twenty minute walk. Frank's father was now in an old age home. One brother lived on a farm for the handicapped, another brother was in the service, but Frank was exempt due to his age. Vera had three children now, and everyone was very happy and contented.

Nina worked, wrote letters to the boys in the service, read book after book, continued with her night school classes, went to church every Sunday, received holy communion once a month, chummed with Jean Collins, prayed for the war to end soon, and dreamed of her love at first sight—the young man named Richard.

One early evening Nina was in her advanced English class when noises were heard coming from the street below. Everyone went to the windows and looked down. Horns blew, people whistled and shouted. Streamers and bits of paper were thrown from windows. People were holding two fingers in the air signifying a V. When Nina reached the street, she learned it was V-E Day. Not long after, it was V-J Day, and all the boys were coming home. Thank God.

A few months later, on a rainy, spring, Sunday afternoon, the telephone rang. Nina answered "Hello."

"Hello, May I please speak to Nina?"

"This is she."

"This is Richard Lawski. Do you remember me?"

"Yes, of course I remember you." Her heart skipped a beat. With her free hand she reached for the woodwork in the archway to steady herself. It can't be true, she deemed. Is it really him? Oh, thank you God.

"How have you been?" he asked.

"Fine, thank you. And how have you been, or should I ask, where have you been?"

"I've been on an island they call Antigua, fighting the war. Thank God it's over."

"I agree," affirmed Nina.

"I was surprised to find your family name in the phone book. I thought you lived in Lily."

"We used to. We live here now." She had to sit down, her pulse was pounding, and she felt dizzy. Touching her forehead, she said, "I can't believe it's really you."

"It's been a long time," he related. Nina could tell from the sound of his voice that he was smiling as she was at that moment. "I would like to see you. I missed you in school in my last year. I heard you had transferred to another school. Are you free tonight?"

"I would like to see you too. Yes, I'm free tonight."

"Would you like to go to a movie?"

"We'll see when you get here. You may think I am ugly and go back home."

"Oh, no, not from what I remember. Is seven thirty all right?"

"Yes, seven thirty is fine."

"Goodbye until tonight," Richard said and hung up after she said, "Bye."

She was grinning from ear to ear, and clapping her hands. *Yes. Yes. Yes. He said he missed me. He cared! Oh, this is too good to be true. And I thought he didn't know I was alive? Huh. Thank you God.*

Chapter Thirty Four

AT SEVEN O'CLOCK SHE WAS DRESSED AND READY FOR HER blind date. She sat in a chair by the living room window, looking out at the street, waiting for his arrival. She was wearing her black suit, a white blouse, and a dainty white handkerchief was exposed in a small breast pocket and showed its delicate lace design. Her long, light brown hair with golden highlights was at its best.

Thank goodness I washed it the day before, she thought, as she went into the bedroom to take one more look in the mirror, and fluffed out her hair. *I hope he likes me. I know I will like him, I just know it. Finally after six years of dreaming, hoping, and living for this day; I am going to see him and talk to him. Why, we said hello to each other only one time. Someday, maybe, I will tell him that I am Polish too.*

She had never known such excitement. She glowed with happiness and expectation. Her dreams were to come true at long last.

A car drove up and stopped in front of the house. A heavy set woman with gray streaks in her red hair and a very stout young man alighted from the vehicle. They were walking up to the house and had reached the stairs.

Nina gasped. "This can't be Richard? Why he got fat and why would he be coming here with his mother? What is this?" she asked aloud.

Sonny heard her from the dining room and went to her. He asked, "What's the matter?"

There was a knock on the door. Nina glanced at Sonny and replied, "I don't know. We'll soon find out." She went to the door and opened it, then exclaimed, "Oh, my goodness. Look who's here." She was trying with all her might to keep from saying, "It's Holey Face and Fatso." She opened the door wide and said, "It's so nice to see you. Please come in."

She turned to Sonny and announced, "It's Mrs. Costello and Nanny."

Sonny smiled and returned, "Oh, my gosh."

"Then you remember us?" Mrs. Costello questioned.

"Sure," responded Nina. "How could we forget? You were our favorite people in Lily,"

She and Bernice Costello shook hands and kissed each other on the cheek. Sonny welcomed Nanny with a hardy handshake. He squeezed the muscles in Nanny's right arm, and then slapped him on the back. "How've ya been?" Sonny asked without addressing him. Knowing how much he himself disliked being called Sonny anymore, he did not want to address his childhood friend by his nickname, yet, he could not remember Nanny's given name. The Durock family never considered the name of Sonny as being a nickname. As far as they were concerned, his first name was Sonny and his middle name was Peter. "It's good to see ya," Sonny added.

Nanny was of the same opinion. He said, "It's good to see you too."

Nina stepped over to Nanny and put out her hand. He accepted it, and she said, "Gee, it's been a long time, Nanny, or should I call you, Tommy, now?" She smiled so widely that her eyes were not visible.

Nanny smiled, and replied, "Naw, you kids can call me Nanny anytime." He blushed, and put his hands in his pants pockets.

"We sure missed you when you left Lily," reported Nina.

"Yeah, I missed you too. I didn't have any friends for a long time when we moved away," Nanny related.

"Aw, gee, that's too bad," sympathized Nina. "Do you know we even changed our goat's name to Billy because we missed you so much? And, we called the road Billy Goat Road instead of Nanny Goat Road after you left. Did you ever hear of a female goat called Billy?"

Everyone laughed robustly. Nadia joined the gleefully united group. She greeted Mrs. Costello warmly and remarked how much Nanny had grown. He blushed again and nervously fingered the contents of his pockets.

Hearing money jingling, more childhood remembrances flashed back into Nina's mind, and she asked, "Hey Nanny, do you still like candy?"

Mrs. Costello answered this question with, "He's on a diet. Look how fat he is."

Nanny's face turned red once more. Consolingly, Nina said, "That's all right, Nanny, don't ever change, we like you this way. It wouldn't be you if you were thin." Always the ever-so-kind and understanding Nina.

"Well," he said, "I still chew gum." He pulled a pack from a pocket and offered a stick to everyone.

Mrs. Durock refused with, "No thank you." His mother said, "You chew my stick."

Nina tucked hers into her suit pocket and said, "I'll save it to remember you by." Sonny accepted and put it in his mouth. Nanny returned the remainder to his pocket and chose not to chew gum at that moment.

"Your son looks just like your husband," Bernice spoke to Nadia. Sonny smiled and looked down at the carpeted floor.

"Yes," agreed Nadia, "he just like his Papa, but he only play baseball. Even in his sleep he playit ball. 'Run, run' he holler. 'Steal home,' he sayit in his dream. Crazy game. I no like it; he sweat too much." It was Sonny's turn to blush.

"That's all right, Mama," Nina said. "He loves the game and he'll be rich some day when he plays in the big leagues, you'll see."

"And look at you," Bernice spoke to Nina. "My, but you're a pretty girl."

"Oh, thank you," Nina expressed appreciation for the compliment, and suddenly remembered that she was waiting for Richard's arrival, hoping that he, too, would pay her the same compliment, or at least discover the same and show it in his eyes and behavior.

Bernice still looked at Nina and said, "I betcha no one's called you Skinny for a long time?" Everyone smiled and Nina replied, "No, not for a long time."

Nadia inquired about Mr. Costello's health and whereabouts.

"Oh, he's fine," Bernice answered. "He's working four o'clock to twelve o'clock today. He remembered you people lots of times and always said we'd have to look you up one day. When we heard everybody from Lily had to move out, we figured you lived here now. Thomas remembered this house. Your children used to point it out to him when they used to go to the show together." She meant the movies.

"I glad you findit us," returned Nadia. "We glad to see you."

Bernice asked, "Where's the rest of your family?" She glanced into the other rooms and asked further, "Where's Butter?"

Nadia answered, "Oh, she getit married. She live with she husband in Virginia. He still in navy. They haveit baby girl."

"Oh, my goodness," exclaimed Bernice. "I wish we had known. I would have sent gifts."

"We not know where you live," responded Nadia.

"Well, I sure am surprised," Bernice expressed as she folded her freckled arms in front of her and sighed. "Where is your husband?"

Nadia offered, "Come in kitchen. I makeit tea, and we can talk there."

Bernice followed her into the kitchen. Nina excused herself saying she was waiting for her date, and went to her room. Nanny and Sonny sat down on the davenport in the dining room. It was the old davenport that had moved with them to Lily and back again to Winsome for a short stay in the living room until Daria had insisted they buy all new furniture for the living room. She helped Alex pay for the maroon carpet, deep blue couch, two maroon chairs, lamps, tables, drapes, and bookcases. The latter lined one and a half walls and were filled with Nina's books. At first,

Daria had not allowed Nina to put any of her accumulated possessions in the bookcases, but, when Daria left, Nina felt free to remove the knickknacks that were on the shelves and placed her books there in their stead.

How foolish, Nina had thought at the time, *to have bookcases without books.* But, Daria was the boss then, and Nina avoided arguments with her like a fly avoids a spider's web. Nina had been the fly who, at one time, buzzed close to home. The spider frightened the fly and she flew to the edge of the forest. She buzzed back home and the spider threatened once again. This time she flew further away. Once more, she returned and this time was caught, hopelessly, torturously, and sought a quick ending by her own hand. The web broke with assistance and this time the spider went away. The fly remained and was now waiting for a sweet, sugary food. The carrier of the nourishment meant survival for the helpless fly who had waited five long years to be fed.

Nina removed the stick of gum from her pocket and placed it in the back of her diary. *I guess I'll always be a sentimental fool*, Nina was thinking. *But, that's how a girl gets when she lives in the past. When you don't have a happy present, and fear the future, you search and remember only the days when you were lighthearted. My heart has been so heavy for so long that it's a wonder I didn't crack up. But, God saved me for this day.*

She put the diary back into her dresser drawer and glanced at the large picture that hung on the living room wall above the couch. Shortly after Daria had moved in, she replaced the picture of the Blessed Mother and Child with a scenic painting of a small white farmhouse bordered on two sides by tall trees. There was no grass in the picture. Flowers covered the fields. Nina focused her gaze on the young boy and girl in the painting who walked hand in hand down the winding path away from the house, looking up into the cloudless sky.

The first time Nina saw the picture, she tried to analyze Daria's reason for the selection. *Daria probably wished our house in Lily looked like that. Or, she knew we thought of Lily as a beautiful place when we were children, and she bought it as a reminder for us. I don't need a picture to remind me, all I have to do is close my eyes. Or, she put herself in the picture as the girl walking away from Lily. When you look at the picture from far away, you can't tell that it's a boy or a girl; it looks like two girls or two boys. Perhaps Daria thought of the children as Butter and me? Then again, it could be Daria and Joe walking together? Only the girl walks half way, turns back, and leaves the boy who walks on and upward to the sky with God, the way her Joe did. Or, the youngsters walk together into the forest and profess their love and everlasting devotion for each other. The boy kisses the girl lightly on the lips and says, "We'll get married some day, you'll see."*

The truth of the matter was simply that Daria chose this picture for its color and nothing else. It had the right touches of blue to correspond with the new couch. Religious pictures in the living room, or in any room, were outmoded, she informed her mother and father. She carried the large, colorful reproduction of Mary and Jesus into the basement and purposely dropped it, shattering the glass that had enclosed and protected the holy picture from dust for seventeen years allowing no chance of it ever entering the living room again. The mahogany frame held, however, and the picture looked even more beautiful with its bright colors exposed. It now hung over the area where Alex had died in the basement.

Words permeated the house: baseball, farm team, class D or C ball, big leagues, fireman. Nina put the words together. They meant, Sonny wants to play professional baseball. Nanny still wants to be a fireman. This is what the two boys were talking about in the dining room when she heard, "Oh, I didn't know. That's too bad. When? My sympathies. I wish I had known," Nina knew her mother was informing Mrs. Costello of Alex's passing.

Then she heard, "Daria. California. She always wanit be movie star," Nina surmised her mother was telling "Holey Face" that Daria went away.

Then, "Butter. My daughter-in-law. Butter and my Thomas."

Oh, my goodness, Nina gasped and immediately knew the main purpose of the Costello visit. Nanny came to see Butter. *Why, he must have meant it the day he left Lily and said to Butter, "We'll get married someday, you'll see." She was his first love. What a shock it must be for him to find out she's married and has a baby already. Why, Nanny must still be in school. He was thirteen years old when he moved away and already he had chosen his mate. And sometimes I think I'm out of my head. Nonsense. One is never too young to fall in love. True love can come at any age. Nanny is a sensitive boy, always was, and always will be. He's capable of loving deeply as I do. We sensitive creatures suffer inwardly. Gee, they would have made a nice fat couple. Butter weighed at least one hundred thirty pounds when she got married. Wouldn't you know it, she'd have to go and fall for a tall, thin boy instead.* She lost weight now, sailors don't make enough money to buy sweets every day the way she did when she worked.

What will Nanny do now? He must be heartbroken, and can't wait to get out of here so he can have a good cry somewhere, alone. Poor Nanny. Why is life so cruel? Will he want to go on? Will he find someone else to take her place? He's young, he probably will. But, he will never forget Butter. One never forgets his first love; it is special. Will he go to bed at night and dream of her all his days, even after he marries another? Knowing how Nanny must feel at this moment, I would like to go out there and put my arms around him and let him bawl.

I'll have to write and tell Butter of their visit. Maybe Butt will write him a nice letter and tell him how happy she is. If he loves her, he will want her to be happy; then, maybe it will be easier for him. We can't let it end right here. Oh, Nanny, I'm so sorry. Now I know why Mama was able to leave my real father and come here to America. Yes, she must have loved him, whoever he was, but Papa was her first love.

She looked into the mirror, then bowed her head, folded her hands, in prayer. "Oh, Lord have mercy on the poor souls who have loved and lost. Give them the strength to go on and find happiness in a way that they can serve thee best," she whispered.

At exactly seven twenty-five Mrs. Costello and Nanny took their leave. Sonny hurriedly changed into his baseball uniform; he was scheduled to pitch a game under lights in Winsome Park that evening.

Nadia left minutes later to see her son play the game for the first time. Her presence in the bleachers would be unknown to him; it would make him nervous to know his mother was watching.

Richard and Nina had the house to themselves that night. They agreed to stay there and get acquainted. "We can't talk if we go to a movie," Nina realized. "Let's just sit here and talk."

A half hour later Nina suggested a walk. She excused herself to get her purse and went into the bedroom. She saw, when she returned to the living room, that Richard was looking at her books. "Do you like to read?" she asked.

"My favorite pastime," he replied.

"Mine too," she returned.

"Nice collection," he remarked.

She acknowledged, "Thank you. I would like to write some day."

"So would I," he smiled.

"My, but we have a lot in common," she said.

"Yes, we do," he agreed. "In more ways than one."

She liked what she was looking at when he came into the house; the same young man she first saw in the library at school—the same eyes, hair, stature, a lot taller, a serious face like hers—and felt she had not wasted the waiting years. He was worth waiting for. She hoped Richard was not disappointed in her.

They left the house. The air was fresh. It had stopped raining at two o'clock that afternoon after Nina received her joyous, surprising telephone call. The rain had washed all the greens of spring. Nina breathed the clean air in deeply. She felt like a newborn baby just beginning life. A few times, as they were walking, Richard dropped back a little behind her. She felt he was looking her over. She didn't mind, he was entitled.

I was a skinny, poor kid from the other side of the tracks a long time ago. I really am a blind date. Feeling a little self conscious, she turned around to him and said, "I'm sorry you thought I was staring at you in school. I liked what I saw and couldn't help it."

He answered, "That's okay. I like what I see now."

They walked to the park and sat down on a bench overlooking Lake Winsome. Richard took her hands in his, and then kissed her softly on the lips.

"Will you be my girl?" he asked.

"I've always been your girl," she replied with a song in her heart. "Let's go watch my kid brother play ball."

She wanted to take off running, but thought it was time to slow down. He took her hand and they began walking to the ball park.

❖ ❖ ❖ ❖

The Polish-Russian Treaty of 1945 returned Papa's land to Russia.